The Colour of Lies

Also by Lezanne Clannachan

Jellybird

The Colour of Lies

LEZANNE CLANNACHAN

ORION

First published in Great Britain in 2018 by Orion Books,
an imprint of The Orion Publishing Group Ltd
Carmelite House, 50 Victoria Embankment
London EC4Y 0DZ

An Hachette UK Company

1 3 5 7 9 10 8 6 4 2

A CIP catalogue record for this book is
available from the British Library.

ISBN (Trade Paperback) 978 1 4091 4694 0

Typeset at The Spartan Press Ltd,
Lymington, Hants

Printed and bound by CPI Group (UK) Ltd,
Croydon, CR0 4YY

www.orionbooks.co.uk

For Michelle Wilkinson, with love
and gratitude

Orange is the colour of lies

At Sissie Golding's party, age seven, Anna realised no one else could see the colours.

There were ten of them sitting in a circle playing Pass the Parcel, a slim packet of gummy bears hidden inside every sheet of newspaper. When the music stopped, Sissie ripped off the paper and began to wail, claiming there were no sweets. But Anna, sitting to Sissie's left, had seen the packet fall into the birthday girl's lap, from where it had been craftily transported to beneath her bottom.

She had no choice but to point out the deception. Birthday girl or not, justice demanded it. When Sissie tried to deny it, the orangey-red fireworks sparking off the crown of her head gave her away, growing brighter and stronger with every lie. Triumphant, Anna had pointed at her.

You're lying, and everyone can see it.

She looked around the circle for verification, and everyone nodded.

We can all see your big fat orange fibs coming off your head.

Which was when the little circle stopped pointing fingers at Sissie and turned their collective scrutiny in Anna's direction, a beast catching a new scent.

Someone had sniggered. *Orange fibs?*

All around her head, stupid. She'd stood up, fists on hips,

I

ready to take them on, but their colours were muddled and confused.

It was then that Billie stepped in. With the authority that came from being eleven when everyone else was seven, she pointed at the birthday girl and laughed. *Orange head, ha ha. Sissie's got an orange head.*

At which point the mothers intervened and Billie and Anna went home without party bags. That evening, still banished to their respective bedrooms, her big sister had sneaked in and hugged her as she cried. Billie wanted to know why she'd said lies were orange. Then she asked lots more questions, which was typical of her, and it turned into a game: *What's the colour if you fart in front of the class? What is Matt Marsh's colour when he looks at me?*

When Billie ran out of questions, she grew serious and said Anna's colours had to be a secret but that was OK because she would always be her protector. Oasis green drifted around her head, proving she meant it with all her heart.

Don't even tell Mum and Dad, Billie had said before slipping back to her own room. *They'll think you're making it up to get attention.*

I

Verdigris

The first time she met Gabriel O'Keefe was in a bar in Soho, ten o'clock at night, standing room only. Ten years as a mother's help and she'd never once been interviewed for a new position by the father of the household, let alone in a bar. In the past it would have been a no-brainer. She wouldn't have gone, knowing something else would come along, because it always did. Only now, in the space of six months, she'd become unemployable. The Sowerbys had seen to that. Last November she'd moved out of their grey-stone mansion in Nochenweem, owed one month's pay and having learnt a lesson about how vicious an animal humans can be when they feel threatened. And nothing is more threatening than something that exists outside of one's understanding, something alien.

It was only down to her sister's efforts that she had a job interview at all.

She was early and had the advantage of observing Gabriel as he arrived. Tall and big-built, a tree of a man, the crowd falling back to let him pass. She knew it was him because he wasn't wearing a suit or a tight pair of pastel trousers but cargo pants, a T-shirt washed to off-white and a hunter's vest. He looked out of place against a backdrop of black marble and blue spotlights, or perhaps she imagined that knowing he was a tree surgeon. The crush of people didn't concern him – a man of

3

Leabharlanna Poibli Chathair Baile Átha Cliath

Dublin City Public Libraries

that brute size cuts through a crowd like a cluster of gnats – but he was giving off a bronze green of intense focus. Verdigris. A beautiful colour, of aged copper spires and church bells. She saw it when people were completing crosswords or engaged in deep discussion, setting the world to rights. It was the feeling of being alive and present, of searching, wondering and scheming. She wondered what was causing the verdigris to rise from the crown of his head. What was once a childhood game, to decipher how people were feeling even as they tried to hide it, was now second nature. She decided Gabriel's bronze green was fascination for an urban setting when he clearly belonged out in the open, under a galactic sky where he could let loose the spinnaker of his chest and unfold his full size.

She waved him over to her spot by the edge of the bar. As he greeted her, the lighting created an interesting optical illusion, his left eye a sun-warmed hazel, his right the hard summer green of unripe apples. But as they spoke, she realised it wasn't a trick of the light and that his eyes were mismatched.

'My wife, Suzie,' he said, leaning forward to put the words in her ear, 'lost someone she was close to recently and it's hit her hard. I go away a lot. I need someone stable and trustworthy to take care of the house and Daniel, my boy.'

The word *trustworthy* reached her on a fizzing bed of red embers. She bit back the familiar surge of injustice. Let him have his say. She'd promised Billie she'd hear him out.

'Suzie insists she's fine, but she isn't. So I need someone with a finer sense, I don't know, an instinct for diplomacy.' He was struggling now, wiping his thumb along his hairline, eyes focused past her shoulder, looking to the script he'd obviously rehearsed in his head. 'I can see from your CV that you've got years of experience and could probably do the job in your sleep, but—'

'You need me to be indispensable without your wife realising it.'

He looked at her properly for the first time and his face opened up with a grin.

'Exactly. I – we – just need someone organised and discreet. And trustworthy.'

That word again. Her sister had told them about the Sowerbys. 'I'm not a thief.'

The same words she'd uttered, disbelieving, faced by a hostile semicircle of Sowerbys in the hall – not the kitchen or the sitting room, but the hallway, as if they intended to march her out there and then.

'Every week, Mrs Sowerby, my last employer, would leave the cleaner's cash on the console by the front door. Then one week it disappeared. They decided to accuse me even though I'd lived with them for almost a year by then.'

She's lying. I can see it. Anna took the money, Martha had said, but behind her booming outrage there had been empty air; no billowing red anger or weighty clumps of brown disgust. All an act. And there was ten-year-old Freddie looking anywhere but at Anna. Guilt is the same deep brown of disgust but it doesn't appear in thick clods. Instead it shivers above a person like a tattered cloth in a breeze, stained with the rusty dread of discovery. Anna knew then who'd taken the money and a glance at his mother suggested Martha knew too. When Mr Sowerby took a step towards her, demanding the truth, orange flared above both mother and son's heads. All Anna could do was deny it. She could hardly point the finger at a child who was afraid of his own father. Besides, the real reason Martha was getting rid of her had nothing to do with the missing money.

'They made me empty my belongings from my room, turn out all the pockets in my clothes, even pull the sheets off my bed, but of course they didn't find their missing fifty-pound note because I didn't take it.'

The memory carried back the humiliation, thick and suffocating as tar. Mr and Mrs Sowerby watching her as she turned her meagre belongings inside out, not a trace of guilt from the woman, whilst a strange hue of magenta pleasure flashed in and out of sight above her husband; something Anna didn't want to think about.

'Their loss, our gain,' Gabriel said. 'If you take the job, of course.'

She watched the space above his head to see what colours might greet her story, but his attention had loosened and slipped away. He wasn't that interested in her. As his gaze lighthoused across the crowd, his colours shifted and folded like sheets of Northern Lights, blues and greens of curiosity. She wondered what it was he hungered for, because she saw that too. A crimson spiral turned around his body, starting at his feet and rising above his head. It wasn't often she saw that kind of active sensuality, someone like herself who moved through the world with their fingertips rather than the cold map of their minds. She watched, fascinated, his attention elsewhere as he asked a few obligatory questions. Then the gentle wave of blues and greens closed like a fan, the spiral vanishing, and his verdigris focus returned. He was watching a group of young girls pushing and nudging inside the doorway, as they tried to decide whether to stay. One of them in particular held his attention, her hair draping down her back like a slow, glacial river, a dancer's expression in her long arms and fine fingers.

He nodded his head in the girl's direction. 'She's very young to be out in a place like this, don't you think?'

'It's hard to tell a girl's age these days.' She smiled at his frown and the protective mauve settling on his shoulders.

6

In that moment she decided to accept the position, because Gabriel O'Keefe was a good and decent man.

There was something about him that reminded her of Lauritz.

Two days earlier, she'd met up with her sister in a deli along from the Montpellier Gardens Hotel, a dreary B & B whose rooms, submarine in size and feel, made a mockery of the grand promise of its name.

Billie preferred not to come to town, the density of people and brickwork weighing on her chest, so it had been left to Anna to choose the venue. To avoid being late, she decided on the deli within walking distance of her room. It was a bad choice, she realised, as soon as she walked in. Billie was confined in a corner by the loos, straight-backed, pulsing with discomfort: a bright beacon in a porridge of grey strangers.

Catching sight of Anna, she rose, her thighs knocking the table edge, rattling the tea set for one. She wore her usual camouflage drapery, a long skirt and oversized cardigan, even now, in her late thirties, afraid of being judged on the size of her breasts rather than her brain. *At least you look clever*, she used to say when they were teenagers, pointing at Anna's flat chest.

'Forgive the orange,' she said now, her hands mapping a globe around her head like an invisible space helmet. 'You know what crowds do to me.'

Billie had learnt her colours by rote, approaching it like a particularly tricky spelling test when they were still children. She knew that orange was an anxious colour with many different nuances; that it could deepen to the burnt ochre of terror or glow with the acid brilliance of lies. At that moment, her mild discomfort appeared as a shoal of tiny goldfish wriggling upwards.

7

'Orange sperm,' Anna said, snaking her hand through the air.

'You're kidding? No fireworks or volcanoes; just spunk. Marvellous.' Billie, Anna had always suspected, was a little envious of her colours, having devoured every book, article and Internet forum on the subject.

Before she could order her own pot of tea, Billie slid a square of newspaper across the white cotton tablecloth. 'I've come to rescue you from Chris.'

Chris, her on-off lover, with whom she'd been living since that day of mud and tar when Ian and Martha Sowerby had stood over her as she packed her case. Chris, who had shrugged as she wept furious tears the colour of oxblood – *Fuck 'em, Anna* – and who, despite the brilliance of his blue eyes, was the greyest human being she'd ever been around. Kind, easy-going but grey. Even in orgasm, he raised little more than a magenta burp.

But it wasn't Chris her sister was saving her from. It was shame, and she hadn't even told Billie the full truth of it.

A precise gold box had been drawn around some wording on the newspaper clipping. *Mother's Help Needed*, underlined in the same metallic marker. Gold, as Billie knew, for ultimate Christmas morning excitement, and for hope.

'What would I do without my big sister?' A well-worn phrase, but she couldn't muster the normal jesty sarcasm. Everything was too broken for that.

'One day, sweets, you'll learn to fix your unhappiness all by yourself. That's what us grown-ups do.' Tough words, gentle smile; her sister all over. Billie tapped the snippet of paper. 'But in the meantime. A new home, spending money and a change of scene in one neat bundle. Plus the added bonus of living mere minutes from your beloved big sister.'

'Do you know them?'

Billie hesitated. 'Not well. Their son is in Lucas's class but they don't socialise. General opinion is that the O'Keefes are quiet, pleasant and keep to themselves.'

Anna asked what the catch was and Billie said there wasn't one. 'But try not to mess it up or sleep with the husband, because I'll have to face his wife at the school gates long after you've scarpered.'

Funny Billie.

2

Water steals colour from its surroundings

The endless downpour has washed away civilisation. Two hours out of town, burst rivers and waterlogged fields replace shopping centres and blocks of flats. Anna slows the Bastard Beetle as the road disappears, sealed beneath a metallic lid of water. The water reaches the wheel arches and the car stalls. She curses its mischievous nature, praying that today is not the day it chooses never to start again. Resting her forehead on the window, she stares at the water lapping at the tyres. It makes her shudder. She's never liked deep water, its opaque surface hiding uncertain depths in borrowed tones of flint and slate and navy blue. Even a puddle can be deceptive. Solitary trees poke through the water, isolated and adrift. At least in the city a person can pretend they're not alone. She thinks about turning back. Billie could call the family and make excuses. Her sister's good at that kind of thing.

As if sensing her misgivings, Gabriel rings. His voice is low and distracting. It fills her head with warm sunset yellows and purples as she pictures him in the Soho bar, his presence like a fortress above the crowd, solid and shielding.

'The thing is, Anna,' he says, cutting through pleasantries, 'we've had a rough time of it lately, my wife in particular.'

She knows what's coming next. The word *thief* might as well be branded across her forehead. A label sticks, false or not.

'You've changed your mind about me.'

'No. Not at all.'

In the pause that follows, she winds down the window to de-fog the glass. No sound enters the car, the rain having also washed away the birds and the wind.

'But I want to be completely honest about our situation.'

Anxious orange sparkles before her eyes. She needs someone to take a chance on her, to trust her again. She needs this job.

'My wife refuses to admit she's not coping,' Gabriel says. 'I think it would help her to have a little time for herself.'

They'd discussed as much in her interview. 'I'm happy to help in any way I can.'

He clears his throat and she wonders what she's failing to grasp. This is the problem with phone calls. It's much easier to pick up on a person's true intentions, those subtle currents that run beneath their spoken words, if she can see their face and read their colours.

'Suzie will appreciate the help once she's used to the idea. If you could just bear with her in the beginning.'

By which she finally understands that his wife doesn't want her there.

Sturford is a huddle of stone cottages around a common, the elongated neck of the church rising above them. On the opposite side of the green is the Moon Hare pub, its sign a rabid hare, up on its hind legs, with goggle eyes and overlapping front teeth, ready to see off newcomers. It's rare to spot another living soul. In her sister's words, Sturford is gorgeous but dead, like sex with a supermodel. Despite the village's hibernatory feel, she loves her sister's house. It never fails to live up to her memories. Whilst her parents' door is always open – her childhood bedroom unchanged, ready to receive her – it is Billie's home she slinks back to, a place of comfort in which to lick her wounds and recharge before venturing out again. Architecturally it's a mess, a stern Edwardian extension shoring up the drunken timbers of a sixteenth-century cottage. The joke, when they bought the house all those years ago, that it was a perfect blend of Jo and Billie. Shabby and slightly falling to pieces relying on stout Edwardian efficiency to keep it together.

She parks on the road by the garden wall with moss stuffing in its cracks and an ancient mulberry tree bowing over it. Maisie and Lucas like to toss its fruit at passing cars from behind the safety of the wall.

Billie is watching for her at the window. She rushes out to meet her, tripping over the broken flagstone in the middle of the path that is like a ship sinking, prow to the sky. A man in slim-fit trousers and a pink shirt is waiting in the doorway, and her heart sinks. She'd hoped it would be family only tonight.

'Try not to gawp.' Billie links an arm through hers, her voice a theatrical whisper. 'A polite reference is fine – you're not blind after all – but don't labour it.'

The trim man with the expensive jeans and styled beard smiles and turns into Jonah. 'Here she is, our free spirit. Ready to wipe snotty noses and dirty bottoms?'

'Jonah?' She tries to remember when she last saw him. It can be no more than six months, nine at a push. She and Billie try to meet once a month, more often if she's living within a few hours' reach, but Jonah and the children belong to this house. 'You're so ... reduced.'

Laughing, he pulls her into a hug, which makes her nose itch with his citrus eau de cologne. He used to have a comfortable smell, a linger of cigarettes and curry, like a room where laughter and good conversation take place.

'Brushed up on your Gina Ford?'

'Heat soup, fold socks, play Uno. Piece of cake.'

'Hear that, Bills? We've been putting way too much effort into the whole parenting thing.'

When he looks across at Billie, who is kicking her red Crocs in the direction of a shoe mound, Anna sees the old Jonah, the one who used to follow her sister like a pigeon begging for stray scraps of attention. He and Billie share a small, private smile. It makes Anna feel like she's come home: Billie and Jonah, one of the few constants in her life.

Dinner is spaghetti with bolognese sauce from a jar, Billie's culinary skills another institution that has resisted change.

When her niece and nephew stampede through the kitchen, Billie takes hold of Anna's shoulders like she's a fairground prize. 'Look who's here, children. Your favourite missing auntie returned to us.'

Lucas and Maisie break their dash to swerve in her direction. She braces herself for their double impact. They launch themselves at her, swinging off her arms, jostling for her attention. She pushes them away, laughing. 'You're like a little pack of hyenas.'

'Will you still be here when it's Halloween, Auntie A?' Maisie's arms have snaked back around her waist, her face raised like a cat begging caresses. 'I already know what I'm going to be.'

'I'm only here for the weekend this time, Maze. But I'll be living close by.'

Before Maisie can ask further questions, she is interrupted by her older brother, who is flipping a plastic bottle of water in the air and letting it fall with a jarring thud on the kitchen counter. 'Watch this, Auntie A, I can land it.'

She plants a kiss on Lucas's head, feeling herself sink into her surroundings, a drop of rain losing itself in a pond. Jonah watches her with a smile and she is struck again by the change in him.

'Anna, stop eyeing up my husband and take a seat.'

'I can't help it. He's irresistible.'

An old joke, but one that doesn't float as easily now that Jonah is no longer scruffy and slack-bodied. At least his smile is the same, easy and affable.

'I hope you're not going to be bored,' he says, once the children are seated and shovelling forkfuls of unravelling spaghetti into their sauce-rimmed mouths. 'There's nothing but balding married men in this neck of the woods.'

'With the exception of you, Jo.' Billie sends him a wink across the table, which Lucas tries to imitate without success.

'What colour am I feeling now?' Maisie's sharp little voice cuts in.

Anna glances at Billie, who shrugs. 'They're old enough to learn about it. In fact Lucas is pretty much the age you were when we first realised you had a condition.'

A condition. No matter how many times she's tried to encourage Billie away from that term, her sister persists with it.

'At the moment, you're giving off a lovely green, like leaves on trees.'

Both children stop eating to stare at her.

'Green is a good colour, one of the best. It's the same colour as peace and curiosity and kindness.'

'And frogs and sick.' Maisie's eyes fill with effortless tears. 'I don't want to be green.'

Billie replaces her cutlery, takes a sip of water and adopts a moment of stillness in which to gather her words, loving nothing better than an educational platform. As she explains Anna's synaesthesia in more scientific detail than necessary for an eight- and a six-year-old, Anna tunes out. Her niece

14

and nephew pretend to listen, nodding at phrases like *colour signatures* and *multi-sensory dimension*.

'How would *you* describe it?' Jonah invites her back to the conversation, though he's sat through many a dissection of her so-called condition over the years.

'I don't see why emotions shouldn't have colours.' Anna shrugs. 'Trees have colour, fruit has colour, why shouldn't anger or love?'

'Lies also have colour,' Billie adds. 'Auntie Anna can always tell when someone's telling lies.'

'Strictly speaking, it's discomfort I pick up on when someone's not telling the truth. The fear of being found out.'

Billie ignores her. 'Our favourite game when we were kids was Truth or Dare because Auntie Anna always knew when someone wasn't telling the truth and then we'd make them do a really horrid dare.'

'Like stick their head in a toilet?' The thought delights Lucas.

Maisie, having given up on tears, declares that love must be red.

'Bingo,' Anna says, though there are variations in tone, from the pale, shimmery pink of friendship to the bloody red of sex.

Whilst the children squabble over which feeling might be brown, her sister oversees the scene with a smile that is both protective and indulgent; as though Anna were a precious heirloom taken from a high shelf to be dusted off and admired, under close supervision.

Jonah sends her a wink of solidarity.

Long after Jonah has put the children to bed and failed to reappear, Billie shows Anna to the guest room, which, much like Jonah himself, has had an upgrade.

'Out with the old, in with the new,' she says. A king-size bed sits where the narrow twin beds used to be, and thick curtains whose hems buckle against a carpet the colour of fresh snow have replaced the flimsy aluminium blinds. The greys and cold blues make Anna think of beaches in winter, but she makes appreciative noises.

'Out with the flamingo-arse colour scheme,' her sister says. 'In with tones of Scandi murder mystery.'

'I liked flamingo arse. It was gentle, like grandma cuddles.'

'You're not immune to a little Scandinavian influence, I seem to remember.'

Lauritz. It can only be Lauritz her sister is alluding to, and yet his name hasn't come up in years, at least not outside of her head. She's surprised Billie even remembers him.

Her sister sways against her, riding the choppy seas of the wine they had with dinner. Billie drank the lion's share whilst Jonah stuck with water. 'I can't tell you how happy I am that you're here. It can get a bit lonely.'

'What about the million people you mentioned over dinner?'

'They're not family. I miss you, Anna. You can be so bloody elusive.'

Anna gives her a hug and is surprised when her sister clings on a moment longer.

As Billie is leaving the room, she changes her mind, swinging herself back round the door frame. 'Gabriel's quite easy on the eye. Did you notice?'

Anna gives in to a yawn. 'No.'

Her sister nods as if this is the answer she expected. 'He acts like he doesn't know it, but he does. He knows full well the effect he has on women. Just so you're prepared. You know, guard up and everything.'

*

Lying in the unlit room, Anna notices how the darkness through the open curtains is saturated and treacly. It has an abandoned, forsaken quality. The way she felt for the duration of that long-gone Copenhagen winter when she walked the busy pavements, alight with the hope that one of the people rushing past might, by sweet coincidence, be Lauritz. It never was.

3

Bubblegum blue for anticipation

On Monday morning, when the Bastard Beetle – unmoved by her obscenities – refuses to start, Jonah offers to drive her to the O'Keefes'. She watches him heft her suitcase with ease from her car and into his black Discovery, and wonders what prompted this sudden focus on his looks. On asking Billie about it, her sister gave a disparaging laugh. *Bless him, silly boy*.

Once in the car, he moves through the radio stations before switching it off. Against the silence she says, 'So. What have you done with the real Jonah?'

'In Billie's words, I've become a boring fitness-fuck.'

She laughs, scrolling through her mobile to find Gabriel's directions. 'We're looking for a white signpost.'

'I know the way.'

On route they stop at an Esso station to fill up Jonah's car. Realising she's about to arrive empty-handed at the O'Keefes', she follows him in as he goes to pay. She browses the sweets section, looking for the packets of Nerds that her niece and nephew love. The packaging is a rainbow confectionery of happy colours. A particular shade of blue leaps out at her as though lit from within. A vital bubblegum blue that matches her mood, one she always associates with the thrill of beginnings, of new jobs, new places, new lovers. She chooses a packet of Skittles because of the colour and joins Jonah at the till, where he has already paid for his petrol. The girl behind the counter is laughing at something he's said as she slicks a strand of her long hair between thumb and forefinger. She points to a tray of reduced-to-clear lip glosses. 'Can I tempt you? For the girl in your life?'

'Why not?' Jonah tips out some coins into his hand. 'My daughter loves dressing up.'

Something about the exchange catches Anna's attention: the way the girl is smiling at him, or perhaps how unfazed he is by it. He must hand over an incorrect amount, because the girl tips the coins back into his hand. 'Start again.'

'See what happens when you hit mid thirties?' He pokes his fingertip through the coins in his palm. 'It all goes to pot.'

'Not from where I'm standing.'

An involuntary laugh escapes Anna. She smirks at Jonah, expecting to catch his embarrassment, but he's meeting the girl's gaze with a cool smile. He offers her his open palm, and Anna watches as the girl slips her hand under his as if to support its weight, counting out the correct change. She has an urge to slap their hands apart.

As they leave the garage, she cranes her head at Jonah, giving him a pointed stare. He pretends not to notice. Once in the driver's seat, he opens the glovebox and tosses in the lip gloss.

'You'll forget it's in there,' she says, and when he meets her with a blank gaze, she adds, 'Maisie's present?'

Just two years earlier, a pretty girl had jumped in his path selling Remembrance Day poppies, making him so flustered he'd come away with three. Anna and Billie had teased him without mercy. This is not the same Jonah.

'Bit young, wasn't she?'

'Who?'

'The girl behind the till?'

'What do you mean?' He frowns, sending her a quick

bemused glance. 'I'm sure they have to be at least eighteen to work there.'

There'd been a holiday in their early twenties with a drunken night of sangria, the three of them skinny-dipping in the black Spanish sea. Anna might as well have been a turtle or a fish, a creature of an entirely different species, for the lack of effect it had on Jonah. She wonders when he started noticing women other than her sister.

At the crook of the road, they find the white signpost and follow the arrow towards Beding. He stops the car to let a pheasant dither across the road.

'Wow. This is rural.' Anna notices her surroundings for the first time. Three roads ribbon away from the grassy hillock supporting the signpost. They lead to nothing but overgrown pasture and forest. Trees line the road ahead, creeping vine knotting them into a high wall of greenery. Through gaps she can see the rain-churned mud of the fields beyond. Far to the left, a dark ridge of hills breaks the horizon like a monstrous wave. She shifts round to look through the back windscreen. Not a single house in sight. A tiny orange bubble of panic bursts in her sight. Without her car, she'll be marooned in this green emptiness.

'Proper marry-your-sister countryside,' she says. 'Sure this is the right way?'

'Yep. The O'Keefes like to keep to themselves.'

You'll see the water first, Gabriel had said in his directions. Within three metres, the grass verges on either side disappear under water. It skims across the road, stealing into dips and potholes. The roof of a single house appears over the trees. They pull up outside and she stares at her new home. A white rectory-style building with square windows and a grey tiled roof. Plain and stern and out of place amongst the riotous green of its surroundings. A man-made channel runs alongside the house, sprigs of weed coming out of the brickwork like insect antennae and willow branches trailing in the water. There are two cars in the drive: a white Peugeot, paintwork gleaming, and a beaten-up old Defender with wings of spattered mud on its flanks.

Jonah turns off the engine. 'Looks a sad place, doesn't it?'

'Everywhere does in the rain,' she says, and tries to recall what Billie had said about the family. A boy, Daniel, in the same year as Lucas; his mother, Suzie, pleasant but reserved.

'If they'd found the body, it would be better. Then the grieving process could start.'

'The body? What are you talking about, Jo?'

'Billie didn't tell you about Suzie's niece? The girl who went missing?'

'No. No, she didn't. I assumed Mrs O'Keefe had lost an elderly relative.'

Jonah looks away from the house, his hands sliding down the steering wheel. 'Lily was just nineteen.'

She turns to face him, incredulous. 'You knew her?'

His colours are springing out like streamers from a magician's hat, too fleeting to read, though a deep blue outlines his head. It's much harder to read a person when they are agitated.

'She used to babysit occasionally.' He twists away from her, undoing his seat belt. 'Not an uplifting topic, is it?'

'But what happened?'

'No one knows.' He gets out, looking back at her to tap a finger to his mouth, indicating the house.

'Wait.' She stays seated. 'I feel odd about this.'

'They're a nice family,' he says, opening her door. 'Besides, it's been three, four months. The drama's over.'

'Are you insane? That's no time at all.'

'I guess.' His tone is non-committal, his earlier colours

having burnt themselves out, leaving behind a smoky grey-blue haze. 'The whole thing's gone very quiet, so it feels longer.'

Having dropped her case by the front door, he kisses her cheek and leaves. She wishes Billie was here. Meeting new people isn't her strength. She learns too much about a stranger within minutes and it can tip her in the wrong direction: either overfamiliar, or withdrawing in the face of repellent colours. She focuses on the parrot green of the young leaves on the beech tree by the garden wall and the dusty emerald pines to the right of the house. Green for calm and confidence. Sometimes she can catch the feeling from a colour, but today it doesn't work.

There's a poster taped to the window nearest the door. A young woman smiles out, head cocked to one side, peering past her long fringe. Vitality and mischief add feathers of happy yellow and excitable indigo to the black-and-white print, colours that only Anna can see.

Lily. Nineteen years old.

Beneath the photograph, a single word in block letters, like a stamp of condemnation.

MISSING.

She looks away before details of the brief paragraph below can lodge in her head. The girl's eyes pain her enough.

Ringing the doorbell, she curses Jonah for driving off.

A boy the same age as Lucas opens the door and stares at her with sombre expectation.

'If I was magic and could guess the names of all the children in the whole world, I'd say yours was Daniel.'

The little gatekeeper doesn't smile or make a move to let her in, so she leaves the packet of Skittles in her bag. A proper present would have been a better idea. Lucas could have helped her choose something appropriate: a football perhaps, or the Match Attax cards that her nephew collects.

'Who's at the door, Daniel?' A woman's voice comes from somewhere in the unlit house.

'Mrs O'Keefe? It's Anna Stevens.'

The woman who comes to the door is small and blonde, with wide-spaced eyes. Her outline is the deep, drenched blue of misery. It surprises her. Strangers are usually bland and colourless because people guard their feelings until familiarity makes them comfortable. Suzie O'Keefe doesn't care what the rest of the world thinks. Letting it all hang out, as Billie would say.

'I was expecting you later,' she says. 'Gabriel is out.'

'Who's that lady?' Daniel wants to know.

'Anna's going to help around the house.' His mother strokes his face. 'For a bit.'

'We need to go to school now, Mummy.'

Anna is shown into a large, sparsely furnished room with a woodburner set into a deep fireplace, a three-piece suite in a mossy, claustrophobic green, and a desk. Despite the two large windows facing the front lawn, the room has an underwater gloom. Blocking out some of the light is a large computer on the desk. The poster of the missing girl adds a further blot on the daylight. Suzie points to the sofa. She'll show Anna the house after the school run, she says, and leaves the room without having made eye contact. Most people take a while to warm to the idea of a stranger in their home, but the red glow throbbing off the woman isn't the usual reticence; it's outright hostility. No wonder Gabriel called to warn her. A year ago, Anna would have picked up her bag and left.

On the coffee table is a boat made from a single lump of clay, with a drinking straw for a mast and a paper sail coloured in crayon stripes of blue and yellow. When she touches the prow, it rocks against the table with a stony grate. She knows how to blend into the background, to assist without intruding;

to become a pair of ghost hands. If that doesn't work, she'll stick it out for six months and then move on.

She studies the room, gleaning clues about her new family. The fireplace has an elaborate surround, with garlands of wooden roses ruined by a shoddy paint job, its carved petals smothered under a thick white layer. On the mantel above it, a dutiful line of family photographs. Most of the pictures are of Gabriel, Suzie and Daniel. The boy fixes the camera with a sombre, distrustful expression, his mother standing over him like a protective shadow, Gabriel a little separate as if waiting to be invited into their private huddle. The girl from the poster is in some of the pictures. She has the same pale hair as Suzie, an echo of similarity in their pointed chins and almond-shaped eyes. Anna leans in, curious and saddened, noticing the boy's hand in Lily's, and how her presence, with Gabriel at her other side, seems to link them all together.

A door closes somewhere in the house and she returns to the sofa, wondering if it caught in a draught. When Gabriel appears in the doorway, he looks equally surprised to find someone else in the house.

'Anna, you've arrived.' Unlike his wife and son, Gabriel smiles. He shrugs off his canvas bag, which lands by the door with a clank of metal. 'Sorry if I scared you. I came in the back door. Have you seen your room yet?'

When she says not, he shows her upstairs. At the top of the landing, a large window overlooks the front of the house, and she is struck again by their isolation.

'Beautiful, isn't it?' Gabriel says, and she manages a nod.

He points to the nearest door. 'Master bedroom, but Suzie'll manage that. One less room for you to keep on top of.'

Daniel's room is beside his parents'. On the opposite side of the narrow corridor are two closed doors, the first of which he opens, indicating Anna's private bathroom. No towels on the rail, no soap on the washbasin, three dead flies in the bath. 'As I explained, Suzie is coping with a lot at the moment.'

The second door he passes without comment, testing the handle as if to check it is locked. This part of the house feels dark and unused, the temperature dropping, the smell of fresh laundry and children's shampoo giving way to mustiness. At the end of the corridor is another room. When he opens the door, it hits the edge of a single bed and they have to skirt around it one at a time to enter a room long and narrow as a coffin. A small window faces the towering pines at the side of the house. Even Gabriel looks appalled at the sight of the naked duvet and the thin, battered pillow, as comfortable-looking as a doormat. Yellow stains bloom in the centre of the mattress. At the foot of the bed is a boarded-up fireplace, and a narrow alcove by the window is crammed with old toys, magazines and age-bleached towels.

'I'll get some sheets.'

'And curtains,' Anna adds before she can stop herself, and he glances at the empty plastic railing above the window before leaving the room.

She sends Billie a text. *I now live in a box room, surrounded by charity-shop crap. Just enough space for a child's bed – lucky I'm a short-arse. Potentially a dead body under the floorboards, given the stink.*

It is Suzie who reappears ten minutes later, with a bundle of white overwashed sheets that remind Anna of hospital beds.

'I ordered the blinds a week ago,' she says, holding out the sheets and a supermarket bag. 'It was my husband's idea to hire you, but Daniel's at school all day. I don't know what there is for you to do here.'

She doesn't wait for a response, closing the door behind her. It slips its latch and butts against the bed frame again. Even the bloody door is broken.

In the supermarket bag are two vanilla candles and three postcards of the local area, two featuring photographs of empty wilderness – as if she needs reminding – and one a Victorian pavilion dressed in snow.

The Petrifying Well, she reads. Seems appropriate.

She lines up the postcards and candles on the windowsill, where they fail to impact the bleakness of the room.

Come home immediately, Billie's text commands, but she's not ready to be rescued just yet.

4

Grey green is the colour of toads and disappointment

On her first morning at the O'Keefes', Anna wakes up laughing. A long-forgotten memory waiting for her on the boundary of waking and dreaming: Lauritz running naked through her parents' garden, his long body flashing through the trees' blue shadows, whooping and hollering to greet the dawn. Anna had watched him from the open window of the guest room, trying to call him back through her laughter, half careless, half terrified of her parents waking up. His scent, the salty-sweet blend of deodorant and sweat, is in the room, fading as she opens her eyes, remembering what was to follow. Lauritz always returns in the hibernation between lovers. Even after all these years.

She gets out of bed and stands by the window, draping the sheet Gabriel has hung as a makeshift curtain around her shoulders. The wind pushes thin, icy fingers through gaps in the window frame, the postcards face down on the floor where it poked them off the sill during the night. The stench rising from the mushroom-tone carpet, a Petri dish of spores and neglect, coats the back of her throat. She digs a fingertip into a swelling in the wallpaper. Rain drips off the pines. If she presses her forehead to the window and looks all the way to the left, she can catch a glimpse of the distant hills behind the house. They are the same grey green as disappointment.

Turning away from the lack of view, she takes a small bundle wrapped in a silk butterfly scarf from her case. She opens it over the bed and a squat ceramic toad rolls out, bulb-eyed with a gaping red mouth, the lacquer of its khaki body wet under the weak daylight. She strokes its head, afterwards rubbing her fingertips together against the imaginary oil slick of its skin. No matter how many times she touches it, her head convinces her fingers the skin is moist and living. She places it on the empty shelf above her bed where it can watch over her, the bunched worm of its tongue ready to flick out and tap her on the forehead.

'Home sweet home,' she says, and the toad grins.

Neither Daniel nor his mother notices her in the doorway, heads bowed over their toast. The contrast between here and Billie's hits her, Lucas and Maisie jumping in and out of their chairs to mess about with each other whilst Billie streams remonstrations that no one pays any attention to, least of all Billie herself.

The boy spots her over his mother's shoulder, chewing his toast and saying nothing. At the sound of her greeting, Suzie looks round, and whilst her grimace is fleeting enough that most people wouldn't have spotted it, Anna sees its colour counterpart – a reddish-orange irritation – flare above the crown of her head.

'You're up early. Didn't Gabriel find you after dinner last night?'

'He did, but I thought as I was up ...'

She'd been invited to join the family for dinner. Going forward, though, she was to take her evening meal either before or after the family. During dinner it became clear that she wouldn't be missing much. Suzie and Daniel had ignored her, discussing homework and the life cycle of frogs, whilst Gabriel drifted in and out of his thoughts, addressing her twice only to ask the same question. What did she plan to do with herself outside of work hours; how was she going to keep herself busy? When she answered, a bronze-green staff of attention shot through Suzie's colours, listening in as she continued to chat with her son. There was a sharp and sparing energy to Suzie, like the thrust of a knife, her every movement precise and on target, from the way she dissected her steak into neat parcels to the fluid snap of her head when Gabriel tried to bring her into the conversation. A woman who didn't miss much.

Half an hour after Anna had escaped to her room, Gabriel had knocked on her door with an instruction for her to have breakfast after eight a.m., when the kitchen would be all hers. In other words, she was to make herself scarce during every family meal.

As Suzie stacks the breakfast dishes, Anna moves forward to help. 'I'll clear the table if you want to get Daniel ready.'

'No need,' Suzie says in a stiff tone, straightening her back and folding her hands. 'I guess you want breakfast?'

'Oh no, I'm fine, thanks.'

'Mummy, we need to go now.'

Suzie's expression changes as she looks at her son, a soft wave of deep pink engulfing her frame. 'We won't be late, I promise. But I have to make Anna some breakfast.'

'Please don't. I just wanted to help.'

Suzie ignores her, water spattering as she fills the kettle, the jarring scrape as she settles it on the hob. Deliberately careless to make a point. She takes a teabag from a jar, waves it like an accusation. 'Will ordinary tea do?'

There's nothing Anna can do but nod and mutter her thanks. When Suzie takes a white loaf from the bread bin, Daniel stands behind his mother, poking the small of her back as her elbow jabs back and forth, sawing off two symmetrical slices.

'My laces, Mummy.' His strident, plaintive tone hits a raw spot in Anna's head.

'Shall I do your laces, Daniel?' She holds her hand out to the boy, who pretends he can't see her. Searching for something to do, she picks up a triangle of hotel jam pots and puts them in the fridge. When she picks up the butter dish – a ceramic hen with a hostile expression – Suzie gets up from tying her son's laces.

'You'll need the butter for your toast.' As Suzie tries to take the dish, a misunderstanding occurs between their hands and the hen falls, held by no one. It hits the floor with a spiteful crash, cracking in half, soft butter slopping across the broad stone tiles. It couldn't have made a bigger mess.

Daniel claps both hands over his mouth. Ignoring Suzie's clipped instructions to leave it, Anna collects the broken pieces and lays them on the counter. Unable to find a cloth, she scoops up the butter cowpat and deposits it in the sink. Mother and son stare at her, hands slathered in butter and yellow splodges polka-dotting her trouser leg.

She offers another weak apology.

'It makes Daniel anxious if we're late.' With a glance that moves about the kitchen like a finger pointing at the burnt toast, the mess on the floor and Anna herself, Suzie takes her son's hand and leaves.

Anna watches them from the landing window. Suzie halts halfway along the garden path as if she's forgotten something, the boy tugging on her arm. Perhaps she's about to return and order Anna to pack her bags. When she reaches the car, she pauses again with the driver's door open, as if one particular thought requires so much energy it stalls the mechanics of her body. From this distance, Suzie's features are too blurred to read. An oily unease slips through Anna. She doesn't like being denied a person's colour. It feels like walking through a forest with her eyes shut.

Daniel's voice is shrill and fretful, spurring his mother into action. They get in the car and Suzie reverses it onto the lane. One final moment of hesitation, where the car stops and she sits motionless with her hands on the wheel. Daniel's body bucks forward in his seat, his fingertips tapping his mother's shoulder. Suzie winds down the window and slicks her hair back from her forehead. Minutes pass before the car creeps forward again.

5

Loneliness, like broken glass

A week into her new position, a Vauxhall Estate in a resigned navy blue arrives. The family's first visitor since she started. The phone hasn't rung once. Considering what the O'Keefes are going through, the lack of outside contact has struck her. As she mops the floor outside the kitchen, she watches Suzie and Gabriel greet the woman in a nervy orange cloud. The woman's shirt is a bold and open-hearted aquamarine. Irrational as it is, it makes Anna like her.

The three of them retreat into the sitting room. A few minutes later, Gabriel leaves the room to make a mug of milky tea and lay out some fancy chocolate biscuits; too absorbed to acknowledge Anna's presence. Back in the room, they speak so quietly she can barely hear the murmur of voices through the closed door. Suzie walks out first, mouse-grey with fatigue and mourning, and shortly afterwards the Vauxhall pulls away.

To avoid Suzie, Anna retreats to the laundry room at the back of the house. She folds Daniel's T-shirts and pants whilst she stares through a thick drapery of rain at the paddock and the forest and the hills. The house is larger than Billie's, with a melancholy, ghost-town feel that makes her tiptoe around, each click of a door or grunt of a floorboard giving her away. The laundry room, where she spends an increasing amount of time hiding, is warm and cosy with its low extension roof and the continuous heat from the dryer, but through her eyes the air has the texture of broken glass, cold and glittery. Her bespoke brand of loneliness.

The only thing that holds the glass splinters at bay is to keep busy.

Despite Suzie's resistance, she's created her own routine, having learnt not to ask, but to do. Offers of specific help get turned down and added to the list of things Suzie prefers to do herself. Once Daniel and Suzie have left, Anna clears the breakfast things, if Suzie hasn't already, and hoovers downstairs. Next she scours the house for anything out of place: a forgotten coffee cup on the mantelpiece, a piece of unopened post that has drifted to the floor, or – thrillingly – Daniel's train set still out on the sitting room floor. A good ten minutes can be used in separating and stacking the wooden tracks. The rest of the day passes in clock-watching agony. By lunchtime she's run out of clothing to wash, dry and iron, and afternoons are spent avoiding Suzie, who only speaks to her when she oversteps an invisible boundary such as offering to help Daniel with his maths. After a solitary evening meal, she'll go for a run, the highlight of her day. That and the occasional chat with Gabriel.

Pulling a giant's burgundy T-shirt from the dryer, she measures it against herself. The hem falls to her thighs, the short sleeves reaching her elbows. It's a colour that pulls her in two directions, as she associates it with both lust and aggression. Though sometimes in the heat of the moment, one doesn't seem so far removed from the other.

'The colour suits you.'

She jumps, turning to find Gabriel. 'I was having trouble folding it.'

'I'll wear it now.' He takes it from her. 'Did you see the flowers outside your room?'

She'd hoped the vase of purple hyacinths might be from

Suzie, a sign of her hostility easing. Gabriel is keen for her to stay, with his daily enquiries into her well-being, and small offerings like today's flowers and the pretty bars of soap, individually wrapped, that appeared in her bathroom. It's one of the reasons she hasn't packed her bag and left, despite the cold front his wife is presenting. That and her own current lack of options.

'Thank you, much appreciated.' She lets her smile tell him it isn't as trivial a gesture as he is making out. Catching herself, she looks away. It would be easy to touch his arm in this confined space or hold his eyes a moment longer. His loneliness is wrapped about his shoulders like a deep blue rug. He doesn't realise it, but her solitude will be drawing him in, like attracting like. Without the assistance of colours, most people take far longer to work these things out.

'You should have asked me to make tea for your friend today. I'd have been happy to.'

'Friend? Oh, Juliet. Detective Adeyemi, to give her official title. Our family liaison officer, to help us through … what we're going through.'

'She seems kind, friendly.' She says it to test the colour of his response and watches a spiral of glowing pinks and greens curl away from him.

'The family is always the first they suspect when someone goes missing.' He puts his hands in his pockets, staring at his feet. 'But Juliet listens. She's on our side.'

Loneliness bowls out of his chest. She doubts anyone but herself can see the pain behind his dignified facade but if she responds to what a person is trying to hide, she can frighten them off.

'It's good you have support.'

'Shame it couldn't have come from our friends.' He gives an apologetic shrug. 'Sorry. I hate moaners and now I'm starting to sound like one. Right, time for work.' He turns away to pull off his grey T-shirt, presenting her for a moment with the wide plane of his back, the muscle working beneath his skin as he lifts his arms over his head. Lava streaks through her. She can't help the visceral response to his naked torso – Billie teases her, says she's a feral little beast – but then she catches the stale smell of fear and is shamed. He must anticipate and dread Juliet's visits in equal measure, never knowing what news she might bring.

He tosses the scrunched ball into the laundry basket and pulls on the clean burgundy T-shirt. 'How's Suzie? With you?'

'Thawing slowly.'

He nods, stretching his chest as he gives in to a yawn. The hem of his T-shirt rises, revealing a band of skin drawn tight over the frame of his hip bones. *Goalposts*, she and Billie used to call them.

He gives an apologetic smile. 'I hope you can stick it out a bit longer.'

'If I'm honest, I'd imagined a busier household.' She'd pictured her parents' home, the constant stream of spinster aunts, teenage godchildren, her mum's coffee circle, her father's business colleagues. Lauritz, washing in on the endless wave of visitors.

There's a beat of silence before he nods. 'Sorry. Just the three of us.' He cricks his neck, stretches out his shoulders as he stares at the rain. 'I should introduce you to some people. There's a local meditation group on Tuesday nights. It's small, friendly. Might be a way of meeting people.'

'Meditation? I can barely sit still long enough to pee.' A laugh escapes her. 'Did I really say that out loud?'

He tries not to smile, then they both give in to laughter and she thinks this silly moment might be the most fun she's had in a long while. Since the Sowerbys called her a thief.

'Something came for you in the post this morning.' He leaves the room, returning a minute later with a parcel in brown paper.

She recognises the rabbity handwriting, the letters scattering in all directions, and smiles. 'From my mother. No doubt something completely pointless.'

'Books?' He stands beside her and the room shrinks to hold the two of them in place. It's been a long time since a man's proximity made her aware of her own breathing.

'Too small for books,' she says. 'My guess is random medication.'

'Travel board games,' Gabriel says, and this time she makes sure not to look up and link their grins. 'Bet you a fiver.' He holds out a flat palm and she claps it with her own.

They are both mistaken. As she opens the brown paper, her stomach drops. Three decks of cards, their colours and pictures as familiar as her own reflection.

'That's a fiver for me,' Gabriel says.

'These aren't games.'

She picks up a deck with a picture of an angel, the battered golds and peacock blues soft and beguiling. A scrap of paper drifts to the floor, but her mind is too concerned with the scolding she's going to give her mother. Gabriel picks up the paper.

'Fortune-telling cards?'

'Oracle cards. And Tarot.'

She sees too late that he is reading her mother's hectic scrawl, no longer smiling. She takes the note from him.

You could give them the answers they need. Love, Mum x

Her mum doesn't believe in fortune-telling or ghosts or souls, anything beyond her five senses. It's her way of telling

36

Anna that she's thinking of her, imagining the cards might be a fun way to break the ice amongst these new people. It's why Anna and Billie never told their parents about her colours. Whilst they'd make every effort to understand, it would be beyond their practical, no-nonsense approach to the world. They wouldn't get it and that would be the loneliest thing.

'You read Tarot cards?' Gabriel's voice is low and quiet, lifting the hairs on the back of her neck.

'Not any more.' She closes the brown paper around the decks.

'Would you read them for me?'

With a muttered apology, she leaves the laundry room, brushing the wall as she passes him, careful not to make contact in the narrow space.

'What about in private?' He overtakes her in the hallway, the solid mass of him bending over her like a tree in a gale. 'If you're tempted to ask the cards about my family, will you tell me what they say?'

'I'm not going to read the cards, Gabriel.'

The Tarot deck grows warm through the paper as if feeding on her energy. After she and Billie outgrew Truth or Dare, the Tarot became their game. It had been easy to fool people into thinking she had a gift for the cards. All she had to do was read a person's colours, the rainbow signposts of fear, hope, lust, shame that guided her forward like flags along a path.

A harmless game until the day she started using them to get what she wanted.

That night, despite what she told Gabriel, she can't resist pulling a card. She pictures him as she shuffles, the cards shucking at speed through her hands. A single card escapes the deck and falls to the floor, landing face up but sideways.

It depicts a heart pierced by three swords against a stormy background. She frowns, returning it to the deck. If it had landed upright, it would have told her that Gabriel was a man consumed with grief. In reverse, it speaks of forgiveness and releasing pain.

The cards are giving nothing away because she has no right to this knowledge.

6

Panic looks like violent orange slashes

From the landing window she watches the O'Keefes leave the house, Daniel over Gabriel's shoulder, yelling with delight, head jolting, as his father jogs to the Peugeot. Putting his son down, Gabriel opens the driver's door for his wife, then takes her face in his hands. They exchange a brief, concentrated kiss. Nothing habitual or careless about it, delivered with feeling, and though Anna can't see their features, their body language is enough to raise an undulating column of pinks and purples. For some reason it surprises her. Even more unexpected are the scraps of envy, dried-out yellow-greens that flake through her sight.

She heads to the empty kitchen, noting Suzie's fastidious efforts at tidying away breakfast, and last night's pans dripping on the draining board. One of her little reminders that Anna is not needed. The front door opens and she prepares to be smiling and cheery. When there is no further sound, she pokes her head round the door and finds Suzie in the hallway. She's facing the open front door, gripping the narrow shelf where car keys and unopened post are kept, her breath coming in gasps as if she's been running.

'Suzie?'

The woman's shoulders draw in but she doesn't turn. Anna approaches, asking if everything is all right. Catching sight of

Suzie's face, she drops back, an instinctive urge to put space between herself and the chaotic slashes of neon orange coming off the woman. Panic is one of the few infectious emotions. She can't witness a person's alarm without it setting her heart into a gallop, adding her own clementine rips to the air.

'What's happened? Is it Daniel?'

Suzie shakes her head, bending over her knees to suck breath through the constricted straw of her throat. Anna sees Daniel get out of the Peugeot, but he remains behind the car door as though it were a shield.

'Hay fever,' Suzie manages to say. 'Makes me asthmatic.'

The orange storm above the woman's head says otherwise.

Something has flowered overnight at the foot of the forest. Anna doesn't know about wild flowers, but their violet blue is making her thirsty. The decor in the O'Keefe house favours Dank Cave and Soggy Moss. She kicks off her plimsolls outside the front door and follows the canal. The grass is long and pinpricked with pink flowers on wavery stalks that are most likely weeds. Rainwater bubbles up from the ground, mud capping her toes. Where the canal disappears underground by the treeline, the floor is hidden by violet flowers with tiny bell-shaped heads. Crouching down, she lets their colour fill her up; the exact tone of friendship. Picking as many as she can hold, she keeps an eye on the trees. She's never understood the appeal of forests, keeping to the lane on her evening runs. Too many shadows and hiding places, which is no doubt why most bad things in fairy tales take place in the forest. There's no fence or boundary wall separating the back garden from the woodland. She's not sure she likes that sense of open invitation.

Heading back, she notices a tall, slim man on a bicycle. He stops at the side of the road, taking his mobile from his slack rucksack and wheeling his bike along the public bridle path on the opposite side of the canal. Eyes still on his screen, he rests the bike against one of the willows, unzips his trousers and takes a long, leisurely piss into the canal. Not so much as a glance at the kitchen window facing him across the narrow waterway. She steps back behind the house, her heart beating hard, a shiver of repelled brown crossing her vision. Having waited a couple of minutes, she looks round the side of the house. The bicycle is still leaning against the willow trunk, partially hidden by its hanging branches, but of the man there's no sign.

With her hands full of flowers, she nudges the front door open with her elbow. The Missing poster catches her eye. This time she reads the details. Lily hasn't been seen since 14 February. Valentine's Day. She wonders if the date is significant. The girl is pretty, with a flirty slant to her eyes that suggests she knows it. She must have had plenty of admirers.

'You shouldn't pick bluebells,' a voice says behind her. The tall man appears from nowhere. He leans against the garden wall, flipping a trowel in lazy arcs and catching it by the handle. He's much younger than she'd realised, pimples lining his jaw like angry red pokes of a pencil.

'Why not?'

He lets the trowel fall by his feet. 'They're protected.'

The front door swings open before she can respond and Suzie is in the doorway with an interesting prickle of reds above her head.

'Am I paying you to chit-chat?'

'Excuse me?' Anna's own reds crackle before her eyes until she realises Suzie is addressing the boy, not herself.

A laugh escapes the corner of his mouth. 'Someone's got to tend your lush garden. Seeing as Gabe's neglecting it.'

Anna's mouth drops open. 'Cocky little—'

Suzie interrupts her with a glare, ushering her inside and slamming the door behind them.

'I don't need *you* to fight my battles, Anna.'

7

Yolk-yellow dust of shocks and surprises

The night is painted on the window, sealing her in. She misses the traffic outside the dingy Montpellier Gardens Hotel; even the screech of seagulls that soundtracked her time in Nochenweem. Honest noises rather than the sly brush of pine against her window or the surreptitious creaks and cracks as the house nestles into its foundations. Twice she gets up, convinced there's someone outside her room.

She shouldn't have spent her first weekend at Billie's; the solitude waiting for her at the O'Keefes' is like a barrel of pebbles she has to force herself back inside, the space closing in behind her every time she leaves. A soft noise in her room sends a zip wire of adrenalin through her. Nothing sinister: a wad of petals dropping from the tulips Gabriel left in her room over the weekend.

She sends Marni a text, knowing she will most likely be awake, mooching about, one of those people who don't seem to need any sleep. *I've ended up in the Hammer House of Horrors.*

Marni's reply comes seconds later. *Get your sister in. She'll scare the pants off the lot of them.* Her closest friend has never been a fan of Billie's.

A little after one a.m., the random noises take on the deliberate and stealthy rhythm of footsteps. She rises on her elbows to listen. A key turns in a lock, followed by the stiff grunt of a door being nudged from the swollen clasp of its frame. Her door has slipped its catch, allowing her to peek out without giving herself away. The room beside hers, the one they keep locked, is now open and a rectangle of coloured light falls onto the landing carpet.

She leans further out. Gabriel is standing with his back to her in the middle of a large room. What she'd imagined was a storage room like her own, crammed with stuff no one wanted, instead contains a four-poster bed and a dressing table with a lamp whose glass shade scatters coloured light across the floor. It's a lived-in space, cluttered with books and trinket boxes, patterned scarves and handbags hanging off the bedposts. An audience of teddy bears is lined up on the bed beneath a rosebud canopy.

A bedroom for a girl.

Gabriel grips the shelf above the dressing table, forehead on his arm as if the act of standing upright exhausts him. The bunch of his shoulder and the muscled length of his arm looks wooden and unyielding amidst the floral drapery, the sunrise crimson and yellows. His boots make deep, muddy indents in the carpet's pink moss.

He slides open the drawer of the dressing table, slowly, as if afraid something nestling within, a bird maybe, might burst out. He takes out a handful of photographs, leafs through them before letting his hand drop away. Loss rises off him, a thick smoke of grey and navy blue. Anna turns away, leaves him staring at the window with its view of the empty night.

A wet Tuesday, where all the colour in the world is washed away, even inside her own head. Gabriel comes home early and his presence lifts the energy. She only ever hears Daniel's voice when his father's at home. Suzie intercepts her on the way to the kitchen.

'You can finish for the day if you like.'

Past Suzie she can see Gabriel and Daniel at the kitchen table engaged in a thumb-wrestle. Gabriel gives her a smile and his son takes advantage of his momentary distraction to win the game.

'Are you sure? It's only three thirty.'

Suzie is quite sure.

It's no coincidence that her working day ends when Gabriel comes home. She lies on her bed and thinks she might go crazy with nothing to do but stare at the dripping pines outside her window. She calls Jonah to ask after the Bastard Beetle's progress.

'Sorry, Anna. Sorry. I haven't had time to get it looked at yet. There's always ... stuff going on.' He sounds so weary she doesn't complain, but for a moment she feels held in place by a boulder and can't breathe properly.

She puts on her running gear. In Nochenweem she went running to get away from the Sowerbys, to seek solitude; here she runs to escape it.

Her trainers are soaked through by the time she returns, rain trickling off her windbreaker, her body itching to peel off the sodden layers. The light is on in her room, the door resting open. She recognises the squeak of her bed frame. Someone is in her room, on her bed. She tiptoes across the landing to find Daniel standing on her pillow. He jumps down with a guilty start, her china toad clutched in his hand. His eyes slide sideways and he makes a break for the door.

'That's my toad.' Blocking his way, she holds out her hand. 'It's called stealing if you take something that doesn't belong to you.'

He hands it back, looking miserable, the toad's skin damp from his hand.

'It's a frog, not a toad,' he says.

45

'How do you know?' She keeps her tone neutral, uncertain how far to press the point about stealing.

'I grow frogs.'

She can't help but smile. 'What, from a frog tree?'

His mouth twitches, not so much a smile as an acknowledgement of her attempted humour. 'If I show you, you can't tell my mum. She doesn't want you to be my friend because you'll be leaving soon.'

She follows Daniel into his room, tiptoeing like a cartoon spy, hoping he'll lighten up and join in, but he doesn't. A large aquarium sits on a coffee table by his bed, giving off an electric hum. The water through the tinted glass is the tropical green of serenity. A scum of frogspawn layers its surface.

As they sit on the edge of his bed, pondering the aquarium, Suzie calls for him to come and double-check his homework. It's an excuse, because Daniel, the anxious little thing that he is, will have put one hundred per cent into his work. Anna's second week at the O'Keefes' and Suzie is still shepherding her son away from her.

'Dan? Your mum's calling you.' Anna's voice is loud, pretending she and Daniel aren't together, bonding over frogspawn. Daniel chews his tongue the way he does when Suzie nags him to tidy up or do his homework; mashing unspoken words with his teeth.

'I'm going to the toilet, Mummy.' Daniel turns his head away, hiding what could have become a grin, as Anna shoots him a look of amused reproach. She gives the tank a shake, the black tadpole beads shivering in their jelly. 'Looks like you could eat it. Like passion fruit. But I'm guessing it would taste like pondwater and frog poo.'

A frown appears between the thin fluff of Daniel's eyebrows. 'When they get legs, you have to put meat in there so they don't eat each other,' he says. Raising frogs is no joking matter. 'Why've you got a toy frog?'

'To remind me of someone.' Before the boy can ask any more questions, she moves the topic on. 'Do you need help naming them?'

His laugh is sudden and straight from his belly. 'You can't name frogs, silly.' Then he looks appalled, catching hold of one hand with the other and squeezing his fingers. 'I didn't mean you're silly.'

'Of course not. Because I'm definitely not silly.' She crosses her eyes, sticking out her tongue. 'Now. All we have to do is make tiny, weeny name tags.'

He doesn't laugh again, his happiness like something bobbing in the sea, briefly visible before the water closes over it again. It's the house. It weighs everyone down. She looks around his room and shudders. Whilst it's a good size for one small boy, the colour scheme makes it shrink inwards, the walls a maudlin blue, the curtains a stormy sky of grey, purple and navy stripes. Facing his bed is a picture of a huge fat-bellied dragon, peering through red slits as it curls its scaled body around a tiny wide-eyed boy.

'That's me,' he says, following the direction of her gaze and tapping the little figure, who does bear a resemblance to him. He runs a finger along the arch of the beast's back. 'And the dragon's my dad. Ready to eat any monsters that come near me.'

'Cheery.' When he turns an inquisitive gaze on her, frowning again, she adds, 'I bet it helps you sleep, having your dragon watch over you.'

He gives an uncertain nod and it occurs to her how different he is to her niece and nephew, more perceptive, more attuned to the things adults say. Lucas and Maisie couldn't care less. They've never needed to be alert to the things grown-ups try to hide. They know they're safe.

'How about a trip to the swings? There must be a playground nearby?'

'There's one in Kirkley.' Daniel frowns, considering the idea.

'Perfect,' she says, all the while picturing the wilderness of muddy nature separating the O'Keefe house from its nearest village. With any luck, Suzie will lend her the car.

'Mummy will say no.'

To their surprise, Suzie says they can go to the playground as long as they are back in time for tea. Whilst she is all smiles, pretending she's easy-going, a nasty red rash burns above her head.

'You can't take the car, though.' She pauses. 'And you can't walk on the road, it's too dangerous. You'll have to cross the fields.'

Anna can't think of anything worse than trudging through mud and ankle-deep puddles. A deterrent against future trips, she suspects. Still, even without wellingtons, it's a treat to get out of the house.

It takes them half an hour, but Daniel doesn't complain, accepting the tedium and muck in a way that Billie's children never would.

'Whose room is opposite mine, Daniel?'

He's reluctant to answer, chewing his tongue again, a play of wary oranges and pondering greens above his head. 'Lily's.'

Anna stops walking. 'She lived with you?'

He nods but looks away, signalling the end of the conversation.

The playground is on the outskirts of Kirkley, between the village hall, a squat flat-roofed building, and a field of green wheat. The place is deserted, the only evidence of life a collection of cigarette butts and two empty cans of Monster Brew by the bench. Daniel runs to the swings, calling for her to push him. She was right to take him out of that house. Here he can be a little boy again. When Gabriel had said it was just the three of them, the loneliness had hit her in the gut but she'd been considering herself. Until this moment she hadn't imagined how that isolation might feel to Daniel.

They fall into an easy rhythm, her hands pushing him forward as he thrusts his legs like arrows into the sky.

'Higher.' He's breathless.

'See if you can pull down some of that horrid cloud.'

'OK.' At the top of the arc, he lets go with one hand and snatches at the sky. Her heart bounds but she stops herself from calling out a warning even as it throws him off balance. Let him be a little reckless.

'I need to go higher, Anna.'

This time he swipes with his whole arm, his body lurching sideways, almost tipping him off the seat. He gives a small cry but then he's bucking with his body to go higher still, so she says, 'Come on, Dan, you can do it. Tear down that cloud.'

It happens in slow motion. The swing rises taut on its chains and with a kick like he's spurring a horse on, Daniel throws himself into the empty sky. Legs and arms flailing, he scrabbles to find a hold as the earth sucks his body downwards. With a scream, Anna runs forward, half blinded by a burst of panic. The empty swing cracks against her hip and she's too late. He's hit the ground. She falls on her knees beside the still little body, afraid to touch him. With a winded gag, he rolls onto his side, his mouth an open cave as he tries to suck oxygen into his lungs. Neon orange rips open the air as she scoops him up and staggers to the bench. She holds him tight, putting him back together. Beads of blood ooze through a cap of sand and gravel on both his knees, but he doesn't cry. When his breathing eases, he gets off her lap.

'I could really have hurt myself,' he says in his sombre

miniature-adult voice, and a laugh of shock and relief escapes her.

'That's the craziest, most daredevil thing I've ever seen. Like Superman launching himself into the sky.'

With a big juddering sigh, he acknowledges this fact. 'I like Superman.'

'Is that so? You and your froglets making plans to save the world?'

'No.' He picks gravel from his right knee, face blank and absorbed in the task. 'I just have to save my mum.'

On the walk home, Daniel makes her promise not to tell Suzie about his fall. As they turn onto the garden path, he takes her hand.

'Can I have your frog?'

'Nope.' She laughs. 'I'm attached to it.'

'But you're too old for toy frogs.'

She swings his arm. 'Still keeping it.'

He gives a sigh, then brightens. 'My house has lots of secrets. Do you want to see one?'

'Of course. As long as I don't have to be sworn to secrecy with blood or spit.'

They find Suzie in the kitchen chopping onions. 'These blasted things,' she says, wiping her eyes on her arm.

Daniel gives her a quick hug and runs out before she notices the bloodied state of his knees. 'Can we watch some telly?'

Anna follows him, relieved to escape the room, which Suzie has filled to the walls with an inky blue-black sea. A dark and drowning place.

The television is on but Daniel ignores it, lifting the clay boat off the coffee table with both hands and giving it to her. 'I made that for Daddy specially, so don't drop it.'

He drags the coffee table towards the wall, then glances into the corridor before throwing back one side of the stripy rug it was sitting on. A glass circle about a meter in diameter is embedded in the stone floor. He presses a switch by the skirting board and a light stutters on beneath the glass, revealing a deep stone shaft. Anna's head spins with vertigo.

'It's a secret well.' Daniel kneels beside her, clasping his fingertips as he waits for her reaction.

'Now *that* is cool.'

'It's got water in it and everything.'

The water lies far below, a faint sheen of light brushing its surface. If she stares too hard, it fades and there's nothing but empty blackness. She swallows, sitting back from the edge.

'I think Lily's down there.'

A rash of goose bumps lifts across her shoulders. Putting the clay boat on the floor, she searches for some colour trace to help her read the boy. Finding nothing, her stomach flips over in alarm. 'Why would you say such a thing, Daniel?'

'Because I've seen her in my dreams. She keeps knocking on the glass.'

Her heart is a canter of hooves in her chest, kicking up yolk-yellow dust. Daniel's face is so pale it has taken on a blue-green tinge, as if stained by the water, but there is still no colour above him. She tries to re-cover the well but he sits on the folded rug.

'I promise you she's not down there, Daniel.' But even as she says it, her heart pounds harder, because what does she know?

'I know that really. It's just bad dreams.' He gives a small shrug. 'She's hiding from the people who were being mean to her. That's what I would do, too.'

Her eyesight fills with warning yellows and oranges. 'What people?'

'On the Internet. I saw on her computer. They hated her. They didn't say it exactly, but they wanted her to die.'

'Dan?' Suzie calls from the kitchen. 'Teatime. Go wash your hands.'

He doesn't move but stares in the direction of his mother's voice. Now his colours come. A messy mix like a paint palette left out in the rain. Anna lowers her voice to a whisper. 'What do you have to save your mum from, Daniel?'

He presses his lips together as he works his jaw, biting down on the things he can't tell her. Hearing Suzie's footsteps in the corridor, Anna lifts him to his feet, kicking the rug flap back into place. It hits the floor with the crack of a whip.

'What's this?' Suzie arrives in the doorway, wiping her hands on a tea towel. To Anna's relief, she's staring at the television, where two men scuffle on the ground, pounding each other's faces. She marches across the room, reaching for her son, her slight frame staggering as she hefts him onto her hip. He looks uncomfortable, holding back from her, his feet knocking against her knees.

'Look how upset he is.'

'We weren't paying attention to the TV.' The coffee table is still out of place, but Suzie is too worked up to notice. Anna points at the clay boat, which has rolled over onto its side. 'We were playing with the boat Daniel made.'

A searing whirl of tangerine moves through her vision. Telling lies is a most uncomfortable thing.

'You may not have been watching the TV, but Dan was. I can see it in his face. We try to shield our son from violence.'

Over his mother's shoulder, Daniel meets Anna's eyes, reminding her to keep their secrets.

~ 8 ~

Envy is yellow-green
like dry leaves

Suzie's humming as she fastens the strap of her silver sandals. It's the closest to happy Anna's ever seen her, as she ruffles Daniel's hair, kisses her husband, applies pink lip gloss. It sparks a dull red resentment in Anna's stomach, having been scolded two days before when Suzie discovered Daniel's injured knees at bathtime. She has been forbidden to take him to the playground again. Yet here Suzie is, giddy as she prepares to escape the house, whilst denying everyone else the same relief.

There's a slight hesitation as Suzie reaches for the car keys, a faint wash of sienna above the woman's head, but then she walks out without a backward glance.

Suzie in her silver sandals and her pink lip gloss, getting the hell out.

Gabriel turns on the radio, raising the volume. 'What's for dinner tonight, Dan?'

His son's eyes widen with mischief as he looks at Anna. Cupping a hand over his mouth, he mutters something. His dad tells him to speak up, he can't hear him.

'Pasta crap,' Daniel says, watching for her reaction.

'Louder, please, or it'll be shepherd's pie,' Gabriel says, and he grins at Anna across the kitchen, including her. 'What do we always have on a Thursday?'

'Pasta CRAP,' Daniel shouts, and Gabriel swoops him into the air, making the boy shriek with delight.

'Show Anna how we do Strong Man, Daddy.'

She's instructed to look away and get her mobile ready to take a photo.

'Now,' Daniel shouts. She looks up to find Gabriel in a carnival strong man lunge, puffing out his chest, Daniel held high above his head, on outstretched arms. She gets a single snapshot before Daniel's rigid posture turns into a loose string of spaghetti and their pose collapses.

As the three of them laugh, something slots into place. It isn't the house that suffocates the life out of everyone.

It's Suzie.

Shortly after she's changed into the T-shirt and cotton shorts she sleeps in, there's a knock on the door. Guessing it's Daniel, she doesn't bother to pull on a jumper, but instead she finds Gabriel. His size is a constant surprise, filling her doorway; he is built like a climbing frame she could spend happy hours clambering and twisting herself around, like the little lust-monkey she is. Seeing that she's ready for bed, he apologises, backing away.

'Is something wrong, Gabriel?'

His feet are bare, she notices, the sight of them oddly intimate, a reminder that she is living in someone's home, inside the heart of a family.

He shakes his head, his pained smile a rebuke to his own weakness. 'Thursdays are tough, that's all.'

'Why's that?' She follows him a step into the corridor, wanting to stop his retreat.

'Suzie has a shift at her parents' pub, the Wells Inn, on Thursdays. It's something she's always done. It makes her happy and gets her out of the house. Which she needs now more than ever.'

Anna hides a smile at his earnest silver greens. He's realised a little too late that a knock on her door could be misinterpreted. 'Do you want a hand getting Daniel to bed?'

'All done. That's my Thursday treat, time with my boy.' He's looking anywhere but at her bare legs and the points of her nipples showing through her top. 'I wondered if you wanted a cup of hot chocolate?'

'You read my mind.' She's never liked hot chocolate, but right now the idea of sitting in the kitchen with Gabriel, just the two of them, is irresistible. There's something calm about him, an oasis of stillness that feels safe and warm.

Lauritz had that same quality.

She pulls on sweat pants and a jumper and follows him to the kitchen, where the air between them is a fluid swirl of pale and deeper pinks, like paint being mixed.

As he moves about the kitchen, pouring milk into a pan and warming it on the hob, she tries not to watch him, afraid he'll catch something in her gaze. On the wall behind the door is the whiteboard where Suzie notes school events, appointments and emergency numbers.

Detective Adeyemi's phone number is on there, in the same weary navy as her car. Gabriel's mobile too, in wasp-sting red. Anna still has his number saved on her phone. If she was a bad person, the immoral little horn-devil her big sister thinks she is, she would send him a text one day. Something innocuous. That's all it would take to open a thread of secret conversation. She won't, of course, but fantasy never hurt anyone.

She watches his shoulders moving beneath the thin cotton of his T-shirt as he stirs chocolate powder into the milk. Imagines the heat of his skin, how he'd smell, how the dip of his spine between those powerful shoulder blades would feel beneath her tongue. As if hearing her thoughts, he looks back at her, smiling, and she glances away, her eyes returning to the whiteboard.

That's when she sees it. Along the bottom of the board, Lily's name and number, rubbed out, only faint impressions remaining. Ghost letters. She wonders who took it upon themselves to erase her details, and how painful it must have been.

Whoever it was had lost all hope.

'Thursdays were my nights with the kids.' Gabriel pours the hot chocolate into two mugs and sits down. 'Once Dan was in bed, Lily and I would hang out. Sometimes we'd watch a movie, her choice, of course: boyfriend dramas and that. Always awful.'

He doesn't seem to notice how half-hearted her laugh is, because it pleases him, a wisp of pink candyfloss lifting away. It's replaced by a deeper tone, an antique rose: the colour of nostalgia and remembered happiness.

'Or we'd drink hot chocolate and talk.' He sighs, those heavy Lily blues never far behind his smile. Infectious too, if she isn't careful. 'During school holidays, Suzie and Daniel would spend the odd night at the Wells Inn. Daniel thinks that's beyond exciting. And then Lily and I would go and climb trees. There are some proper ancient beasts out there.'

He runs out of steam, giving her a sad smile, grateful to have been heard, whilst she tries not to imagine Lily and Gabriel climbing together, hearts pounding, breathless as they lift themselves up and out of the world. Yellow-green confetti falls around her, the hungry colour of leaves sucked dry by the sun.

Whilst she will never send Gabriel a text or touch him in a way that wakes up his body, she can't deny her colours.

9

Storm clouds are the
colour of lost hope

'What's he like?' Billie looks tired, drawn. The light through the café window is unkind, picking out the loosening skin along her jaw and the netting of fine lines beneath her eyes. *This is my Saturday face*, she'd said when she arrived, blaming it on the dinner party they'd hosted the night before.

'Gabriel? Nice. Friendly. We chat sometimes. He made me hot chocolate the other day. Most effort anyone's made since I arrived.'

'How very charming of him.'

She gives her sister a look. 'He's trying to make up for his wife, that black hole of humanity.'

'There's a general consensus amongst the school mums that Gabriel's a sexy beast.' Billie has that look, one that hounded Anna throughout her childhood, amused and knowing. 'There's no way he's escaped your keen eye.'

'You're the one who keeps mentioning him. Might it be *you* who has a bit of a crush?'

'Please.' Her sister gives a disgusted grimace.

Billie likes to tease Anna for her *keen eye*. Usually Anna laughs along, keeping to the roles assigned during childhood. To Billie's soaring eagle of intellect, she's always been the scrappy little fox, following its nose and appetites in meandering loops.

57

'All I know is Suzie's the least warm human being I've ever met.'

'She's not so bad.' Billie gives an amused huff, stretching out her legs. The Bandstand Café is empty apart from themselves and an elderly woman breaking chocolate cake into crumbs for the pigeons. Earlier, they'd taken a walk so Billie could show Anna the sights. It had taken under ten minutes, the village consisting of a single road leading in and out, and a cobbled square with a row of oak trees and a dilapidated Victorian pavilion in its centre. *Everything you could need*, Billie had said, pointing out three tea shops, a chemist's, a Tesco and a lingerie shop.

Nochenweem with fancy knickers, Anna thought.

Her sister had made no reference to the posters of Lily taped to lamp posts, phone booths and the windows of flint-fronted houses.

'Don't forget what Suzie's been through.'

Something about the comfortable manner in which Billie refers to the missing girl bothers her. 'Jonah says you knew Lily.'

'He said that?' Billie's gaze is vague, as if trying to recall an acquaintance's name. 'She used to babysit for us when our regular girl couldn't make it. Do they ever talk about her?'

'Never. What happened?'

'She didn't come home one night.' Billie straightens, plucking her blouse away from her stomach. 'But given what she was like, it's not terribly surprising.'

'What she was like?'

'Wayward. Out of control.' Her sister shifts in her seat, adding two lumps of sugar to her coffee. 'Look, no one wants to speak ill of the dead.'

'No, of course not. I shouldn't have—'

'But she was a little piece of work.' Leaning back in the

58

chair, Billie folds her arms across her belly. 'Still. As a mother, it doesn't bear thinking about.'

Having declined Billie's offer of a lift home, Anna strolls around the small square, delaying the moment of return to the mouldy tomb of her room. She studies the pavilion's antiquated beauty, its roof undulating outwards from a central pinnacle, like a lady's parasol. Above the door, a brass plaque gleams in the sun.

The Kirkley Petrifying Well

Entry 5s.

Take the Waters for Health and Beauty

She climbs the ironwork steps to peer through the elongated windows. The glass is rippled with age but she can make out tables with upturned chairs, and large cabinets lining the walls between the windows. She scrubs the window with her thumb, trying to get a better look at the objects on display. There's something curious about them, all the same dirt-grey colour, crude and misshapen as lumps of rock. She follows the windows round to an entrance with a sign above it that says: *The Petrifying Well Tea House and Museum* in letters of acidic tangerine so sharp and aggressive she feels them in her stomach like a sudden cramp.

'I wonder how many poor Victorians died in agony looking for health and beauty.'

She glances round to find Suzie at the foot of the steps, turned out of thin air like the unhappy ghost she is but making small talk as though they are quite comfortable with each other. Friends, no less. Anna gives a ridiculous little wave in greeting whilst Suzie regards her with the same grave expression as

Daniel's. Her thin arms, straining with the weight of super-market bags, look like they might snap under a firm breeze.

'What's the Petrifying Well?'

Suzie puts the bags on the ground, rubbing the red welts in her palms left by the plastic handles. 'A natural spring. In the cave beneath the pavilion.' She reaches for the bags then changes her mind, straightening again. 'There's a myth about a girl back in the sixteenth century who got herself pregnant. She wouldn't say who the father was, so her family were convinced she'd slept with the Devil. She ran away and raised the child in the cave. Which is where her father found them and killed the child. She cried and cried and her tears ran into the water and cursed it.'

'And then some Victorian marketing man bottled it and made a mint. Clever. I might have to get some.' To date, their longest conversation.

'It's closed at the moment.' Suzie picks up her bags, their collective weight making her huff with the strain. 'The amount of rain we've had has made it unsafe. It's not a nice place. I wish they'd tear the whole thing down.'

As Suzie turns away, Anna tries to think of something to prolong their conversation, as if a couple more words might be all that is needed to build a bridge between them.

'I just want to say...' The woman's eyes have become glass marbles, cold and deflecting. 'If there's anything you want me to do...'

Suzie doesn't respond, but nor does she walk away.

'Gabriel thinks you should have the room next to the one you're in at the moment. But it belonged... belongs to my niece Lily.' Suzie can't meet Anna's eyes now, addressing her words to the pavilion, and Anna can't bring herself to study the sorrowful roll of blues and greys; an endless surf of loss. 'I'm not ready to pack up her things yet.'

Before she can assure Suzie she has no interest in the room, the other woman interrupts, a rough grain of defence in her tone. 'I don't care what anybody else thinks. I *have* to believe she's coming back.'

But the storm-cloud grey says her hope is long gone.

10

Beige doesn't give a shit

The well in the house fascinates her father, who bends at the waist to study it. His left hand is behind his back, his stiff fingers pointing outwards like a dried flower head. She pictures Gabriel's hands, their loose, unbound strength, the skin across his knuckles patterned with scars like fossils embedded in stone. How recklessly he must treat them.

Her father wants to know the history of the house and what kind of dwelling existed on the spot previously. Her mother ushers him into an armchair, fixing him in place with a cup of tea.

'I think, despite that awful little room, this is a good decision. It must be nice to focus on just one child rather than a whole pack of them.' Her mother perches on the chair arm, her hand finding her husband's, a gesture of casual affection that Anna doubts either of them is aware of. 'Billie's over the moon, of course, having you so near.' She makes it sound as though Anna had had options.

With a grunt of agreement, her father lifts the cup and saucer to his chin and takes a careful sip.

'I've had Marni on the phone, grilling me for details of your new life. Apparently you've abandoned all your old friends,' her mother says.

Anna rolls her eyes, trying not smile. 'I've called her plenty of times. It's an excuse to catch up with you, Mum.' Her friends always loved her mother, whose flame, whilst not one to cosy up to for warmth and comfort, is bright and humorous and draws everyone into its light.

'We comfort each other in your absence.' Her mother winks, planting a kiss on the crown of Anna's head as she gets up and excuses herself. Once she's left the room, her father puts down his cup and saucer and rocks himself out of the chair. He collects a plain plastic bag from the hallway. 'Before I forget, some bits and bobs I found whilst clearing out the garage. I can't tell what's yours and what's Billie's.'

He hands her the bag, his gaze falling on the poster of Lily in the window.

'I remember reading about that poor young girl in the papers,' he says. 'She's been missing about four months now.'

Anna nods. 'So you've made the connection.'

'*I* have, but not your mother. Do they have any idea what happened to her?'

Upstairs, a door closes, her mother having clearly allowed herself another little tour before finding the bathroom.

'They don't mention her at all.'

'I read a statistic the other day about how many teenagers run away in this country,' he says, optimism lifting his neat white eyebrows. She is struck by a wave of love for her father, for the retired GP in him that still wants to reach out and save people. 'They simply vanish, no communication, no reasons offered. Often they come back.'

'Let's hope that's the case here.' She looks inside the bag. With an exclamation of delight, she takes out a ballerina made of coloured glass, one long leg pointing behind her, arms stretched out in front as though preparing for flight. Her childhood treasure; at the age of seven, the most precious object she'd ever owned. She touches the delicate fingertips, the ruffle of the full skirt, amazed to find them intact.

'I still remember opening the box and finding her inside.'

Her father smiles. 'And I still remember your little face.'

She holds the figure up to the light, its pinks and reds and purples coming to life. In the centre of the ballerina's breast-bone is an air bubble, a tiny disfigurement that she hadn't noticed until Billie, finding her wooden chess set a little dull in comparison, had pointed it out. After that, the bubble was always the first thing she'd see, and as much as she loved the figurine, the rapture of those first few moments never returned.

Without doubt, the most unkind thing her sister had ever done.

She puts the ballerina on the coffee table beside Daniel's lopsided clay boat and feels through the rest of the bag's contents. An envelope catches her attention, the flap still sealed and intact. The stamp depicts a cartoon man in a green jumper, smoking a cigarette, with the word *Danmark* above. Her name is on the front, above her parents' address. The room gives a carousel swirl, her vision filling with wild flares of crimson and sun-yellow anticipation.

'What's this?'

Her father isn't sure. It's one of the items he'd come across in the bottom of a cardboard box. He holds up his finger, remembering. 'It fell out of a book, I think. One of Billie's old mathematical texts.'

Before she can ask any further questions, her mother enters the room. Obeying an old guilt reflex, Anna drops the letter into Daniel's train-set box. Her father notices but makes no comment.

'I was just telling Anna what a taskmaster you've been recently, making me clear out all those boxes in the garage.'

But her mother's not listening. 'I thought the O'Keefes only had one child?'

'They do. Daniel.' Anna can't concentrate. Her father is watching her with a frown of concern, and any moment now, her mother's maternal instinct, keen as a bee's antennae, will kick in. 'I'm starving. Shall we go?'

Her mother looks back towards the hallway, pursing her mouth. 'Who's the young man upstairs then? He gave me quite a shock.'

She runs upstairs, heading for her own bedroom until she realises the door to Lily's is wide open. The boy from the garden is sitting on the four-poster bed. Somehow she knew it would be him. There'd been something territorial about his manner as he'd leaned on the garden wall making pathetic insinuations. He doesn't look up at her approach. A small hand-crafted doll with gauze wings dangles by its yellow cotton hair from his finger and thumb. Engrossed, he swings it through a lazy arc.

'What are you doing? You can't be in here.'

He drops the doll beside him on the bed and looks up at her.

'I can, as it happens. I was a friend of Lily's.' He leans sideways, a casual arm held out to shake her hand. 'I'm Ben, and you must be Anna.'

She has an urge to slap his smug face. 'But how did you get into the house?'

'I've got a key to the back door. Gabe and Suze know they can trust me. I'm no thief.'

She narrows her eyes, studying his expression as the air fills with soot and smashed reds like paint stepped across a floor. He can't know.

'Well. It would have been considerate if you'd let us know

you were here. You gave my mother quite a shock.' She hates the haughty note in her voice. It lets Ben know he has her at a disadvantage. She's not sure why he makes her uncomfortable. She's never been one to cross the road to avoid a huddle of teenage boys.

He doesn't reply, but picks up the little doll again. Turning it upside down, he jams his middle finger through its cardboard base and up into the stuffed cone of its dress. He bobs the impaled doll at her, grinning, pleased with himself.

'Hello, Anna,' he says in a breaking falsetto. 'My name's Lily.'

She shakes her head in disgust, retreating to the corridor. 'What's wrong with you?'

'I miss Lily,' he says, but above his head there is only gelatinous beige. He's not sad or filled with dread for his missing friend. He's bored.

Lunch turns into the longest two hours of her life, the letter like a burning ember dropping through her thoughts. She struggles to eat and repeats questions until her mother asks if there is anything wrong, observing that she has been out of sorts since she went upstairs to confront the young man.

'Confront?' Her mother's choice of word irritates her. 'He's a weedy kid, not some hardened criminal.'

She pleads the beginnings of a cold, a lie that excuses her from an afternoon at Billie's. Once home, she notes with relief that Ben's bicycle is gone. She heads straight to the toy box in the sitting room, but the envelope with the Danish stamp is no longer there. She upends the box over her lap, scattering tracks and painted blocks on rubber wheels across the floor.

'Anna?'

Gabriel is in the doorway, his expression amused and questioning.

'I didn't see your car.' She starts collecting up the toys.

'I walked back after dropping Suze and Dan off at the Wells Inn. I wasn't in the mood for a long family lunch.'

She smiles. 'I faked a cold to escape an afternoon at my sister's.'

'So we're both as bad as each other.' Gabriel breaks eye contact, holding up a finger as if something has just occurred to him. He leaves the room and she hears a drawer open in the kitchen. 'You're looking for this?' He returns with her envelope. 'I'm not sure how it got in Dan's box, but I put it aside for safe keeping.'

She takes the letter and rushes upstairs to her bedroom, throwing her bag against the door to keep it shut. The flap peels back with ease and whilst age may have dried up the glue, something tells her it had been opened and carefully re-sealed a long time ago.

This is her second letter from Lauritz, the first one also posted to her parents' address, where Billie had intercepted it. Finding her in the kitchen, grabbing her by the wrist and dragging her upstairs. *Danish stamp*, she'd whispered, waving the letter out of Anna's reach. She had stood over Anna as she'd read it, and watched her heart break.

His wife is pregnant, Anna had said.

You should be happy for Lauritz. It's what he wanted, but then Billie had sat on the bed beside Anna, hugging and rocking her as she'd cried.

Unlike the first letter, this one has been typed, setting a formal, disconnected tone, and it is brief. Black words on white paper read through a shifting screen of rusty dread and hopeful greens. If only his words could be imbued with the colour of his emotions, but they can't. For that she'd have to see his face.

67

Dear Anna,

I hope you will not be angry with me for contacting you. It has been so long since last we saw each other. By now, you are a grown woman, running her own life, and maybe you have forgotten me already.

You are asking yourself why am I writing. It is because I think of you so often still. I spend many years trying to guess what you'll be doing now and what your job will be and what kind of man you married or plan to marry.

So instead of becoming crazy with these questions I think I will write and ask you. It is your decision if you send me the answers or decide not to. But I hope you will choose the first option.

I don't know what is the right way to sign off. I hope you remember me.

Lauritz

She reads it through three times. The address in the right-hand corner is one she recognises. The big white house with the black-tiled roof overlooking the Øresund, whose waters freeze into rippled waves against the shoreline during winter. Folding the page in half, she tears off one long strip after another until it is shredded and illegible.

Lauritz hadn't offered a single piece of information about himself.

Picking up the pieces, she returns them to the envelope. The postmark is June 2007. Four years after the summer she turned nineteen. Their summer.

How it ended up amongst her sister's things when Billie had already moved out of their parents' house, she can't guess, but it has sat in a box for nine years, giving Lauritz his answer. Not that it matters. He'd written out of curiosity, nothing more.

She thinks how she scolded Daniel for pulling the shell off a snail, allowing his idle curiosity to destroy a small life. It's excusable in a boy of eight, unforgivable in a grown man.

II

Gratitude is a mauve mist

'Anna? Are you in there?' Suzie's voice is a panting rasp, her knuckles going full pelt against the bedroom door. It wakes Anna with such a violent start that she flails out, a bony crunch as her elbow connects with the wall. The door falls open. 'You're still sleeping?'

The one day she has allowed herself a lie-in. She's about to remind Suzie that no one needs her in the morning, but the colours above Suzie's head dry her mouth. A storm of tangerine is making holes in the air.

'What's happened?' She finds herself breathless in response.

'Dan needs to go to school. Now.' Suzie holds the car keys out, her hand shaking. 'Can you drive?'

Suzie offers no explanation, speaking only to give directions. Whatever caused her panic is gone. She is pale, her hair damp and lifeless against her skull. It's a twenty-minute drive through narrow roads. Occasionally they break out of the trees to hilltop views of open land like a gasp of fresh air. Anna loses track of the many turns, each one leading to an identical lane, until, without warning, they reach a signpost for Lodswold. Past it is a tiny hamlet, a single house deep on either side of the road, with a village shop, the Barn Owl pub and the primary school, a large Edwardian building. Suzie instructs her to pull over some distance from the pedestrian crossing opposite the school gates.

Anna waits in the car, watching Suzie and Dan fall in with the other parents and children heading through the school gates. As people slow to greet each other, Suzie picks up her pace, moving through the crowd like water trickling through a rock pile. On her return, she insists on driving. They don't speak for the entire journey, Suzie's rusty, iron fortress warning Anna not to attempt small talk.

'Don't tell Gabriel what happened this morning,' Suzie says, as she pulls into the drive and switches off the engine.

Anna hesitates. 'What *did* happen?'

'Nothing. I was tired, that's all.' Suzie checks her reflection in the rear-view mirror. She flicks life into her hair, her energy returning to its usual sharp precision. As Anna opens the car door, Suzie stops her with a hand on her wrist. 'Thanks for driving. I mean it.' A soft mauve mist rises out of her, breaking over Anna like lapping surf.

'I can help with drop-offs and pick-ups if you like?' Here, finally, something she can do.

Suzie's gratitude sifts away, her blue core returning. 'OK,' she says after a moment. 'You could do the morning school run.'

'Great.' Anna fails to keep the surprise from her voice.

'On the condition you don't tell Gabriel.' Suzie unlocks the front door, then pauses with the key still in the lock. 'You have to let him think I'm still doing it. He'll worry otherwise.'

'My lips are sealed.'

For the first time since she arrived at the O'Keefes', Suzie gives her a genuine smile.

Late evening, the light greying through the cloud. When Anna opens her window to feel for rain, a confetti of dry paint falls away from the sash frame. She brushes the paint scraps out

71

over the ledge and decides to go for a run. There's a knock on her door as she is tying her laces. The door swings open of its own accord.

'You're going out?' Suzie says, eyeing Anna's trainers, her own feet bare. In cotton pyjama bottoms and one of Gabriel's T-shirts, she looks ready for bed though it's not even eight.

'For a run.' In her head, she begs the woman not to ask her – now of all times – to do a chore. Once she's dressed to go running, a signal reaches her blood and her body's ready to go. She might stop breathing if she has to remain inside a minute longer.

'Never understood the appeal.' Suzie grimaces. 'Can I tempt you to a drink instead?'

'A drink?'

'Sure, why not?' Suzie's face blooms with mischief. It makes her look young and vital. Unrecognisable. 'After all, I'm not getting up for the school run.'

'Gabe's gone to see a man about a dog,' Suzie says as she skips across the kitchen to a heavy oak sideboard, swinging back both doors. The action lifts cords of muscle on her slim arms. Her petite frame makes her look delicate, but Anna suspects there's a strength to Suzie that isn't immediately obvious. 'Or should I say a man about a log? Get it? Because he's a tree surgeon?'

Anna gives a good-natured laugh, but she's thrown. It's rare for someone to surprise her. A person's colours betray their light and shadow long before their actions do. In Suzie she'd seen only the grey metal of her loss. She should have known better. People are never a single colour.

Suzie can't seem to slow down. Two shot glasses taken from the sideboard, and from the freezer a bottle of brown liquid with a green label, all delivered to the table with movements sharp and keen as a dancer's. Above her head, streamers of happy marigold and a lively shade of turquoise that heralds fun.

'Jägermeister?' Anna holds up the bottle. 'I was picturing a sedate glass of wine.'

'Do it properly or not at all. Applies to drinking and marriage.' Suzie pours two measures and holds up her glass. 'Here. This is to seal our secret pact. About the driving.'

They clink glasses and down the shots. The liquid heats a path down to Anna's stomach. She refills their glasses. To hell with it. She's always been dry tinder when it comes to a harmless bit of fun. The second mouthful follows the first and lights a happy flame in her chest. Her time here is about to improve.

When it gets dark, Suzie takes a bag of tea lights from beneath the sink, lining them along the sill. Their flames twist and flicker, reflected in the window, catching silver grains of rain as it drifts just beyond the glass. The bottle is half empty and Anna's brain is bobbing in oil, spinning and tilting as she leans forward for her newly refilled glass. Suzie gives a series of neat burps, three perfect bubbles. The woman even belches with poise.

'Guess how many times Gabe asked me out before I gave in?'

'Tell me.'

'Four.'

'Why the resistance?'

'I thought he was a big oaf.' Suzie stretches, arching her back, and sighs. 'I assumed he'd have the manners of a pig and walk around farting and grunting with not an original thought in his big head.'

'What changed your mind?' A verdigris column breaks through her drunken fug.

'Because I was mistaken. Gabe's sharp and intuitive. He

has a kind of animal wisdom. And he's a little wild, which sometimes I am too.'

A day ago Anna would have given a disbelieving laugh at the notion of Suzie's wild side, but she's been invited to meet the real Suzie tonight and finds her all the more likeable for her initial reserve.

'Besides, he wrote me a poem.'

The idea makes Anna laugh. 'Now that I *can't* picture.'

Suzie laughs too. 'Have you any idea how ridiculous a pencil looks in that big fist of his?'

'Let me guess. Roses are red, violets are blue, I'm in love, Suzie, I hope you are too.'

'Something like that.' Suzie presses her lips against a grin. 'I might let you read it one day. If you prove trustworthy, of course.'

Anna sobers. 'I didn't take the Sowerbys' money.'

Suzie gets up to clear their glasses, and whilst she doesn't stagger, her actions are tight and concentrated. 'There are plenty of worse things a person can do than pinch a bit of cash. Believe me, Anna, I know.'

The next morning, with a head that feels swollen and fit to burst like the mercury bulb in a cartoon thermometer, she feels her way downstairs. To her relief, only Suzie is in the kitchen, pale but steady as she drinks a cup of tea by the window.

Anna gives a rueful grin as Suzie slides an open can of Coke across the counter.

'Drink that.' Her tone as cold and flat as the greys washing around her.

'You look remarkably unscathed.'

Suzie gives her a dull, humourless stare. 'Why wouldn't I be?'

With that, the good feeling from the night before is gone. Once more Anna is the unwanted help, an outsider, a thief.

12

Dislike is a burnt and sooty black

Suzie gives her the night off, wanting time alone with her son whilst Gabriel goes to the local climbing wall. She'd been increasingly frosty as the day had progressed, making sure Anna didn't mistake an evening of drunken silliness for the beginnings of friendship.

Billie, delighted with an excuse to get out of cooking on a Tuesday evening, offers to take her out. As they leave the O'Keefes', Anna tries to mention Lauritz's letter, but her nerve fails her. Billie won't understand the impact. Without intending any hurt, her sister will say something dismissive, because it makes no logical sense for a love affair that ended thirteen years ago to matter still. She never told Billie the reason for her lonely year in Copenhagen, how she'd read her Tarot cards and divined some message urging action; to chase after what she wanted. Over family lunch she announced that she'd been offered an au pair job in Copenhagen – she hadn't – whilst under the table her fingers twisted the napkin into a rope as she waited for someone to mention Lauritz. No one did, though she'd caught a flash of calculation in Billie's eyes.

Billie has a hankering for spaghetti carbonara. She knows a place but it's forty minutes away, near the coast. The distance appeals to Anna. Maybe there'll be something to see. A bit of life.

'We'll take the scenic route,' Billie says, but it turns out to be more of the same. A long road unravelling between fields and tiny villages with thatched white-stone cottages and not a soul in sight. Anna lowers her window, letting the muggy breeze mess with her hair, ignoring Billie's complaints about the rain getting in. When they reach a derelict garden centre at the side of the road and her sister announces that they've arrived, she laughs, assuming it's a joke, until Billie turns into the gravel car park.

The Pizza Pasta Parlour, once the garden centre's cafeteria, sits in the lee of the disused greenhouses. Through mould-ridden glass Anna can see trestle tables with empty terracotta pots, a section of strip lighting hanging down like the broken branch of a tree.

'My guilty pleasure,' Billie says. 'Jonah has banned flavour from my house.'

There's a lone VW camper van in the car park and no other buildings as far as the hills on the horizon. No danger of eavesdroppers, thinks Anna.

Inside the restaurant, the wooden bench tables have red-and-white checked cloths and floral centrepieces made of dry pasta. As soon as they are seated, Billie's questions begin. She wants to know how the atmosphere is, whether Anna has sensed any tension between Suzie and Gabriel and if Lily's name is ever mentioned.

'Anyone would think you'd planted me there as a spy,' Anna says.

Billie is offended. 'It's called being sympathetic. If you'd heard the conclusions people have leapt to, you'd appreciate my interest in facts rather than hearsay.'

Two oversized bowls of linguine arrive, tacky with cream sauce and pimpled with squares of ham. Billie shakes two full tablespoons of Parmesan over hers. 'Jonah nags me to watch my diet, but the day these curves vanish, he'll be a starving man.'

Anna pictures the flirty exchange between Jonah and the young garage attendant, and how he took it all in his stride. 'Are you two happy?'

'Of course.' Billie replaces her fork with its plump roll of linguine. 'Still madly, wildly, hornily in love.' Lifting her wine glass, she finds it empty. 'Remind me why we ordered wine by the glass rather than a bottle? It's like foreplay without the sex.'

Anna risks a glance above the crown of her sister's head. A flicker of oranges and reds, a blue heart at the centre of the flame. Visible only for a matter of seconds. The thought of Billie and Jonah being unhappy frightens her. Their stability is the bulwark of her jellyfish existence, keeping her safe.

'He used to be quite a hit at school, with both teachers and parents, back in the days when his charm button was switched on,' Billie says.

'Jonah?'

'Gabriel. Try to keep up, sweets.' Her sister makes a disparaging face and Anna is tempted to point out how often Billie brings the conversation back to Gabriel. 'There's something a little superior about his wounded-animal act.'

'Act?' She sees Gabriel in Lily's bedroom, gripping the shelf, his loss filling the air like dust. She swallows a gluey, half-chewed mouthful. 'Lily was part of his family. There's no act.'

'You forget that us mere mortals can't see through people's facades.' Billie pricks the air with her fork. 'To some, it looks like an act.'

'You don't like him.'

'What gave it away?' Her sister waggles her fingers above her head. 'Red? No, black, isn't it?'

And even though Billie's right and there's a cloud of soot above her head, Anna says, 'Your words, big sister.'

77

'I could ask why *you* like him. You're the people-reader.' Billie dabs her lips with the paper napkin. 'The thing is, Anna, most people believe Gabriel had something to do with Lily going missing.'

Billie refuses to elaborate. 'I shouldn't have said anything. You know how I feel about gossip.' She declares herself in a food funk, growing quiet, but when Anna suggests they head home, her sister gives a non-committal shrug. *No rush.*

'Daniel said Lily was getting nasty messages online.'

A geyser of ember reds shoots up from her sister's crown. Billie always insists she is off limits, so Anna tries not to stare. *If I want you to know how I'm feeling, I'll tell you.* Ruled by logic, her sister has always kept her emotions tight to her scalp, little more than muted flickers.

'Poor girl.' Billie scrunches up her napkin and tosses it onto her dirty plate. 'It's shocking the way some people behave.'

As uncharacteristic as her sister's colour display is, Anna is relieved to see it. Until now, Billie had seemed unmoved by the girl's disappearance.

'Daniel says she was scared.' She sits back, unsettled by another red burst above her sister's head.

'What did the girl expect? If you're going to stick your hand in someone else's sweetie jar, you'd better be ready for the reckoning.'

'Ready for the reckoning? Wow.'

Billie pulls a scornful grimace, plucking at the waist of her blouse. 'I'm sorry she's gone, of course I am. But she didn't help herself, the way she carried on.'

Anna takes an outraged breath, but stops herself from speaking. How they've found themselves on opposing sides over a missing girl, she's not sure. In the silence, Billie shakes the last drop of wine from her glass into her mouth and refuses to make eye contact.

'I had lunch with Mum and Dad on Sunday.' It's always down to Anna to break the silence.

'Oh yes, was it nice?' Billie, all brisk cheer.

'Dad's been clearing out the garage. He found stuff from when we were kids.'

'Photos of us with dodgy hairstyles?'

'A few of those.' She pushes her half-empty glass of wine across the table and Billie accepts it without comment. 'There was a letter inside your old maths book. For me. From Lauritz.'

Her sister nods, raising her eyebrows to feign interest. Not quite ready to relinquish her sulk. 'The one about his pregnant wife?'

'No. A later one. Sent to Mum and Dad's nine years ago. In 2007.'

There's a subtle shift in Billie's expression. 'The year Jonah and I got married. I stayed at Mum and Dad's before the wedding. Oh, I think I remember a letter. The Danish stamp, of course.'

'And the fact that you read it.'

'Did I?'

Anna nods, waiting for her sister's full recollection to catch up, reining in the angry red strands like raw whiplashes between her and Billie.

'How naughty of me. Sorry, obviously I didn't mean to keep hold of it. I must have been distracted, what with getting married and going on honeymoon.' Billie makes a sarcastic *silly me* face.

Anna had known she would treat it as a joke.

'I can't remember what it said. Don't tell me he was leaving his wife?'

Anna stares at her. 'Even if he had been, I got it nine years too late.'

'Ah well. We all get over our childish infatuations. Oh, don't look like that.' Billie pulls her into a hug across the dirty plates before getting up to pay the bill at the counter. She returns with a bottle of red wine. 'A little appeasement for poor Jo stuck at home.'

Back in the car, Billie wedges the bottle in the passenger seat footwell.

'I didn't think Jo was drinking at the moment.'

'All the more for me then,' Billie says, steering the car towards the exit. A large black vehicle passes them on the main road. She lurches over the steering wheel to watch it pass. Then she pulls out behind it, accelerating with an alarming wobble. 'That was Gabriel's car. What on earth is he doing all the way out here?'

'It's not him, Bills. He's gone climbing. What are you doing? We can't follow some random car.'

'I'm telling you, it's Gabriel. And there are no climbing walls around here, just the marina or the beach. What the fuck is he up to?'

Billie speeds up as they round a bend, Gabriel's tail lights appearing once again. When Anna tells her to stop being ridiculous and turn back, her sister claps her knee. 'I thought you were the adventurous one out of us two?'

Gabriel's car indicates right as he reaches a large wooden sign by the side of the road that says *Cranley Marina* in disappointed green letters. There's no traffic, so they wait a moment before following him along a narrow avenue bordered by thin strips of manicured lawns, past which there is nothing but endless farmland and neat hedgerows. Winding down the window, Anna sniffs the air but smells only earth. They must be close to the sea and yet she has no sense of it.

'He'll be meeting someone,' Billie says.

'But who?' Despite herself, she is curious.

The car park is empty, no sign of Gabriel's Defender. Beyond it is a yard where yachts and speedboats are stationed out of the water, perched on precarious-looking wooden struts. Billie pulls over behind a yacht, pointing out its name. '*The Wanderer*. Apt, wouldn't you say?'

Anna pushes her tongue into her cheek, trying not to grin, but Billie's mischief is infectious.

They walk past the swollen bellies of dry-docked boats, the wind whining through their masts. The place has a twitchy, watchful feel and Anna keeps snapping her head towards imagined movements. She quickens her pace.

'Do you need me to hold your hand?' Billie says, and Anna pinches her on the arm.

The marina clubhouse has an open deck facing the harbour wall. Past it are the jetties with moored boats, the swaying stalks of their masts silver in the light. The deck is crowded with diners. Fairy-light yellows and pinks float in Anna's vision as she scans the tables for Gabriel, the colour of her anticipation coming as a surprise.

Billie holds out an arm and they pause beneath the hull of a cruiser. Gabriel's car is parked in the shadows.

'There's a bar inside,' Billie says in a low voice. 'Bedrooms, too.'

Anna is about to follow her sister when she spots a dark outline in the driver's seat. 'Wait, Bills. He's still in the car.'

'Definitely waiting for someone,' Billie says, stepping back out of sight.

Minutes pass and Anna's had enough. 'We can't stand here spying on him.'

'But he's here for a reason.'

Gabriel is sitting very still, staring ahead. She follows the line of his gaze. Past the jetties, the inlet is flat and smooth as black ice, the sky above it vast and filled with stars. The join between water and sky is invisible. A person could sail out and find themselves in outer space.

'Perhaps he's looking for some peace,' she says, and Billie makes a disdainful noise.

Back at the O'Keefes', she finds a section of ceiling the size of a dinner plate collapsed on her bed. It looks like a giant bird's nest has burst upon her covers, a mess of wet plaster and matted horsehair insulation. Rainwater trickles off the ceiling's broken timbers, dripping brown onto her pillow. The attic joists are visible through the hole, and in the dark space beneath the roof, there's a flutter of motion; a draught or something alive, she can't tell.

She makes a bed on the sitting room sofa with her summer coat as a blanket. In the morning, a gentle hand on her shoulder wakes her, a mix of concern and amusement in Gabriel's mismatched eyes. The halo around his head is a sunrise of violet and coral.

'There you are, Anna.' Her name, in his voice, runs like a silver bead down her spine. 'Your bedroom door was still open this morning and your coat wasn't in the hall . . .'

His concern floods her with sugary pinks and she gives him a warm smile. 'Here I am. Safe and sound.'

She hears too late how clumsy her words are, as Lily steps into the space between them and Gabriel leaves the room.

13

The Lily Blues

She finds her ceramic frog in Daniel's bed as she changes his sheets. It makes her smile, shaking her head. She plays with it when she's brooding and low, rolling it around in her palm, stroking the wet shine of its skin. Perhaps it comforts Daniel too. Still, it's hers, not his.

She leaves Daniel's room to find Juliet, the family liaison officer, standing in her bedroom doorway, drying her fingers on a hand towel. The woman steps aside with a warm, open smile, unfazed at being caught mid snoop. 'That's not good.' She shakes the towel at the hole in the ceiling and the bucket on the mattress catching drips. 'Lucky for you you weren't in bed when it happened.' She laughs, the glint in her eye matching the mischievous saffron of her shirt. 'Where will you sleep tonight?'

Anna's smile falls away as she points to Lily's room. 'In there.'

'Lily's room?' Juliet's tone is light, her fingers working the towel under her wedding ring. 'That must have been a tough decision for Suzie and Gabriel.'

Gabriel had offered her the room with Suzie looking on in pinched silence. When Anna tried to decline the offer, Suzie had stalked out of the kitchen, leaving a trail of bruised disdain, as if seeing through her niceties. Anna couldn't think of anything worse than sleeping in the missing girl's bed.

'Tricky for you too, I'm guessing. You know, I'm here for all members of the family, and that includes you.'

Above the woman's head, with her expression still radiating concern, a new colour sparks into life, a bronzed green that Anna sees when Billie is about to pick someone's opinion to pieces.

'We can always have a chat, in confidence of course, if anything is worrying you.'

First Billie with all her questions, and now the FLO; both hoping she'll spy on the family.

Once the detective has left, Gabriel asks for Anna's help in packing up Lily's room. His booking to clear a fallen tree at Daniel's school had been cancelled five minutes earlier. He says little, but a glaze of deep red tells her he doesn't believe the excuse given.

As he unlocks the door to Lily's room, blue and red splinters burst around his hairline. It's an impressive effort at composure. Anna always pays extra attention when colours are kept close like a cap, because that's when someone is afraid to give themselves away. He stops in the centre of the room. Anger is an artificial red that doesn't occur in nature; that of ketchup and postboxes. For a brief moment, Gabriel's reds stamp away his deep shadow blues.

'We need boxes,' he says, and leaves the room again.

Standing very still, Anna tries to get a feel for the room, to see if she can sense something wrong. It's a corner room, as is hers, except Lily's is twice as large and has two windows, one overlooking the flat roof of the laundry room extension and one facing the canal at the side of the house. Sunlight pours in, cooking up a soup of girlish smells. Floral perfume, sharper deodorant, a Christmassy cinnamon and clove from a glass vial with scented sticks. She moves to the window overlooking the tar roof, letting the sun warm her face and arms. A dream-catcher hangs from the sash lock, large as a dinner plate, with blue beads woven into the web and three long pink feathers. She pushes it aside to stare at the fields. Last night's rain sits in silver stretches across the ground, the house shipwrecked, cut off from the rest of the world. The atmosphere inside is the same, the four of them marooned together by Lily's dis-appearance.

Lily used to stand in this same sunny spot, she thinks, and somehow knows it to be true. She lets go of the dreamcatcher and moves to the other window. Ben is crouched by the canal, his back to her as he pulls up nettles with a gloved hand. She steps back as he turns to stare up at the house.

The room's silence is thick and intent, making her feel observed. She can't bring herself to go near the bed. The duvet cover is a joyous candy-stripe pink, but its soft, rumpled state tells her the bedclothes haven't been changed since Lily last slept there. Poking out from under the bed is an open book lying face-down, waiting for the girl to pick up where she left off. The title on the cracked spine is *Witchlore: sex and magic*. On the dressing table there's a porcelain hand draped in glass beads. Clothes hang over the back of a chair, a careless layer of discarded tops and ripped jeans. Beneath the dressing table, a pair of silver glitter trainers. Too much information about a girl who is never coming home. She doesn't want to know Lily. She stands in the centre of the room, an unwelcome guest, afraid to touch anything, her colours painting the air with discomfort and a growing irritability over how long Gabriel is taking. Fear too, that burnt ochre haze. Afraid of what happened to Lily, who read about sex and magic but still loved teddy bears and glitter. The room tells her Lily was loved and looked after. It wasn't enough to keep her safe.

'Good. You're still here.' Gabriel comes in with an armful of flattened removal boxes and a roll of bin bags. Depositing the lot on the floor, he sits on the bed, runs his hands through his hair before tying it back into a small messy sprig. He takes a deep breath.

'Are you OK, Gabriel?'

His gaze is blank, not really seeing her, eyes red with fatigue. It turns the hazel of his left eye into a deep amber blaze. It had been close to midnight by the time he got back from the marina. Lying on the sofa, Anna had watched the beam of his headlights sweep the sitting room walls and realised she'd been listening for his return. Did Suzie question him about his late return, she wonders, and did he tell her where he was?

'We've been putting this off,' he says, rubbing his eyes.

'Suzie doesn't want me in this room, does she?'

'There's nowhere else for you to stay. She knows that.'

Anna looks away, hiding a grimace. 'Your gardener says he was friends with Lily.'

'Gardener? Oh, Ben. He works for me on the tree business but it's been a bit quiet recently so he does odd jobs for us here. He's going to see if he can patch up the ceiling in your room.'

She glances at the crown of his head and sees how those billowing blue greys – the Lily Blues as she has begun to call them – have shrunk under an irritable orange rash. He doesn't wish to discuss Ben.

As he assembles a box, she notices the swollen knuckles on his right hand, the skin taut and discoloured.

'What happened to your hand?'

'Nothing.' He doesn't glance at it. 'This has been Lily's room since she was twelve. She came to us in January 2009. Daniel wasn't even a year old. Can you imagine that? First time parents still trying to figure out the baby stuff and suddenly we were responsible for a teenager as well. A traumatised one at that.'

It isn't right to study a person's colours when they're raw with pain, so she looks away. But she has learnt something. There is no way Gabriel is linked to Lily's disappearance. The colour of his devastation tells her so. Billie can listen to all the rumours she likes, but she's mistaken.

Anna lays a hand on his arm. The contact sends a spray of hot pink through her vision and she is glad no one can see it but herself. 'When you said Suzie had lost someone, I had no idea it was something like this.'

He stops making the box to look at her. 'Is it too much for you? I'd understand if it was.'

'I don't shy away from tricky situations.'

Gabriel nods, still studying her. 'I saw that in you the first time we met. A resilience. I think you and I are quite similar.'

A slow curl of shell pink lifts from his crown, cerise streaks running through it. There's nothing more compelling than watching an attraction take hold, of witnessing her effect on another person. She looks away, taking a breath. Sometimes, in a forbidden situation such as this, it would be far easier not to see a person's colours. In the silence, she knows Gabriel is reading her too.

He clears his throat, passing her the box to complete, his injured hand stiff and useless as a puppet's. 'Suzie's sister was quite a bit older and a lot wilder. They didn't have much to do with each other. Angie didn't even come to our wedding. We knew she had a child but we'd never met Lily before she came to live with us. Angie was hit by a car and that was that.'

'Poor Lily.' The missing girl snaps her from her daze. 'What a terrible thing.'

He nods. 'She was a mini adult when she arrived. But we took good care of her. She adored Dan from the minute she saw him. It was like she remembered how to be young and silly again, playing with him.'

From under the bed he pulls a black suitcase, plastered with stickers of dazzling lips, saucer-eyed cats and comic-book words – ZAAPP, POWW, BOFFF – the edges curling away from the nylon. He opens the cupboard door. 'Her clothes can go in here. I'll tackle the shelves.'

He hugs his elbows, staring up at the shelves above the dressing table. Between the books, there's a row of angels with pipe-cleaner arms and glitter-glue wings, identical to the one Ben had impaled on his middle finger. Anna wonders how Gabriel's colours would react if she told him, but something tells her not to make an enemy of the boy.

In the cupboard she finds a checked shirt, pink sweat pants, several pairs of leggings and a white cotton dress. T-shirts and hoodies fill the shelves running up the left side. Her fingers are cold and nervy as she folds and refolds, trying not to notice how small the tops are or their worn scent or the odd stain like spilled tea or juice where Lily tossed them in the cupboard rather than washing them. Careless youth. Careless with youth. She understands why Gabriel can't touch her clothes.

'I guess these can be emptied now.' On the shelf above the angels is a cluster of glass jars with sealed lids, each filled with clear liquid. Gabriel takes one down and flicks open the catch. The lid opens with a corked pop and he tips the contents into the sink in the corner of the room, as if dashing out the remains of a guest's wine. It never fails to surprise her how deceptive a person can be in order to hide their feelings. But unlike everyone else, she can see through his casual tone and the nonchalant sling of his arm.

'What are they?'

'Lily's magic potions.' The side of his mouth goes crooked, a sorrowful half-smile, teasing a ghost. 'She had a little business, making these angels. She sold a few online and at the Petrifying Well.'

He takes an angel off the shelf and peels open the Velcro on the back of its stiff conical dress. Inside the cotton-wool stuffing is a small glass vial with a tiny cork stopper and liquid shivering inside. 'The River Kirk is said to have magical properties. It runs under the pavilion and used to draw people from all over the country back in Victorian times…' He stops talking as if his breath has run out.

'Suzie told me the story about the girl and her devil child.'

'This area is full of ghosts and witchcraft.' He shrugs. 'If you believe in that kind of thing.'

'Luckily I don't.'

His eyes are distant again, staring at the white sky. 'Lily loved all those old wives' tales. She made love potions from the water and put them in her angels.' He gives another unhappy lopsided smile. 'The power of marketing and all that.'

His Lily Blues are so dense she has to look away to breathe easily again.

On the floor of the cupboard is a wooden doll's house. Clicking open the lock that keeps the two halves together, she finds it empty except for a thin pile of tracing paper, held flat by a paperweight, two red cherries in their glass suspension. When she lifts the weight off, the pages jump into life, curling in on themselves as if to hide their pencil drawings. She flattens them against her lap. On every page the same image of an angel wing has been repeated and reworked, the feathers rendered in intricate detail, the wing a majestic drape.

Gabriel squats down beside her, takes the pages from her hand, his manner slow and hesitant as though she might move them out of his reach at the last minute. Air rushes in and out of his nostrils. The space between them warms, then closes as his shoulder touches hers, a rocking movement as he balances on the balls of his feet.

'These can go …' He stands, bows over the case, then changes

89

his mind and shoves the sketches in an empty black bin bag. 'We've still got all her sketchbooks.'

From the corner of her eye, she sees him retrieve one of the sketches and fold it into his back pocket. A flash of wasp-sting red breaks through his deep, suffocating blue, raw and angry but fleeting; perhaps nothing more than the passage of a tangential thought, like the recurring nag of an unpaid bill.

A single sheet remains inside the house, its unfurled edges having caught between the walls. This one she keeps.

She stands by Lily's bed in her damp running clothes, the rain having returned as soon as she left the house, like the joke of a spiteful child. Someone has left a pile of clean bedclothes outside her door, but it feels cold and callous to strip the bed and shove the sheets into the washing machine. Removing the last traces of the girl. People cling to those traces. When her grandmother died, her mum walked around with Nana Farley's handkerchief in her pocket. She'd catch her burying her nose in it. *It smells of her awful cigarettes*, she'd say, laughing at herself, tears in her eyes.

Something shifts in the atmosphere, goose bumps lifting on her arms. Glancing over her shoulder, she finds Suzie in the doorway.

'What's wrong?' Suzie's voice is sharp. It releases jagged little bolts of red into the air above her head.

'I'm not sure what to do with Lily's sheets.' Whatever she says is likely to enrage the woman, but she has to be honest. 'I feel bad about taking them off. I don't know if you want me to wash them or . . . I'm sorry if that sounds stupid.'

To her surprise, Suzie's jagged reds soften to grateful mauve. 'It doesn't sound stupid, Anna. Not at all.' As she stares at the bed, Anna is struck by how small and vulnerable Suzie looks, like a punished child. 'I should change the sheets myself, but I just can't.'

'I'll do it. I'll leave them in a bag at the bottom of the airing cupboard so you can decide in your own time what to do with them.'

Suzie thanks her with such a wash of pinks and indigos that Anna is left feeling ashamed. How childish of her to take the woman's coldness personally. Under different circumstances, they might have been friends. They might still be.

Pulling herself together, she tackles the bed. First she pushes the mattress up onto its side, thumping it with her fist to release old dust. The fine particles left by Lily's body, a thought she blocks or she'll never make herself sleep in the bed. In the base of the airing cupboard she finds a thick woollen blanket, musty from disuse, and lays it over the mattress, adding a base sheet and plumping the pillows. Having made the bed, she scans the rest of the room, her eyes falling on the pipe-cleaner angels. In the morning she'll move them to Daniel's room. Her own clothes are still on the rail in the tiny box room, but she can't bring herself to hang them in Lily's wardrobe. Aside from the angels and the coloured glass lamp, all that remains of Lily's belongings is the dreamcatcher, hanging in the window to guard the girl as she slept. Anna considers taking it down, but a superstitious shiver prevents her. Instead she lights a candle and puts it on the windowsill, the flame twisting and ducking in the draught, the dreamcatcher in a slow twirl above it.

Having showered, she returns to the room with its happy yellow candlelight and freshly made bed. The candle gutters, and in the violet dusk, rain flickers in the air. She turns Lily's angels to face the wall, their bead eyes glittery and alive with candlelight. Rubbing her arms, she swallows on a dry throat, heart thudding.

'I'm not trying to take your place,' she whispers. The sound of her voice in the empty room raises the hairs on her arms. She is being ridiculous, thinking herself into a fright. Taking a breath as if to dive into cold water, she flips back the duvet and lies down. Through the sheet she can feel the blanket's stiff woollen prickles. Sleep couldn't feel further away.

Shutting her eyes, she listens to the dreamcatcher clicking against the windowpane. With a sudden slither and tap, the light behind her eyelids snuffs out. Bolting upright, she finds the room in darkness. She gets out of bed, legs weak with shock, and finds the dreamcatcher on the floor, its knotted loop having come undone. The candle has been knocked over, spilling wax over the lip of the sill and down the radiator. She decides to leave the mess for the morning. If she doesn't make herself get back in the bed now, she never will.

As she lies there trying to ignore the itchy heat of the blanket, she has the oddest sensation of sinking into an existing outline, her body slotting into Lily's shape.

14

Clods of dark-brown revulsion

On Thursday morning, Gabriel stays home, his morning's work cancelled. He waves the three of them off whilst Suzie manoeuvres the car through the gate, her hands making sticky sounds against the steering wheel. Halfway down the lane, she slams on the brakes and spills from the car, bending and swaying over the verge to catch her breath. Anna moves into the driver's seat, and once Suzie is able to get back in the car, Daniel asks what's wrong.

'Hay fever,' Suzie says.

In the rear-view mirror, Daniel sits in a cloud of murky green disbelief, shot through with little red lightning bolts. He doesn't believe his mother and he doesn't like being lied to.

'Hay fever can make you a bit asthmatic,' Anna says. 'It makes you feel like you can't breathe.' She is convincing enough to disperse his cloud.

After they've dropped him off at school, Suzie's damp, chilled fingers find her hand.

'I'm beginning to wonder what I'd do without you, Anna.'

It's a heady thing to be so needed. At that moment, she might have done anything Suzie asked of her.

*

The upstairs corridor smells of Suzie's perfume as she gets ready for her shift at the pub. Anna imagines what she'll do if Gabriel knocks on her door once Daniel's in bed. She tells herself she'll turn down his offer of hot chocolate, pleading a headache, but her treacherous yellows fizz with anticipation. Suzie comes to find her as she's putting on her trainers.

'Gabe and Dan are coming with me to the pub,' she says.

'You don't feel up to driving?'

Suzie shakes her head, a small, desperate plea in the look she gives Anna. 'I told Gabe I have a migraine.'

'I won't say anything.'

Suzie gives a reassured nod. 'Dan'll sleep in my parents' flat above the pub until my shift ends. You're OK on your own until we're back?'

'Of course.' She is touched by this consideration, even more so by Suzie's trust in her. If a shiver of toad-green disappointment crosses her vision because Gabriel will be out too, she refuses to acknowledge it.

As soon as they leave, the rain comes, an ocean emptying over the house, cancelling her evening run. She puts the television on and then, out of curiosity, lifts an edge of the rug. The water in the well has risen, the surface giving a slight heave and roll, quietly breathing. With a shiver, she leaves the room.

Lily's room is as silent and watchful as ever. Even the rain sounds muffled and distanced. The thought of climbing back into the missing girl's bed fills Anna with dread. The angel figurines are still on the shelf because Daniel didn't want them in his room. Lily had joked that they came alive at night and had a party. Anna notices for the first time that beneath the yellow wool caps of their hair, the angels have caramel beads for eyes; as if Lily had created an angelic likeness of herself in her little figures. She turns each angel to face the wall, then changes into her nightclothes, her movements hasty, hiding her bare breasts with an arm as she reaches for her T-shirt; fighting the ridiculous notion that if she glances up, she'll find Lily watching her from a corner of the room. She gets into bed with her laptop, clicking on promotions for beauty products she'll never buy, wasting time until she's exhausted enough to fall asleep. Then she types *Lily O'Keefe* – the name given on the poster – into the search engine, wondering if Gabriel had officially adopted her.

She has to scroll through several pages before she finds a single YouTube clip of Lily, uploaded a couple of years ago. As she presses play, a nervous jangle of yellows and rust shoots across her vision.

Lily is cross-legged on her bed, smiling into the frame, twisting her hair into a rope over her left shoulder. 'I'm Lily and I'm seventeen. And in lots of ways I guess I'm just a regular teenager. I'm still at school, I smoke a bit, I drink a bit. I don't come home with love bites – I mean, who does after fourteen, right?'

She has a way of fixing her eyes on the camera that makes her seem much older than seventeen. She's mesmerising. Anna turns down the volume, trying to pinpoint her allure. Buttery skin, wide caramel eyes, and full, round bosoms beneath her pink T-shirt, but whilst her youth plays a large part in her attractiveness, there's something more. An awareness of the effect she has on people.

Lily places her hands one over the other between her breasts.

'Anahata, the heart chakra,' she says. 'In Sanskrit, *Anahata* means unhurt, unstruck and unbeaten. Being young doesn't protect you from pain or hate.' Tears rise but she doesn't let them fall, lifting her chin a little. 'But beneath our wounds beats Anahata. It is infinite and it can't be broken.'

Anna pauses the clip, pressing a palm against her chest

95

where her own heart is beating hard. She doesn't know Lily and yet she can hardly bring herself to watch, knowing that in a few years' time, something will happen and the girl won't come home. She takes a deep breath. The clip has been viewed over six hundred times, with three hundred and twelve likes and no dislikes. There's a single comment.

Little witches deserve to be drowned.

With a horrified gasp, she leans back against the pillows, closing her eyes.

Before she can watch the rest of the clip, a noise downstairs distracts her. It's too brief and indistinct to tell what it is. Grabbing her mobile, she opens her door a fraction and switches off the light. With a tiptoe dash, she reaches the landing window and looks out over the front lawn and the drive. Gabriel's Defender hasn't returned. She listens again but hears nothing. Feeling braver, she heads downstairs. The light is on in the kitchen. She could have sworn she turned it off before heading to bed.

'Hello?' Her voice is timid, pathetic.

The kitchen is empty, nothing out of place. She sips a glass of water, waiting and listening. Thinking about the missing girl. Detective Adeyemi's number faces her on the whiteboard and she decides it's probably a sensible idea to save it to her mobile. As she does so, the ghost letters of Lily's name and number catch her attention.

Before she can consider what she is doing, she keys in Lily's number and presses the call button, her heart drumming in her ears. For one off-kilter moment, she is convinced a young woman's voice will answer.

A long tone sounds. The mobile is dead.

She switches off her own phone, deriding her foolish behaviour, and heads back upstairs.

A man is standing inside the box room, half hidden by the

door. Shock bursts brilliant yellow in her vision. Dropping back a step, she crouches close to the floor. His skinny height gives him away. He's wearing an oversized pair of headphones and she can hear the rhythmic bass buzz from across the landing. The bedroom door has slipped its catch and come to rest against his back, shaking as he jiggles to his music. She straightens, but before she can march up and give him a piece of her mind, she realises that the source of the motion is his right arm, bent at the elbow, moving with a hectic judder. His trousers are low and lopsided on his hips, the buckle of his belt bouncing and swinging by his right leg, keeping time with his jerking hand. Her mouth dries, clods of dark brown in her vision. With his headphones on, she might reach Lily's room unnoticed, but the thought of him spinning round to face her makes her feel sick; that and the possibility that the unclosed door is deliberate, this act taking place for her sake.

Her limbs are loose and watery as she creeps back downstairs. In the laundry room, she wraps a towel around her bare legs, slots herself between the wall and the dryer and waits for Ben to leave.

15

A scarlet plume of infatuation

Suzie's perfume has a strong, androgynous scent, something between tangy shower gel and a man's cologne. Her lipstick is a stubborn red, highlighting the flat line of her mouth. She keeps plucking at the material of her grey blouse, adjusting it across her shoulders, a pale suggestion of cleavage showing through its transparent mid-panel. Gabriel, in a clean pair of cargo pants and a blue sweater, looks how he always does once he has showered away the work day. He is making an effort with his comments, though.

'The girl I married, just as beautiful, if not more so.' He looks across at Anna. 'Mrs O'Keefe scrubs up well, doesn't she?'

She smiles back, but there's no need to answer because Suzie isn't interested in her opinion. One of her frosty days. In the grip of the Lily Blues. She hands Anna a piece of paper with the landline for the Spice Tree in East Mawsey and reminds her that their mobile numbers are on the kitchen whiteboard.

'His bedtime is strictly seven.' She looks past Anna's shoulder to where Daniel is reading a school book on the floor by the coffee table. 'He'll ask you to sit outside his bedroom, but don't leave until you're positive he's fast asleep.'

Anna nods. Daniel is a clockwork toy compared to some of the children she's looked after; all she has to do is point him in the right direction.

'Lily was always Daniel's babysitter,' Suzie adds.

'Will Ben be here tonight?'

'Unlikely. He's not one for putting in the extra hours.' Suzie ties the belt of her raincoat. 'Look, he's a little creep, but what can I do? Gabriel and his waifs and strays.'

'He was here last night. But he wasn't working.' She can't bring herself to tell Suzie what Ben had been doing. How it hadn't felt like a private sexual moment so much as an act of aggression against her. It would sound ridiculous out loud.

'Maybe he has a crush on you.' Suzie watches Gabriel reverse the Defender into the lane. Not paying attention.

Anna clenches her teeth. 'Maybe someone could have a word with him about turning up whenever it suits him. Just because he has a key...'

'Ben doesn't have a key, Anna.' Suzie hugs her middle, staring out. She doesn't acknowledge Gabriel's beckoning wave. 'I'm not bothered about going out tonight, though. If it's a problem.'

The rusty clouds that have been following Suzie grow dense, changing shape, forming slashes in the air. Anna will have to raise the issue of Ben again when her employer is in a more stable state.

'There's no problem. I'm fine, honestly.'

With each passing day, it seems to take Suzie a little extra effort to leave the house.

Once Daniel is in bed, Anna settles herself into the frame of his doorway with a magazine. His eyes open and close a few times, checking she's there, but by seven thirty, he's out cold.

Restlessness descends, an itch to go roaming. She heads for Suzie and Gabriel's bedroom and stands at the foot of the bed whose sheets she is not allowed to change. On one bedside table is a box of supermarket tissues and a thin gold necklace curled around itself like a snake in a nest. She opens the drawer on the opposite side of the bed. Loose coins and condoms slide across the base. A spare carabineer and a packet of batteries. She studies Gabriel's items through a tattered layer of brown, telling her to leave the room, reminding her this isn't who she is. On her way out, she tweaks the door back into its half-open angle.

Going back to Lily's old room, she passes the box room. The door is wide open, the bed and the railing where her clothes had still been hanging gone. She finds her clothes in a layered stack on Lily's floor, still attached to their hangers, and hates the thought of Ben having touched them. He must have been in the house while she and Suzie were doing the school run and the weekend shop. She scans the room, knowing in her bones that he will have wandered about touching her things, but there's no telltale evidence.

She sits at the dressing table and opens her laptop on the paused clip of Lily's YouTube video. When she presses play, Lily looks away from the camera, fiddling with the twisted rope of her hair.

'Like all teenagers, I'm in love.' Lily falls silent. A plume of scarlet rises off her crown. 'My best friend, my kindred spirit, my lover.' With a sigh, she remembers her virtual audience and faces the camera again. 'It's tough being young, right?' She is laughing at herself, but her eyes glitter with tears. 'We always want what we can't have.'

Lily's words tumble in Anna's stomach. She knows the pain of wanting something you can't have.

Closing the laptop, she sits back. Wonders whom Lily had been in love with. She remembers the angel-wing sketch still hidden in her jeans and gets up, hoping Ben didn't push his grubby hands through her pockets.

There's a shuffling outside her room. Her door edges open.

'Who's there?'

Please let it not be Ben.

The door stops moving, but she can't hide under her covers like a terrified child. Wrenching back the door, she finds Daniel in his pyjamas, looking as shocked as she is.

'Can I sleep with you tonight?' He points to the roll-out mattress behind him; the one that lives under his bed in case a friend ever comes to stay. His pillow and duvet are shaped into a small hillock, a conquering teddy balanced on top.

'Sorry, Daniel, no.' She hasn't the patience for this. 'The room's too small.'

'But my mattress can easily fit beside Lily's bed.'

'Not tonight.'

'I could sleep outside. You can leave the door open. Then I can put my pillow a little bit in your room and still see you.'

If she relents, the angel-wing sketch will have to wait until morning. 'Why don't you jump into your mum and dad's bed? They should be home soon.'

'I can't. At night it's Mummy and Daddy time.'

'Daniel. Back to your own bed. Now.'

Leaving the spare mattress in the hall, he returns to his room, turning his back on her as she tucks him in, fixing his wide, exhausted eyes on his tadpoles. She hesitates, then reminds herself he'll be asleep within minutes.

To her relief, the folded paper is still in her jeans pocket. She takes it back to Lily's room and unfolds it on the bed. With her fingertip she traces its ornate pathways, wondering what is was about the picture that had sparked a reaction in Gabriel. When she reaches the tight whorl of the feathers in the wing's soft hollow, a shape materialises. With a gasp, she holds the paper up to the light. Now that she's seen it, it stands out.

The letter G has been worked into the pattern.

G for Gabriel? Had Lily been in love with Gabriel?

She presses the sketch against her chest, her heart thudding through it. No wonder there are rumours linking Gabriel to Lily's disappearance. Young girls talk, especially when they're in love. She wonders whom Lily had confided in. In all the time she's been here, not one person has called for him or invited him to the pub. He is utterly alone.

She closes her eyes, seeing Lily holding back tears, and wishes she could have met the girl. Soft blue sadness rises like steam from her skin. Sorrow for Lily, and for Gabriel, implicated by a young girl's infatuation. And for herself, the young, naive girl who'd bought a flight to Copenhagen on her twentieth birthday.

She'd known where Lauritz and his wife lived because her father kept all his contacts in a mahogany box file. During the flight she drank two miniature bottles of white wine, then took a cab to the house straight from the airport. Her plan, to ring on the doorbell and let what would happen happen.

She remembers studying the house from across the road, the sea behind her frozen into white ripples of ice, the narrow beach striped with black seaweed. The sky was winter white, the colour of a migraine, reflected in a colourless sea. An omen she'd ignored.

The front door had opened whilst she was still plucking up courage on the other side of the road. Out came Lauritz, as if drawn by the force of her desire. He didn't see her, looking back into the house as he waited. His wife joined him on the porch, smiling up at him. When she raked her fingernails through the thick hair behind his ears, Anna could feel its texture beneath her own fingertips. When Lauritz planted a long, slow kiss on his wife's forehead, Anna walked away, hating everything about herself.

She folds the angel wing away. 'You and I, Lily, fell in love with the wrong men.'

In the listening silence, she can feel the girl's presence.

The photographs in the dressing table. She has the oddest feeling of being guided, someone whispering in her ear. When she and Gabriel had packed away Lily's belongings, she'd seen him open the drawer, his hand like a heron's claw about to snatch up a fish, then shut it again, unable to touch the pictures. She rustles the photographs together and climbs into Lily's bed.

The bed feels different. She lies back, testing the notion. The crawling anxiety that hounded her first few nights in this room is gone. As though she has passed through a barrier, she and Lily now on the same side, bound by their love for a man they couldn't have. She rubs the goosebumps on her arms and turns her attention to the photographs.

Teenage faces holler silent messages, laughing and flushed, eyes glassy, arms slung around each other in sagging human chains. *Look how wild we are, look how much fun we have.*

Lily is easy to pick out of the crowd. If her friends are sitting on a wall, Lily is balancing on her toes. Whilst they're lined up for a snapshot, she's propelling herself off their shoulders. Even in solo images, she is throwing her body into shapes to catch the eye, pirouetting, star-jumping. There are no boys in the pictures.

A draught reaches her. It stirs the open curtains, the beads of the dreamcatcher tapping like a fingernail on the glass. With a shiver, she replaces the photographs, running her hand over the splintery base of the drawer first to see if she has missed anything. Her fingertips come into contact with a stiff piece of paper, lodged in the back of the drawer. A business card for the Dragon Ink Tattoo Parlour, a scaled dragon curling around the margin. The name *Bozie* is scrawled across the back, a heart replacing the dot above the i.

Anna draws in a sharp breath and returns to the angel-wing sketch with the secret letter at its heart. The same image that had been drawn and perfected until its lines were crisp and clear. The girl had loved Gabriel with such intensity she'd needed to mark it on her body.

Lily had been designing a tattoo.

~ 16 ~

Rust-coloured dread

Something's happened. When she opens her bedroom door ready to drive Daniel to school, she hears a woman crying. She finds Daniel in his bedroom, shoving his pyjamas into his crocodile rucksack. 'Why aren't you in your school uniform?'

Gabriel steps out from behind his son's door, his colours an explosion, too chaotic and overlapping to read.

'Oh God, what's happened?' A screen of rust slots across her sight.

'Nothing.' He sends a warning glance in his son's direction. 'We all just need a day off. Dan's going to have a sleepover at his grandparents', lucky boy and . . .' The sound of his wife's sobbing cuts him off and he closes his eyes.

'Shall I go and see . . .' Anna starts to say, but his colours sharpen. Hard, punchy reds and rust browns. She's never seen anger on him before. It's not moving towards his son or herself, which means it's a reaction to his private thoughts. Without thinking, she steps forward to pull him into a hug, but he half turns, presenting her with a shoulder. Too angry to be comforted.

She swallows, the blood draining from her face. 'I'll make myself scarce.'

*

Closing her bedroom door, she sits on the bed. She has no idea what to do with herself. A run, perhaps, to see if she can escape the turmoil of colours breaking out of her skull. She falls back against the mattress.

On the shelf, Lily's angels stare down at her. Someone has turned each one back to face the room. Cold branches through her but it gives her an idea. She starts up her laptop and types *Lily O'Keefe angels* into the search engine, and up comes Lily's website and blog.

A simple page opens with a row of the angels against a blue background, a live Twitter feed and three heart-shaped buttons with the words *Love*, *Lust* and *Respect*. When she clicks on these, a different angel appears, each with a twelve pound price tag. *Love* holds a red felt heart in her pipe-cleaner hands, *Respect* has her hands on her hips, bold and demanding, whilst *Lust* cups her small foam-ball breasts. Despite her mood, Anna smiles, enchanted by Lily's mischievous invention.

Returning to the home page, she scans the blurb, a potted history of the area's obsession with the River Kirk, spiced with witchcraft and ritual killings. *The river*, it concludes, *runs with ancient energy bubbling up from the earth's deepest forgotten layers. An energy that is older and wilder and more powerful than anything our limited brains can grasp. But because we humans think we can conquer a thing by labelling it, let's call it magic.*

A new message appears on the Twitter feed. A customer complaining the angels are still out of stock. An irrational firework red breaks over Anna as she resists the urge to reply, to shame the woman with the knowledge that whilst she's bitching about lack of professionalism, Lily hasn't been seen in four months. Scrolling on, she finally finds a tweet from Lily. Dated end of January.

Perfect gift for Valentine's Day #whodoesn'tlovelove?

Her heart beats harder as she clicks on it, afraid of the

responses she might find. Daniel said Lily was being trolled. There's a single reply.

@lilysangels Slutty Angel? #newidea #bestseller #guaranteedto makeakilling

Charming. She kneads her fingers, which have grown cold and clammy, but she can't stop now, scrolling on through the feed. The ugly comments are hidden among messages from satisfied customers like pieces of broken glass across a floor.

@lilysangels Will-suck-cock Angel? #bestseller #guaranteedkilling
@lilysangels Maneater Angel? #guaranteedkilling

The house is empty as she runs down to the sitting room and takes a piece of paper from the printer under the desk and a pen from the drawer. Back upstairs, she writes down every malicious tweet she can find. When she's finished searching the Twitter feed, she checks each page on Lily's website and then moves on to her blog. There are only four entries, but with each new one, the troll's venom escalates.

Little Lily. You're no angel. One day someone's going to come and clip your wings.

The troll, Anna notes, uses a new email address each time but always opens the message with the words *Little Lily* as a way of identifying themselves; making sure the girl understands she has an enemy.

She finds a single response from Lily.

What's your problem? Why are you doing this?

The response had come hours later, a little after three in the morning, the troll's hate a compulsion driving him or her out of bed in the middle of the night.

What's my problem? Check YOUR conscience, Little Lily. Think a pink feather dreamcatcher's going to keep you safe? #whoswatching whenyousleep?

Her hand drops away from the computer. It would have been easy for someone to clamber up onto the extension roof and look in. She stubs her toe against the bed leg in her panicked rush to reach the window. Holding her breath, she scours the asphalt roof, her heart jolting and bumping as she searches for footprints, but the rain lies in reflective pools across the surface, concealing evidence.

Lily's dreamcatcher stirs, the glass beads winking in the sunlight, sending out signals. She yanks it off the window catch, breaking its suede loops.

A heavy squall arrives out of nowhere. The noise of water so loud that when it stops as abruptly as it started, the silence is overwhelming. She can hear the workings of her own body, a whine of hunger from her stomach, a gurgle of air moving up her throat as she swallows. She shifts in her chair to stare out at the colourless sky. A small noise, a flap and tick behind her, makes her start. Her list of malicious messages has fallen to the floor. If she doesn't pull herself together, the sound of her own breath is going to startle her. She heads for the laundry room, needing the distraction of a practical, mundane task.

Whilst she is pulling a twist of warm clothing from the dryer, a figure walks around the side of the extension, setting her heart off yet again like a bird bursting into flight. It pounds harder when she recognises Ben, a dirty canvas bag over one shoulder, carrying a toolbox and a large saw. He doesn't spot her as he releases his load to the ground and bends over the terracotta pot outside the door. Rolling up his sleeve, his mouth working out his distaste, he plunges his arm in. His hand comes out wet, with a key.

She moves further away from the door. The light is off and he still hasn't seen her. With relish, she anticipates the shock he'll get when he does.

He catches sight of her before he's fully through the door. He doesn't flinch, not so much as a ripple of surprise disturbing his expression. She recalls some pseudo-medical article she once read that listed the traits of psychopaths. Apparently they never startle.

'Thought I wouldn't see you?' he says, smirking as he unzips his jacket.

'They haven't given you a key at all.'

'Spare key, my key.' He shrugs. 'Makes no difference. I'm pretty much part of the family. I can come and go as I please.'

When he leaves the room, she closes her eyes, reaching for her phone in her back pocket.

Her sister's mobile goes straight to voicemail and no one answers the landline. The surface of the canal boils under a fresh downpour. She sends Jonah a text.

I need to know what's happening with my car. Please? Without it, I'm trapped in this bloody house.

Taking a shuddery breath, she sends a more considered message of apology. It's not fair on him, she writes, considering how busy he is. She'll find a garage herself as she should have done from the start.

Right now, car or no car, she needs to get the hell out of this house.

By the time she reaches the outskirts of Kirkley, her grey suede boots are destroyed, her socks soaked through, water running off her scalp, but the rain has stopped. She stands by a railing where the road bridges a stream and looks over the edge. When she and Daniel went to the swings, it had been little more than a thin liquid cover for the stony bed. Now it is swollen with rainfall, cascading out. Part of the bank has collapsed, exposing mud the colour of scorched earth, the reeds and wild flowers washed away.

The heavy gush of water takes her breath with it. She remembers Daniel peering into the well in the floor, terrified but compelled. An image hits her from nowhere: a young girl's naked body trapped underwater. The picture is stark and brutal in its detail, Lily's hair anchored in weeds, her caramel eyes staring up at nothing.

With a cry, she pushes herself back from the rail. She should never have read the girl's blogs or watched her YouTube video, so candid and intimate, inviting her in. She would have liked Lily, the girl's reckless spark reminding her of herself at that age.

Except that now, when she thinks of her, she sees a body in the water.

'There you are.' Gabriel pokes his head round the door to her bathroom, where she is on her knees, scrubbing at yellow stains in the bathtub. A place to hide whilst Ben crashed and hammered and whistled in the box room, making sure she couldn't forget his presence. Gabriel perches on the rim, and something about the way his gaze reaches down to her as she kneels by his legs, close enough to stroke his calf, feels too intimate. It sends a scarlet fizz through her, like a mouthful of pink champagne bubbles. She joins him on the edge of the tub, levelling their eye contact.

'I'm sorry about this morning. Some days are like this.' His hands are on either side of him, holding onto the bath rim, his fingers almost touching her. 'I understand if you want to leave.'

'I'm not leaving.' *You need me, Suzie needs me, Daniel needs me.* And in some strange way she can't explain, Lily needs her too.

17

Bravery is orange fear and green determination

Suzie isn't feeling well, so Anna and Daniel have been building a Lego fortress for his frogs to play in once they're fully grown. They've been in the house all day. As has Ben, who'd popped into Daniel's room to eat a sandwich earlier, his knee barging Anna's thigh as he'd dropped onto the floor between them.

She gets up to stretch her legs, staring out at the forest. In the miserable light, it becomes permanent night inside the trees. Daniel joins her, tapping at raindrops through the glass. Briefly, a golden shaft of sunlight cuts through the cloud.

'Someone's died and now they're going to heaven,' Daniel says.

'What are you two plotting?' Gabriel says as he walks in. He catches Anna's eye, imparting some grim fleeting message before he smiles at his son. Suzie, she thinks.

'Let's go find some fun,' he says.

'With Mummy?'

'I think we should let Mummy have a rest. It's her Saturday too, isn't it?'

But Daniel doesn't want to leave without his mum. Between them, Anna and Gabriel offer suggestions – the playground, ice cream in Kirkley, even the long drive to the sea – but the boy dismisses each idea without consideration. Meanwhile Ben has sauntered out into the corridor, busy on his mobile, a few sparks of age-green bronze around his crown. His colours might relate to what's on his phone screen, but something in the pit of Anna's stomach tells her he's listening in.

'I want to go to the pavilion.'

It's his father's turn to protest, but Daniel insists.

'Do I need to change into my ball gown?' Anna's question breaks through the deadlock as father and son stare at her, equally bemused. 'It sounds posh, the pavilion.'

'You can't wear a ball gown.' The horror in Daniel's voice makes Gabriel smile, and he gives in, as long as Anna promises not to wear her ball gown.

Following Gabriel to the stairs, she glances back at Ben who has been rifling through his toolbox during the entire conversation, and catches him staring.

They wait by the Defender whilst Daniel looks for his favourite trainers.

'The school mothers tiptoe around Dan like he's an injured fawn,' Gabriel says in a low voice. 'Always commenting on his serious little face and blessing his little heart. They treat him like he's made of glass.'

'Well, they're mistaken. I've seen how brave he is.'

A flourish of gratitude rises from his crown, a lustrous and velvety mauve that is a close cousin of love. 'I'm glad you're here, Anna.' He glances at the closed curtains of his bedroom. 'We've been walking around holding our breath for too long.'

The rain has washed Kirkley clean, pedestrians and litter swept away with the downpour. A lone dog-walker passes them in the street, the woman tilting the wide brim of her hat to offer them a greeting. With Daniel holding both their hands, they become a family in the eyes of a stranger. Gabriel, with his unshaven face and his thick, unruly hair falling about his ears and neck, a weathered tree of a man; Daniel, who could be mistaken for her child, with his dark hair and large eyes; and herself, wife and mother. It wakes a greedy ache, a singed yellow-green.

The pavilion is unlit, an abandoned supermarket trolley on its side by the entrance. 'Won't it be locked?'

Having righted the trolley, Gabriel takes a set of keys from his pocket, grinning as he gives them a triumphant shake. A key ring with the face of a cat sticking its tongue out catches the street light in its pink glass gems.

'This is where Lily used to work when she stopped school,' Daniel says.

The lock is stiff and rusted. When it finally gives, Gabriel pushes the door open and steps aside, a hand on his son's shoulder, the other on the small of Anna's back, his touch gathering them into a single unit.

'Sometimes Lily would bring me here at night when she was babysitting,' Daniel says, and Gabriel's hand falls away from her back as he frowns at his son.

'What?'

Daniel doesn't answer, taking a cautious step into the pavilion. Gabriel tries the light switch, which gives an empty click, the place remaining in darkness. Anna takes Daniel's hand. They stare at the upturned chairs on the tables, like the remains of a forest fire in the ashy light.

'Spooky old place,' she says cheerfully, and rubs his cold hand.

They're standing inside an elongated oval room with high ceilings, the floor crammed with tables and the bulky display cabinets against the walls. There's a counter with a till to the right, and behind it, a rail of shelves selling books and miniatures of the pavilion. Her heart gives a yo-yo bound as she recognises Lily's angels, their bead eyes and glittery wings reflecting the dim street light.

Gabriel stands a way off, hands in his pockets. It's too dark to make out his expression, so she's denied her usual clues, though the hunch of his shoulders says how uncomfortable he is. It sets off her own orange screen of anxiety and she takes a deep breath, wondering why Daniel wanted to come here. An unpleasant smell hits the back of her throat: stale air with a rotting, vegetal undertone. She points to the nearest cabinet with its rows of soot-coloured objects. 'What are those things?'

But the boy isn't interested in the displays, tugging her across the room, his short fingernails digging into her hand. To the left of the counter is an arched doorway with an iron grille. Past it, a flight of stone steps that sag in the middle, worn smooth by countless feet and leading down to darkness, the exact texture of the tarry blackness she associates with violent rage. She prays the door is locked, sensing movement in the sightless dark, a dank breeze funnelling upwards and a constant rushing sound.

'I hear water.'

'The River Kirk,' Gabriel says, and then turns to his son, who is trying the handle. 'The answer is no, Daniel.'

The boy brings his face close to the grille, his hands squeezed into fists, held out from his sides like he's summoning a super-power. 'We have to go and look at the water, Daddy.'

'The lights aren't working, Dan.'

The boy fumbles a penlight from his hoody pocket and slides his whole arm through the grille, slashing its rapier beam backwards and forwards. Objects embedded in the wall above the stairwell pop out in the fleeting light, small and yellow as old teeth or knuckles of polished bone.

Gabriel sighs, leaning towards Anna. 'Two minutes and we'll get out of here.'

He takes a large torch from inside his coat pocket. In its steady, broad light she sees the mosaic of a fountain, a spring of water gushing from it, the words *Eternal Health and Youth* caught in its froth. Not teeth or bone at all, but hundreds of tiny shells in gentle pinks and yellows and iris blues. Colours that would normally soothe but are drowned out by the clamour in her head telling her to turn and run. Gabriel says something, his breath warm against her cheek.

'Sorry?'

But before he can repeat himself, Daniel has pulled open the door and started down the stairs. Gabriel lurches forward, his fingers missing, clawing air.

'Daniel, stop.'

'I want Anna to see the river.' Daniel's voice is high and shivery.

Gabriel chases after him, and after a moment's hesitation, Anna follows the jagged light display of their torches. The steps are steep, ending in what looks to be a cave, the torchlight swooping over grey rock. The sound of the water fills the space, reverberating off the walls.

At the foot of the steps, Gabriel holds his arm out, preventing her from moving further into the cavern. 'Careful. The floor ends in a few feet.'

He runs his torch along the lip, where the ground falls abruptly away. A flimsy railing is all that prevents visitors from pitching over the edge. Past it, the river barrels along with the speed of a train, smashing itself against the cavern walls, sending fine spray into the air. The floor gleams, oily with moisture, making Anna's legs ache in anticipation of a slipping foot. She's finding it hard to breathe, the weight of rock and water filling her head like the dizziness before fainting.

Daniel yanks his hand out of his father's grip and walks to the rail. 'Come on, Anna.'

She's about to say no when Gabriel takes her hand.

'This is the Petrifying Well.' His hand releases hers by the railing. He lifts his torch from the water's hurtling surface to a huge boulder of rock jutting out over the river. A natural shelf splits the rock almost in two, and in the gap a row of objects dangle from thick grey twine. Water trickles down the rock face, dripping off the suspended items. 'If you look at it from the side, in profile, it looks like a skull.'

The torch beam picks out a doll, a shoe, and three masks with holes for eyes and mouths in frozen yawns of agony.

'The water turns everything it touches to stone.'

'How?'

'Magic.' Daniel interrupts his dad, whose hand is locking him in place, a huge, bunched manacle on his shoulder.

'I don't believe in magic.'

'The village sits on ancient chalk mines,' Gabriel tells her. 'The flooding from the last two winters has broken through several of the old shafts, which is why the place is closed.'

'Sounds unstable.' She attempts a silly face, a silent scream for Daniel's benefit. The boy tries to smile back, and in the torchlight she glimpses curls of orange and determined green. It reminds her of when he was on the swing, terrified but wanting to go higher.

'If you imagine a bone eaten away by...'

'Daddy...'

'...osteoporosis, that's pretty much the foundation.'

'Daddy?' Daniel's voice swoops upwards into a high panic. 'In the water.'

Gabriel points his torch across the broken surface, the waves cartwheeling over themselves in the current. 'There's nothing, sweetheart.'

'There. There.' Daniel, in the grip of terror has grabbed Anna's arm, his fingers like pincers on her bare skin as he lifts onto his tiptoes, pointing to the far side of the river.

'Dan, there's—' Gabriel makes an odd sound, as if the air has been punched from his chest. With a plastic clatter, the light disappears and Daniel cries out in alarm, flailing his arms, the penlight see-sawing through Anna's vision. Pulling the boy into a hug, she murmurs a rush of nonsense in his ear whilst he falls silent, a tremor running through his thin frame like an engine turning over.

'Fuck, *fuck.*' Gabriel crouches down, groping for his torch. His voice is breathless. Orange sparks burst in Anna's vision. He sounds afraid.

'Got it.' The light lifts along the cavern walls as Gabriel climbs onto the lowest rung of the railing, directing a shaking beam beneath the face of the Petrifying Well.

A long shape is hanging low in the water. Rising and submerging, the river tries to suck it back under, but the tangle of its hair is caught in the rock.

'Gabriel? What is that?'

Daniel presses his face against her and covers his ears with his hands. Gabriel is breathing in harsh gasps as he climbs onto the next rung, steadying himself with his shins against the handrail. Anna looks away as he points his torch at the thing floating in the water.

Dropping back onto the floor, he slips and rights himself. 'Nothing. It's nothing.' He lifts his son into a hug. 'A bit of broken tree, Dan-Dan, that's all.'

Daniel recovers first. By the time he has climbed the stairs, he is calling for Anna to come and see the museum. She waits with Gabriel as he shuts the door. His hands are shaking.

'Are you all right?'

He nods, but his colours say otherwise. Orange leaves a lingering stain.

'Look, Anna. A real baby.' Daniel taps the glass of a cabinet, skipping on his toes, giddy with sudden energy.

She hides a grimace, needing to get the hell out of the place. For Daniel's sake, and perhaps because Gabriel is watching her, she leans in to study what looks to be a rough clay approximation of a newborn baby. Its eyes are sealed shut under a coating of dried mud, body frozen in a cradled position, head bent towards its midriff, rocking on its naked bottom as Daniel's hands patter against the cabinet.

'So, what's the deal with these things – and don't say magic.'

'Read that.' The boy points to a framed handwritten notice, the lettering brown with age. 'Out loud.'

'"In the olden days, people used the water from the Petrifying Well to kill love rivals and preserve stillborn babies."' She looks up at the stone-caked baby. 'That's not real, is it?'

Daniel's glee falters. He glances at his father, growing uncertain.

'No, of course not. It's a doll.'

Anna says nothing, her body overcome with sudden weariness, the river rank in her nose. She needs air. Her thigh catches the corner of a table, pushing her off track as she turns to leave. Gabriel catches her arm, steadying her.

'It's limestone,' he says. 'The water's saturated with it.'

'Chemistry, then. Not magic.'

He holds her gaze. 'Nothing wrong with a bit of chemistry.'

Whilst Gabriel locks up, Anna heads back to the car with Daniel.

'My dad keeps Lily's key in his top drawer with his socks and pants. So we can come again. Just me and you.'

'Why would you want to come back, Dan?'

He juts out his jaw, glaring at her as if she is being deliberately obtuse. He doesn't answer, but she already knows what he's looking for in the water.

～ 18 ～

Suspicion is the colour of roadkill, blood and feathers

Daniel falls asleep as soon as the car engine is running. Gabriel drives for a few minutes, then, having checked his son in the rear-view mirror, brings the car to a halt in the middle of an unlit lane. With the headlights off, the night wraps around them, making them invisible. An approaching car would spot them too late.

'What's wrong?' Anna looks back, past Daniel's crooked head, his thumb sliding from his slack mouth, to the road behind.

'Lily was last seen getting off the train from London.' Gabriel addresses his words to the steering wheel. 'She'd been shopping for the day. She met a friend at the station pub, they had a drink and then Lily said she was off to meet someone.'

'You don't have to do this, Gabriel.'

He nods, falling silent. She wants to ask him about the angel-wing tattoo to see if he knows what it is. Lily can't have gone through with it, because the Missing poster doesn't mention a tattoo. She wonders if he has spotted the secret declaration of love worked into its design.

'The police can't decide if she's run away or something's happened to her. Without a body . . .' He swallows, choking on the word.

'Might she have run away?'

'No.' He pauses, running his palms along the steering wheel. 'Maybe.'

He moves a hand to the key but doesn't turn on the ignition. 'Lily was a bit wild and careless. I think she upset someone. She kept a blog and was getting trolled; that's the term, isn't it?' He shifts in his seat, straightening his legs as much as the floor space allows, writhing with discomfort. 'A lot of malicious stuff has been said about her. And about me.'

She can't admit she's already seen those venomous messages. None of them had mentioned Gabriel, which means there are more to find.

Tweaking back his shoulders, he lowers the window. The air that seeps in is heavy and moist. The water is everywhere, in the air, running beneath their feet, impossible to escape.

'What's being said about you?'

Billie, alight with drama, telling her in a lowered voice that Gabriel was linked to Lily's disappearance.

'It's been suggested I was the person she was going to meet.' He clears his throat. 'That I ... did something unspeakable.'

He closes his eyes, injustice lacerating the air around him, making it bleed.

'I know exactly how it feels, Gabriel.' She squeezes his arm. 'To be accused of something you haven't done.'

He says a quiet thank you, glancing over his shoulder as Daniel stirs and sighs.

'How are you and Suzie coping?' she says as he starts the engine.

'Suzie wants to sell up and leave, but I won't be chased out. I've done nothing wrong. Suzie'll be OK. I'm taking care of her.'

'And you? How are you doing?'

He looks at her for the first time since they got in the car, a long, inscrutable gaze. 'No one ever asks how I'm doing.'

The look on his face fills her with sweetness, a lemony-pink butter-cream swirl. The way she used to feel when Lauritz laid his head on her stomach, curling his body around hers. *Happiness is easy with you*, he used to say.

She doesn't believe in ghosts. And yet here she is, pausing outside the closed door to Lily's room, listening. The room sounds empty, which of course it is. But that doesn't stop the clementine sparkles that wave her through the door. One day she'll walk into the room and the girl will be there. It's a conviction she can't shake.

The glass lamp spreads pastel pinks, neon limes, sunflower yellows around the room; happy colours that lift her mood, the way smiling releases endorphins. She lays out the photographs of Lily and her friends and the tattoo sketch on her bedcovers and studies them. In piecing together the girl, she might discover what happened to her.

A knock at the door startles her and she claws the photographs and sketch together, flinging them under the bed.

'Anna? It's Suzie.'

She's guessed as much from the rapid fire of knuckles against her door. Suzie looks red-eyed and disorientated, her hair sleep-ruffled. She sweeps her gaze around the room before making eye contact. 'Have you seen Gabriel?'

'Isn't he putting Daniel to bed?' Anna takes an instinctive step back. Suzie's hunting for something, the roadkill colours of suspicion, flayed reds and feather browns, giving her away.

Suzie doesn't reply, reaching into the room to straighten a crooked fold in the four-poster's canopy, her eyes darting across the bedclothes.

'Well, he's not in here.' Anna's tone has a snap of indignation. She tries to soften it with a silly show of looking under the bed. 'Nope, definitely not in here.'

'He'll have gone out for a bit of air. He does that,' Suzie says, shame like a rice shower against her bloodier colours as she leaves the room.

Anna watches the door, listening. Then she shuffles under the bed on her belly, gathering the scattered pictures. As she wriggles back out, something catches her hair. Her fingers feel paper as she tries to free herself. She rolls onto her back. A plain brown envelope is taped to the underside of the bed. Inside it, the edges of three photographs are visible. Leaving the envelope in place, she slides them out, then scrambles from under the bed, banging her forehead in her haste.

Something taps at the window, a quiet, surreptitious noise that makes her start. Lily's dreamcatcher stirring in a draught. Someone has fixed its broken loop and hung it back up in the window. She takes it down, throwing it to the back of the cupboard before sitting on the bed to study the photographs.

'Whoa...Jesus.' Three pictures of Lily sprawling on a sofa, naked beneath a blue-checked blanket that reveals more than it hides. In the muted light, her eyes are luminous, the colour of liquid honey. With her gaze locked on the person behind the camera, her body arches, catlike with lust. The sofa has an ugly, distinctive pattern of falling horse's heads. Anna wonders where the photographs were taken, and by whom.

Her heart double-bounding, she puts the photographs face-down on the bed, their raw intimacy all the more shocking for Lily's youth. She looks younger than in her YouTube video, not even seventeen.

19

Lava-glow lust

It was Billie who insisted Anna read Lauritz his cards.

Her sister was always trying to catch his attention. She liked his Danish accent, said he had lighthouse eyes. *They sweep across you like you're naked.* When Billie had failed to impress him with her opinion of the Iraqi war, boasting about taking part in the largest demonstration in British history, she reverted to their old childhood games.

Lauritz Kellerman was the son of their dad's best friend at school. Anna had grown up with the stories of their schoolboy escapades – the stolen cigarettes, cider binges and late-night rendezvous with girls from the local school – each recounting more heroic than the last. She knew that Lauritz's father, Klaus, was blind in one eye after falling out of a tree, that he was married to a Finnish ballerina who was famous in Scandinavia, that he drank schnapps with his herring to keep the fish alive in his stomach. Of his son, she knew almost nothing. Lauritz worked for his father's shipping business. He wore a wedding ring and was attractive in a sandy, wind-blown way. To her and Billie's mortification, their dad always asked him the same question at the start of every visit: *Any little bundles of joy on the way yet?* Lauritz would shake his head, joking about his poor efforts. Only Anna could see the flare of pain that billowed above his head like a sail catching a breeze.

But that painful, swollen blue wasn't what caught her attention. On his third visit, she noticed his colours change when he looked in her direction. It made her curious about her own power, so she agreed to read his future.

What a dangerous gift you have, he'd said with a smile that was both lazy and hungry, a lava glow rising from his body. Even now, a residual heat returns with the memory.

And he was right. It had been a dangerous gift, one she'd misused.

The ceramic frog eyes her from its sentry post on top of the gilded Tarot cards, daring her to ask a question. She wonders what the cards would say about Gabriel and Lily.

Leaving the frog lolling on its side, she shucks the cards from their battered box. They slide out in an oiled rush and she closes her eyes, letting her hands remember them. Despite the chill in Lily's room, the cards are skin-warm. She shuffles until the falter in rhythm lets her know they're ready. A card flips out, landing on her lap. If three or more drop out, it's an accident, but a single card is a message.

I can feel your heart knocking, Lauritz had said the first time he pulled her against him, locking her in place with his arms. Her heart is knocking now, trying to break through the cage of her ribs.

She flips the card over with a sense of already knowing what it is. Her old friend the Seven of Swords. A thief sneaks out of a palace in broad daylight, clutching an armful of swords, looking back over his shoulder to meet her eye in acknowledgement. A fellow trickster.

Motive and stealth are its messages. Or it can refer to tiptoeing around a tricky person. Suzie, she thinks with a sour smile.

Above all, the Seven of Swords is the card of deception and betrayal.

When she was nineteen, manipulating the cards' messages to

persuade Lauritz back to her bed again and again, the deceiver had been herself.

It still might be, she thinks, because her every thought of Gabriel glows a deep, carnal pink.

The next morning, she is in the kitchen trying not to eavesdrop on the conversation between husband and wife in the hallway as Gabriel puts on his work boots. He comments on how tired Suzie looks, concern a soft ribbon in his voice. 'I can take Dan to school today, sweetheart,' he says. 'Then you could go back to bed for a bit.'

'Bed is for lazybones,' Suzie says. 'You'd better scoot or you'll be late.'

She hears the quiet noise of a kiss, once, twice.

As soon as the Defender has left the drive, Suzie comes to find her in the kitchen. She slides the car keys across the table.

'Can you take Daniel on your own today, Anna?' she says, no trace of the sprightly woman from moments before. As if the energy it takes to hide her fragile state from Gabriel has sucked her dry.

Late afternoon, and Anna has just returned from the supermarket, the key still in the door, when she hears a crash. Loud and startling, it is the sound of something shattering, followed by silence. She runs into the sitting room and finds Suzie sitting on the floor, staring at two objects in her hands, neither of which Anna can identify.

'I dropped Daniel's boat.' She holds up two large, uneven clay rocks, the imprint of Daniel's small fingers showing through the patchy yellow gloss. 'He's going to be devastated.'

'Where is he?'

'He's trying out football club.' Suzie's hands are shaking as she moves the pieces around as though she might find a way to press them back together. 'Gabe's getting him.'

Crouching beside Suzie, Anna smells sweat beneath the woman's deodorant. 'How about some glue?'

Suzie tucks her skirt between her knees so Anna can see the debris lying on the floor beneath her: a rubble of clay chips, the paper sail torn away from the pencil mast. A sweep of light moves across the wall, followed by the crunch of tyres on the drive.

'Shit.' Suzie rakes at the mess, her panic clawing orange marks into the air. 'Shit.'

Anna tries to help, brushing up the coarse sand of dried clay with the edges of her hands.

'What am I going to tell them? Dan made it for Gabe's last birthday.' Suzie sounds like she might cry as little brown shards keep falling out of her overfilled hands. 'How can I say I dropped it? It looks so careless.'

The front door opens, Dan's voice in mid-story, his father chuckling.

'Blame it on me. I'll say I was dusting and knocked it over.'

'Mummy?' Daniel's voice is in the hall now. 'Where are you?'

Suzie blanches, her eyes wide and panicked, staring at the doorway.

Gabriel spots them from the hall and steps into the room, his eyes moving between them. 'What's happened?'

Standing up with a brisk clap of her hands, Suzie nods in Anna's direction. Her look is one of restrained reproach, as if she's trying to be fair.

'I'm afraid Anna's managed to drop Dan's boat.'

20

An unhappy confetti of purple, blue and red

Gabriel is quiet and distant, Anna's presence forgotten. They've been driving for twenty minutes so far, having passed through Kirkley and up into the Black Downs. The road rides the spine of the hill, rising and dipping, with fields falling steeply away on both sides.

They pass a hand-painted sign as they descend into the valley. *April's Gaff.*

'Almost there,' he says. 'Think you can sit still long enough?'

'I'll do my best.' She smiles. Whilst he hasn't mentioned the broken clay boat again, his brief flash of disappointment when she'd taken the blame still smarts. It's curious how desperate Suzie is to hide certain things from him.

The lane breaks into tarmac ice floes, the car dipping and lurching through the gaps. At the end is a small tile-hung farmhouse in the lee of the hill, surrounded by neglected outbuildings, one of which must be the meditation studio. The sky is a thirsty blue, with thin wind-raked clouds like desert-bleached ribcages.

'So this is where the sun's been hiding,' she says, and the way he smiles at her lifts her mood. Perhaps she's forgiven.

Four cars are parked alongside a tractor whose giant wheels are sewn into the ground by creeping ragwort. Apart from a goat licking the corner of a weather-beaten garden table, the place is deserted. A wind chime hangs by the kitchen door, brass tubes and ornamental bells butting each other in the breeze, their notes a metallic rainfall.

'Gabriel, you gorgeous hunk.' They are greeted by a middle-aged woman with a rough halo of brown curls. Passing the chime, she reaches out to rub the Chinese coin embedded in its wooden windcatcher. For luck, Anna guesses.

'You must be Anna, my new girl, ay? I'm April. The woman Gabe should've married.' The woman laughs, enjoying her own joke. Her accent has a guitar-string twang, Australian or New Zealand. She takes Anna's hand in a warm grasp. 'Know anything about meditating?'

'Not a thing.'

'A beautiful blank sheet. Just how I like them.'

April's studio is a wooden hut, the colour of honey, in the centre of an apple orchard behind the derelict barns. Comfort descends as soon as she enters its bright, warm interior. Six people are seated in a circle. Heads turn to study Anna, tentative smiles as they regard her. On April's instructions, she removes her plimsolls. She's grateful that her painted toenails aren't too scrappy until she spies April's big toe poking through her khaki sock and smiles to herself.

April directs her to an empty chair. It's when the introductions start that she becomes aware of an unpleasant bristle of oranges and reds behind those quick smiles. They don't want her here. So much for love and light.

Taking a breath, she tells herself it's growing pains; a tight band of people having to shift and stretch to accommodate a stranger.

To her right is Jo, a thin stick of resentment. Having given her name, Jo turns her head away, passing on the introductions like a child's party game. To her left is Milly, a tiny, plump woman in her fifties whose feet don't reach the floor.

'Welcome, Anna.' This from the youngest member of the group, late teens or early twenties, softly spoken, with a single strip of pillarbox red running through her dark hair and a dimpled smile. 'I'm Margaret, though I prefer Greta.'

When it comes to Gabriel's turn, he says, 'Anna and I already know each other. Anna's our new mother's help.'

The atmosphere thickens with interest, eyes flitting between her and Gabriel. He looks different in this setting, legs stretched out before him, shoulders back, as if he can finally inhabit the full capacity of his body away from the house. Away from Suzie.

Marble pinks and spring greens flow towards Gabriel as he speaks, though he remains quite contained, possibly unaware of the group's goodwill and support.

Anna knows only too well that feeling of isolation, when human connection is so unexpected it can be missed entirely. On the day of Sissie's party, when she learnt she was different to everyone else, she stepped off the world and onto her own island. At least she has Billie. She wonders if Gabriel has someone to help with the loneliness.

Distracted, she forgets to pay attention to the rest of the introductions until April, having lit candles around the room, settles in a large leather beanbag, feet planted on the floor. 'I'm April Showers. And yes, that is my birth name, because my parents were hilarious fuckers.'

Gabriel sends Anna a wink, smiling.

'This is how it works, Anna. I tell a story and you follow it in your head. Let the pictures come. If your shopping list or tonight's dinner muscles in, acknowledge them and put them kindly to one side. That's the tricky bit, stilling our busy minds.'

The room sinks into a deeper quality of silence. Anna's chair creaks as she shifts, trying to get comfortable. Jo twitches her head in her direction and Anna freezes in position. Her eyelids are jittery and spring-loaded. She thinks Gabriel might be watching her, but when she opens her eyes, she's mistaken.

'Bring attention to your breath but don't alter it.'

Her heart, for some reason, is rapping out a fast beat.

'You're standing on the banks of a clear stream. The water moves over smooth white stones on the sandy riverbed. There's a breeze on your face, the scent of pine and mountain flowers.'

She pictures herself stepping into the river, letting the chilled, crystalline water wash over her feet.

'Move into the river,' April says, and Anna almost utters a small *ha!* of triumph, finding herself a step ahead. An urge, strong as thirst, comes over her. She wants to lie down in the water, letting it run over her skin, through her hair and clothing.

'Time to let go,' April says. 'Release all the negative things from your past, the hurts, the nasty words you've given and received. Let the water wash away all that black sludge.'

Strings of black tar issue from Anna's feet and fingers. These aren't her colours. Black is the colour of violence.

'Guilt. Let that go too. And shame. Both poisonous.'

She closes her inner eyes, feeling the water run over her. It's shallow, the colour of cut sapphire, so there's nothing to be afraid of.

Something brushes across her face, tickling.

She opens her inner eyes to find the face of a young girl inches from her own. Pale brown eyes stare down at her, the girl's white-blonde hair trickling across her cheeks. She knows that face from every photograph in the dressing table drawer. Lily is on the riverbank, leaning over her.

Her body reacts before she can stop it, lurching forward in her chair with a rasp. Eyes open and close in a Mexican wave as the group surfaces and goes back under. Aware that Gabriel is watching her, she rushes for the door.

The grass soaks into her socks as she runs across the orchard.

'Anna, wait,' April calls, breathless, arms crossed beneath the weighty judder of her bosom as she jogs along, Anna's shoes clutched in her hand.

'I'm not going back inside.'

'That's OK. At least put your shoes on.'

April shows her to a bench beneath an apple tree, the wooden slats slippery and swollen with rain.

'Meditation can bring up all sorts of buried shit. Sit with it a while. Breathe through it.'

Anna can't meet her keen gaze, something too knowing in April's eyes. Gabriel is watching from the doorway. She mutters an apology for disrupting the session.

'Everyone has an off moment. Come back inside in half an hour so we can close off.' She makes it sound necessary, like putting the cork back in the bottle.

Smiles of quiet camaraderie greet her when she returns, as though she's passed a test. Margaret holds back her red hank of hair as she leans towards Anna to whisper, 'Kudos for coming back.'

'Now, my darlings, close your eyes and place a bubble of golden light in the centre of the room.'

Keeping her eyes on her feet, Anna tries not to pay attention to April's voice, waiting for the session to be over.

'In this light we place all the people who need healing.'

There's a moment of silence before April continues. 'And as always we send out a healing light to Lily in the hope that it might guide her safely home.'

The girl's name bursts like an orange anemone in Anna's chest. There's a silent criss-crossing of looks between the group.

Gabriel keeps his head lowered, staring down at his scarred hands.

'Never giving up hope,' April says. Beside her, Margaret starts to cry.

Gabriel hands Anna the keys and asks her to wait for him in the car. He catches up with Margaret, who has lit a cigarette, still wiping her eyes. It's a short, unhappy exchange, the girl stroking the red stripe of her hair, flicking ash off her cigarette, a jitter of discomfort. What he says makes her shake her head with such vigour that even at this distance it throws out a miserable confetti of purple, blue and red.

'Are you all right?' Anna says when Gabriel returns to the car, his face set into blankness.

He gives a curt nod and starts the engine. Before they can pull away, April rushes across the yard, something held between her finger and thumb.

'For Suzie,' she says, reaching the car. 'One a day. It'll help her sleep.'

Gabriel lowers his window, holding out his palm. She hands him a brown glass vial filled with tiny circular pills on it. He closes his hand, catching her fingers in a brief, grateful clasp.

April rests her forearms on the ledge of the open window and leans in. 'You're quite intuitive, aren't you, Anna?'

Anna studies April's outline for clues, but the woman's tranquil green aura is steady and unchanging, a rarity when most people's emotions flicker and flare like a dry storm. She gives a casual shrug. 'I'm not sure.'

'Unusually so. It's a good thing, by the way. You shouldn't try to hide it.'

Anna's laugh is short and brittle. 'I'm not hiding anything.'

Gabriel is watching her with sudden interest. She has the

uncomfortable sensation that April is poking about inside her head.

'You have a gift, Anna.' The woman's voice is soft, beguiling. 'It's a blessing.'

Anna turns her face away from their combined scrutiny, the words popping out before she can stop them.

'A blessing doesn't cut you off from the rest of the world.'

21

Black is the colour of violence

'You need a drink,' Gabriel says.
      'If you don't mind, I don't want to talk about April or her notions.'

'OK. *I* need a drink.' He smiles at her. 'I won't ask any questions. Trust me, I'm the last person to pry into other people's business.'

She should say no, but she can't resist a little stolen time in his company.

He conducts a tricky U-turn on the steep, narrow road and they descend back into the valley, this time turning away from April's farm. Five minutes later they pull up outside the Wells Inn, wisteria-clad, with crooked eaves and a signpost swinging in the wind. The cloud has returned and a mean spatter of rain hits the windscreen.

Gabriel points to a wood stack where a tree has been chopped into roundels, sawdust greying in the mud by the edge of the car park. 'My work. Not that I got paid for it. This is my in-laws' pub.' He gives a grim laugh. 'I still owe them for stealing away their daughter.'

'I've never seen a tree being cut down,' Anna says. 'Can I come and watch sometime?'

To her disappointment, he shakes his head. 'Lily used to come and watch. That was my first mistake right there.'

She's not sure what he means, but his colours are burning low and defensive around his head, so she doesn't ask. He glances at the two other vehicles in the car park, growing wary. She can see him shrinking back into his body, trying to reduce his size and become unremarkable.

'Lily came with me when I took down April's oak,' he says. 'It made her cry even though I explained the tree was already dead. She said it broke her heart to see the branches stripped away. She was crying for its loss of dignity.'

'Did Lily…' She stops, but it's too late, she has his attention. 'Did she have any tattoos?'

He frowns. 'Not that I ever saw. Why do you ask?'

'I wondered if that's what the sketches in her room were.'

A bronzed green opens like a fan above his head. 'What is it? This gift of yours?'

'You said you wouldn't ask.'

His gaze is direct, unwavering, though his colours are kind, telling her she can trust him. But she's made that mistake once before and it cost her a job and her reputation.

'It's what April said. I'm intuitive. It basically means I'm good at guessing things.'

His greens deepen, blotting out the bronze. He knows there's more to it but he lets the subject go and they get out of the car. He holds the pub door open for her, ducking his head as he follows her in.

It's a hermit's cave inside, empty, dark and unaired. The ceiling is close overhead, beer jugs and horseshoes dangling off its beams. It reeks of slopped ale and vinegar. Gabriel asks what she wants to drink and she says a vodka with tonic.

'Double?' He raises his eyebrows, teasing, and she pokes her tongue out, the lightness that was between them before the meditation returning. He turns to the lad behind the bar. 'Keith in?'

With his back to her, she can't read his reaction when the barman says no.

She chooses a small table by the unlit hearth and decides she likes the place after all. It's a den, not a cave. A place where they can hide out for a while. With any luck, Ben will be gone by the time they return. Earlier in the day she'd peeked into the box room to check on his progress, only to find that despite the great clamour of activity, he had done nothing but round off the hole's ragged edges. She'll tell Gabriel how uncomfortable Ben makes her. She's seen his protective streak, a strong silver band that rises up like an extension of his backbone.

The door opens, bringing in a blast of rain and two men in open-necked shirts, their hair styled into slick identical crests. They notice Gabriel, and Anna's stomach flips over as they share a look, their colours turning to soot. When they spot her, drawing conclusions, the grimy dust cloud reaches for her too.

Despite the choice of empty tables, they take the one next to her. The man sitting closest, bulldog handsome with a diamond stud in his ear, leans back, straightening and crossing his legs so his feet end up inches from hers. He fixes her with an open stare, setting off a prickle of damp heat in her armpits whilst Gabriel and the barman chat on.

Her temper flares and she meets Bulldog's eyes. There's a moment where they contemplate each other, then he shoots out a stiff arm to shake her hand.

'And who's this young lass then?'

'Anna.' She makes sure to take his hand with a firm grip.

His companion lets out an amused snort, giving Bulldog a casual slap across the ribs with the back of his hand. 'You need glasses, mate. That's no young lass.'

Anna moves her eyes to him, determined to remain composed despite the heat that bursts in her face.

'This one's quite obviously a *lady*,' he adds.

'Smooth,' she says, and they grin, the graze red of their attention softening, falling away. It's not her they're interested in.

Gabriel pulls his wallet out of his back pocket, taking his time, counting out change.

'There he is. Big Gabe.' Bulldog shifts forward in his chair, flicking a glance at Anna. 'Look at that brute strength. Gets the girls all wet, eh?'

Gabriel turns, a drink in either hand. He hasn't heard what Bulldog said, but with an orange flicker, he recognises the men. Then his face goes blank, his colours drawing in. Anna finds herself holding her breath as he approaches, but no one speaks. Bulldog picks up a menu, passing one to his companion. His feet jiggle beside hers, the toe of his shoe brushing her ankle. She shifts her foot. She's holding herself in an uncomfortable position, her body tensing away from him, but she won't give him the satisfaction of moving her chair.

Gabriel sips his beer, oblivious or wary she can't tell, because the space above his head is clear. 'Group's not for you, I take it?'

The men listen behind their menus.

She doesn't want to speak, her mouth dry, waiting for it all to kick off with her caught in the middle, whilst Gabriel is blind to it all. 'Possibly not.'

'I could never persuade Suzie to give it a go.'

The words are repeated under Bulldog's breath, passed on to his companion. *Give it a go.*

'Give what a go?' his companion wonders.

Anna meets Gabriel's eyes, raising her eyebrows, trying to convey her own message. He shrugs, returning to his pint. She thinks about mentioning Ben, but she can't concentrate under the men's scrutiny.

A loud snap makes her jump as Bulldog closes his menu. 'I'm not that hungry, mate.'

'Nor me. Lost my appetite.'

The two men get up and Anna focuses on her drink, turning it round and round, her fingertips slick with condensation. Now. Whatever is going to happen. It's now.

Bulldog rests his knuckles on their table, leaning towards Gabriel. 'Give my best to Suzie, won't you?'

'Sure.' Gabriel sniffs, rubs his nose. 'Who are you again?'

'Funny fucker, aren't you?'

The moment Gabriel and Bulldog lock eyes, the black shadows come, bursting from the crowns of their heads; something she's seen on newsreels but never in real life. The glass spins out of her fingers, tipping over, clear liquid spilling across the table.

Bulldog straightens, dips his fingertips in the spilt vodka and flicks it in their general direction as he turns to walk away.

Anna rounds on Gabriel as the door closes behind them. 'What the hell was all that about?'

Gabriel reels in his black shadow, giving nothing away with his blank expression and the relaxed slouch of his body. Only she can see the effort of self-control, because after that, there's no colour at all.

'The charming one is Suzie's cousin.' Having drained his pint, he looks at her. 'Flexing his muscles, that's all.'

'I'd like to go home,' she says.

Gabriel pauses in the pub doorway, watching the rain smash pockets of water into the gravel. 'Maybe Suzie's right about leaving this place.' He is ash grey with sudden weariness, swaying on his feet, as though the rage has burnt him hollow. She'd had no idea how much fury he carries.

She reaches for his hand, stroking her thumb across the patina of scars around his knuckles. 'How awful for you to live like this.'

He lets his head drop to her shoulder and she pulls him in, her cheek to his, the heat of their breath mingling. A car passes, cutting a wave from the grey water pooled at the side of the road, and he pulls back, taking his hand from hers.

Still jangled and nervy, she follows his gaze, but the car is gone. 'What's wrong?'

Gabriel steps into the rain. 'I'm sick of being watched.'

22

Sticky possessive caramel

A noise startles her from the depths of sleep, heart pounding, though she couldn't have said what the sound was. The wind and rain, perhaps, breaking against the side of the house like the sea. There's a ticking noise inside the room, and when she switches on the lamp, she sees water dripping off the windowsill, hitting the same wet spot on the carpet. It's almost two in the morning, but she's wide awake.

She walks past Daniel's room. He's curled up, a tight nut inside the shell of his covers, frowning, anxious even as he sleeps. The door to his parents' room is slightly ajar. She tiptoes down the stairs, the carpet tacky with damp, and notices the light on in the kitchen. She stalls in the doorway, finding Gabriel sitting at the table, his wife leaning over him, her hands in his hair. Mortified and full of apology, she's about to back out, thinking she has stumbled on an intimate moment, when she sees the bloody cloth in Suzie's hand.

They look at her in unison. The sight of Gabriel's face makes her suck in her breath, a noise that seems unnaturally loud in the quiet room. His lower lip is swollen and puce, the skin split and seeping blood across his chin. His left eye is a blue bird's egg.

Suzie places herself in front of her husband. 'This isn't your business.'

'What happened?'

Neither speaks. Suzie turns back to Gabriel, dabbing at his lip, her other hand resting on his forehead like a mother feeling her child's temperature. There's mud tracked across Suzie's normally pristine floor from Gabriel's outdoor boots, his climbing bag in the middle of the room where it has been dropped, a knot of rope beside its open lip. His hair is wet from the rain.

'Was it the men from the pub?'

'What men?' Suzie's voice is hoarse, her eyes raw with tears. The bloodied cloth hovers in front of Gabriel's left eye. He lowers it, cupping her hand in his own. The tenderness of the gesture makes Anna's chest tighten, and she blinks away caramel yellow that is both hunger and envy. A strangely sweet colour for something so bitter.

Suzie starts to cry. 'Everything's so fucked up.'

'Were you climbing? I don't understand how they found you.'

Neither of them answers or even looks at her. She walks out, closing the door behind her.

Suzie's cousin would know where they live. She follows the smeared earth of Gabriel's footprints to the front door and opens it a fraction. Nothing out there but the rain.

The hot water runs out before the bath is half full. She slops lukewarm water over her body like some beached sea mammal, trying to get warm, trying not to think about Gabriel. She hadn't slept again after the shock of his beaten face. Suzie had taken Daniel out after lunch, and when Anna had gone looking for Gabriel to offer him something to eat, she'd found him sleeping, stretched fully dressed across his bed. The hem of his T-shirt had risen to reveal the tight band of his stomach. It would have been easy to slip her hand underneath it and let her fingertips count out his ribs.

Except she was never going to be that person again. It was seeing her, an unknown woman, out with Gabriel that had infuriated the men, of that she is certain.

She pulls out the plug, wrapping herself in a towel. She can hear Ben crashing about in the box room, where he's been all afternoon, having hauled a stepladder upstairs. She has the distinct feeling the noise is for her benefit. Letting her know he's just the other side of the flimsy wall.

When she leaves the bathroom, he is in the corridor.

'How about that then?' His grin is sly and calculating. He makes a point of staring at her bare legs beneath the hem of the towel. 'Gabe's face mashed to fuck.'

When he walks past, the back of his hand grazes her hip, by accident or not she can't tell, but it sets off an involuntary shiver of revulsion.

Opening the door to her room, she finds Suzie sitting on the bed, Lily's photographs from the dressing table drawer in her hands. A toffee yellow flashes before her eyes, a possessiveness she has no right to. Suzie glances up, registering the towel, Anna's skin marbled with cold. She holds up the pictures.

'For the last seven years I've been Lily's mum. She wasn't easy to win over. Like a little wolf cub. I promised her I'd never let anything bad happen to her again. I did my best, you know. The number of times I got her out of trouble, gave her alibis for skipping school, nursed her through hangovers. I really tried.'

'She was lucky to have you on her side.'

'Not many people were.' Suzie picks a photograph from the pile, one of Lily looking sleepy in a pink terry-towelling bathrobe, her cheek resting on her knees, hair falling to her toes. 'Look at that sweet face.'

Anna brushes away a droplet of water running down her arm. 'She's beautiful.'

'But difficult sometimes. She could be selfish.'

'That's teenagers for you. You don't mean to hurt anyone. You just get carried away.'

Suzie looks at her. 'Did you?'

'Yes. Though I never meant to. In some ways...' She stops, knowing she has gone too far.

'You were going to say that in some ways you were a lot like Lily.' Suzie gives a clipped laugh. 'Anna, we were *all* a lot like Lily at that age.'

Anna can't hide her shivering, but Suzie either doesn't notice or doesn't care.

'Have you seen this one?' She holds up a picture of Lily lounging against the horse-head sofa, and Anna curses herself for not double-checking that all three photos had made it back into the envelope taped under the bed.

With one pointed finger Lily tugs down the edge of the checked blanket to reveal the swell of her breasts, a playful grin on her face, her tongue between her teeth.

'You see. She wasn't always sweet.'

'Who do you think took that photograph?' Anna says.

'Who knows. Lily had a line of blokes trailing after her.' Colours clash above Suzie's head, fiery embers butting up against hopeless slate, but that roadkill suspicion is missing. Anna wonders when Suzie lost her hunger for answers. Gabriel too. Only Daniel is looking, and Anna herself.

'She was in someone else's house.' She points at the sofa with its horse's heads tumbling out of a white silken sky. 'Will you show it to your family liaison officer?'

'I can't show this to anyone.' Suzie's hand is splayed against her chest, the sound of her breathing audible. 'Look at her. What would they think of her?'

A hot bile of anger rises from Anna's stomach. 'They'd think she was a beautiful young girl, full of life, and that somewhere out there a monster is getting away with...' She stops short of the word *murder*.

Suzie's body bucks forward as if to run, the photograph pinched between her fingers. She staggers upright, the picture falling and crinkling beneath her foot as she rushes out of the room.

'Suzie. Wait. I'm sorry, I shouldn't...'

The bathroom door bounces off the wall, followed by an agony of retching, wave upon wave without a breath, as if Suzie's body is trying to turn inside out and purge itself of the poison.

23

Shame is a migraine white

In the dream, she is lying in Lily's bed when the window lifts open and a figure climbs in, hands and feet first, followed by a body. At first she can't see who it is because her eyes won't stay open. When her vision clears, Lily is on the bed. With an impish grin, the girl slides her hand beneath the duvet and pinches Anna's big toe. She wakes with a gasp, her toe hot with the fading pain of imaginary fingernails, to startling clarity.

Lily wants to be found and she's asking Anna for help.

Getting out of bed, she dresses and texts Billie to let her know she's up, having been invited to spend the day with them. She tucks the pictures of Lily on the horse-head sofa and the angel-wing sketch into a pocket inside her bag.

Opening her door, she listens to the house and then steps into the corridor. One small, inert foot pokes out from under Daniel's bedclothes; the door to Gabriel and Suzie's room is still closed. Once the front door is shut behind her, she breathes more easily until she spots Suzie at the end of the garden. Barefoot, wearing only cotton shorts and a vest, shoulders hunched, clasping a steaming mug beneath her chin. They haven't seen each other since Suzie ran out of Lily's room to be sick. The woman watches her approach, her face giving nothing away.

'I'm so sorry about yesterday.'

'But you were right,' Suzie says, shivering and blowing into the mug. She is bleached with exhaustion and misery, the last of her hope scrubbed away. 'There *is* a monster out there.'

Anna's own colour segues in, a snow-blind white, the colour of migraines, remembering how she complained to Billie about the box room, the boredom and her employer's coldness; scratchy grains of sand compared to what Suzie must wake to every day.

She asks if there's something she can do to help, anything at all.

'You can make me a promise,' Suzie says, and a rash of lipstick-red speckles fills her aura.

Anna's stomach flips over. 'OK.'

'Promise me you won't be seen alone with Gabriel again.'

'I—'

'You can't go anywhere alone with my husband. There's enough talk about my family as it is.'

Suzie may be worn and weary, but she's still battle-ready.

Jonah collects her by the white signpost at the end of the lane. When she gets in, he offers a bashful wave like he used to, back when he was awkward about greeting with kisses. His hair struts out at sleepy angles and the neckline of his jumper is fraying, cotton balls catching his stubble. With a rush of affection, she gives him a hug because he is kind and familiar and she's in need of a friend.

'Sorry I'm such a scruff,' he says. 'I've been running after the kids all morning.'

'Where's Billie?'

'Still in bed.' He looks away, preventing her from reading his colours.

'Is she ill?'

'No, just tired.' He checks his reflection in the rear-view mirror, one hand attempting to smooth out his hair. 'I've got some quotes for the Bastard Beetle. There's one last place I haven't tried yet. We pass it on the way. I'll see if they can look at it sometime this week.'

Five minutes later, they pull into the garage they'd stopped at on her first day at the O'Keefes'. Inside, she can see the pretty young attendant who'd flirted with Jonah.

'Won't be a minute,' he says, combing his fingers through his hair again. She decides to stay in the car, where she can openly observe them. Their interaction is playful, judging by their grins, but short-lived.

'No luck there,' Jonah says on his return.

So what, she tells herself, *if he's learned to flirt a little?*

A dull white throb has started up behind her left eye, amplifying sounds. The closing of Jonah's door, the car's rumbling acceleration reverberate in her head like a struck bell. They drive through Lodswold, past the children's school, and ten minutes later reach Sturford. Now that she's experienced the isolation of the O'Keefes' house, the village no longer strikes her as remote and deserted. Despite the muggy rumble of thunder, a cricket match is under way on the green.

They park by the garden wall. The front door opens before they can reach it, and something white sails out and jabs her on the lip. A paper aeroplane falls to the ground by her feet. Maisie and Lucas appear from behind the doorway, shrieking with laughter, pelting them with more paper planes. Jonah laughs, then catches Anna's eye, his smile fading.

'Sorry, they're just excited to see you.'

She pulls her niece and nephew into a hug. 'I've got a headache, that's all.'

He suggests she waits for Billie in the quiet of the study, the only room the children aren't interested in.

The study, once used to house defunct sports equipment, outgrown toys and extra guests, has been given a makeover, much like Jonah himself. Now it is a grown-up space with bookshelves, a computer on a desk, a giant television screen above the mantelpiece, and a small sofa covered in rugs and cushions, ready to sink into. From the room's pristine state, it's obvious it doesn't get much use. She considers heading upstairs to kick her sister out of bed, but the pain in her head dissuades her. Instead she jiggles the mouse to wake up the computer. The password is on a Post-it note by the keyboard, in Jonah's handwriting: M4isieLuc4s.

She brings up the YouTube clip of Lily at seventeen. Everything she learns about the missing girl suggests she'd have liked her. Putting it on mute, she reads the emotion in Lily's face, a full palette of love, defiance and hurt, the metallic green verdigris of determination. The pain in her head swells. Sitting back from the screen, she notices a thumbs-down icon. Someone has pressed dislike since she last viewed the clip. A new comment has appeared below.

Poor Little Lily. If only you'd kept your greedy little pussy under control and stayed away from Gabriel OKeef.

The anger that bursts in her sight is a scraping cardinal red. With a groan she presses the heels of her hands to her eyes, though the colour cannot be escaped. Somewhere close by, concealed in their home, is an individual so warped with hate they cannot keep their malice to themselves, even now. The troll knows Lily in person – has stood on the laundry roof and looked into her bedroom – which means he knows she is missing, and still he vents his hatred. Behind the headache, a watery nausea is rising.

She straightens as the study door opens and Billie walks in, but she's too late to close the page. Her sister, tuned in as she is to Anna's every mood, approaches, eyes widening in concern.

'What are you looking at?'

She moves to one side. There's no point trying to fox Billie.

'I found a YouTube video that Lily made.' She breaks off with a shrug. 'It made me sad.'

As Billie leans over her to study the screen, a waft of stale alcohol hits Anna. She notes her sister's newly washed hair and the fresh glimmer of pale bronze on her eyelids. Neither conceals how drawn and pale she looks.

'You changed your mind about spending the whole day in bed, then.'

'When you have cherubs of your own, you'll appreciate the luxury of a six-monthly lie-in.'

'But you've been drinking, haven't you? I can smell it.'

'Two glasses of wine at a parents' social evening. On an empty stomach. That's as wild as it gets around here.' Billie sits on the edge of the desk, blocking the screen. 'Now. Listen up. What happened to Lily is a tragedy, but you didn't know her. This isn't something for you to get involved in.' She narrows her eyes. 'You've got your headache, haven't you?'

Anna lets her head rest back on the chair, nodding. Her sister, always her saviour, orders her to lie down, promising one of her famous cheese toasties. Anna does as she's told, curling up in the arm of the sofa.

Billie hesitates in the doorway. 'Look, I get it. I understand why you might be fascinated by Lily. But the similarities between the two of you don't mean anything. They're coincidental.'

'Similarities?'

'Both of you at nineteen, stunning girls, headstrong and a bit spoilt. For you there was Lauritz. For Lily it was Gabriel.'

'How do you know how Lily felt about Gabriel?' She has to close her eyes again, colours bursting and layering like dashed paint.

'Everyone knows everything in a place like this.' Billie takes her hand. 'Leave it be. Don't get drawn in.'

'I saw Lily when I was meditating.' The pain in her head is

an overfilled glass of water, the slightest movement threatening to tip it into a full-blown migraine. 'She just appeared. How is that possible?'

For once, her sister doesn't have a ready answer. She tugs the blanket away from the sofa, where it is tucked into the cushions, and wraps it around Anna's shoulders. 'Meditating is similar to dreaming. Our heads plant stuff.'

Her bag is within arm's reach, the three photographs and the angel-wing tattoo inside. 'I found something in her room.'

'I always said you'd make a world-class detective, Anna. What've you got?'

She cracks open an eye. Billie, whose colours usually sit like a skullcap on her head, is sending out geysers of lemon yellow. Anna is suddenly unsure about exposing those intimate pictures of Lily to her sister's powers of clinical observation, which can sometimes lack magnanimity. Shaking the photographs into the base of her bag, she takes out the sketch.

'I think it's a design for a tattoo. I found a card for a tattoo parlour as well.'

Her sister takes the picture between her fingernails and holds it up to the light, studying it in silence for a moment. 'Have you seen what's in the centre of the wing?'

'The letter G.'

Billie gives the paper a smart rap with the back of her hand. 'You see. No smoke without fire. Have you shown this to anyone?'

'Not yet. I wanted to see what you thought first.'

Billie narrows her eyes. 'You need to take this to the police.'

'The police? But then it looks like I'm interfering. And who's to say they haven't seen it already?'

'You found the sketches hidden away, you said.'

'Not hidden ...' She can't think; the pain in her head is

a manacle around her thoughts whilst her sister's are racing ahead.

'You're trying to protect Gabriel,' Billie says. 'You brought this to me hoping I'd shrug and say it's nothing, don't worry about it.'

Anna shakes her head, closing her eyes with a groan of pain. 'Not true.'

A distant thud and howl above them elicits a huff of frustration from Billie. Getting up, she points at the sketch. 'This links Lily and Gabriel. It's proof.' She leaves the room, calling her children's names.

The pain in Anna's head is bulging and hard as pack ice. The last thing she needs is a call to action. Her sister is reading too much into the sketch. At most it suggests that Lily had a crush on Gabriel. Who is even to say the letter stood for Gabriel? Other names exist – Greg, George, Gareth.

Maisie's voice rises into a muffled wail. With a groan, Anna turns her face to the sofa. A small horse's head fills the frame of her vision. She blinks, sits bolt upright, then stumbles backwards off the sofa, taking the blanket and several cushions with her.

The sofa in Jonah's study is covered in floating horse heads.

24

Love is pink and purple

The migraine lasts two days. Anna drifts in and out of sleep, waking with the passing noise of the family. Gabriel comes to see her every day with aspirins and tea. Daniel visits her twice. Once she wakes to find him sitting on her bed, rubbing his arm above the elbow. He shows her a red patch on his skin but doesn't answer when she asks how he hurt himself. He leaves the room without having said a word, but the pain, and the nausea tacked onto it, pins her to the bed. Daniel's second visit is to tell her that Billie is on the telephone. She doesn't take the call. Her head is filled with fog that rational thought cannot penetrate. She can't understand what it might mean, Lily's naked body on the sofa in her sister's house. All she knows is that Jonah is no longer shabby and sweetly risible. He flirts with young girls. Those photographs could blow her sister's marriage apart.

On the third day, she wakes without the pain. She is staring at the syrupy light behind the blinds and praying for sunshine when there's a knock on the door. Gabriel comes in with a tray. The swelling around his eye is gone, leaving only a circle of yellow bruising, the gash on his lip held together by the taut zip of a scab.

'You need to eat something,' he says, and she sees him note her bare shoulders above the covers. He's brought her a bowl of minestrone soup, a bread roll, and an apple sliced into neat segments. The effort touches her and she stops him before he can leave again. He turns his back whilst she pulls on a T-shirt, crinkled with dried sweat, discarded during the night.

'I can't tell you how nice it is to see another living being.'

He takes a seat on the dressing table stool whilst she eats. She holds back a smile, seeing how his bulk reduces it to a child's chair. He massages the knuckles on his right hand, fresh blood bubbling from under the raised lid of a scab.

'Are you all right, after ... the fight?'

'I'm used to it.' He shrugs. 'At twelve, I grew two foot taller than everyone else, and since then it's like I'm a fairground attraction. You know: *Come and have a go if you think you're hard enough.*'

He tries to smile, the tender flesh of his lip straining white around the gash. He gives another shrug, dismissing the subject. 'You look like you're feeling better. I'm sorry we've neglected you.'

'I've not been much use, have I?'

'On the contrary,' he says, feeling out the chair legs as they creak beneath his weight. 'You've brought a bit of light and happiness to this house. It's been a long time since my boy laughed or clowned about. He's missed you these last few days.'

Love rises from him at the mention of Daniel. Glancing up, he gives his pained smile. 'What are you looking at?'

'I can see how much you love Dan.' She takes a breath, makes a decision. 'I see it rising up in long, soft waves from your whole body. It's deep pink and purple.'

'That's what you see?' He gives a soft, wondering laugh, watching her intently, a green curiosity joining the pinks above his crown.

'According to my sister, it's a medical condition, not a blessing.' She gives a wry smile. 'It's called synaesthesia and it's where more than one sense comes into play. For example, you experience sounds with your sense of hearing only, but a synaesthete might taste them too, or see them as colours as well as hear them. It's very individual how it manifests.'

'And for you?'

She is right to trust him. His reaction couldn't be more different to Martha Sowerby's. That evening with the snow falling, whilst the children slept and Mr Sowerby was at Christmas drinks, she'd helped Martha hang garlands and been lulled into a sense of friendship. The more she'd tried to explain her synaesthesia, the darker and rustier the woman's colours had turned. Martha Sowerby had been afraid of what secrets Anna might learn. Two days later, she was accused of stealing.

'For me, every emotion has its own shape and colour. Right now, there are thin lines like fishing reels lifting off you. They're a nice colour, a greeny blue, because even though you're confused, you're open and interested.'

'April was right. It sounds like a gift,' he says.

'I'm just really, really good at reading body language and facial expression. The colours are an extra tool, that's all. Not special, not spooky.'

'You don't tell many people, do you?'

'No. I made the mistake of confiding in my last employer, and that's when it all went pear-shaped. I think she was afraid of what I'd see when I looked at her. Or her husband.' Her smile falls away at the memory. 'You have to know who to trust.'

'Yes. You do.' He too grows sober, staring down at his injured hand. Then he straightens and gives her a tired smile. 'OK. What colour am I giving off now?'

'Still dark pink, almost purple, but it has fizzy scarlet edges,' she says. 'And it looks like a giant ostrich plume.'

'Sounds manly.' He laughs. 'I was thinking of the first time

I saw Suzie. She was working behind the bar at the Wells Inn, laughing and teasing the old boys who refused to be served by anyone but her.'

She tries to picture a younger, happy Suzie, the one she'd glimpsed the night they got drunk on Jägermeister.

His gaze slots into hers. 'And now?'

This time it's more difficult, because her own colour screen is interfering, sparked by the quiet, intimate tone of his voice. She is conscious of her unwashed hair and the sour smell of her T-shirt.

'Crimsons, fuchsias, tinged with red. But the shape is loose, shivery, like leaves on a tree.'

'A pink-leafed tree.' He smiles and she has to look away.

'What are you thinking about?' she asks, stirring strands of pasta through her cooling soup.

'I wasn't thinking. I was just looking at you.'

She meets his eye, her body bursting into heat, the walls of the room collapsing inwards to pin the two of them in a secret place. The look between them is a click of recognition, one she feels deep in her stomach.

Somewhere in the house, a phone rings. Gabriel gets to his feet and moves towards the door. 'That's probably your sister again.'

The ringing stops and he pauses with his hand on the door handle. 'Does guilt have a colour?'

'It's like a piece of brown cloth, all torn and sometimes stained with rust.' She knows where this question is heading.

'So if you asked the right people questions about the night Lily didn't come home, could you read their colours and learn the truth? Could you tell if they're hiding something or lying?' His own colours are painting hectic slashes in the air: burnt orange peel, parrot yellows and greens; as excited as he is frightened by the idea.

'Yes. I can tell when people are lying.'

He nods, staring at his feet, the spin of his thoughts visible in the tension of his body.

'Margaret,' he says, finally. 'The girl with the red stripe of hair in April's group who's always crying. She knows something but she won't say what it is.'

The ceramic frog sits on her stomach, riding the waves of her breath. She strokes its cool, slippery head and tries to picture Lauritz but sees Gabriel instead.

The frog seems to be gathering weight, pressing down in the centre of her stomach, and she bucks her hip so it falls on the floor. It had been a present from Lauritz on his third visit.

Did you know the Egyptians worshipped the frog goddess? he'd whispered in her ear as he placed the little figure on her naked stomach. *Heqet, the goddess of fertility.* Then he slid his long body on top of hers and the frog rolled between their stomachs, like it was trying to work its way into her womb. Afterwards she licked their sweat off its glassy skin and observed how it made his eyes glaze over.

Then she took her Tarot from her bedside table.

What do you see for me, Anna?

She had held up the Empress, letting him gaze at the seductive power of the woman with her warrior stance, wild hair and powerful hips.

I see new beginnings.

And what does this one say? He'd tapped the Seven of Swords. He didn't notice her hesitation.

That one says if you want something badly enough, you'll find a way to have it.

Only she could see the clementine brilliance of her lies.

25

Mourning grey

Anna is hiding in the laundry room, avoiding Suzie, who is an electrical storm of prickling colour, toxic enough to fire off another headache. She'd walked in on Anna and Gabriel talking in the kitchen and pinned them with a glare, not bothering to hide her displeasure. Gabriel's response was to pull Suzie into a hug, kissing the crown of her head, soothing her, nothing but love and patience in his face.

In the corner of the ceiling a leak bubbles, releasing the odd drip, slow as treacle. Outside, a fine mesh of rain blows across the open fields. All she can hear is rain in the gutter. She folds Daniel's boxer shorts into tiny squares and looks out over the forest. Before Suzie had walked in, Gabriel had been telling her about a river that used to run through the woods, hundreds of years ago. A place where they drowned women suspected of witchcraft. It's no longer visible, having sunk down into the earth, but its arteries still exist, threading through the ground, feeding the River Kirk and its tributaries. She shivers, seeing those women, bound by chains, sinking to the riverbed. One frozen January night, he and Lily had tried to find its source.

'After the women drowned, they were burned,' he'd said, his mood grey and mournful as the day itself. 'Their ashes were washed into the river. Lily said the women won by becoming part of the endless water cycle. They defeated their persecutors by becoming eternal.'

It has started to hurt her to witness the depth of his loss.

Her mobile buzzes with a text, a welcome distraction.

Is there a problem with your phone? Billie wants to know.

Anna finds Suzie in the sitting room, staring down into the well. 'I'm sure Daniel's shown you this,' she says, frowning. 'I'm worried about the water levels with all this bloody rain.'

Anna stays by the door, far from the well. 'I was wondering if I could go out for a few hours. I'd be back in time to pick Daniel up from school.'

Suzie doesn't look up. 'Fine. You can't take the car, though. I might need it.'

They both know this is untrue. Disappointment slicks a toad green smear across Anna's vision, followed by a single slash of orange panic. Everything is conspiring to keep her hostage in this house – her broken car, Suzie's spite, even the weather.

She wonders if she should let Gabriel know how little his wife has left the house recently, but then her thoughts return to Billie and another uncomfortable conversation waiting to be had.

Billie arrives in a battered VW Golf. She gets out, waiting for Anna with her head back, inviting the rain on her face. Anna hesitates by the front door, wondering if she should change out of her jeans, seeing as her sister is wearing a tight wraparound dress and heels.

Suzie walks her up the drive as if to see her off the premises. To her surprise, Billie and Suzie greet each other with a hug. When Suzie turns back towards the house, there's a smile of genuine warmth on her face.

'Jonah's taken the family car, so we'll have to make do with his crappy runaround.' Billie opens the door and points to the passenger seat which is sitting too far forward with little leg space remaining. 'It's been stuck for ages, I'm afraid. You'll just have to cope with having your knees up around your ears.' She barks out a sudden laugh. 'Mind you, you're probably quite familiar with that position.'

'Naughty.' Anna sends her a look of mock-outrage. 'How long have you and Mrs O'Keefe been besties?'

Billie manoeuvres the car through an arduous U-turn in the lane. Up close, the effect of her glamour is diminished, hair pulled into a greasy bun, her eyes bald and unmade-up. As she huffs over the steering wheel, the car fills with exhaled booze, and Anna stares at her through a pale tangerine haze of worry. Sooner or later she'll have to discuss her sister's increased drinking with Jonah or their parents, who are nothing if not practical.

'I didn't like the way the other school mums were avoiding her. So I made an effort. She's in desperate need of a friend.'

Billie to the rescue, as always.

'I thought we'd have a picnic, by the way.'

As the car hits a pothole, there's a clink and rattle from a large wicker hamper in the back seat. Anna lifts the lid and finds a bottle of champagne and two ham and cheese sandwiches from a garage. She's about to comment on the lack of sunshine when another wave of alcohol reaches her as Billie puffs with concentration, squinting over the wheel.

'How was your morning, Bills?'

'Unproductive. I meant to clear out the attic and instead found myself reading my old textbooks. I mean, that stuff was mathematical acrobatics, Anna. I tried to follow some of it but my mind's become a fat slug. I literally had to lie down on the floor to recover.' A laugh escapes through her nostrils. She takes a hand off the steering wheel to wipe her nose, the car sailing in languid motion into the opposite lane.

'Did you have a little drinkie whilst recuperating on the floor, Bills?'

'Not so little.'

'Are you wasted?'

'If you can call a bottle of Cinzano being wasted. We had a Cinzano phase, didn't we?'

'Pull over.'

Billie fixes her with a baleful glare, and Anna realises just how drunk, and angry, her sister is.

She takes hold of the wheel, giving it a little jolt.

'Fuck, Anna. Trying to kill us?'

'Trying to save us. Pull over. I'm driving.'

The car bumps onto the grass verge. Billie crosses her arms, seaweed hair escaping her bun. 'Why've you been avoiding me?'

Anna takes a deep breath. 'Something to do with the crippling pain in my head.'

'A poor excuse. I'm guessing you've not made it to the police station either with that picture Lily drew.'

'Again, paralysing agony. I'll show it to the O'Keefes' family liaison officer when she comes next.'

This may be the first outright lie she's told her sister, she and Billie having always been on the same side. When Gabriel was in her room yesterday, his eyes painting the sweetest colours over her skin, she knew then she would do anything to spare him further pain. She won't be showing the angel wing with its incriminating secret to anyone, least of all the police. Billie would think it a physical thing, nothing more than sexual attraction, when in reality it is a deeper connection. In some ways, it was inevitable. She, the loneliest woman in the world, was always going to fall in love with Gabriel, the loneliest man in the world. Their bond the grinding injustice of being wrongly accused.

'If you don't get the opportunity,' Billie says, 'I can always drop it round to the police station for you.' With a groan, she lets her head loll against the headrest. 'God, I'm wasted. Can't believe you made me drive.'

A few metres ahead there's an empty car park at the foot of a hill surrounded by soaring pines. They haven't travelled far, but it's a road Anna doesn't know. It has brought them close to the hills that are visible from the back of the house. She suggests the car park for their picnic, away from the road at least. Billie grumbles about a lack of view, but relents. It affords Anna a few extra minutes in which to summon her courage.

'How often did Lily babysit for you?' she asks once they've parked.

Her sister lowers the window, closing her eyes as a light mist of rain comes in. 'I'd say a maximum of six times. Why?'

'Did anyone ever come with her? A boyfriend, maybe?'

'A friend came with her sometimes. A girl with this awful dyed fringe that Maisie tried to copy with my red lipstick.' Billie pushes the hair from her face. 'Actually. Sometimes she brought Gabriel.'

She can't show Gabriel the intimate photos of Lily now. If he recognises the sofa, he'll confront Jonah, or worse, go to the police. She'd wanted to watch his reaction, hoping – if she were honest – to spot a flare of toad-green disappointment. It might help him to view Lily as an ordinary, flesh-and-blood girl who sometimes fucked up, same as everyone else.

'Tell me, has he made a move on you yet?' Billie, in a sudden flurry of activity, gets up on her knees and reaches into the hamper for the champagne.

From her bag, Anna takes the pictures of Lily on Jonah's sofa and the list of all the malicious messages she's found on

Lily's blog and Twitter account. She'll hand over everything she knows. Billie can handle anything. She'll apply that superior intellect of hers and everything will slot into place.

The champagne cork pops, hitting the back window and making her flinch. Billie cackles in her ear as she drops back into her seat, taking a huge slug of champagne. 'Well? Has he?'

'You keep asking. The answer is still no.'

Billie tilts the bottle to her lips, the champagne backwashing and spurting over her chin. 'Did you notice the bruises on Suzie's wrist?'

'Bruises? No.'

Her sister shrugs. 'Apparently Gabriel's got a vicious temper.'

'Utter crap. You need to stop listening to village gossip.' But as she scolds her sister, Anna sees again the black rage punching out of Gabriel's crown like a fist as the men goaded him in the pub. 'I've seen his colours when he speaks about his wife. Seriously, you've plummeted in my estimation.'

'Really? Our sisterly bond is broken for ever?'

'Irreparable.'

Billie pulls a pitiful face, which Anna ignores. When her sister waves the opened wrapper of a sandwich under her nose, offering it up like a gift for the gods, she relents with a tight smile. Billie leaves the second sandwich untouched.

'You've had quite a skinful, haven't you, Bills?'

'Lot of skin to fill, dear sister.' Billie points the champagne bottle at a path which leads through the pine trees and up the slope. 'Not quite the picnic spot I had in mind. See the plaque on top of the hill? That's dedicated to all the women burned for being witches in these woods.' She glances across at Anna. 'Hey, what've you got there?'

'Promise you won't freak out?'

'Have you *ever* known me to freak out?'

Anna unfolds the list of nasty messages, keeping the

163

photographs face-down. Billie ignores the paper in her hand and reaches for the pictures. 'Ha. Little…' Recognition breaks over her in a sickly amber. She takes a slow slug of the champagne, her eyes on the trees beyond the car.

'Bills?'

Her sister wipes her mouth on the back of her hand and takes another audible gulp from the bottle.

'Are you OK, Billie?'

'Why wouldn't I be?' Billie turns her head away, staring out of the driver's window. When Anna cranes her head, trying to catch her sister's expression, Billie's hand lashes out, delivering a slap on her bare arm. 'Don't do that, Anna. Don't fucking do that.'

Anna rubs the hot stinging spot and waits. Billie goes through the photographs one by one, then hands them back with a scathing smile and a shake of the head. 'On my bloody expensive sofa.'

'That's all you have to say?' Anna watches her sister give an expansive yawn and stretch.

'What do you want me to say?' Red crackles along Billie's hairline. 'That she's a slutty little minx who messed about on my sofa whilst my children were sleeping upstairs?'

'But who was she with? Who took the photos? We need to…'

Billie opens the door and strides away from the car, kinking over on her high-heeled ankle and stopping by the foot of the path.

Anna catches up with her. 'Whoever took the pictures was in your house.'

'The question is, who was the girl fucking? There's a long list of suspects.'

'Is it possible…' she takes a deep breath, tries to fill her head with green courage, 'that Jonah took the photographs?'

Billie's laugh is punched out. Raising her hands to her crown, she fireworks her fingers in the air, making explosive sounds. But there is nothing above her head because she's reined herself back in. 'For God's sake, Anna, this is the man who blushes when his mum kisses him.'

'True.'

'Look. It's awful about Lily. The problem is, she was carrying on with a lot of men. And when you behave like that, stepping on people's toes, there's always a reckoning.'

'A reckoning?' She suddenly remembers Billie using that odd, old-fashioned word at the Pizza Pasta Parlour, but Anna can't shake the feeling she's come across it more recently. Orange sparkles fill the air, making her dizzy as the realisation hits her. She runs back to the car to retrieve the list of vicious messages. With a hand on the bonnet to steady herself, she reads out the seventh one. '"Little Lily, if you're not careful, there'll be a reckoning." Billie? Was it you?'

Billie pulls her hair from its ponytail, smoothing it back from her face, over and over. 'Well,' she says at last. 'What do you want me to say?'

'Why? What possessed you to send such nasty filth to that young girl?' Anna folds the list with shaking fingers whilst her sister says nothing. 'I can't believe it. I'm looking at you and you're not denying it and …'

The silence opens up between them. She feels it as a solid thing pushing them apart.

'Look at me,' Billie finally says. She makes her fingers into a bird's beak and jabs at her own midriff, digging her fingertips deep into her flesh. 'Look. At. Me.'

Jab. Jab. Jab.

Anna can't remember the last time she saw her sister cry.

'Stop it, Bills. Don't do that.' She throws the list in the

car and rushes back to her sister, pulling her into a tight hug. Covering her face with her hands, Billie cries quietly on.

'We'll work this out, but we have to discuss it, OK?'

So this is what it feels like to be the carer, she thinks. The one who offers comfort and finds solutions. Until this moment it's always been Billie. An overwhelming rush of love turns the air pink.

'If you got in, there's a way out. Isn't that what you always tell me?'

Her sister steps back, wiping her face. 'You think I'm a monster.'

'I think you're finally human.'

Billie gives a weak smile. 'It made me sick, all her free-spirit shit, taking whatever she wanted. As though being young and pretty and skinny meant she was entitled to it. She was like a little cat rubbing herself against everyone's husbands. She needed to learn a lesson. There are consequences when you fuck with other people's stuff. No one else was going to teach her. Yes, she flirted with Jonah and he enjoyed it – or maybe he was just in shock – but really it was Gabriel she wanted.'

'You know your messages implicate him, don't you?'

'So they should. I walked in on the two of them.'

Disbelief, smoky and grey-green as trees in winter. Anna blinks. 'What did you see?'

Billie wobbles, her shoes catching small pebbles as she heads back towards the car. With an irate grunt, she scuffs off her pink heels. Perching on the edge of the passenger seat, she digs her stockinged toes into the mud and gravel. 'I didn't *actually* see them getting it on, but I opened the door and there was a ... palpable tension. Something had been going down.' She gives a drunken laugh like a hiccough. 'Lily, probably.'

'You can't joke about this.'

'I can. It's what us humans do. We take the piss out of the things that scare us, like death and middle-age spread.'

Anna picks up her sister's ruined heels and drops them into the footwell. 'Those messages about Lily's dreamcatcher and watching her as she slept. That was you too?'

Billie blinks, strokes invisible hairs back from her forehead. 'I don't remember all the things I said. I was always wasted.'

Anna rubs her eyes. 'Jesus.'

'You're not going to tell anyone, are you?' Gripping the edge of the seat, Billie hefts herself onto her feet and takes Anna's face in her hands. 'I had *nothing* to do with Lily going missing. Do you understand? Look at my goddamn colours, sister mine. Go on.'

'I don't need to.' Anna closes her eyes. 'I know you didn't. I know *you*, Bills.'

The rain comes, sudden and heavy as a crude theatre effect. Billie picks up the list, scanning it once. 'You're such a nerd, Anna.' Scrunching it into a ball, she shoves it in her mouth and starts to chew.

Anna gapes at her. 'You're kidding.'

Her sister spits it back out, grinning and wiping away a line of saliva. She tosses it out of the window, then starts to fiddle with the handle of the jammed seat.

'Thing's driving me crazy.'

She swings her legs out of the car, oblivious to the rain, and rifles through the glove box. With a triumphant grunt, she holds up an adjustable wrench, then gets out and crouches down to stab at the runners.

With a groan, Anna climbs back out of the car, recognising the grim determination on Billie's face. They're not going anywhere until the blasted seat is fixed. The rain soaks into her scalp. Rain saturated with the death of innocent women. She shakes the thought from her head.

'Stupid Jonah and his stupid clumsy ways.' Billie hands her the wrench.

Anna peers beneath the seat, the rain on her back like fingers tapping for attention. As she feels along the tracks, something bites into her finger, a bubble of blood expanding on the tip. 'There's something stuck in the runner. Help me, Bills. Press down on the handle with your foot, and when I tell you, give the seat an almighty shove.'

With some difficulty, she fixes the wrench about the small twist of metal wedged into the track. Their first few attempts fail, her sister losing her footing, collapsing forward on top of her, snorting with helpless laughter.

'One last try, Bills.'

It happens in a rush, Billie's weight finding its mark, the seat shifting a few inches with the metal squawk of a braking train. They both lean in. Caught in the jaws of the wrench is a ring, an enamelled fish with blue and purple scales suspended on its broken silver circle.

'One of Maisie's?'

Billie takes it and throws it in the glovebox. Then she changes her mind and retrieves it, bouncing it in her open palm as if it burns. 'I can't give it back to Maisie like this. She'll be heartbroken.'

Closing her fist, she veers round, casting herself off balance as she launches the broken ring high into the air. It disappears into a deep tangle of bushes. Then she drops back into the passenger seat and closes her eyes. 'You know that awful sinking feeling when you realise you've royally messed up? I've been living like that for months now. Since Lily went missing.'

'It's fine. We're going to get through this, you and me.'

'Now you sound like me. Role reversal. I might quite enjoy

being the irresponsible one for once.' Billie cracks open an eye, smiling.

Anna starts the engine and reverses out of the car park. 'Does Jonah know?'

'No.' Billie puts her dirty feet on the seat and hugs her knees. 'We're trying for another baby, by the way.'

She dismisses Anna's startled questions, a finger to her lips. 'Hush now, driver. I need beauty sleep before the baby-making starts.'

26

Blue and purple fish scales

She wakes to a text from Billie.

What a terrible wastrel I am. Puked twice. Come over tomorrow or Friday once you're free so we can carry on sleuthing.

As if nothing had happened and the small matter of her online bullying is closed.

Anna leaves Lily's room and goes downstairs. It's gone seven forty-five, and even in this drowning house, where everything takes place in underwater silence, there should be more signs of life. Daniel's school bag is outside the kitchen. Through the open doorway, a pair of naked feet on the kitchen floor, toes scrunched up.

Suzie is wedged into the corner between two cupboards, hugging her knees to her chest. She's crying with her whole body, shuddering, mouth racked open but making little sound. A string of slime links her top and bottom lips, expanding and contracting to let out her gasps.

'Suzie?' Anna rushes into the kitchen, but the woman fends her off with the palm of her hand, hiding her face. A sweep of goose bumps alerts her to another presence. Daniel is at the breakfast table, wide-eyed, a lump of food in his cheek. Behind him, on the far side of the room, is Gabriel, kneading his wrist, eyes fixed on the window.

The stillness unnerves her, no one moving, no one speaking.

Suzie and Gabriel's colours clashing and shifting, unreadable, whilst Daniel is blank and colourless. She crouches beside him and strokes his arm. 'Daniel?'

He bends his head over the plate and spits out a brown cud of chewed sausage. His mother gets to her feet and leaves the room, Gabriel following without acknowledging Anna's presence. As if she were now the ghost. On the table a bowl of muesli is soaking up milk, beside it a plate with a fried egg on toast, half eaten.

'What's happened, sweetheart?'

Daniel pokes his knife carefully into a sausage and holds it up in the air, contemplating it. 'My dad wants to take me camping but Mummy says no.'

Anna lowers his hand, trying to meet his eyes. 'Did they have a fight, Dan?'

'I don't know.' His tone is matter-of-fact.

'You do know.'

'I can't remember.' He dabs his sausage at the ketchup on his plate. 'I was eating.'

'Why did your mum say no to the camping trip?'

With a small hike of his shoulders, the conversation ends, but as Anna begins to clear the plates, he says, 'Mummy has to stay living here so why should me and Daddy get to go away and have fun.'

She scrapes the leftover food into the bin. 'That's a shame.'

'And Daddy has to do what Mummy says because he owes her big-time.'

Keeping her voice neutral, Anna asks why. He says he doesn't know, but the orange ring around his head says otherwise.

Because of Lily, Daniel says, he's allowed to have the day off school sometimes, like today. Taking Anna's hand, he leads her to the sitting room. A pale yellow mist lifts from his head as he explains that he's going to make an angel.

Anna listens for Suzie and Gabriel, but the house is dead. They should have left half an hour ago for school. Daniel stops by the coffee table, lifting a corner of the carpet to peer through the glass, burnt orange sending cracks through his happy yellows.

'No fish today.' Relief washes away the burnt orange. 'Come on, Anna.'

He switches on the computer, tapping in the password with a stiff little finger. 'How to make angels by Lily O'Keefe.' He says the words out loud as he types them into the search engine. Lily's smiling face appears, freeze-framed. Anna lowers herself onto the arm of Daniel's chair.

'It's called a vlog,' Daniel is saying, and she makes an impressed sound.

It's a clip she hasn't seen before, with almost two thousand views, hundreds of likes and a single dislike. Her eyes are drawn to the comment section, her stomach tumbling as she reads the first message.

Sweet Little Lily with her sweet little angels and love potions. You're still just a dirty, little

The rest of the comment is lost beneath the screen. With a surreptitious slide of the mouse, she makes sure the entire message is hidden from Daniel. Billie has always been pithy and outspoken, but never cowardly. Anna sees again her sister stabbing at her stomach and waist, making the flesh wobble. Self-loathing will drive a person to do terrible things. It's the only explanation for Billie's behaviour.

In the clip Lily wears a headband of cloth roses, the fringe of her hair bunching and spilling over as if she had slept in it. Glitter sweeps out from the corners of her eyes. Anna can't shake the sense of recognition, a connection with a girl thirteen years her junior and whom she'll never meet.

This is Evangelista, Lily says, *my nineteenth angel. An angel for every year of my life. She's not for sale, I'm afraid. I'm giving her to someone special.* Here she meets the camera's eye. *You know who you are,* her look says.

She picks up a tiny gold-wire crown studded with sapphire-blue beads. *Cute, right? I must have stuck the wire in my finger about a million times.*

Anna glances at Daniel's rapt face, his fingers clasped in his lap, absorbing the instructions as Lily shapes the wire cone for the angel's body and stuffs the cavity with balls of cotton wool, laughing as one of her rings catches on a loose twig of wire and she has to pick it free.

'Wait.' Lurching forward, Anna pauses the video. Cinnamon bursts in her vision as she stares at the ring on Lily's right thumb. An enamel fish with blue and purple scales winking in the light.

She taps the screen. 'That ring.'

'The fish one? I bought it for her. With all my pocket money. Do you like it?'

All she can see is her sister's face as she jiggled the ring in her palm like it was made of burning metal before throwing it as far as she could. The air rots, turning shades of spoilt orange, blood and feathers.

It means nothing, she tells herself, but the colours don't believe her.

People lose rings. Rings fall off.

Billie had known who it belonged to.

Back upstairs, she finds Ben leaning against the wall outside the box room, foot jiggling, a distant thud from his earphones.

'Morning, Anna.' His eyes are dark slits.

'There you are, Ben. Lurking as usual.'

He huffs out a humourless laugh. 'Waiting for G.'

She closes the door behind her with a shiver, her body

shaking off the sticky residue of his gaze. Daniel had found a box of Lily's angel-making supplies in a cupboard in the kitchen, so she has some time to herself. She spreads all the photographs she can find of Lily across the duvet.

'Tell me what happened,' she whispers.

She studies each photograph until she begins to recognise the different faces. Ben doesn't feature in a single one, but in a cluster of teenagers around a fire pit, a swatch of red catches her attention. Bringing the picture closer, she studies Margaret's plump, smiling face leaning on Lily's shoulder. Margaret, who burst into tears when April sent out a prayer to bring Lily safely home.

Gabriel said the girl knew more than she was letting on. Perhaps Anna should give April's meditation group one more go.

Suzie, in a rare moment of kindness, offers her the car to go to April's meditation. *Gabe's out and I won't need it*, she says. It's been over a week since Suzie last drove anywhere by herself.

Anna wonders where Gabriel is. Just before lunch, he and Ben had heaved the swan-necked machine that turns branches into sawdust onto the open-backed truck he keeps in the garage. She can't ask Suzie where he is, can't speak his name for fear of betraying herself.

She lowers the windows as she drives, the evening sun like a miracle. On the radio, an old Fleetwood Mac song that strikes her as perfect as the hills roll away into a sunset sky of happy colours. She gets a little lost and arrives late.

There are three empty chairs. One of them is Gabriel's, which she avoids in the hope he might still arrive. She chooses the seat she sat in last time but for some reason this sets off a thorny prickle of red from the sour woman, Jo, who sends a silent enquiry to April.

April only smiles and says, 'You're good there, Anna.'

Neither Gabriel nor Margaret shows up: a wasted journey. Whilst April leads the group into a meditation, Anna plays a childhood memory game, trying to memorise April's paraphernalia and list as much as she can in her head. Lump of rose quartz, jar of white feathers, small chest used as an altar with five tea lights, a poster of a human outline showing the chakras. Prayer beads. Within minutes she's bored and finds herself listening.

April is talking about rising up through the blue sky, and higher still into the endless drift of space, where they are surrounded by points of light. The lights glide towards her, taking shape to become golden figures. Each figure sends out a fine thread of light, connecting to her until they are linked like stitches in a golden carpet.

'Your soul family,' April says in her low, gruff voice. 'The people you love, the people who've hurt you, the stranger who smiled at you on the train. As you move through your lives, these connections, fleeting or lasting, bind the whole of humanity together. Holding you in a place of love.'

For a moment, Anna is moved by a sense of belonging. It reminds her of being a little girl on birthday mornings, opening presents in her parents' bed. But then the good feeling is gone, chased away by the fish ring and the naked photos of Lily.

'You are never alone,' April says.

Bullshit, she thinks. Billie is the person she's closest to, and she has no idea what's going on with her. By the time she returns to the meditation to escape her thoughts, April is talking about a fire inside a circle of stones and a spirit animal stepping forward to assist them. Nothing steps forward for Anna. She's afraid to focus in case Lily appears instead.

'No one got a fish?' April asks during the round-up after-wards. 'I could have sworn I saw a fish, stunning it was, with blue and purple scales.' She scans the circle and her eyes meet Anna's for the briefest moment. She can't come back. The woman can see inside her head.

27

Isolation is a shipwrecked grey

The next morning, she wakes as the sun is rising in a bowl of honest blue. The sight propels her out of bed. It's barely six a.m., but Daniel is often awake at this time. She dresses and heads to his room, only to find his bed empty. Heading downstairs, she calls his name, but she can feel the emptiness of the house. By the front door is a pair of Ben's trainers, lying as if he's kicked them off against the wall. She can't remember if they'd been there the night before. Red pricks the air. His possessions are deposited around the house, taunting her, keeping her on alert.

Back upstairs, she risks a peek into the box room and finds an irregular patch of plaster where the hole had been. Ben's excuse to lurk around the house will be redundant soon. There's still no sign of Daniel. The door to his parents' room is wide open, she notices. Holding her breath, she looks in.

Daniel is lying between Suzie and Gabriel, awake and sucking his thumb. He moves his fingers in a small wave when he sees her. Gabriel is on his back, fast asleep, an arm slung above his head, the covers pushed down to his waist. Anna steps back as Suzie stirs, her hand finding her son's face to stroke his cheek before reaching for Gabriel. At his wife's touch, he turns towards her, folding her hand in his and bringing it to rest against his mouth.

Anna tiptoes away. The sight of their small family knotted together fills her with a familiar shipwrecked grey.

'Is this how you felt?' She whispers the words to the listening room. 'Never belonging?' A breeze comes from the open window and she fancies the bed's canopy shivers harder in response to her voice.

She used to be proud of her freedom. Her friends used to envy it. April said you couldn't move through life alone, everyone bound together by strands of human connection, but Anna had glided, cold and glass-like, through the last thirteen years and nothing had ever taken hold. Not since Lauritz. With some effort of recollection, she could break up that featureless chunk of time into smaller bites. Most recently, her three-year relationship with Chris in that tiny grey-stone village in Scotland where she'd landed, having run out of ideas. Thinking herself so damn lucky when a local family, the Sowerbys, hired her. Before that, a stint in Bristol with Josh, who admitted after nine months that he couldn't get over his ex. London, Michael – brief but intense, burning itself out with the same ferocity with which it began. Lovers and other people's families like stepping stones in an endless river.

Beneath the cotton folds of the canopy, spider webs loop like necklaces with tiny dust beads. The threads that hold everyone else in place, binding wives, husbands, children, never found her. She can't understand how she never got stuck.

Getting to her knees she swipes the cobwebs away.

'I'm going to find out what happened to you, Lily,' she says, and the breeze dies away.

Suzie tells her to take the day off. Gabriel's home for the day and he's keen to do the school run. Regrettably, Anna can't take Suzie's car, though. There's no discernible pattern to the woman's moods. No way of knowing when she'll be bordering hostile or disarmingly considerate. Every day's a lucky dip. That day in the car when Suzie said she didn't know how she'd manage without Anna, her colours were pure, the intensity of her gratitude straight from her heart.

But Suzie's goodwill never survives the night.

She's lucky with the bus connections and makes it to East Mawsey in less than an hour. The bus drops her by Waitrose at one end of the high street. According to Google Maps, the tattoo parlour is at the opposite end. Halfway up the street, between a dry cleaner's and a bookie's, there's a fish and chip shop, the smell of vinegar and frying fat hanging like a curtain in the street. A girl is walking out of the chip shop as Anna passes, the red stripe in her fringe catching her eye.

'Margaret?'

The girl takes a moment to place her, then waves her bag of chips in the direction of a window above the shop. 'I actually live there. You'd think I'd get sick to death of fish and chips, wouldn't you?'

'I was hoping I might see you at April's last night,' Anna says.

'Oh, shame. You went back? We could have gone for a drink. It's what we do sometimes.' Margaret's smile slides away. 'Actually, the last time we went was with Lily.'

'Lily used to go to April's group?'

Margaret nods, picking through her chips with navy finger-nails. 'Where did you sit last night?'

'Where did I sit?'

'Yeah.' Margaret blows on a chip. 'Where'd April park you?'

'Between ... I think it's Jo to my right, and on my left ...'

'Milly whose feet don't reach the floor? In the chair directly opposite April?' Margaret doesn't wait for her reply. 'April's put you in Lily's old place. Which some of us find weird. But I guess it's worse to face her empty chair.'

The electric prickle of antagonism Anna had experienced both times at the group had nothing to do with her presence as a stranger; it was about the chair she'd been put in.

'Honestly, it's OK,' Margaret says, seeing her shiver. 'We're not mad at you. We were just a bit surprised at April.'

Anna sleeps in Lily's bed, sits in her place at the meditation group, and in her bag is the sketch with the secret letter worked into its centre, Lily's declaration of love for Gabriel; the same man who fills her waking thoughts. Piece by piece, Lily's life is becoming hers.

In the reception at the Dragon Ink Tattoo Parlour, a stone Buddha grins out of the fireplace and a sharp chemical incense rises like mist from a fake bonsai tree on the counter. The girl manning the desk is wearing a pretty floral tea dress at odds with the skeleton bones tattooed along her arms and fingers.

'Hiya. Have you got an appointment?'

'No, I was hoping to catch Bozie between clients. He did a tattoo for a friend of mine.' Anna hands over Lily's angel-wing sketch, an eye on the perimeter of air around the receptionist, but the soup of stable green and beige remains unchanged.

'That's pretty,' the girl says, taking it with a cursory glance. 'I'll see if he's free at all.'

If Anna had had to imagine a tattoo artist, Bozie would fit the picture. Tattoo-sleeved, silver rings through his nose and lower lip, bottle-black hair spiked and shaved at the sides to reveal a spray of stars behind his left ear. But the wash of colour radiating from his aura is unexpected; a man unafraid to wear his emotions. It makes him seem instantly familiar, an old friend. Her warm greeting throws him and he asks if they've met before. Her face grows hot. She never learns.

Bozie's character may be warm and approachable, but to him she is a blank stranger.

'My cousin, Lily, was thinking about having this angel wing done.' The lie makes her heart beat harder. 'You might remember her?' She watches for a shift in colour or texture when she says the girl's name, but his rainbow glow remains steady and untroubled. He doesn't know Lily, or at least he hasn't made the connection to the missing girl.

'Do you remember doing this tattoo?' It occurs to her that she has no idea how long ago Lily might have had it done. Legally she would have had to be eighteen; Anna knows, having flirted with the idea of a tattoo herself as a teenager.

'I remember wishing it was one of mine,' he says. 'Pretty fine skills. You after the same thing?'

He has a flirtatious eye and it makes her relax. She knows how to play this. 'You'd have to rework it a little. Lily may have been in love with the mysterious G,' she traces the letter with her finger, 'but I'm not.'

'I remember. Clever, that.' Glancing up through his long eyelashes, he catches her smiling at his colours, fizzing lemon sherbets and pink candy stripes. 'What? My hair out of place?'

She grins, thinking this is the most fun she's had in a while. Finally she's allowed to breathe. 'Thing is, I'm a bit scared.' She offers a playful flash of her shoulder. 'See. Tattoo virgin.'

His eyes sweep over her bare skin, showering her in scarlet leaves. Returning his attention to the tattoo, he taps the paper. 'I think I remember the girl. Lily, did you say her name was? She was nervous too.'

'Really? I'm surprised. She talked a big game about it.' The chances she is taking. Her armpits have grown damp.

'People do.' He gives a short laugh. 'Nah. She wasn't up for it. She was with her friend and they'd both had a drink. She was doing it to impress some fella. That was my take on it.'

'Did she go through with it?'

'She did. Two and a half hours without a squeak.'

'Do you remember when that was?'

His colours change, a leafy green curiosity opening up above him but no sign of wary orange, so she presses on. 'Might her name be in your appointment book?'

'I remember because it was Valentine's Day and I was chuckling to myself. Like I said, a present for a fella.' He meets her eyes. 'You're not after a tattoo, are you?'

She holds up her hands in a gesture of surrender. 'Lily's taken off and I'm trying to work out what was going on with her before she left.' Rust flakes off the air. Any minute now, he's going to make the connection to the missing girl.

'Oh. Right.'

'It was in the papers a while back, in fact.'

'No shit? Sorry to hear that.' His fingers worry the tiny beaded ring at the edge of his eyebrow, but his colours are honest and clear. It gives Anna a punch of sorrow for the O'Keefes. How a tragedy that reduces a family to rubble casts only short-lived tremors soon forgotten or missed entirely.

'Do you mind if I ask a few questions?'

'Go ahead.' He flips out his palms, open, willing to help, whilst empathy, a purple sea, rolls off him.

She leaves with Bozie's number in her phone – in case she needs anything more from him – his slow smile moving through her like a mouthful of honey. He couldn't recall much more than he'd already told her about Lily. He remembered Lily's friend more clearly, a big, sexy girl, the way he liked them, with a red stripe in her hair. Holding Lily's hand and saying it was OK if she wanted to change her mind.

The bus connections don't work in her favour on her return. It's gone four o'clock by the time she arrives back at the O'Keefes. Daniel's school bag is in the hall, the sight of it lighting a pink sparkler of anticipation, surprising her with how much she is looking forward to seeing him.

'Where've you been?' Suzie stops her in the hall, barring her way to the kitchen, where Daniel is doing his homework.

'East Mawsey. The buses were erratic, to say the least.' She doesn't shy away from Suzie's cold disapproval. There is only so much she will take, for ninety pounds a week. Daniel's head lifts, his pencil stalling as he pretends not to listen.

'I had to collect Daniel alone.' Suzie unfolds her arms, her chin jutting forward. 'You know how I feel about driving at the moment. You are in fact the *only* person who knows, and still you let me down.'

The air turns red. It fills the hallway. 'One minute you need me, the next you don't. I wish you'd make your mind up.'

'Don't be angry at my mum, Anna,' Daniel says from the kitchen, his tone pleading.

'In case you've forgotten, you're here to make yourself useful.' Suzie clenches her hands into fists, drawing a breath. Daniel's chair falls backwards as he gets up and runs over to his mother.

'I feel sick, Mummy.' He puts his arms around Suzie, pressing his forehead into her chest, his face hidden from Anna.

I just have to save my mum. That was what Daniel had said the day he flew off the swings.

'It's all right, Dan,' Anna says, but the boy keeps his face hidden. Suzie shoos her from the kitchen with a ferocious glare.

Back in Lily's room, the boy's panicked rush plays over in her head. The chair falling, the way he'd pushed himself between them, throwing his arms around Suzie. Saving his mother from Anna. The thought is unbearable.

28

White feathers

When, a few hours later, Daniel beckons her into the bathroom, asking if she wants to see another secret, her emphatic response makes his mouth twitch into a smile. Relief, similar to hope, is a shaft of golden sunlight.

He kneels on the floor by the wooden surround of the washbasin, butting the heel of his hand down the length of one plank.

She gives his hair a playful ruffle, which he doesn't acknowledge. 'What are you, Master O'Keefe? Some kind of part-time plumber?'

His answer is a small smile, revelling in his own secrecy. A section opens inwards, a wooden door without a handle. Inside the cupboard the floorboards are unvarnished, spattered with old plaster and black mouse droppings. She coughs on the dust, which doesn't seem to bother Daniel as he feels about inside. He takes out a folder. Sellotaped to the front cover is a picture of him with Lily. He's writhing with laughter, half falling off the sofa as she tickles him. She too is laughing, hair escaping a messy ponytail, more child than adult.

Before he opens the folder, he makes sure she understands the honour being bestowed upon her. 'Not even my mum has seen this.'

She puts her hand over his. 'You know you don't have to save your mum from me, don't you?'

When he doesn't answer, she repeats the question, pressing him. He gives an irritable little shrug and a nod, then opens the cover. It's a scrapbook, every page with a photograph of Lily. The print quality is poor, the edges gently scalloped by small scissors, but a wave of greed, canary yellow, washes over Anna. Daniel lets her take the book. With each new image, Lily takes shape, coming to life.

'I take Mummy or Daddy's phone when they're busy. I know how to plug it into the computer and print their photos. I figured it out by myself.'

'Genius,' she says. 'Sneaky but genius.'

Something slides out from between the pages and lands in her lap. An iron key with a cat-face key ring poking out its tongue. 'Isn't that Lily's key for the pavilion, Dan?'

His colours take on a mischievous shade of sunflower. 'I got it from Daddy's drawer. It's OK, he won't notice, because he doesn't want to go back there ever again. He said so.' He puts the key inside a plain envelope stuck in the middle of the scrapbook, then flips to the back cover, where six white feathers have been taped.

'Lily leaves these for me when I'm missing her.'

'Where does she leave them?'

'Mostly in the drainpipe by the front door because she knows that's where I look for bugs and toads.'

Snapping shut his book, he returns it to its hiding place. Anna would have liked a little more time to study it, and suspects the boy knows as much and is enjoying his guardianship of the treasure. So many pictures of Lily she still hasn't seen.

Gabriel comes home after dark, dropping his climbing kit on the kitchen floor and drinking milk straight from the carton. His hair is ragged with sweat, a leaf caught in his T-shirt. She tells him Daniel's asleep and that she is going out.

'Suzie upstairs?'

'Yes.' She almost adds, *Since lunchtime*, but it isn't her business.

'Bed for me too,' he says. 'I'm cream-crackered.'

But he isn't tired at all. His energy is a fizzing, brilliant scarlet.

Anna picks up her rucksack. Inside is the pavilion key, which she took from Daniel's secret scrapbook whilst the shower was running to conceal her activity. Now she's the sneaky one. There's also a torch in the rucksack and Lily's photographs from the dressing table. She hurries to leave the house. Not because Daniel will discover she's taken the key – he's already in bed – but because sometimes, late at night, Suzie moans, soft and high, in pleasure. It used to amuse her; now she can't bear it.

Besides, she has an experiment in mind.

April had called her synaesthesia a gift. What if, she's been thinking, there's something more to it than a neurological quirk? As she closes the front door, she notices a small object, startling white against the darkness, close to the ground. A single white feather is caught in the drainpipe that runs down from the eaves. She plucks it free, rolling the quill between her fingers, wondering if Daniel could have planted it there, though she can't think when he had the opportunity. She replaces the feather in the drainpipe's metal join.

It must be from a pigeon. She often has to scrape their shit off the landing windowsill where they gather. But something in the air shifts, her colours turning shivery and phosphorescent with the possibility of inexplicable things. After all, some waters turn objects into stone, and she herself can read the truths a person hides inside.

*

186

The fear doesn't hit her until she's walking down the stone steps, greasy with moisture, towards the Petrifying Well. The rush of water is louder than she remembered, and as she points her torch beam downwards, she recoils in shock. The water has risen to the bottom step, the platform breaching and disappearing under a restless skin of water.

Five minutes and then she'll go. With her waterproof jacket as a cushion, she sits halfway down the steps, closer to the entrance than to the water. Taking out Lily's photographs, she holds them like a spread of cards in her hands, the torch trapped between her knees. She closes her eyes and pictures the missing girl, trying to summon the figure who appears in her meditation and, increasingly, her dreams.

'Were you here the night you died?' The river drowns out her words.

She waits, hoping for a colour, alien and separate to her own, to appear.

A breeze rushes her back, a shuffling noise behind her in the closed-up pavilion. Swivelling, she catches sight of a dark shape. In a cold panic, she grabs her torch and shines it into the centre of the room.

'Bloody hell.' April staggers back, blinking in the light. 'Who's there?'

'It's me. Anna.' Collapsing over her knees, she breathes out, her heart bumping against her thigh. 'Fuck, April. You scared me.'

The obscenity tastes bad in her mouth, a noxious bile. Curse words and sex, the only things in her experience that mingle taste with colour.

Fucking, basically, as her sister once so drolly put it.

She pushes the photographs into the rucksack as April, one careful step at a time, comes down to join her.

The woman claps her on the knee. 'What on earth are you doing here?'

April, she suspects, has her own inbuilt lie-detector. 'Looking for Lily.'

'Me too.' April shifts her buttocks on the step. 'She used to sneak in here with friends sometimes, in the middle of the night. I saw her once or twice, naughty thing.'

'Did you tell anyone?'

'Nah. She wasn't doing any harm.' April takes a breath, settling with her palms resting upwards on her thighs. 'I thought I'd come and get a feel, dip my finger in.'

'Mind if I stay?'

'Sure.' April shrugs. 'Not much of a spectator show, though.'

They watch the river heaving through the iron rail, dashing against the steps. A minute or two passes, then April stretches her back. 'Yep. Something not very nice happened here.'

'Like what?' But Anna knows she's not going to share.

'There's a lot of discordant energy down here. Some of it ancient, from when they used to drown women like you and me.'

Whilst she shivers, the inclusion – *women like you and me* – gives her a coral burst of pleasure, like a child being handed a class commendation.

'I feel Lily's energy here too. And violence.' April's voice has a faraway quality. 'Not life-threatening, but damaging.'

Anna's chest is tight. She takes little sips of air into her lungs. 'Someone hurt her?'

With another handclap on her knee, April pushes herself to her feet. 'Yep. Someone hurt that poor child down here.'

29

Green for honesty, brown for guilt

Some days her colours are a blessing, as April suggested. On other days, they exhaust her, rising and fluttering, so many different messages to be deciphered. She hasn't slept well since her visit to the Petrifying Well. Her dreams are full of glimpses and snatches: Lily by the window mending the dreamcatcher, Gabriel on the edge of her bed. Twice she is woken by finger-nails trickling over her back. April asked her not to tell the O'Keefes what she'd sensed in the pavilion. It would only add to their pain. And nothing could be proved.

She takes the bus over the top of the Downs and gets out at the start of April's lane. The trees at the side of the road are in heavy leaf, draping her in calm and peace, with the occasional drip of last night's rainfall. In the grass, wild flowers on long stalks, sugar yellow and plum purple, giving her a fleeting happy buzz like the unexpected smile of a stranger.

She's early for the group. When she reaches April's bound-ary fence, she waits, hoping to catch Margaret. She hasn't been there for long when the girl appears on her bicycle, wobbling and jiggling along the rutted lane.

'Back again?' Margaret hoists a leg over the bicycle seat and dabs sweat from her upper lip and brow before giving a broad smile. Her skin is flawless, a delicious plumpness to her cheeks, everything about her generous and giving. Anna can see why Bozie was smitten. 'Stick with it. It's been a life-saver for me.'

'Really?' It's all she needs to say. Margaret is one of life's sharers.

As they walk, the girl tells her about being kicked out of her mum's home at sixteen, about uninhabitable bedsits, a leaning towards self-destruction, life's slights and injustices collected like Brownie badges. Her colours are bright and open, enjoying an audience, until Gabriel's Defender passes them in the lane; then a dark ochre snakes away from Margaret's crown. It's more complicated than dislike, though Anna can't quite place it. She's seen them together and there is a strong familiarity between them.

'I hope you've got good friends to support you.'

Margaret hesitates. 'Lily was my friend.' Easy tears glitter in her eyes. 'We were at school together. I was two years above her, but we just clicked. Kind of a soul recognition.'

'I've heard so much about Lily. I almost feel like I know her.' Anna waits to see if she has gone a step too far.

'You live in her house,' Margaret says. 'You take care of Daniel. You're part of her family now.'

'They've given me her old room.'

Surprise shoots out of Margaret like a fountain, though she tries to hide it. She leans her bicycle against the side of April's house. Through the orchard, the group is gathering. Gabriel stands away from the huddle, hands in his pockets, studying an apple tree whose boughs almost reach the ground.

'I found some sketches of an angel wing in Lily's room. It looked like a design, for a tattoo maybe.'

'I doubt it's a tattoo.' Margaret stops walking. Her surprise has changed colour, curdling from a curious yellow to a muddled orange. 'She just liked drawing.'

People who hate lying are the easiest to spot, her telltale

orange like a flying saucer above her head. She tugs the cuff of her sleeve over a tattoo on her wrist.

'Are you OK, Margaret? You've gone very white.'

'I miss her.' The orange fades, replaced by an honest, heartbroken indigo.

April's words come back to her. Someone hurt Lily in that awful place. She mustn't think about it.

'Gabriel misses her too, but he tries to hide it,' she says, watching the space around Margaret's head. 'As if he doesn't have a right to mourn her when he was the only father she'd ever had.'

Margaret's colours turn autumnal, their texture crackling like dry leaves. 'The police questioned him a couple of times.'

'They did?'

'He was the last person to see her. Apparently.' The girl picks up speed. 'We need to go inside. April hates it when we're late.'

Warm tropical sea, a serene turquoise, rocking her weightless body. She is right there.

'A whale swims up from the deep waters beneath you,' April says, 'and lifts you on its back as it rises.'

It makes her smile, going along with it, enjoying the calm. Until something grips her hand. Hard, cold fingers digging in. Looking down, she finds the water has changed, no longer a shimmery blue, but solid black, the sea in the dead of night. Rising out of its depths is a shivery white form. Its features shift and ripple but she knows who it is. Her breath gets stuck in her chest as the water closes like a skin over her face, laughter bubbling out of Lily's mouth as she drags her downwards. With a gasp, she forces herself back into the safety of the studio, opening her eyes to look straight into April's thoughtful gaze.

She sits out the rest of the meditation with her eyes closed. This really is the last time she'll return. The session closes with the same prayer for Lily's safe return and her hand burns as if bruised by those cold, hard fingers. As soon as the door is open, she is out, racing ahead to duck both Margaret and Gabriel. He catches up with her as she reaches the lane.

'Are you OK, Anna?'

'Not really.' She keeps her eyes on the road ahead, the concern in his voice enough of a distraction. He offers her a lift home.

'I'll take the bus. I promised Suzie I wouldn't be seen alone with you.'

He hesitates. 'Take a walk with me then. Until you feel better.'

Their eyes meet, an unspoken acknowledgement of stealing time together. She follows him past the farmhouse, where April and Margaret are in close conversation by the kitchen door. Margaret is wiping her face whilst April gives her shoulder a reassuring squeeze. Gabriel's mouth curls in disdain.

'Everyone was suddenly Lily's best friend after she...' He can't finish the sentence.

'Did the police speak to Margaret about Lily?' They are following a choppy path through a meadow, heading for a ragged wall of pines. Looking back, Anna catches Margaret studying the two of them as she sets off on her bicycle.

Everyone watching everyone.

'Margaret probably volunteered herself.'

She can't tell him about Lily getting the angel-wing tattoo and Margaret going with her. He'd wonder why she was so interested, and then he might remember that Lily used to babysit for her sister. The link is there between Billie and the missing girl. She mustn't bring attention to it.

They fall into single file and she observes his easy walk, the sure-footed pick of his feet over embedded rocks, the sun across his shoulders. His hair is pulled up into a small, messy bun, a glint of red in the baby hair at the nape of his neck. His outline is a crimson blur, her colour not his. A shallow ditch cuts across the path and he turns, offering his hand. The sunlight exaggerates the leaf and bark of his eyes. It's easy to see how a teenage girl could be swept away, her adolescent dreams shaping themselves around the giant trunk of his body.

She looks from one eye to the other. 'Green for honesty, brown for guilt.'

'Is that what your colours say?'

But he's smiling, teasing her. She follows him through the pines to a steep riverbank, where the water spills off a shelf of tree root into a lower pool.

Pulling off his work boots, Gabriel sits on the grass, feet in the river, the water soaking the cuffs of his trousers. 'Lily and I used to come here after the group. A bit of peace and quiet before going back to real life.'

'You loved her very much, didn't you?'

He looks sharply in her direction. 'Reading my colours again?'

Getting up, he wades into the centre of the current, staring upriver with his back to her.

Ask the questions, let the answers take shape in the air.

'You have an unfair advantage,' he says, as if hearing her thoughts. 'You can know everything about a person but keep your own thoughts secret.'

The water flows fast, with deep, hidden pockets – a thing without colour, never to be trusted – and yet she has the oddest feeling he's waiting for her. She kicks off her plimsolls, her breath cutting with the cold. River mud oozes between her toes, sucking her foot downwards.

'When I was nineteen, I fell in love with a thirty-year-old man,' she says. 'His name was Lauritz and he had a wife who neglected him because all she could think of was having a baby.'

Billie had walked into her room one morning, catching her at the mirror, her fingertips exploring her lips, swollen from his hard mouth, the bristle of his unshaved skin, his teeth. *You've seen the ring on his finger, right?* Her tone light, disinterested, one of the few references she ever made to the affair.

Anna had noticed his ring, in passing, and understood what it signified, but it had been no more real than an overseas war; her head lamenting the loss of lives without feeling it in her heart.

Gabriel turns his head to the side, listening. 'Did your married man love you back?'

'Yes.'

'How could he not?' he says, but he doesn't meet her eyes, his words a careless kindness like a pat on the shoulder. He takes a pebble off the riverbed and skims it across the water's surface. Two skips and it disappears back under with a gulp.

'I've known Lily since she was a child.' He turns to face her. 'I taught her how to climb trees, how to throw a punch and how to deal with jealous, unkind kids. Me, not her mother, who was busy partying until the day she stumbled under a car. Not even Suzie, because Daniel came first. Me.'

Waves of green and blue and purple snake high above him. He means, and feels, every word. 'I was her father figure, her big brother and her friend.'

She takes his hand and kisses it. The rough skin of his knuckles against her lips sends an arrow from her mouth into her stomach. 'Does anyone take care of you, Gabriel?'

He gives a quiet laugh, shaking his head. 'Not until you came along.'

'When I was meditating today...' She hesitates, questioning how much she should tell him. 'I saw Lily. She tried to pull me underwater.'

He licks his lips. 'I don't know what that means.'

'Might she have run away? My father's a GP. He says it's much more common than people realise. Is it possible she might come back?'

His colours flatten and die under a grey pall. He shakes his head.

'But April is still hopeful, isn't she? Sending out her prayers.'

'She's not coming back.' He moves closer, his fingers, cold as the water, moving up to her wrist, a physical plea to make her stop.

'But how can you be sure?'

'Lily is not coming back,' he says again.

Then he puts his hand around the back of her head, a glint of tears in his eyes as he closes the space between them, his mouth on hers.

30

Desire is crimson and magenta

She can't sleep. Gabriel's kiss has left a scratchy restlessness in her body, like a fading high. The sound of the rain washes over her. Kicking off the covers, she wishes the ceiling would open and let the rain break against her body. The room is hot and airless, her skin too tight for the bubbling, stewing heat inside her. She pulls off her T-shirt, then her shorts. Letting the air find her naked body, she imagines the door opening, quietly, quietly, Gabriel coming in without knocking. She presses the palm of her hand between her legs, crimson and magenta ribboning from her, plaiting in the air. Her fingertips start a slow circle as she plays over in her head the way his mouth felt, the tip of his tongue meeting hers. Her fingers move faster, with increasing urgency, but twined around the deep pinks is a thwarted reddish brown, the colour of a scab. She flips over onto her stomach, pressing her hips against her grinding fingers, but the harder she tries, the more elusive release becomes. It hovers just beyond reach until she gives up, sweating and raw. Self-contempt moves in, a jagged and bitter red. Putting her clothes back on, she goes to wash her hands. Lets the water run until it scalds her fingers.

He doesn't belong to her any more than Lauritz did.

*

She is woken in the middle of the night by Suzie's voice, high-pitched and beseeching, her words coming in broken bursts. Thuds and crashes reverberate through the house's skeleton. She gets out of bed, listening for Gabriel, but either he's whispering or Suzie is ranting alone. A shatter of glass makes her jump, the noise painful inside her head. She opens the door a fraction, her heart hammering out orange bolts. Daniel is standing outside his bedroom, still as a desert plant.

'Dan?'

At the sound of her voice, he runs into her room and climbs under her covers, thumb in his mouth. She hesitates before lying down beside him, her body a stiff margin along the edge of the mattress. With his bent knees and the covers bunched behind him, there isn't much space left.

'Mummy's sad about Lily.' He wriggles his head further onto her pillow, a sharp knee catching her stomach.

She's about to send him back to his room when the sight of his sombre face, eyes gazing at nothing happy, hits a tender spot deep inside her; a place she didn't know existed. With a tentative hand, she strokes his hair. Letting his eyes shut, he snuggles closer, yearning towards a gentle touch. The urge to protect him bursts in amethyst lights. In all the years of piggybacks and bear hugs with her niece and nephew, she's never been moved to tenderness. She loves them because they're Billie's children, but they don't need her. There's nothing she can offer them other than play fights and sweets. She flips Daniel over so the twin points of his knees face the wall, and scoops herself into a safe hollow around him.

'Anna? Are you going to stay here all night?'

'That's the plan, Dan-Dan. It is my bed, after all.'

'But if the plan changes? Will you wake me and tell me if you're going?'

'I promise I'm not going anywhere.'

With her promise, he falls asleep within seconds. But Anna can't close her eyes, straining to hear what's happening on the other side of the house. The fight has ended, no noise coming from Suzie and Gabriel's bedroom.

She keeps seeing the look on his face as she broke out of the kiss.

What are you doing, Gabe?

His reply: *Everything in my life is broken.*

'Anna, Anna, come here.'

Daniel has fallen into the well. He's crying for her help, but he's so far down she can only see his pale face, a tiny white pebble with terrified eyes.

'Anna.' His voice is against her ear and she wakes, scrambling upright, still caught up in the horror of her dream. It's dark, still night-time. Daniel has her hand, trying to pull her out of bed, towards the window. 'Hurry, she's there.'

'What?' Fresh panic breaks over her. The covers coil around her ankle as she tries to follow him, and she stumbles. He lets go of her hand and rushes to the window, pressing his forehead and palms to the glass. 'Lily's outside.'

The curtains are wide open, and on the floor is Lily's dreamcatcher, its pink suede loop broken again. Anna's vision pinballs between the trees by the canal, the towpath and the paddock beyond.

'Can't you see her?' Daniel cranes his head, but his voice has lost its conviction. His hands slip off the glass. 'She *was* there.'

With a shudder, she steps back from the window. 'You were dreaming, Dan.'

His fists clench by his sides, above his head blue devastation rather than anger. 'But I saw ghost lights in the forest. That means she's out there.'

'Dan ... do you think Lily is a ghost?'

'I think she is now.' He won't look at her. 'Otherwise she'd have come home.'

She draws him back from the window. The moon is large and unnaturally brilliant, the trees, the paddock fence and the canal wall standing out in sharp relief. There's no threat out there, she reminds herself, a sick swipe through her stomach as she remembers – as she does a hundred times a day – that it was Billie sending those messages. No one is watching the house.

But if she stares hard enough, she too might see the ghost of a lost girl.

~ 31 ~

Cardinal haze

She wakes to find her door wide open. From her bed she can see Ben's toolbox, a pair of paint-spattered overalls heaped on top. Daniel walks into the room before she can close the door, clutching her frog in one hand, a pair of green climbing shoes in the other. Instead of school uniform, he's wearing baggy shorts and his favourite Arsenal shirt.

He's even more solemn than usual, his thin arms poking from the wide bell of his sleeves, the brittle nuts-and-bolts of his elbows and wrists. Again she feels the unfamiliar weight of care. 'What's wrong, Dan?'

'Daddy's not taking me climbing now.'

She attempts a casual tone. 'That's because it's a school day.'

'No. It's an inset day. And my dad's gone.'

Disappointment feathers from his head, brown and khaki green, curling over like dying ferns as he walks out of the room. He doesn't answer when she asks where Gabriel has gone.

Grabbing her towel and fresh clothes, she takes a long, cowardly shower until the water runs cold and forces her out.

Suzie calls her name as she leaves the bathroom. 'Have you seen my casserole dish, the big orange one?' There's tension in her voice, as if the effort to keep it light is a dumbbell she's struggling to lift.

'Sorry, no.' Wetness seeps up from the carpet under Anna's

bare feet. A thin, broken line of spilt liquid runs from Daniel's room towards the stairs. Dark slops mark several of the steps.

His room is empty, as is his aquarium, the water level halved, much of it pooling on the desk and the floor beneath. As she returns to her room to dress, there's a flutter of movement outside the window overlooking the back of the house as a crow lifts upwards, its wings battering the air. Opening the window, she looks past the flat roof to the patio, where a birds' feast is taking place, crows and seagulls cawing and skirmishing over a dark stain of water that writhes and gleams in the light. A seagull breaks away, passing close enough that she can see two tiny frog's legs spasming against its beak. In the middle of the garden is the still figure of Daniel, his mother's casserole dish by his feet, watching the birds peck and jab at his beloved froglings.

Stepping back, Anna drops her head into her hands. The only thing she can think of is to call her sister.

Billie doesn't ask questions, not even when Anna instructs her to avoid the front of the house and collect her from the stile by the back of the paddock. In the corridor outside her room, she listens for Daniel and Suzie. The box room is empty, though the light is on, and the overalls are no longer lying on the toolbox. As far as she can tell, Ben has made no progress since she last looked in, the patch of naked plaster still rough and unpainted. She wonders where the little creep is. It unsettles her when she can't pinpoint his whereabouts.

The television is on in the sitting room. She heads in the opposite direction, carrying her plimsolls so her bare feet are quiet as velvet on the floor. She makes it to the laundry room without being seen and out onto the overgrown patio, where a puddle of water is all that remains of Daniel's frogs. From there, it's a quick dash across the sumpy back garden, more mud than grass after the heavy rains, and over the timber fence into the paddock. As she runs across the field, the sun appears as if to shine a light on her escape.

Her sister pulls up as she is clambering over the stile, throwing open the passenger door and revving the engine for effect.

'Need a new identity?' she says, checking her rear-view mirror and pulling away in a leisurely fashion.

'Gabriel kissed me.'

The car comes to an abrupt halt, jolting her forward.

'I warned you, right?' Alarm is casting off Billie's crown like fishing reels.

Anna rubs her neck. 'Bills, can we just drive?'

But her sister wants to discuss it right there in the middle of the road, firing questions and cutting her off before she can answer, chopping her to pieces.

The air between them splinters into colour like a church window shattering. She can't tell which colours are hers and which Billie's. This is her sister, the person she is closest to, her team. They never fall out. She notes Billie's dishevelled look: unbrushed hair, no make-up, a baggy white T-shirt with the outline of colourless stains like stepping stones down the front. Her sister is unravelling.

'A man simply doesn't lunge at a woman without the confidence that she'll respond in kind.'

She has a ridiculous urge to burst into tears and cling to her sister's hand, begging forgiveness. Billie is right, as she always is. All those unguarded moments when she let Gabriel see what was in her eyes. If she'd shown him a blank wall rather than a mirror, he wouldn't have kissed her.

'You're looking at me like I disgust you,' she says.

'Not you. Your behaviour.'

A cardinal haze, all hers, paints out her bewilderment. Lily's ring wedged into the seat runner; naked pictures of the missing girl in her sister's house; the messages like poison darts that Billie had attacked the girl with. Billie hasn't exactly got her shit together either.

'You don't know how lonely I've been in that house.'

'You're always lonely.' Her sister snaps a band off her wrist, checking the mirror as she yanks back her hair. 'This is Lauritz all over again.'

His name shocks her into silence. They drive back to Billie's without speaking but halfway through the journey her sister's hand finds hers, her grip hard and damp. *Holding on for dear life*: a phrase their mother likes to use.

When they pull up outside Billie's house, her sister says, 'It's only because I love you, Anna. You know that, don't you?'

'Why did you mention Lauritz? He was a lifetime ago.'

'Had you forgotten him?' Billie quirks her eyebrow and gets out of the car.

Maisie and Lucas run to greet Anna at the front door. She buries herself in effusive hugs, drawing them out with tickles and helicopter swings. Looking after Daniel has tenderised a part of her that had been stiff and unused, still in its protective wrapping. It's an unsettling feeling, she thinks, to believe herself an adult and then discover there is still so much she doesn't know about herself.

Jonah comes out to view the commotion. He's in a pair of tracksuit bottoms slung low on his hips, a tight T-shirt and bare feet. While Billie goes to shower, he offers Anna breakfast. She realises only then that it is barely eight in the morning.

'Not working today?' She watches Jonah scramble eggs, slice sourdough, mash avocado. There's something self-satisfied about the way he moves, she thinks, and then feels unkind when he offers her a plate of food with his shy smile. The problem is that there are now two Jonahs: the old one, comfy as a shabby sofa, and the one who'd flirted with the attendant, his colours bold as nail varnish.

'I work from home on Fridays.'

'How's the baby-making going?'

His frown releases orange tendrils. 'It's some mad notion of Billie's. I don't know where it's coming from.'

'Your mid-life crisis, maybe?' She winks to soften her words. 'Maybe your toned biceps have made her look at herself in a questioning light.'

'My fitness is about health, not vanity.' Two dull patches of red appear on his cheeks.

'Sure you haven't developed an eye for pretty girls, Jo?'

Her words are turning the orange strings into thick rope above his head, but there are no aggressive reds to fend her off. Jonah hates confrontation. With her sister out of the room and his anxiety making him vulnerable, now is the time to take out the photographs of Lily. She searches through her bag, certain she'd put them in the inner pocket and zipped it closed, but they aren't there.

'Did you ever drop Lily home after she babysat for you?'

He pretends to give it some thought. 'Only when Gabriel couldn't fetch her.'

'In the Golf?'

'What's this about?' He pushes his hands through his hair, as if he could brush away the telltale oranges. It's making Anna equally nervous. She wants to know and she doesn't want to know.

'Did you and Lily ever go for a drive before you dropped her home?'

Jonah strides out into the corridor to call his children for breakfast, then answers in a quieter voice. 'Of course not, Anna. Why would I do such a thing?'

But his denial means nothing if she can't see his face.

She hides out for the whole of Friday at her sister's house, having found a quiet moment before lunch to apologise to Jonah, blaming her behaviour on the stress of living with a ghost. He accepts her apology, but a pale shade of injured blue remains. She needs to be more cunning in her search for answers.

When the light begins to fade, Billie takes her home. 'Time to face the music, little sister.'

'I can't get used to the new Jonah,' Anna says as Billie fiddles with the radio, swerving across the road in her distraction.

'I did warn you he'd become a boring old fitness-fuck.'

'But why? What's he looking for?'

Billie looks across at her, and though her expression suggests surprise, there's nothing more than a headband of even colours, none of which dominate: a common factor amongst people ruled by their intellect rather than their heart. 'If it doesn't bother me, why should it bother you?'

But there's something up with her sister and she can't work out what it is. Ironic that the person she's closest to is the hardest to read.

Outside the O'Keefes' house, she waves Billie away, needing a minute alone to find courage. Gabriel's Defender still hasn't returned. A faint light issues from the top floor, the house as always so damned quiet. She is startled by the front door opening, bringing her face to face with Suzie. There's no light in the hall, the woman's face in shadow, the only colour her own burnt sienna.

'You were out a long time. Daniel's been missing you.'

Her tone is friendly but a warning switch trips in Anna's chest. Daniel tears out of the kitchen to throw his arms about her waist. Conscious of his mother's eyes, she gives him a brief squeeze before extracting herself.

'Have you had a nice day, Dan?'

Suzie answers for him. 'We've had a lovely day. We made biscuits.'

A band of tension loosens around Anna's chest. Gabriel hasn't confessed to the kiss after all. Daniel takes her hand, his fingers their usual chill stickiness. 'We saved some biscuits for you and for Daddy when he comes back from Nana Trish's.'

Suzie smiles as if all is right with the world.

That night Suzie invites her to join them for Daniel's bedtime story. The aquarium is gone, in its place a carnival of Lego boats, toy cars and plastic dinosaurs. Pale stains remain in the carpet, making the room smell of pond water and rotten ham. She wonders when, if ever, she should ask Daniel about his missing froglets. Whilst Suzie reads, Anna sits on the floor, rigid with best behaviour, and when it's her turn to say goodnight, she gives Daniel a perfunctory hug, aware that Suzie is watching in a shroud of possessive yellow.

'Glass of wine?' Suzie says. A reward for passing a test.

Suzie pours a single glass for Anna from a bottle of Riesling that was opened days ago for a risotto. For herself, a carton of Ribena, as if to make it clear this is not a repeat of the night they drank shots together. She pricks the juice carton's foil with the tip of the straw, a sharp and precise movement as if she were bursting a balloon.

'I've been struggling without Lily.'

Anna nods, taking a sip of wine, unsure what to say. It is astringent, pickling her tongue, but she can hardly tip it down the sink. The sun is setting, bronzed light shining through horizontal tears in the cloud. A blackbird sings in the dusk, its song scrolling away in silver curls. She can imagine how the air would smell, rinsed and fresh as cut grass. If she could be anywhere but this kitchen…

'Daniel is very fond of you.'

'He's a lovely boy. His manners put my niece and nephew to shame.' This last intended as a joke.

'Some of the boys in his class have been teasing him.' Suzie's face doesn't change, but her colours stain red. 'They say things like "Your dad's Killer O'Keefe."'

Anna hears the implication that Lucas is one of them.

'I found some photos under Daniel's pillow this morning.'

She doesn't have to ask which ones. 'They disappeared from my bag.'

'Why were they in your bag?' The red stain above Suzie becomes long and thin, taking bloody swipes out of the air. Anger always looks like wanton destruction. 'Who've you shown them to?'

'No one. I didn't want to leave them lying around.' She takes a deep breath.

The sound of the front door closing with a reverberating slam makes them both straighten. Gabriel's home. Relief, a golden dust, floats in her vision, but it is Ben who looks into the kitchen.

'Evening, ladies. Looks like I missed dinner.' He sends Anna a wink before heading upstairs, a large canvas bag slung over his shoulder.

'It's better than being here alone,' Suzie says, her gaze still to the window. 'With Gabe away.'

'Ben's staying here?' Anna's voice is louder than she intended.

Suzie's shoulders hiccough into a short, angry shrug. 'I don't feel safe on my own.'

'But you're not alone. I'm here.' She pictures the hectic motion of Ben's forearm, the thrust of his hips pointing at the single bed she'd slept in, and wonders how she'll close her eyes with him in the house at night. 'We don't need him.'

Suzie gives the juice carton a slow squeeze until a dark red bead of liquid dribbles down the straw.

'Someone was threatening Lily online. He mentioned the house. He knew which room was hers.' Suzie presses out another droplet of juice and watches it run down the side of the carton. 'We should have told you, I guess. I'm sorry.'

Anna's throat dries. She takes a gulp of wine, coughing on an awkward swallow. 'Don't apologise. Don't those online trolls usually turn out to be harmless? Bored housewives and the like?'

A burst of streamers, the plastic red of brake lights, flails away from Suzie, including Anna in a generic rage against the world.

'A bored housewife?' Suzie says, staring out of the window. 'Lily wouldn't be missing if that was the case, would she?'

Once the glass of wine has been forced down, she heads upstairs. The shower is running in her bathroom. Closing her bedroom door, she calls Billie's mobile. It rings unanswered three times. On the fourth attempt, it goes straight to voicemail. The shower stops and she hisses out a rushed message.

'Billie, you've got to tell Suzie it was you. She's living in terror. She can't even leave the house. You've never been a coward. Tell her.'

There's a knock on her door. She knows it's him and ignores it. Another knock. She flings open the door and there is Ben, a towel tucked in a loose fold over his hips. His chest is hairless and pale, with a wet plastic sheen, like the individual slices of cheese Billie buys for the kids' burgers.

'I used up all the hot water, I'm afraid.'

'Fine.'

He leans against the door frame, his fingers curling around

the wood. She can't shut the door without trapping his hand. It's tempting.

'A lot of good memories in this room,' he says. With a sideways grin, he drops back and she slams the door.

She calls Billie's mobile one more time.

'They think there's a link between the messages and Lily going missing. Which means they're looking for Lily in the wrong place. They're looking for you.' She takes a breath. 'Do it for your own sake, Bills.'

Shortly after she turns off her light and gets into bed, there's a quiet but persistent tapping. It's coming from the wall that divides her room from the box room.

'Night night, Anna,' Ben says, and she is horrified by how close he sounds, as if a curtain rather than a wall separates them. 'Sweet dreams.'

32

Simmering orange

The next morning she walks into the kitchen to find Ben standing in the centre of the room, his back to her as he shovels food into his mouth. An empty packet of Cheerios – Daniel's favourite – lies on its side by the sink. His teeth crunch down on the cereal. He sounds like he's eating bones. She hates the noise he's making, hates the chicken-peck movement of his head as he goes in for another spoonful. Hates his elbows poking the air. She stands there burning in her own flames, hating most of all that she can't escape him. He turns, sensing her, a bubble of milk in the corner of his mouth as he grins.

'Sleep well?'

'Very.' The lie will be obvious in the black marks beneath her eyes. Several times in the night she'd been jolted into panicked wakefulness by the sound of someone outside her bedroom. 'But *you* can't have. What were you doing wandering about the house?'

There's the tiniest flicker of hesitation, but his colours are so sparse she can't read what it might mean.

'I was on foot patrol, of course,' he says. 'Isn't that what I'm here for?'

When he leaves the house shortly afterwards, her energy returns, cut free of the tight net of his presence. She changes into a chirpy yellow dress and lays out a picnic rug in the back garden. Cool air ripples across her thighs and arms, the sun's heat dabbing through in pockets of stillness. She tries to fight it but her mind keeps dropping into lazy thoughts of Gabriel. First his kiss, running through her head like melted plastic, fuchsia pink, followed by the grey plummet of his sudden departure. If she could only see him. He wouldn't have to talk, she'd know what was going on in his head.

The heat is startling after weeks of rain. The white roses and lilac clusters in the front garden release their scent, wasps darting and drunk in the bloom. Daniel rides his scooter in the lane, and after a while Suzie comes out with a bowl of apples and the compost bucket. Sitting down, she splays her small, neat toes in the grass.

'I thought we'd make an apple crumble. It's Daniel's favourite.'

Last night there'd been a movie, popcorn, chocolate biscuits. Little treats, Anna suspects, to sweeten his dad's absence.

She helps Suzie peel the apples, neither speaking, competing in friendly silence for the longest ribbon of unbroken peel.

'Whole apple.' An irregular curl of apple skin is caught in Suzie's peeler. With a triumphant grin she swishes it in Anna's direction, teasing her. In response, Anna tears off the peel and pops it in her mouth, chewing with vigour, eliciting outraged laughter from Suzie. It gives her a pang of regret, a powdery chateau-blue pebble. Under different circumstances they would have fallen so easily into friendship.

Leaning back on the blanket, face tilted to the sun, Suzie says, 'I was convinced Gabriel hired you to spy on me.'

'Why would he do that?'

'To make sure I don't run away.'

Anna drops the last apple into the bowl of water and watches it bob amongst the other pale globes. Without their

211

skin, they no longer look like apples. 'Is that what you want? To run away?'

'I think about it all the time.' Suzie picks up the bowl of apples, handing the compost bucket to Anna, and they head inside. The apples empty into the kitchen sink, with a rolling thud like distant thunder. 'Gabe refuses to leave, and I could never go without Daniel.'

She straightens, staring out of the window. With a sharp dart of her body, she leans forward to rap on the glass. 'I'm not paying you to sit on your arse and text your girlfriend,' she shouts through the glass. On the other side of the canal, Ben shoves his mobile into his back pocket, rights the wheelbarrow and ambles off, slow as an old man. A puff of soot blows across Suzie's brow.

'Why do you keep him on?' Anna says.

'Gabriel insists. He's good at the tree business apparently.' The gritty dust fades. 'Ben's all right. He's practical. He can fix just about anything, despite being ... Lily's age.'

'He says they were friends, him and Lily.'

'Does he now?' A faint dusting of soot returns.

Taking an apple from the sink, Anna starts to cut it into segments. 'I can tell you don't like him.'

Suzie gives a brisk flap of her hand. 'He's a bit of a piss-taker, but I need him to stay here. It makes me feel safe while Gabe's away.' She turns the radio on, her face changing as she listens. 'Mine and Gabe's song. An oldie, but so good.' Bruce Springsteen, 'I'm On Fire'.

The apple pieces, still wet, slip about in Anna's grasp as she cuts out the core. If she appears to be fully absorbed in her task, Suzie might reveal more of the small, telling details that make up the cement of their marriage, invisible to an outsider.

'We fell in love like they do in the movies, Gabe and I. Once I stopped being stubborn, that is.' Suzie gives a soft laugh, sunrise pink and mauve waving from her. 'I still love him like that. On the night Lily disappeared...' she keeps the same conversational tone, but her colours are shrivelling, 'I told the police he was home with me. But he wasn't.'

She measures out flour, humming as if she had merely commented on the weather. Anna takes another apple from the sink and drives the tip of the knife into its crown. She can't think what to say.

'What was I supposed to do?' Suzie asks over her shoulder. 'Tell them he was out climbing trees all night long? Tell that to my mum and dad?'

Anna is making a mess of the apples, the segments uneven, the core breaking and scattering pips. 'Is that what he was doing?'

'He likes the forest at night. There was a big moon.' Suzie hugs her arms, fingers digging into the flesh above her elbows. 'I can see how ludicrous it sounds from your face. And I know *you* want to believe it.'

She wonders what Suzie is implying. 'I think many people would have done the same thing in your position.'

'Exactly.'

She tries to breathe away the fireball blasts of horror, the trailing smog of disbelief, whilst Suzie sits at the table rubbing together butter, flour and sugar for the crumble topping. Her back is to Anna, military-stiff, her voice toneless as she speaks again. Not a scrap of colour to be gleaned.

'Gabriel changed after Lily disappeared. There's an anger growing inside him, filling him up until he can't keep it in. That's when he goes looking for a fight.'

Her fingers pinch and squeeze the lumps in the mixture. The room is airless and hot, the sun glinting off the stainless-steel sink, the fridge handle, the silver clip in Suzie's hair. When

Anna leans over the sink to open the window, Suzie glances up. Both of them trying to read messages in the other.

Billie had said something about Gabriel's temper. She pictures Suzie on the kitchen floor; her hysterical weeping a few nights ago; her panic after she dropped Daniel's boat, the present he'd made for his father. She sees the shadow fist punching out of Gabriel like a call to violence as he faced the men in the pub.

Even the kiss in the river. A man teetering on the edge of the world.

The silence draws on, the conversation settling like dust. After Suzie has put the apple crumble in the oven, she gives Anna a quiet pale-pink smile.

'I like having you here, Anna,' she says. 'I don't have many friends.'

33

Amused custard yellow

She wakes in the middle of the night and the realisation is there waiting for her like a torch shining on her face. A false alibi. Suzie's confession has made her an accomplice. Ironic, she thinks, given how much she longed to be part of their family. Now she can't find a way out. As she sits up to bash some shape into her pillow, she notices the dressing table stool lying on its side. The last thing she did before going to bed was push it against the door. Through an orange flare she notices that the door is open, wide enough for someone to poke their head in and stare at her as she slept.

She peers into the unlit corridor. The door to the box room is closed, the house silent. This time when she pushes the stool against the door, she heaps a book, her shoes and a few toiletries on top to serve as a more effective alert.

She'll never sleep now. Not with Ben in the house and the secret Suzie has dumped in her lap.

Get a grip. Breathe.

Billie asked if she'd seen bruises on Suzie's wrists. She hasn't. If Gabriel was capable of hurting anyone, she'd have seen it in his colours. Aggression is a deep burgundy stew, always present, bubbling quietly until the heat gets turned up and it boils over. Very different from the odd flash of anger.

She doesn't want to think. Lying very still, she closes her eyes, willing on sleep.

Her bed gives a tiny jolt. Above her head, the canopy shivers. Her body must have given a jump as she dropped into sleep, she tells herself, pressing a hand over her thudding heart. A second jolt, harder this time. She scrambles out of bed, the duvet trapping her legs, tumbling her to the floor. There's not enough air in her panicked lungs to scream as she kicks her way out of the covers, simultaneously scrabbling for the stool and hauling it out of her way.

The quiet mutter of a voice stops her dead. Holding her breath, she steps forward. A man lies wedged between the cupboard and the bed. His knees are bent, his torso slipping sideways down the cupboard door, his feet pressed flat against the bed frame. He gives a soft laugh and slowly rolls over to push himself up with his hands.

With an inarticulate cry, she backs away, her head colliding with the edge of the shelf. Ben rises to his feet. He's naked except for a pair of boxers sagging off his skinny hips. He moves closer, shambling and unsteady, hands reaching for her.

'Get out of my room.'

Furious tears prick her eyes, her voice shaking. But he keeps coming, head down, backing her into the corner of the room. His foot bears down on hers and she loses balance, falling back against the wall. Making it easy for him to catch hold and pull her up against him. Breathing in her ear as his hips make little thrusts. The soft, heated package of his genitals butts gently against her stomach and her gorge rises. Her vision is gory with rage and revulsion. With a mighty shove, she is free, surprised by how easily he falls back. She kicks the stool aside, half aware of a searing pain in her right toes, opening the door so hard it rebounds against the wall. Runs into the corridor. Turning, she finds him still standing by the foot of her bed, looking down at his feet. He mutters something, half breath, half voice.

'Get out!' she shouts. He looks in her direction, but there's something odd about the way his eyes don't appear to see her, his gaze restless and blind.

'What's wrong with you? Are you drunk?' Though she hadn't smelt alcohol on him, just a bitter soup of sweat and sleep-sour breath.

'What's going on?' Suzie is rushing along the corridor, dragging Daniel behind her.

Pushing past Anna, she looks into Lily's room and switches the light on. Ben blinks, pushing a hand through his hair.

'What the fuck?' he says, and tucks his hands into his armpits, staggering past a wide-eyed Daniel and Suzie, who ignores him.

'You scared Daniel half to death,' Suzie says, her voice straining with the effort to remain calm and friendly, but she can't hide the brown stick of disapproval from Anna.

'I woke up with Ben. In. My. Room.' The anger in her voice makes Daniel blink, but she can't worry about that now.

Suzie pinches her lips together. 'Can't you see he was sleepwalking? You need to calm down and stop being so hysterical.' Hefting Daniel up onto her hip, she returns to her bedroom.

Giving in to helpless, angry tears, Anna goes back into her room and perches on the edge of Lily's bed. She can't turn off the light.

If she had her car, she'd pack her shit and be gone.

She opens the window, drawing in cool, damp air. The surface of the canal is ruffled like feathers. Past it the trees move with an underwater sway, everything in slow motion. Except for a single rigid shape beneath the largest willow tree, the only thing that isn't rolling with the wind. She tries to puzzle out what it might be. A tiny ember flares before it. At first she mistakes it for her own sting of anxiety, but then it falls, drawing a lit trace in the shadow like a shooting star. A cigarette.

Someone is hiding in the shelter of the trees, watching the house.

She drops below the windowsill, hugging her legs, panting with shock. On hands and knees, she reaches the opposite wall and switches off the bedroom light, which must be illuminating her room like a television screen. Waits for one long moment before risking another glance. The figure is gone. In her overwrought state she may have imagined it. Perhaps Suzie is right. She's being hysterical.

If she gives in to fear, both inside and outside the house, she'll have nowhere left to go.

She is woken by Daniel poking her shoulder, solemn and persistent.

'You have to come outside and play football with me,' he says.

She sends him downstairs for a bowl of cornflakes whilst she gets up, sluggish with lack of sleep. There's no sign of Ben, but she double-checks the bathroom lock before she showers. By the time she comes downstairs, the kitchen is empty, no breakfast bowl or milk drippings on the table. She goes outside, calling for Daniel as she crosses the tiny footbridge, her bare feet slipping on the waterlogged wood. Gold beads are scattered in the grass where sunlight catches the dew, the air humid, swollen with gathering heat. A heron stands one-legged further down the stream, bees drifting through the willow sprays, the scent of grass drying in the sun; ridiculing last night's terror. Something catches between her toes in the long grass. With casual inspection, she flicks it away then stops to take a closer look. A roll-up smoked down to its browned filter.

Suzie is in the kitchen, radio on, laying rashers of bacon in a pan. She sends Anna a muted look the colour of weak tea but says nothing.

'I'm sorry about last night,' Anna hears herself say, and burns with the injustice of it. 'It's quite a shock to wake up to a man in your room.'

'Hardly a man,' Suzie says, then adds, 'But I guess it startled you.'

Anna opens her palm, wondering if she is going to be accused of being hysterical again. 'I found this on the other side of the canal.'

'Hate cigarettes.' Suzie gives a small grimace. 'It's a public footpath. We get dog-walkers. And sometimes people who want to have a good gawp at the house the missing girl lived in.'

Anna allows that unpalatable fact a moment of space before she presses on. 'I thought I saw a man there last night.'

'What?' Suzie's hands fall away from the pan, a piece of bacon still caught on the fork. 'Are you sure?'

Before Anna can reply, Suzie tilts her head as if to catch a sound.

'Where's Dan?'

They rush together for the front door.

Whilst Suzie searches the lane, Anna crosses the canal, heading for the copse of oak and beech trees, past the willows. Every time she calls his name and he doesn't respond, a piece of her chest closes. Disbelief lays its dirty, green-tinged smoke over the empty path and in the gaping spaces between the trees. Suzie's voice rings from the other side of the house, metal-edged with anxiety. Anna runs along the bridle path towards the paddock and the woods behind.

If only she'd told him to wait in his room.

If only she'd gone downstairs and made breakfast for him.

Reaching the paddock, she grabs hold of the wooden rail, breathless, dizzy with the unthinkable. The field is empty. She drops her head on her arms. A fleeting noise like the cry of a gull catches her attention and she looks up. Ben is running out of the forest, Daniel on his back, whooping and laughing.

'What do you think you're doing?' she shouts across the field as they approach. 'Taking off with Daniel? Not letting us know?'

Daniel slides off Ben's back, the smile leaving his face, whilst Ben's smirk remains. She holds his eye, a snow-blind veil of shame across her vision. Out of the house, under a sunny sky, Ben is nothing but a teenage boy with a pimply face and bony arms. When did she become so weak and afraid?

'Poor Dan here was bored and all alone.' Ben gives Daniel's shoulder a squeeze, hard enough to make the boy squirm, though his adoring gaze stays fixed on the older boy.

'You want to apologise for last night?'

He puffs air through his lips, disdainful and amused, looking away, but she catches a tiny cluster of beads, the colour of strong coffee, trickling through his aura. A twinge of embarrassment.

'I'm hungry,' Daniel says, tugging at her hand, and they head back towards the house. When she glances over the little boy's head to read Ben, she finds no residue of colour.

'Ben was Lily's first boyfriend,' Daniel says.

'Give it a rest, Dan.' Ben pretends to swing a punch, cuffing the top of the little boy's head, knocking him off balance. Daniel giggles, finding it all hilarious.

'Dan, there you are.' Suzie's cry makes the boy hesitate, a confusion of surprised yellows and greens above his head. 'I didn't know where you were.' Dropping to her knees in the grass, she clutches her son in a tight embrace, giving in to muffled sobs.

Daniel pats his mother's head, stricken and awkward, while

Ben strolls away, fine strands of custard yellow lifting off his crown. Finding the whole thing amusing.

Something wrong with that boy, Anna thinks.

She waits until Ben has left on his bike and Suzie is cuddled up on the sofa with Daniel watching *Monsters, Inc.* before leaving the house. Afraid of being overheard, she calls Billie from the paddock.

'You need to come over today and tell Suzie about the messages.'

'So you keep saying.' There's a pause on the end of the line. 'It's never going to happen.'

She tells Billie about the man hiding under the trees.

'It's a horror tourist, that's all. The stalker doesn't exist, remember?'

'Exactly. We need to separate the real threat from the ... false. That's why you have to tell Suzie.'

'So she can call the police? Would that make you feel better?' Billie's voice has a dangerous red edge. 'Your own sister in jail?'

Anna takes a deep breath and tries to think clearly. Falling out with Billie uncobbles her brain. 'Explain how Lily's behaviour made you feel – Suzie's admitted she could be tricky. And let her know how sorry you are.'

'Say sorry and it'll be OK? You're so bloody naive, Anna.'

'Suzie won't go to the police. She told me something. Something major.'

Billie goes quiet. When she speaks again, her voice has changed, low and keen with sudden interest. 'What did she tell you?'

Anna swallows, realising she's made a mistake. Billie is convinced of Gabriel's involvement in Lily's disappearance. This is what she's been waiting for. 'Billie ... why did you get me this job?'

'What?' Her sister is thrown. 'To save your unemployable arse, of course.'

'But why the O'Keefes? Why all that effort to put me in with a family going through such trauma?'

Billie gives an impatient tut. 'Stop changing the subject. Tell me what the big secret is.'

'You put me there to spy on them, didn't you?'

Billie gives a growl of frustration. 'Tell. Me. Now.'

'Only if you tell Suzie what you did.'

Her sister sucks in a breath. 'Fucking forget that.'

'If you're not going to, I will.' Anna's hands are shaking as she ends the call.

34

Mustard jealousy

The next morning, Suzie makes pancakes for breakfast, humming and swaying her hips to a tune inside her head. With her hair still wet from the shower and her face without make-up, she looks startlingly young. For the first time, Anna sees the powerful resemblance between her and Lily.

There is much laughter as Dan squirts lemon juice across the table and into Suzie's tea. Anna, happy to be included in this small, tight unit, is still surprised by the woman's sea change. One day brought to her knees by fear, the next light and play-ful. What can't be denied is that Suzie is more consistently cheerful without Gabriel.

'Is Daddy coming home tomorrow?' Daniel wants to know, and the yellows around the room fall away.

'Yes, maybe.' Suzie smiles, but a sprig of red and orange branches from her crown. Seeing it, Anna loses her appetite.

'Your sister has invited us over for Sunday lunch.' Suzie licks Nutella off her fingers and passes a chocolate-filled pancake to Daniel.

'I don't want to go to Lucas's house,' he says in a quiet voice. 'He doesn't like me because I'm in the C team for football.'

'Want to know a secret?' Anna cups her hands around her mouth and whispers in his ear. 'Lucas wet his bed until he was seven years old.'

Her reward for this disloyalty is a huge grin, though he claps his hands over his mouth to hide it.

'I don't know what I would have done if it weren't for your sister,' Suzie says. 'She's a life-saver.'

'I didn't realise you were such good friends.'

'When everyone else avoided me like the plague, for the unforgivable sin of having lost someone ...' a sideways glance at Daniel, who pretends to be absorbed in eating his pancake, though Anna can see he is listening, a sharp cone of verdigris above his crown, 'Billie stuck by me. The only one.'

'My sister can't bear injustice.'

Suzie isn't eating any pancakes herself. There's a pallor beneath the fresh gold of her tan from when they sat in the garden peeling apples.

'She was a good friend to Lily as well. Lily was in awe of her, for obvious reasons.' She waits for Anna to acknowledge whatever these obvious reasons might be with a nod of the head before continuing. 'Billie's the opposite of my sister, Lily's mum. Smart, educated, funny. Head screwed on. She got Lily through her GCSEs, persuaded her to do A levels. She was talking to her about going to uni ... not that long ago.' Suzie spreads a new pancake with chocolate and hands it to Daniel, though his first one has been left half eaten on the plate. 'Billie was as devastated as we were to lose Lily.'

Anna nods, her stomach writhing. Suzie's opinion of her sister is about to take a devastating plunge. She wonders if Billie will make her confession before or after the meal.

'I'm not hungry any more, Mum.'

Suzie lets her son leave the table, her eyes following him up the stairs. Then she turns back to Anna. 'Did Billie tell you about Lily getting pregnant?'

*

After Suzie and Daniel have left for Billie's house – Suzie having turned down her offer of a lift – Anna scrapes the un-eaten pancakes into the bin and washes up the pan, thinking about Lily. Pregnant at sixteen. When she'd asked who the father was, Suzie had grimaced as if she'd bitten into something rank and pointed at the ceiling. It had taken her a moment to understand.

You're kidding? Ben?

Suzie had sighed with a shrug. *First love. Who can explain it?*

Lily had told Billie about the pregnancy first, something that still causes Suzie some hurt, given the fan of deep indigo that had unfolded. Anna wonders how her sister had reacted on the inside. She would have presented a calm and sensible exterior, but few people know that a puritanical streak runs through the core of Billie's being. It's why she married Jonah, the first and only man she ever had sex with. An unplanned pregnancy, at such a young age, would have appalled her.

She goes for a run to clear the electric crackle of acid yellows and tangerines. Instead of fading, it seems to intensify with every step. So many secrets, like doors to hidden rooms, opened and shut again before she can fully grasp them. Suzie has secrets, Daniel too. Even the house, with its concealed well. She wonders what doors Gabriel is holding shut and then realises she herself is behind one of them, with a kiss in the river. She has lost her position as idle witness.

The moment she gets in from her run, she calls Margaret and invites her over. The young woman interrupts her directions. She used to visit Lily all the time, she says, a tremor moving through her voice.

It takes Margaret an hour to cycle from East Mawsey, the stripe in her fringe damp with sweat, turning it a dark liverish red. As Anna leads her to the kitchen, she stops by the foot of the staircase.

'I'd like to see Lily's room.' Smiling bravely through a surge of tears. 'Just to feel her energy one last time.'

As they stand in the doorway to Lily's room, she watches rose gold flicker in Margaret's hair like raindrops bursting on the surface of a pond. The disdain she'd felt for the girl's ready tears shames her. Margaret had cared deeply for Lily.

'Makes my fingers tingle like electricity's running through them, my temples too. I have ants crawling through my hair.' Margaret gives a quick, embarrassed laugh, checking Anna's expression. 'I'm sensitive to energy. Lily was too. Not in the same league as April, of course.'

Moving around the room, she touches the bed's canopy, the little angels, running her fingers down one slim feather of the dreamcatcher. When she opens the wardrobe, her hands fall away from the doors. A spear of indigo pain darts from her crown. 'All her clothes are gone.'

'Gabriel asked me to pack them. They're in a case under the bed.'

Margaret crouches down and pulls out the case. As she rummages through Lily's clothes, Anna watches a sharp, metallic green rising from her.

'What are you looking for?'

Margaret sits back on her heels, a chiffon scarf with a butterfly design trailing from her hand. 'What happened to her boots?'

'I don't remember seeing any.' Something about the girl's hungry, focused colours puts her on alert.

'They were her favourite.' Margaret takes her mobile from her red suede shoulder bag and scrolls through her photographs. 'Here. These.'

In the photograph, Lily faces away from the camera, looking

back over her shoulder, grinning with delight as she points to her feet. She's wearing a pair of brown leather boots with angel wings embroidered in gold thread above the heel. 'Took her six months to save up for them.'

'I wonder where they've gone?' Anna thinks back to the description on the poster of Lily's clothing on the night she went missing. 'She was wearing trainers, wasn't she, the last time she was seen?'

Margaret bunches the butterfly scarf beneath her nose, inhaling as she nods. The rose-gold flicker above her head arches upwards into a solid crest of rich, simmering magenta.

'You were in love with Lily.'

The girl's eyes startle open. With a sigh, she lets the scarf unravel, smoothing its creases with her fingers. 'That obvious?'

'And Lily?'

Margaret looks away. 'There was only one person for her.'

'Gabriel.' The room falls silent around his name.

Margaret turns down the offer of a drink with a glum shake of her head. The wild plume of her love for Lily has shrivelled into a battered pewter. Anna can sense her getting ready to leave. As she takes the photos out of the dressing table drawer, inspiration hits. 'We should make a new poster, Margaret. Using a better picture. One that is more... Lily.'

Margaret considers this with a slow nod, then, as the idea catches, spreading out like sunlight on water, she squeezes Anna's fingers. 'You're right. And I prefer Greta. Margaret is so over-fifties.'

'What about this one?' Anna holds up the photograph of Lily sleepy-eyed in her dressing-gown, gentle, vulnerable. 'We need to get people thinking about her again.'

Margaret nods, squeezing her hand once more, her gratitude like purple flowers opening out their petals. Anna finds herself warming to the girl. Beneath the flakiness and melodrama, there is kindness, her lack of guile making it acceptable to be less than perfect.

'If I knew where she was,' Margaret says, feeling her words out, 'I could get on with my life.'

'Do you have any idea? Even a wild theory?'

'Nothing at all.' But a tiny orange flame like a struck match bursts into life. Gabriel is right. Margaret knows more than she's letting on.

The girl moves towards the doorway, rubbing her wrists and tweaking the unbuttoned cuffs of her white blouse. The edge of the tattoo, pointed like a snake's tail, shows through the slit. Noticing Anna's scrutiny, Margaret rolls her sleeve to her elbow, revealing the silhouette of a girl's face, her hair falling in long waves, wild and sharp-tipped.

'Lily. Of course.'

Once again Anna has the feeling of slipping away from the secret nub of the matter. She takes the angel wing from the envelope beneath the bed. 'This is the sketch I told you about the other day.'

She lets Margaret unfold the paper, giving herself a moment to sit back and read her reaction. There's a clash of green pleasure and navy heartache, then spoiled mustard, twisted as a piece of rusted wire, cuts through it all; the same colour with which Margaret views Gabriel. She knows then what it is. Jealousy.

'I'm certain it's a tattoo,' she says, tracing the letter G. 'And I ... sense she went through with it.'

'Sense?' The girl's eyes are wide and wary.

'I get a feeling about things. Like the way I knew how you felt about Lily.'

Margaret acknowledges this with a slow nod, her tongue poking at the light sheen of sweat above her top lip.

'You can trust me.' With a steadying breath, Anna tries to

calm the yellow and green screen of her own anticipation so she can keep reading Margaret. The colours above the girl's head have started shivering and darting like fire coming to life around a piece of paper. 'We'll never know what happened unless we put the pieces of the puzzle together, Greta.'

The girl nods. 'I met Lily off the train from London on the day she disappeared. She'd been shopping. We went to the Railway House for a few drinks. The police know this. She had a couple of vodkas for Dutch courage.' No tears now, but she is shivering with tension. The recollection hurts her. 'We went to a tattoo place in East Mawsey that stays open late some nights. It hurt like hell but she didn't make a noise.'

'I guess she was determined to have it done. She worked hard enough on the design. I found pages and pages of it.'

Margaret looks away, fighting back the tears for once. There's more to it, a tiny complex knot of pain that Anna can't decipher, but she needs to take it slowly or the girl will clam up.

'What happened then, Greta?'

35

Colourless

Margaret sits on the edge of the mattress, stroking the stripe of pillarbox red behind her ear, gathering in her colours. 'When we left the Dragon's Ink, I went home. Lily was off to find Gabriel.'

'Did she find him?'

The girl drops back across the bed, folding her hands over her stomach. 'I don't know.'

A murky green wave of disappointment spurs Anna to her feet. She stares out at the forest, flicking the dreamcatcher so it taps the glass. Margaret's careless collapse across Lily's bed, her stubborn silence, fills Anna with a prickling rash of irritation.

'Someone knows where she is,' the girl says. 'Out there. Someone knows.'

'True.' Anna nods at her own reflection in the window.

Downstairs, the front door shuts with a slam that shivers up through the walls. 'I'd better go,' Margaret says, sitting up, her shoulders rounded with defeat.

Anna recognises the rapid chuck-chuck of feet on the stairs. 'It's only Ben.'

There's nothing but a faint green mist from Margaret's crown as she leans forward to look through the doorway. 'All right, Ben?'

Ben pauses, removing an earplug, eyes skimming past

Margaret, registering equal lack of interest. His eyes meet Anna's before making a pointed journey down her figure. But it's all just for show, the air above his head empty. It strikes her then, the thing that unsettles her about Ben. His lack of colour.

She listens for the sound of his door closing as he retreats to the box room, but it doesn't come. The faulty catch, or the door deliberately left open so he can eavesdrop, she can't tell.

'Daniel says Lily and Ben used to date.'

Margaret gives a dry laugh. 'For about a week. He had the charisma of a dead leaf, she used to say.' She takes an angel off the shelf, stroking the silver gauze of its wings, nudging the brass wire halo above its head.

'Keep it if you want.'

She puts it back on the shelf. 'I have one already.'

Unable to persuade Margaret to stay any longer, Anna follows her outside. Swinging a leg over her bicycle's crossbar, the girl checks the lane for non-existent traffic. 'Thanks for inviting me over.'

'There was just one more thing... Greta.'

Little red bubbles burst above Margaret's head.

'Daniel says he gave Lily a fish ring.' It has taken her a full hour to summon the courage to ask. 'Was she wearing it the last time you saw her?'

'I didn't notice.' With a backwards wave, Margaret pushes off into the lane, so keen to be gone she doesn't question why Anna wants to know.

She wakes up close to midnight with an overwhelming thirst. On her way to the kitchen, she decides to look in on Daniel. Having gone to bed early, she'd missed their return. Billie can't have confessed to those nasty trolling messages because Suzie would have banged on her door.

Tiptoeing into Daniel's room, she finds his bed empty, the

231

covers thrown back. Alarm flashes through her until she notices the still figure at the window.

'Dan? What are you doing?' But she knows. Looking for Lily.

'Mum and I saw a light in the woods when we were driving home from Grandma and Grandpa's pub. Mummy said it was just people camping.'

'I'm sure she's right.' Anna joins him at the window, an arm around his shoulder. 'How was Lucas at lunch today?'

He shrugs, not wanting to discuss it. 'Mummy's *not* right. They're not humans. They're called will-o'-the-wisps. A man called Will tried to trick the Devil and now he can never go to heaven.' He climbs onto his bed and takes a large hardback book off the shelf. On the front is a picture of a wild-eyed man following a dancing flame into the woods. 'There's loads of stories from all over the world about ghost lights. If you find them on a grave they're called ghost candles.'

'Nothing but fairy tales.' She replaces the book on the shelf. 'I've lived for thirty-two years and never, ever seen a ghost light.'

'That's because you never lived here before,' he says, his face solemn with the wisdom of a child.

Water gushes through the house, the noise deafening.

'I'm coming,' she cries, fighting out of her covers, her chest filled with horse's hooves. The water is running through the corridor, a river cascading down the stairs. It takes her feet from under her and she plunges downward. When she stands up in the hallway, the river reaches her thighs. She wades into the sitting room, the coffee table floating past. The rug drifts away to reveal the glass circle.

A young girl's face shines out of the water, one eye pressed open against the glass, its colour leached away.

When she screams, her mouth fills with water.

On all fours, Anna stares at her own reflection in the black glass.

The floor is dry, the roar of water coming from the storm outside. Saliva floods her mouth and she spits it into her palm, thinking she might be sick. She sits back on her heels, shaky and disorientated, closing her eyes to calm the kaleidoscope flicker of colours. When her limbs feel trustworthy again, she finds the light switch behind the sofa, approaching the lit well with dread. The water has risen, a matter of centimetres separating it from the glass. Crumbled brick and black leaves rock with its restless surface.

The horror of Lily's face trapped beneath the glass rises again. She can't stay in the house a moment longer. She opens the front door and finds the rain has run itself out, the night newly washed, water dripping from the trees and gurgling through the gutter where she'd found the white feather. A gust of wind blows in, speckled with rain. Gabriel's wellingtons are by the door, his work jacket with the reflective safety strips hanging beside Daniel's school coat like a collapsed tent. She steps into the cold boots, feeling herself hampered by the slop of space around her feet as she shuffles sideways to unhook his jacket. His smell surrounds her, a tang of old sweat and something sweet like apricot. Unmistakably him. Pressing her nose to the collar, she sends him a silent plea.

Come back. Wherever you are.

Moonlight falls across the garden in broken strobes as the trees shift in the wind, the rush of air soothing her. Blowing the cobwebs away, her dad would say. Her nightmare sloughs away. Keeping close to the house, she heads for the bench outside the laundry room. Tugging the hem of his jacket down, she sits on the edge of the wet seat and breathes in the night air.

It's time to leave, she tells herself. It is not up to her to find

Lily or dig her sister out of trouble, though God knows Billie's done it enough times for her. The thought fills her head with lonely grey cement, comforting almost in its familiarity. She has always fallen so readily into other people's nests, blending in, making herself indispensable; only it isn't real. The Sowerbys were a reminder of how easily she's discarded once the fit is no longer comfortable.

The O'Keefes need her – Suzie relying on her so she can pretend she's coping, Daniel hungry to be loved and listened to, and Gabriel's need the most compelling of all – but the nightmare is a warning. Time to pack her bags and head to Billie's. She checks herself. They haven't spoken since she begged Billie to come clean to Suzie. Her parents' house, then, where her childhood bed is always made up, ready to receive her.

As she heads back to the front door, her eyes pick out a long shape, solid and motionless, beneath the willow branches. A figure standing under the trees by the wooden canal bridge. She breaks into a run, the boots lurching around her feet. Adrenalin rushes through her body, her skin hypersensitive, anticipating a grapple of fingers. The door is open, no more than two metres away. Afraid to look back, she stumbles forward and somehow makes it.

Inside, she falls against the door, the noise reverberating through the house as it slams shut. Freed from the clumsy weight of the boots, she runs upstairs, fleet as a startled deer. From the landing window, she studies the driveway. When she returns to her room, the sight of Daniel huddled in her bed stops her en route to the window. She's never seen him cry before. A painful mewling like an injured kitten.

'Dan-Dan, what's happened?' The top of her head clips the bed's curtain rail in her scramble to reach him. Scooping him up, she hugs him tight, the pounding in her head nothing compared to the sight of his distress. He stops crying, wiping his face on her shoulder, and she doesn't care about the snail trail he leaves on her T-shirt, only that she has managed to comfort him.

'I came to find you but you were gone.' His voice unravels like a thread, the tears returning. He swipes them with the back of his hand, trying to be brave.

'I went outside for some fresh air, that's all.'

'I thought you'd gone.' He takes a few shivery breaths. 'I ran into Mummy's room and I thought she was gone too.'

'Your mum's gone?'

Daniel shakes his head. 'No, she was under lots of covers.'

'Everything's fine, Dan. No one's going anywhere.'

'Promise?'

She promises through a snowstorm. How can she think of leaving when it is the thing Daniel most fears?

36

Sky the colour of a grease stain

On Monday morning, Daniel knocks on her door.
'You have to call school and say I'm not coming in today,' he says, and his russet and ochres twist and flail, setting off an adrenalin ache in Anna's stomach.

'Let me go and speak to your mummy.'

He gives a vigorous shake of the head. 'Mummy wants to sleep.'

Having cast off his school uniform, Daniel insists on football practice, racing around the back garden, fists clenched, face puce with exertion whilst the ball eludes him, contrary as a cat. Anna joins in until Ben takes the lawnmower out of the shed and starts to cut the overgrown grass, his eyes fixed in her direction.

When Daniel's foot finally connects, the ball soars over the canal. He crosses the footbridge with a victorious crab dance to retrieve it, then squats down by the willow tree, studying something by the roots. 'Look what I found.'

Anna rushes across the bridge, afraid of what he might have stumbled on. 'If it's another snail, Daniel O'Keefe, you leave his little house on.'

To her relief, it isn't a cigarette end but a white feather sticking out from the ground like an odd-shaped flower.

'Can we go for a walk?' Daniel is asking, pointing along the bridle path. 'Me and Daddy found a sinkhole. Please, Anna? It'll take my mind off my lousy football.'

Slipping her arms beneath his, she twirls him in a circle, his legs windmilling out. 'When did you become so crafty?'

At least inside the trees, Ben can't stare at her.

They follow the bridle path along the canal, past the paddock and into the mouth of the woods. At first, her heart beats hard and fast, orange fireworks wherever she looks, but the sunlight breaks up the solid block of trees until it no longer feels dense and sinister. According to Gabriel, the ancient river runs beneath their feet, but with the sweet smell of sun-baked pine and the exhilarated greens of beech and oak, the thought fails to unnerve her. Daniel takes her hand, pointing out squirrels and jays and early mushrooms. He has a good eye, he explains, like his dad. Overhead, young trees create a cathedral spire from which leaves and pieces of twig fall, dislodged by birds and breeze, everything curiously animate.

Breaking out of her grasp, he runs ahead. A happy, careless eight-year-old, the way he should be every day.

'Found it.' Pointing at the ground, he urges her on.

In the middle of the path is a huge and inexplicable crater, large enough to swallow a car, a dim reflection of water at its base. Daniel's feet are on the edge, where the earth is thin and wrinkled as a pair of toothless lips. She yanks him backwards.

'Sinkholes happen when there's been lots of rain,' he says, unfazed, and it occurs to her that perhaps he stood close to the edge to test her reaction. 'It makes tunnels under the ground and then it just goes poof.' He illustrates his scientific knowledge with finger fireworks. 'Sometimes houses fall inside the holes. And people.'

'Where are the signs or fences to stop people from falling in?'

'Only me and my dad know about it.' He picks up a handful of stones and throws them over the edge. They land with a faint splash. 'If I was a monster, this is where I'd hide. I'd wait here until someone walked by and then jump out and pull them down.'

'Thank you for that particular nightmare, Dan.'

He doesn't smile, edging closer again, pelting stones and twigs into the crater.

The wind has picked up, muscling through the trees, its movement creating imaginary figures in the corner of her eye. She's forgotten to let Suzie know they were going for a walk. She holds her mobile up, trying to fish a signal out of the sky, but there's no service this deep inside the forest. Daniel insists the path ahead is the quickest way home. 'It's the loop Daddy and I always take.'

She figures he found the sinkhole easily enough, but when they reach a split in the path, he stops. 'I think it's this way.'

'You think or you're sure?'

He's pointing to the track on the left, which feels correct if they are to loop back towards the house. The path on the right drops away, cutting into the bank like a lightning scar. His grip tightens as they walk on in silence, the spring and buck of his energy lost, his colours muddled and collapsing like storm surf. It isn't how a child should feel. She strokes his head, wishing she could brush away those rough seas. For one curious moment she thinks it's worked, as a column of lemon yellow shoots up.

'Hey, there's a tent.'

Where the forest opens into a clearing, a hammock is suspended between two sturdy trunks, a tarpaulin roof slung across a second, higher rope to hold the rain off.

Daniel's hand slips out of hers, his clear child's voice cutting through the trees. 'This is so cool.'

Beside the ash pit of an old campfire lies the white stub of a roll-up.

'We need to go home now,' Anna says.

Daniel grows quiet, glancing around the clearing. His sudden wariness makes her shoulders tingle, a crawling sense of being watched. A T-shirt and a pair of shorts have been stretched across a bush, the bony points of twigs poking through the sagging material.

'It's like the invisible man.' Daniel's voice is a whisper.

As she hurries him away from the clearing, she glances back at the T-shirt pinned against the bushes, noticing its pulsing burgundy, the colour of lust and aggression. Hope bubbles up her chest, a golden champagne froth, but she can't see the size, draped as it is against the twigs.

Suzie is by the stile as they run out of the woods. She is hugging her elbows, crows' feathers glistening blue-black above her crown. Anna feels the woman's displeasure in her stomach. Daniel stops running, wary as he approaches his mother.

Suzie gives him a quick hug, meeting Anna's eyes over his head. 'Dan, sweetheart, run ahead and put your pyjamas in your sleepover bag.' In contrast to the dark fury of her expression, her voice is gentle and light, the disparity unnerving.

Anna starts to apologise, but Suzie holds up a hand, cutting her off.

'Where are we going, Mummy?'

'To Grandma and Grandpa's.'

The thought sends out happy shoots of yellow, which muddle with amber as his eyes move between his mother and Anna. 'Is Anna going to come?'

'Run along now, Dan-Dan.'

Suzie waits for him to reach the canal. Out of earshot. 'I

let you into my family. I shared my pain, my vulnerability, my *secrets.*'

Anna knows what's coming. The poison yellow of jealousy, the angry red and injured blue, all blending into the dusty fig purple of betrayal.

'And in return you kiss my husband.'

He told her. Gabriel confessed.

There's a beat of breath in which Suzie searches her face for the impact of her words. But Anna, more than anyone, knows how to batten down her colours.

'You need to be gone by the end of the day.' Suzie starts to walk away, then hesitates. 'Just so you know, I'm considering whether to report you to the police. For stealing money.'

'What?' The word breaks the seal on the storm surge inside. She must look stricken, because a fleeting satisfaction moves over Suzie like a tiny multicoloured hummingbird.

'I have to protect my family.' Suzie looks away. There's no pleasure left, just fear, and Anna understands this isn't about revenge.

'I won't tell anyone, Suzie.' Now she puts all her colours into her voice, beseeching violet blues, the metal conviction of green bronze. 'I won't tell a soul you gave Gabriel an alibi. I swear it.'

Suzie listens but says nothing.

Sick and shaken, Anna waits by the paddock fence for Suzie and Daniel to pack the car and leave. The white Peugeot reverses in short, erratic bursts into the lane, stalls, starts up again. She can't see Suzie's colours, only the determined lift of her chin. Further along the lane, behind the row of trees, the car comes to a sudden halt. Suzie will have to cope with her panic attacks alone, though Anna feels bad for Daniel.

After a couple of minutes, it moves on again.

*

There's no answer on Billie's mobile or landline. When Anna tries Jonah, his mobile goes straight to voicemail. It takes her less than five minutes to gather her belongings. Sitting on the floor beneath the dreamcatcher, she looks around the room.

'I'm sorry I couldn't help you, Lily.'

As she is leaving the room, the doorbell rings and she runs downstairs, convinced it's Billie, her sisterly instinct like an antenna picking up her distress. Instead she finds April, who steps forward to pull her into a long-lost hug. She bites the inside of her lip to stop herself crying. Despite everything, the woman's presence lifts her.

'How are things?'

'Bluey grey.' She can't confess she's been fired because Gabriel kissed her in the river. April will see it, that fraction of time before she pushed him away. When she'd kissed him back.

'I'm looking for Gabriel. Is he about?'

Anna shakes her head, adding that Suzie and Daniel have gone to stay at the Wells Inn.

'Well, I had my hopes set on a cuppa, so you'll have to do.' April puts an arm around her shoulder and gives her a squeeze. 'Chin up. Everything's temporary, you and me included.'

At the kitchen table, April sprawls out her knees, hands clasped in her lap beneath her belly, her eyes rising and dipping around the room as if reading messages on the currents of air.

Leaving the teabags in, Anna sets the mugs on the table, her eyes on the space above April's head; both of them reading signs in their own way.

'Have you been back to the pavilion?'

April shakes her head. 'I'm not too fond of that place.'

'But you might learn something new.' Anna wraps her hands around her mug, cold and shivery to her core. 'You seem to know things that other people don't.'

April pinches out the teabag and gets up to throw it in the

sink. 'If I knew everything, my love ...' She hoists one buttock up on the countertop, her heel butting against the cupboard. 'Now. Where's Gabriel?'

'He went away on Friday. Suzie says he's visiting his mother, but she's not telling the truth.'

'Nope. That she isn't.' A shiver of pale tangerine moves through the steady emerald of April's halo. 'His mother passed away a couple of months ago. They haven't told Daniel yet. Too much loss for that little one.' She squints up at the sky, a frown on her face. 'Did they fight, him and Suzie, before he left?'

'I heard shouting, yes.' Anna pokes at her own teabag, the freshly boiled water scalding the tip of her finger. He couldn't have told Suzie about the kiss that night. She has been too friendly and relaxed, warm even. No one can sustain an act at that level for long.

'Suzie OK?'

'Yes.'

April knows she's lying. She can feel it without having to look up.

'At least the rain's stopped. Though that sky is odd,' April says, changing the subject. 'Did you know, Anna, there are rivers of energy flowing through our bodies? Nadis, they're called. They get blocked by all the shit we throw at them, our anger, our old heartbreaks. When your rivers can't flow properly, you feel alone and isolated.'

She doesn't need a lecture on being lonely. 'Rivers inside, rivers outside. No escaping the water around here, is there?'

'Nope. Nor the forest.' With a grimace, April looks across the canal to the forest behind.

A shiver runs through Anna. 'Do you think the forest's haunted?' She sees Daniel at his window, searching for ghost lights.

April turns away from the window. 'Violent deeds leave an energy behind. It's not got a nice history, that forest.'

The skin on Anna's arms prickles. Foolish of her to start this conversation when she's alone in the house, overlooked by the forest. She checks her mobile; still no response from Billie.

April tips the remains of her tea into the sink. 'Better head off.'

Following April to the door, Anna wonders what impulse sent the older woman here. She could beg a lift to her sister's house, but the shame outweighs her unease. Billie or Jonah will get back to her soon enough.

They stand on the porch, looking up at the sky.

'Most of us try to live a decent life, but we're human,' April says, giving her a smile. 'We fuck up.'

She avoids April's colours. 'True.'

'Think I prefer the rain to that sky.' April points upwards. The sun is hidden behind a solid bank of cloud with a sour yellow colour like a grease stain on white cloth. The sight of it fills Anna with oily unease.

Once April has left, she tries Billie's mobile again.

'Please come and get me, Bills. I messed up, like you knew I would. I've lost my job.'

37

Red fire, singed edges

The sky works through injured tones of violet, and reds like fresh hand marks. Anna lowers the blinds before it gets dark, trying not to look at the dense mass of the forest but a single fire-yellow light amongst the trees by the canal catches her attention.

Ghost light.

Her hand drops from the blind's drawstring, orange paint-balls bursting in her vision, until she realises it is only the ceiling bulb reflected in the glass. She thinks about the hammock in the woods and the burgundy T-shirt. Imagines herself going to find it, walking alone through the unlit forest, testing herself to see if she's brave enough. Only it can't be him. It makes no sense for Gabriel to be camping out just minutes from his own home.

She has never spent a night alone, retreating to the comfort of her parents' house or to Billie's in the lull between one warm body in her bed and the next. She can't understand why Billie hasn't contacted her. To pass the time, and by way of apology, she mocks up the new poster of Lily on the computer in the sitting room. The result pleases her. A sweet, vulnerable girl, a simple plea.

Help us find our beloved girl, Lily, missing since February. New information needed. No detail too small.

As she unpicks the old poster from the window to replace it with the new, a silver van slows to a halt in the lane, the driver leaning out to stare at the house. Heart thudding, she sees him catch sight of her and withdraw his head. When he moves on, she spots the cartoon logo on the back of the van, a surprised rat in a net. Nothing sinister. Just Pest Arrest looking for his next booking.

As if in answer to her distress, her mobile rings, the shrill tone unnaturally loud in the quiet room. She scrambles to answer it, slumping back into the chair as she hears Jonah's voice.

'Thank God, Jo. When are you coming?'

In the pause, the air turns reptilian green and her stomach churns. 'You *are* coming to get me, aren't you?'

'Not tonight. Sorry. Billie's not here and ... Well, it's tricky.'

Her thigh bumps the edge of the table as she gets to her feet. Copies of Lily's poster slide off the pile and drift to the floor. 'Where's Billie?'

Jonah breathes out heavily through his nose. 'She's gone off for a few days.'

'What are you talking about? My sister doesn't just go off for a few days.'

'Yes she does, Anna.'

Striding back to the window, she slips on a poster, which rips beneath her feet, pitching her onto one knee, the pain like the red slice of a knife.

'Since when? Where?'

'I can't talk now. You'll have to call your parents this time.'

'This time?' But the line is already dead.

*

Her parents' landline rings on until her mother's recorded voice announces that the Stevenses are probably out playing golf, please leave a message. They never hear their phone and her mother's mobile will be sitting forgotten at the bottom of a bag. Panic swells in her throat. She tries the only two taxi firms listed in the area. One doesn't answer; the second has a single driver working on a Monday night and he's on an airport run. She can't walk to her parents' and her sister's isn't an option. She's trapped.

Back upstairs, she knocks on Ben's door. It falls out of its catch, swinging open on an empty room, but his clothes are there, folded into neat stacks by the bed. It will be just the two of them tonight in this big, empty house in the middle of nowhere.

In Gabriel and Suzie's room, she sits on the edge of their bed, her sense of transgression warping from a shivery yellow orange into the golden-brown treacle of guilty pleasure. She lets herself imagine Gabriel's naked back arcing like a bridge over Suzie's slight figure. *Mummy and Daddy time*, Daniel had said. Lying back, she thinks about Gabriel's mismatched eyes and the way he'd kept them open as he kissed her. It's possible she'll never see him again.

The rain stops. She's become used to its steady sizzle, and without it, the silence has a stiff waiting-room quality that makes her aware of her own breathing. A door clicks shut somewhere in the house, moving on a draught. She runs downstairs to double-check the laundry door. Passing the kitchen, she realises the window has blown open. As she leans over the sink, reaching for it, she sees the man. Under the willow tree, a dense black shape against the charcoal smudge of shadows. He makes no effort to conceal himself. A sob balls in her throat. From the tilt of his head, she knows he can see her. By the time she has slammed the window shut and locked it, he has disappeared.

Her hands are shaking so hard she presses the wrong number twice as she tries Gabriel's mobile. He won't answer, she tells herself. But he does, after two rings.

'It's me.' She clears her throat. 'Are you coming back tonight?'

'Anna.' The line is bad, his voice segueing in and out. 'Not tonight.'

She pictures Lily in the new poster, sleepy, her smile innocent and trusting. Thinking herself safe. 'Please come back.'

The signal picks up strength, bringing Gabriel in close for a moment, his breathing in her ear. 'What's wrong?'

'Suzie's taken Daniel to the Wells Inn for the night and I'm—'

'I'm glad you called,' he says, interrupting her.

She closes her eyes. He's going to say something tricky but heartfelt; she can hear it in his voice.

'The thing is, Anna, I love Suzie with all my heart.'

'*You* kissed *me.*'

There's a pause, in which she hears her role leading up to the kiss as clearly as if he'd spoken it aloud. A slow red storm gathers, swirling around her like strands of candyfloss, twisting and thickening.

'I shouldn't have,' he says. 'I need to be stronger than that.'

'Is that why you told Suzie? To get rid of me?'

'I haven't said anything ... Anna?' His voice sharpens with horror. 'Does Suzie know?'

The twisted red strands are gone, vivid yellow shock in their place. She presses her palm over her heart.

'But if it wasn't you, who ...'

A mottled plum purple, the colour of a deep bruise, opens before her eyes.

Billie.

She hangs up.

When she was Daniel's age, she caught Billie cracking open her piggy bank with the handle of a kitchen knife. Her reaction was to smash Billie's ceramic castle in return, wild with the hunger for revenge, whilst her sister took one look then ran to get their dad to witness Anna's destructive fit of temper. Getting in there first, devising a strategy to deflect blame, even at the age of twelve.

Making Anna's weakness work in her favour.

She bends over her knees, giving in to her reds with a growl of rage, letting the rusty, bloody flames incinerate everything in her sight, the edges singed with soot.

Her mobile rings again, Gabriel's name on the screen.

'We need to speak, Anna. Come and find me.'

'But where?'

In the pause, she hears him draw on a cigarette. He exhales, long and slow. 'You know where I am. You and Daniel found my camp earlier.'

The phone cuts out before she can ask anything more. She thinks about him smoking. It is Gabriel watching the house at night, not some sinister stranger. All she has to do is stick close to the canal then run through the woods to his camp. There's nothing to fear out there.

In the ashy dusk she can see the willows and the open paddock behind, but the trees of the forest are glued together by shadow, a dark mass waiting for her. April said violent deeds had taken place there, a bad energy left behind.

Of course he's in the bloody forest.

Before she leaves the house, she takes the Tarot deck from her suitcase in the hall and shuffles through the cards, acknowledging the delaying tactic. It doesn't matter what message she divines, it can't keep her safe. She lays a three-card spread on the hallway floor.

Seven of Swords for deception.

The Moon for illusion and losing your way.

The High Priestess for something hidden. Or, the booklet reminds her, for mutual attraction.

With her ceramic frog and Daniel's pencil torch in her pocket, she leaves the house. She doesn't falter until she reaches the end of the canal, where the water gushes underground. A weed with white blossom grows on the mound of earth covering the tunnel entrance, solitary and conspicuous, like flowers on a grave. Beneath her feet, the river that sank into the ground carrying its record of deaths, still feeding everything.

~ 38 ~

The glacial blue green of sincerity

The forest feels different from earlier in the day with Daniel. Viewing it through a child's eyes, it was a place of small wonders. On her own, she notices only the shadows and the relentless crackle of leaves and branches. Rolling her frog in her hand, she picks up speed.

A loud snap to her left makes her start, dropping the frog in the dirt.

'Gabriel?' She doesn't like how pathetic her voice sounds and tries again in a louder, more assertive voice. 'Is that you, Gabriel?'

No answer. What if it isn't Gabriel who's been watching the house at night? She rubs the mud off her frog and walks on. Something hits the back of her heel, making her skip round to face the path behind her. A large stone is lying by her foot.

'Seriously, Gabriel? This isn't funny.'

In reply, another stone launches out from the trees and rolls past her toes. Her body goes rigid, unable to decide whether to run or confront whoever is hiding there. The figure that steps out from behind the trunk of a sprawling oak is too slight to be Gabriel.

'Ben. You little shit. What are you doing here?'

The boy laughs, mimicking her frightened sideways skitter with a falsetto squeal. 'Wondering what you're up to. Looking for Gabriel, are you?'

He shuffles a footstep close and her mouth dries. 'What's wrong with you? Deliberately scaring me when a girl's gone missing. Your ex-girlfriend, in fact.'

'Hardly call her that.' He is no longer laughing, staring down at a collection of small, dirty stones in his palm. The sight of his long, big-knuckled fingers raises a brown mist of disgust, imagining them raking and pawing at Lily.

'And yet you got her pregnant.' She watches the blank space above his head.

He barks out a surprised laugh. 'Oh yeah. Forgot about that.'

But the prickle of colour, faded as it is, is wrong. Where she would have expected defensive reds or pale shame, she finds a faint self-satisfied clover green.

'You *were* the father, weren't you?'

The stones make a gritty, scratching noise as he grinds them together. 'Yeah. What about it?'

Above his head, she can just make out a tangerine ring.

She watches until Ben is out of sight, then breaks into a run. The trees draw in, the path existing only a metre ahead. Past that, there is nothing but nebulous layers of shadow on shadow. Light-headed with adrenalin, she picks up her pace, running on the balls of her feet. She switches on Daniel's torch, but its string of light only illuminates what it touches – segments of crenulated bark, the dirt path a step ahead – turning what remains in darkness darker still.

As her eyes adjust, she settles into her run, the light crunch of grit beneath her feet keeping time. She gives the sinkhole a wide berth. The smell of burning wood reaches her, fresh and acrid. In the clearing, a rope of smoke twists out of the extinguished fire; the hammock and clothing are gone. Gabriel is gone. She let him wait too long. All the fearful thoughts she's been holding back step in with nightmarish suggestions. She's been tricked. Something's happened to Gabriel.

And Lily. What happened to Lily?

Her eyes fill with tears. She listens hard, too afraid to move or shout his name.

Her mobile spins and flicks through her fingers, falling to the ground. Crouching, a hand over her mouth to smother the sound of her breathing, she huddles down in her squat, trying to be small and inconspicuous, a tiny frightened mouse. There's no signal. No matter how many times she presses his number, the connection won't come.

A slow, steady crackle to her right as something starts to close in. A branch snaps like the crack of a starter pistol and she is off, ripping through the undergrowth. The noise of her bolting tears open the forest. Trees loom towards her, the path swerving, sending her knee-deep into bushes, birds swooping at her head. The crater opens its sly mouth, the earth beneath one foot crumbling away, making her stumble. In the corner of her eye something is matching her speed, crashing through the forest just off the path, stealth abandoned, the pursuit in earnest. She can't even scream.

Ahead is the paddock. If she can just reach it.

The thing breaks out of the trees and into her flight path. With a cry, she throws herself off course, no choice but to head away from the field and the house beyond. Her name is being called but she can't break her terrified hurtle until something ropes around her middle, hard as metal chain, cutting into her midriff and stopping her dead. Two hands are knotted against her stomach, Gabriel's voice in her ear.

Gabriel turns her round into a fierce hug. She presses her face into the hard skin of his waterproof, his body heat coming through it, the hammering of his heart against her cheek. He strokes her hair, once, before disengaging, leaving her to sway, weak with the aftershock, a feeble vine after his solidity.

'Can we go home now?' She sounds pitiful.

He shakes his head, his hands on her shoulders in a light and comfortless touch. She looks up at him, and even in the moonless night she can see something is wrong with his face. He winces as she shines Daniel's torch at him, and pushes her hand away, but she's seen enough.

'Is this why you can't come home?'

His head drops, the tips of his fingers feeling out his split eyebrow, the grotesque puff of his right eye. 'Daniel doesn't need to see this.'

'So think about that before you go looking for a fight.' Her words snap out.

'Looking for a fight?' His fingers keep prodding at his injured face as though he could rearrange its distorted putty. 'Is that what Suzie told you?'

Something is circling in her head but she can't quite grasp it; like the shadow of a bird moving across the ground. 'Isn't it true?'

Even in the dark, something about the tilt of his head, the evasive shift of his eyes, sends a ripple of snowflakes through the air. Shame. But there's more to it. She can feel it. 'Who did this to you, Gabriel?'

'Do you really not know?' he says. 'How have you lived in the heart of our family and not worked it out?'

Suzie on the floor in a cage of orange slashes, Daniel's boat smashed to pieces around her. Pinching the lumps out of the butter and flour mixture, clinical in manner, as she talked about Gabriel's temper. Suzie's voice raised, never Gabriel's.

'But your hands,' she says. 'Aren't those fighting injuries?'

He stretches out his fingers with a bitter laugh. 'Sauce-pans, drawers slammed shut. This one...' he points to a thick two-centimetre-long scar between the knuckles of his ring and index fingers, 'tip of the bread knife.'

'It's Suzie, not you.'

Suzie's panic over Daniel's broken boat wasn't fear of Gabriel's reaction but fear of her own behaviour being found out. Her rage makes her look weak, as do the panic attacks that prevent her from driving her son to school. Anna sees Daniel pushing himself between her and Suzie as they'd argued. Saving his mother from her own anger. Protecting Anna.

'I'm so sorry, Gabe.' Inside her surge of indigo is an opal bubble of elation. Suzie's violence releases them from the guilt of that brief kiss. She'd understood from the day she entered the house that she was being asked to take sides. She made the right choice.

He drops his head back, damaged face to the black layer of cloud blocking out the stars and the moon. 'What a mess. I assume she's asked you to leave?'

'By tonight.'

'I'm going to head off for a few days.' The way he's looking at her, his voice low, raising a shiver as though he'd stroked his fingers along her skin. She waits for him to ask her along, knowing she'll say yes without hesitation. Sod the consequences. Billie's disapproval no longer matters.

'I'll give you a lift, if you like, to your sister's?'

Toad-skin green, a thick and suffocating pall.

'No thanks,' she manages to say in an even voice. 'It was Billie who told Suzie about us.'

He considers this, then nods. 'Your sister's never liked me.'

When she asks why, he gives an unconcerned shrug. 'No idea. So, where am I going to drop you?'

'My parents' house. Please.' Thirty-two years old and still running home to Mummy and Daddy.

He'll walk her back to the house to collect her belongings,

he says, and then on to where his car is parked; concerning himself only with the practical element of her leaving his house for good. When his fingers brush hers, she thinks he might take her hand, but he doesn't. It's irrelevant how he feels about her or that he kissed her. He is held firmly in place by the threads of his life. Unless she can find a way to break them.

'Suzie says she gave you an alibi for the night Lily disappeared.'

'Yes. She did.' He stops walking. 'As soon as she discovered Lily hadn't come home, she wanted to go to the police. I asked her to wait. I was so sure...' his breath cuts out, 'that Lily would be home before the end of the day. But Suzie was in a wild panic. I don't know why, because Lily stayed out sometimes.' His words are stilted with the effort of maintaining a calm, measured manner. 'Suzie pretended she was off to the shops the next morning but went to the police instead. She came home acting like she'd done me a favour.'

'But it does sound strange, Gabe. Climbing trees at night.' She's not concerned with the answer. All she wants is for him to press his mouth on hers again.

'The moon was as big as a television screen that night. I'd never seen anything like it.' He inhales, face angled to catch a scent. 'The forest is full of magic when it's dark. Can't you feel it?'

She breathes in. The air tastes of wet tea leaves and mushrooms and mud. It fails to raise the peach and coral candy stripe of wonder, a rare favourite.

'Why didn't you go to the police and tell them the truth?'

'How could I do that, Anna? She's Daniel's mother. And her lies made me look guilty.'

He slips his hand into her jacket pocket and she wonders what he's doing until he takes out Daniel's torch. Switching it on, he passes it to her, turning it on himself. In the light, his one good eye is a startling forest green.

'Read me,' he says. 'Ask me if I've done anything wrong.'

She steps back to widen the halo of light around his head. 'Ask me.'

'OK. Have you done anything wrong?'

'I've done nothing wrong,' Gabriel says, and the colour rising from his crown is the glacial blue green of a mountain lake. The cold purity of truth.

39

Libido red

His hand finds hers as the moon breaks through the cloud, the crowns of the trees and the paddock turning milky white; the night another world where only the two of them exist. She slows her pace, in no hurry to reach the house. Once they've crossed the canal, he heads for the garden wall and rolls a ragged string of tobacco into a cigarette paper.

'I didn't know you smoked?'

'Only when I'm banished,' he says. 'For her handiwork.'

He lights a match, the end of the roll-up clamped between his swollen lips as he draws on it.

'You've been watching the house at night, haven't you?' she says.

'Ben's not a whole lot of use.'

Once she's collected her suitcase, it takes them twenty minutes to reach Gabriel's car, but to her relief, they avoid the forest, keeping to the lane until they find the lay-by with a short track leading off-road. At the end of it, the Defender is half hidden by a scrub of bushes and small trees. As they drive, she winds down the window, closing her eyes as the air rushes in, stagnant with unspilled rain. She thinks about all the questions she could ask, those missing details, but each one would return them to the lives waiting outside this moment, so she says nothing.

From a late-night garage, she buys flowers for her mother. Only four bouquets of gerberas remain, in libido red, wistful pink and yearning fuchsia, their colours making her hot and restless, despite the brown fringes of their turning petals.

'What do you think?'

'Not bad for garage flowers.' His glance is swift, uninterested, and she is struck, as she often is, by how unmoved people are by colour. At this moment, with the flowers making her feel sweet and heady, she is sorry for everyone else. Gabriel is in no mood to talk, so she gives in to fantasy. She pictures him on the forest floor, waiting for her to climb on top of him. His naked chest, the polished rock of his shoulders, the roller-coaster dip from ribcage to pelvis. The two of them rolling on the bare earth, grinding themselves into mud and sharp stones.

Soon he'll drop her at her parents' and drive away.

What is kept inside her head hurts no one.

Her dad's car is in the drive, the same pristine Mercedes he has lovingly tended these last fifteen years. It is a biscuit beige, the colour of complacency and boredom. Nothing changes. Her life is a miniature Ferris wheel. Parked on the kerb behind the Mercedes is a small black rental car with a Hertz sticker in the window.

'OK?' Gabriel says when she sighs. She'd hoped, seeing as it isn't the weekend, their house would be free of guests. He pulls up outside the neighbour's house, the Lawrences', whose front lawn hasn't changed since she last lived in Wonersh Close, with its square of grass and the stone bird bath they never fill because Mrs Lawrence is afraid of mould.

'I won't get out,' he says, pointing to his face. 'Don't want to terrify the neighbourhood kids.'

He makes no move to touch her, so with a quick wave, she climbs out, takes her suitcase and refuses to look back as he drives away. With the flowers clamped in one arm, she checks the time, then rings the bell. It's gone ten, so the guests will have eaten, unless her father cracked open a bottle or two of fizz beforehand. At least there'll be leftovers; her mother always cooks to feed double the number of guests. She rings again. Through the frosted-glass panel she sees the sitting room door open and recognises her mother's shape: short, slim, with the blow-dried bouffant of hair that she and Billie secretly refer to as the tea cosy.

It's rare to see her mother look startled. 'Annie, what are you doing here? We didn't know you were coming.'

'I left messages on the answer machine.' She lowers her armful of flowers. 'I tried Billie first, but she's unavailable. Is it inconvenient?' She knows how she sounds, silly and plaintive as a child, but her mother smiles, shaking her head as she pulls her into a hug, the flowers' cellophane wrapper crackling between them.

'Of course not. We've got someone visiting. But I've made enough curry to feed an entire country.'

'Is that my youngest I hear?' Her father appears in the doorway, another figure following behind.

'Annie, do you remember Lauritz?' her mother is saying across a huge distance.

40

Regret is a fine blueberry powder

She drops the flowers on the kitchen table, presses her shaking hands flat against the surface and closes her eyes. Those few minutes face to face with Lauritz are blurry and fragmented, as if they took place under a strobe light. She knows she spoke and that her father was saying something about Klaus and a heart attack and Lauritz had radiated slate-blue grief but still smiled deep into her eyes.

Her mother comes into the kitchen and asks if she wants a hand with the flowers.

'No, I'm fine. I'll grab a shower though before we eat, if that's OK?'

They haven't eaten yet; her father's G&Ts had been hitting the spot.

How will she sit opposite Lauritz after all these years and eat and speak like a normal human being?

Her mother sets out a couple of vases and a pair of scissors and leaves her to the empty kitchen with the quiet tick of the wall clock and the gurgling rice cooker. She fills the vases with water, taking care not to spatter the counter, trying to draw calm and serenity from precise action. Having sliced open the first cellophane wrapper, she shakes a single gerbera from the bunch. The head pitches forward, broken-spined. The next flower does the same, the crush of her arms having snapped every one of the thick, velvety stalks.

They are already seated at the dinner table at the far end of the sitting room, the conversation drifting to a halt as she comes in. The shock of seeing Lauritz hits her again and she can't look in his direction as she sits down. Her hair, still wet from the shower, has dripped on her coral blouse, leaving dark orange stains, the back already soaked through, making her skin itch. She can feel him watching her whilst her parents busy them-selves opening bottles of Tiger and dolloping rice onto plates.

They know, she thinks. Her parents know what happened between her and Lauritz. She can't bear to imagine how they might have discovered it. She takes a deep breath. At the very least, she owes it to them to diffuse the tension. 'I'm so sorry to hear about your father, Lauritz.'

Saying his name aloud ignites a powder trail of memories, stirring an ache in the pit of her stomach.

'Thank you, Anna. At least when it happened, he was doing what he loved the best.'

'Working, no doubt?' her father says, nodding in agreement with his own suggestion.

'No,' Lauritz says, and she recognises the quirk in the corner of his mouth, a precursor to mischief. 'He was in bed with my mother.'

Whether or not this is true, there's a finger snap of silence before her parents erupt into scandalised laughter. Lauritz grins, bowing his head. Afraid to meet his eye, Anna rips off a chunk of home-made naan. Doughy and undercooked, like a wedge of Play-Doh, it absorbs her saliva and seems to expand in her mouth. She chews through it with dogged determination, unable to focus on the easy chatter around her. But when his attention is elsewhere, she takes him in, reacquainting herself.

He is tall and broad in an elegant, understated way compared to Gabriel's unrefined, organic strength. Clean-shaven, clean nails. His hair is a little longer than before but still doesn't reach his shirt collar. Thick as ever, though its sunshine vigour has faded to the colour of sand under a winter sky. His eyes are the happy blue of postcard seas and whilst this is a good colour, it had always been about the way his gaze made her feel; his eyes shining a light on all that was good and beautiful about her.

He is saying something about his father, but she can't listen to his words, only his voice. She knows this voice; its timbre is unremarkable, neither light nor low, and yet she hears it in the deep pit of her stomach, in the hollow between her legs.

His accent is still strong, trimming away the frills of the English language so that everything he says sounds to the point, essential.

Her mother's curry is overloaded with chilli, her mouth flayed within a few mouthfuls, a light perspiration breaking out on her forehead. She shovels it in, between mounds of rice and gulps of beer, listening. He's here to close the UK arm of his father's business. After this visit, there'll be no reason for him to return.

'I can't believe you've left it so long to visit us, Lauritz,' her mother says. 'It must be four or five years.'

'Six.' He meets Anna's eyes as if this might mean something to her.

'That long? You were here, Anna, remember?' Her mother is trying to draw her into the conversation. 'With that lovely teacher boyfriend you had at the time. Graham?'

'Michael.' Lauritz hasn't been back since then. She pushes the curry and rice to one side and closes her cutlery on the plate, unable to continue eating.

'Well, Lauritz is a workaholic like his dad,' her father says.

Her parents' conversation stops and starts, pouncing on

a safe topic before pausing to find the next plank across the void of unmentionable things. One of them being his wife and the child they had been expecting when he wrote his first devastating letter.

'You look well, Anna,' Lauritz says in a brief lull.

'Thank you. You too.' She spoons mango chutney onto her plate in an effort to avoid his eyes but then can't resist a glance at the space above his head. What colour had she expected? Where there were once snaking bands of magenta, she sees only the dried rose of a remembered love, and over it all, the fine blueberry powder of regret. He had spoken so often of his wife's desperate need for a baby, of the perfunctory, mechanised sex, the joy sucked out of everything. She hadn't seen his equal longing for a child because she hadn't wanted to.

She'd read his Tarot cards and the Fool, with its promise of new beginnings, had appeared repeatedly. She'd allowed herself to believe that the golden hope rising from his crown was because of her but perhaps, whilst she'd been hinting at a blossoming relationship, he had been praying for a child.

Wiping his mouth on his napkin, he picks up his cutlery and she takes another opportunity to study him. Over the years, her memory of him has become two-dimensional, a paper cut-out of the man all other men failed to live up to. She holds Gabriel up to him, and finds to her horror that it is Gabriel who shrinks.

Lauritz is back, flesh and blood filling him out again.

After dinner, she pleads a headache and leaves them to coffee and mints, unable to face his proximity on the sofa. She leans against the door of her childhood bedroom and her colours move through the air like a shoal of tropical fish, swooping and breaking to escape a predator.

Six years ago, this same event had taken place, except that

time she hadn't been alone when she arrived unannounced. She'd met Michael in a coffee shop, started talking, and hours had turned to days. A kind of pirate's-treasure elation had propelled them forward. They couldn't believe their luck at having found each other. Come and meet my parents, she'd begged one Sunday afternoon, and he'd laughed. *Ten days in?* When she'd retreated from the suggestion, he'd grown serious, insisting he wanted to meet them. It felt like a threshold moment. She'd arrived at her parents' house convinced she was about to embark on a new life, only to find Lauritz there. Michael recognised it before she did and left in the night.

She empties her bag onto the bed she's had since she was a child. Her sister's double bed remains along with her desk, but all Billie's childhood belongings have been boxed or sent to charity. In pointed contrast, Anna's old bedroom stays trapped in time, a safety net to catch her when she falls. The assumption that she *will* fall in the ready-made bed and dust-free surfaces.

A reel of memories waits for her on the narrow mattress: his hand running the length of her body, painting a streak of shimmering magenta, his touch making her beautiful.

Watch my hand, Anna, he'd said. *Watch where it travels.*

By the foot of the bed is the wooden cradle her grandma gave her, teddies and bald-headed dolls crushed in, bulging over the sides like a sagging bouquet. She tips them out, along with the thin foam mattress, and finds her old photographs.

She flips through them. Some faces come with a follow-on story, others she can't put a name to. There's one of Jonah and her sister, newly dating, sitting on the sofa, not quite touching, their faces plump and shiny with youth. What she's looking for is herself, nineteen-year-old Anna. She finds the picture. She's staring at the camera, a secret in her half-smile, new knowledge glowing in her eyes. Lauritz hadn't been her first, but she'd grown up in his arms. There are two shadowy figures in the background – Billie, posing behind her left shoulder though the flash hadn't reached her, and Lauritz. His face is in profile, looking away, trying to avoid capture. Even in shadow, the fact of his youth hits her. Younger than she is now, Lauritz had been standing on the apex of his life, the steep side of youth having been scaled, the descent not yet embarked upon; steady in his perfect moment.

She hadn't stood a chance. Any more than Lily had.

She wonders if Gabriel has any idea how the girl had felt about him. With a shiver, she relives the crush of his arms as he'd caught her in the woods, the way he'd held on until she'd stopped struggling, his heart beating against her back. She'd seen a documentary once of a cheetah catching a baby antelope. First the ferocious bucking, then, hindquarters trapped in the hunter's jaws, a beat of stillness in which both animals stopped wrestling and caught their breath. The moment of acknowledgement. Only now Lauritz's voice is rising up the stairs, saying his goodnights as he makes his way to the room that was once Billie's.

41

Dread's rusty sword

One o'clock in the morning in her parents' home, the time when, thirteen years ago, her door handle would twist, with such oiled lack of effort it seemed to move of its own accord. Sometimes she'd been awake, watching for it. Other times, it would be the shift in the mattress, the sudden naked draught as her covers lifted, and then the warmth and solidity of him, the hairs of his legs against her thighs, his breath on her neck.

She tries not to stare at the door, but her eyes won't close. Lying in bed this past hour and a half, curled around her cramping stomach, the spicy food she'd pushed down bulging and writhing through her digestive system.

He won't come, she tells herself, her body strung with tension.

Sleep, when it finally arrives, brings snatches of dream, hallucinogenic snapshots of naked skin and intertwined limbs, the faces interchangeable; sometimes Lauritz, sometimes Gabriel. She rouses to imaginary noises, then wakes at one point to the noise of a storm, convinced there's another body in the bed beside her, only to find she is clutching her own arm. Lightning flickers through the thin curtains, thunder like a beer barrel rolling down the road.

It's still raining by early morning, when she gives up on sleep, flattened by the knowledge that Lauritz hadn't come.

There is nothing she can do about her puffy eyes and limp hair. She sips hot water and lemon, staring at the garden through the kitchen's French doors. Half the patio is under water.

This time Billie isn't going to save her. She's not sure how they're going to move past her sister's betrayal. Her stomach lurches as the kitchen door opens, but it's only her mother, looking harried as she always does when woken too early, clutching the front of her dressing gown.

She holds out the house phone. 'I was knocking on your bedroom door but there was no answer.'

The thought that her mother may have done the same thing all those years ago and drawn an uncomfortable conclusion makes her feel a little sick.

'It's Suzie.' Her mother puts the receiver on the table. 'Apparently your mobile is off.'

She hasn't told her parents the reason she was asked to leave the O'Keefes'. With an encouraging nod, her mother leaves the kitchen, not quite shutting the door and Anna knows she'll listen from the corridor.

'I need you to come back. Now. For Daniel's sake.'

Suzie's voice goes through her like the slash of a rusted sword, sharp and high-pitched with urgency. She gets to her feet. 'What's happened?'

'Half the square in Kirkley has collapsed because of the rain.'

'Is anyone hurt. What—'

Suzie interrupts. 'They found something.'

From the corner of her eye, she sees Lauritz appear in the doorway, watching her.

'What?' Dread dries her mouth.

'I don't want to talk about it over the phone. Can you come back? For Daniel's sake,' Suzie adds again.

She looks up and meets Lauritz's concern, realises she's been pacing the kitchen, her hand in her hair. 'My parents aren't really up yet. I'll come as soon as I can.'

When she hangs up, Lauritz offers her a lift. She notices how tired he looks.

42

Placid greens

Lauritz looks ridiculous in the confined space of the rental
car, his long legs jammed up under the steering wheel.
He winds down the window to release an elbow, and the air
rushes in, carrying the smell of his shower across to her. She'd
forgotten how he always smelt fresh and clean. As she clicks
in her seat belt, careful not to touch him by accident, she sees
the wet curl of his hair behind his ear and down the nape of
his neck and remembers how it felt under her fingers. She lets
the seat belt retract.

'Wait. Stop.'

He pulls over by the sign for Wonersh Close. 'Are you
OK?'

'Give me a minute.' *You and me in this tiny space.* 'I need to
get my head together.'

'Tell me what's happening?'

She shakes her head. 'I wouldn't know where to start.'

'Have you eaten today?'

The notion of food seems ridiculous. 'No.'

'Maybe we should eat some breakfast first then?'

She shakes her head again, and then it lands on her, the
full weight of her restless night, the shock of seeing Lauritz,
Gabriel's smashed face, the dread of what has been found. The

blood drains from her cheeks and she lurches over her knees, head in her arms, until she stops feeling faint.

Lauritz waits for her to compose herself. He doesn't try to touch her.

What throws her as they arrive at the O'Keefes' house is the lack of activity. She'd been picturing police cars, a continuous trample of strangers, horror tourists on the towpath, iPhones raised and ready. The storm has turned the lane into a silty ribbon, whilst the canal has swollen over its brick lip, sending liquid tentacles through the grass.

Gabriel's Defender is there, Detective Adeyemi's car behind it, but the front door is shut and the curtains are drawn in the sitting room. Lauritz gets out and opens her door.

'Do you want me to come inside with you?'

'No, I'm fine.' The front door opens. Gabriel, with Daniel in his arms, stands in the doorway, leaving her no choice but to get out. As Lauritz turns to go, she remembers to thank him for the lift, feeling herself pulled between two opposing forces: Lauritz moving away, Gabriel pulling her in. He comes out to meet her along the path, Daniel still wrapped tight about him. When he glances in Lauritz's direction, she catches a fleeting moment of calculation, a thin shoot of curious verdigris scrolling off his crown.

'Thanks for coming back.' He lowers Daniel, who resists being released, his fingers locking about his father's neck.

'What's happened?' Anna mouths the words above the little boy's head, but Gabriel puts a finger to his lips. In the light of day, his face looks less raw. His eye has opened a slit; the gash running from his lip to his nose has sealed under a scab that tugs at the corner of his mouth.

'They found Lily's shoes.' It's Daniel who answers, and she

is disconcerted by his absence of colour. As though he were reciting a plot from a story book.

She meets Gabriel's eyes, but all she sees is utter weariness.

'We were wondering if you could take Daniel somewhere for a few hours?'

Daniel takes her hand and they watch Gabriel retreat into the quiet, unlit house. The sky bulges with fresh rain clouds, and neither she nor Daniel is wearing a coat or appropriate footwear. The little boy has his Superman flip-flops on and her plimsolls already have a tidemark where the water has soaked into the pink fabric. When she turns away from the house, she sees Lauritz's rental car waiting just past the drive. He leans across to the open passenger window. 'Is it all OK? Your mother will ask me.'

'Where are you from?' Daniel says.

'Denmark. The land of Vikings and butter.'

'We're fine, thank you.' Anna gives Daniel's hand a little shake. 'How about the playground. A little birdie told me you love the swings.'

The boy folds his arms, tucking his hands beneath his armpits, reminding her of Ben in her room that night. 'I want to see the big hole where they found Lily's shoes. The pavilion almost fell into it.'

'It's on the news,' Lauritz says, and he opens the passenger door.

The road leading into Kirkley is cordoned off by the narrow bridge. Parked cars line the grass verges, which are disintegrating under the churn of wheels, mud slicks smeared across the road. Lauritz executes a tricky U-turn, his forearm resting on Anna's seat as he twists to look out of the rear window. She inches her shoulder downwards, away from his dangling hand, the swing of the car threatening contact.

Daniel begs them to stop, pointing to three people walking in single file past the police tape. Anna glances at Lauritz, who says, *Why not?* and she wishes she'd told him about Lily on the journey over. What if it isn't just her shoes they've found? The thought makes her jittery, tears not far behind. She doesn't know the girl and yet the drama of it is a tidal wave sweeping her away.

They park and walk along the middle of the road to avoid the muddy streams on the verges. Lauritz and Daniel are chatting, the boy's words rushing out, breathless and punctuated with sudden, nervous laughter.

Lauritz, walking beside her as if he'd never left.

In the centre of the village, fire engines and police cars block the road outside the tea shops. The square has been taped off, the pavilion conspicuous and deserted, the focus of activity to its left, where the roof of a police tent rises above the crowd. Everyone stares in the same direction, their bodies packed together, a slight shift and crane of their heads as they search out a better view. Light-headed, she stops walking.

'Anna?' Lauritz takes hold of her shoulder as if to keep her from collapsing, their first physical contact in thirteen years.

'Some of the trees have shrunk,' Daniel says, teetering on his toes.

There's a gap in the line of oaks, the leafy canopy having dropped in one place, the branches fanning out over the roof of the forensic tent. A uniformed man ducks his head beneath the jut of a thick bough as he opens the canvas door.

'Wait here with Lauritz,' she tells Daniel and pushes her way into the crowd, ignoring the tut and glare as she forces a path to the edge of the cordoned-off area. A crater like the one in the woods has opened in the ground a few metres from the pavilion, swallowing up two of the trees. The oaks have fallen towards each other, their trunks crossing in the middle.

'X marks the spot,' a familiar voice says in her ear.

She glances round to find a grim-faced April.

'It's a . . .' she tries to recall the name Daniel had given, 'a sinkhole.'

'That would be the scientific name. I'd be tempted to call it an act of God.' April draws her away from the crowd and lowers her voice. 'Lily's trainers were found, tied together by the laces, inside the hole.'

'But how did they get there?'

'Gabriel says the hole's most likely been caused by flooding underground,' April says. 'Somehow her shoes got into the waterways underneath the village. But they could have come from the river outside town or . . .'

'Or the Petrifying Well.' Anna meets April's eye. 'Have they found her? Tell me the truth.'

'Not yet.'

Daniel shouldn't be here. She can see him from the corner of her eye, head bowed whilst Lauritz crouches down to speak to him.

'You've known all along, haven't you?' The placid greens above April's head strike her as an outrage; the woman's detachment in the face of what is happening. 'Despite the prayers and the light to guide Lily home. It's a load of bullshit. You know she's never coming back.' She stops talking, because there's a danger she'll start to cry.

'I don't know anything of the sort,' April says.

Before Anna can reply, someone knocks into her, pushing her to the side. Margaret, sobbing wildly, slings her arms around April's neck. 'Have they found her? Is it Lily?'

She leaves April to comfort Margaret. From the sombre look on Lauritz's face, she guesses Daniel has told him about Lily. She takes the boy's limp hand and hurries him away from the square. She keeps wanting to say *It's OK*, but it isn't. When she suggests they go and see Lucas, she pretends not to notice the further slump in his small frame.

She needs Billie. They'll shout, they'll cry, and life can move on. She needs her sister back.

As they reach the bridge, she looks back at the square where the crowd watch the police looking in the wrong place. Sometime soon they'll work their way to the Petrifying Well, where people once brought their keepsakes, the things they couldn't let go of, to be turned into stone.

43

Appalled barbecue-sauce brown

Lauritz agrees to drive them to Billie's. As Anna gives him directions, her voice cracks, the threat of tears rising again. Catching it, he looks across at her.

'Billie and I have fallen out.'

He takes her hand and she tries to ignore the soft pastels of his sympathy, those neutral tones more painful than a slap. 'What happened?'

She hesitates. 'We both behaved badly. It seems neither of us has really grown up.' *Billie still needs to be the goody two-shoes and I'm still messing about with married men.* 'My head understands what she did, but still.' It was the piggy bank all over again. Billie had turned Anna into the enemy so that Suzie would never listen to anything she had to say now. Battle strategy, that was all. Not even personal.

'Come in,' she says as they pull up outside Billie's. His presence had always woken up her parents' house, her dad cracking jokes, her mother opening the port. Billie teasing him, pitting her superior vocabulary against his, whilst Lauritz, unfazed, swatted away her provocations with his easy laugh and quick tongue. 'Billie would love to see you again.'

He sends her a quick smile as he shakes his head. 'They're waiting for me at my father's company.'

He gets out of the car, a regretful blue-grey coming off him in waves. 'I leave on Monday,' he says. 'I hope you will meet with me one more time. Then we can talk together.'

'Good idea.' But she won't meet him again. She doesn't want the details of his life, and when it comes to her turn, he'll hear the emptiness and know it's because of him. She gives him a hug. The wide hoop of his arms barely touches her.

Jonah opens the door before she has a chance to knock. 'Billie's not here. I told you.'

She blinks at his sharp tone, the sizzle of reds and oranges aimed at her. 'Where is she? I need to speak to her.'

He looks past her shoulder, his eyes following Lauritz's car. 'I can't tell you.'

The air catches fire. 'You have no idea what Billie has done to me. You—'

'She told Suzie you kissed her husband.'

Daniel's hand tightens around Anna's fingers as he stares up at her. She catches Jonah's flash of apologetic blue as he looks at the boy. Then he calls back into the house. 'Lucas. A friend's here to see you.'

Daniel drops her hand, stepping sideways to stand alone. The play of colour above his head is the same as the day on the swings when he urged her to push harder as he tried to break through his fear. It makes her want to swoop him up and run.

Lucas comes skidding around the corner in his socks, stopping dead as he sees Daniel. Brown contempt curls off his head as though he smells something rotten.

'Run along, boys,' Jonah says, and Lucas turns away, wearing his disgruntlement like a big sweeping cloak.

She catches hold of Daniel's shoulders and whispers in his ear, '*Seven* years old.'

When the boys have gone, Jonah leads her into the kitchen, where takeaway boxes lie open on the table with half-eaten pizza crusts and crushed cans of Coke. Until then, she'd suspected Billie was hiding upstairs. He stacks the boxes, then sits at the table without offering her a chair or a drink.

'OK, so I messed up,' she says. 'But do you have any idea what Billie's been doing? She was terrorising Lily. All the while pretending to be the girl's friend. Her *mentor*, for fuck's sake.'

'Anna, please.' He drops his head, holding up a hand, defeated. 'She's been trying to make up for her actions. They've been so passive, the O'Keefes. They wouldn't speak to the press or the local news stations. It was Billie who organised three days of search parties to comb the area. Did you know that?'

She pauses, taking this in. 'No. Why hasn't she—'

'And the poster? Who do you think made and distributed the poster?'

Fatigue sweeps through Anna's body. She pulls out a chair and faces Jonah over the takeaway boxes. 'Why don't I know any of this? Billie gave me the impression she hardly knew the O'Keefes.'

His helpless little shrug fills her vision with red nettle rash.

'And why did she hate Lily so much?' she says. 'Why don't we talk about *that*?'

Jonah avoids her eyes, squeezing an open pot of barbecue sauce, an appalled russet brown. It gives a viscous bulge, threatening to spill over.

With a sigh, he tosses the dip inside a pizza box. 'Lily reminded her of you. That's what she hated.'

The idea is so ludicrous she almost laughs but then she sees his earnest, unhappy face.

'I think Billie *did* see similarities between me and Lily. That's why she tried to help the girl. She was trying to keep Lily on the right path.'

Jonah looks away, refusing to listen, determined to believe the nonsense Billie has fed him to cover up her behaviour.

Anna narrows her eyes, watching him through a screen of fine orange sand.

'Jonah. You're effectively saying my sister hates me.'

He still doesn't react.

'Which is ridiculous.' Orange darkens to red. 'Saying Billie hates me is . . . is like saying she hates her own hand. It's—'

The kitchen door opens, bouncing against the counter. Jonah straightens, a puff of green relief above his head, rescued from the conversation. Lucas stalks in, head down, his jaw jutting, two furious red spots on either cheek as he tries not to cry. He comes to stand by his father, who puts a distracted arm around his waist. Daniel wanders in, stopping by the doorway, apparently captivated by the wall calendar with June's frog-eyed pug in a party hat.

'Are you hungry, boys?' Jonah says. Lucas shakes his head, his mouth in such a tight scowl it reminds Anna of a dried apricot.

'Can we go home now?' Daniel says, meeting her eye with a glimmer of a smile, a victorious parrot-green feather stuck in his crown.

'I think that's probably a good idea,' Jonah says, still not meeting her eye.

44

Heartsick indigo

They walk to the village green and stand by the Moon Hare sign. The plaque makes a metallic caw as it moves in the wind, the hare's goggle eyes watching them.

'Is someone coming to get us, Anna?'

She chews her bottom lip, going through options and scoring them out one by one. She can't face her parents. She doesn't have a number for Lauritz. Gabriel has bigger things to concern himself with. Suzie isn't even a consideration. She can't think straight, still seething over the conversation with Jonah. He'd like to believe Billie's problem with Lily was somehow Anna's fault. Otherwise he might have to admit that New Jonah quite enjoys the flirtatious attention of young girls and it makes his wife feel crap.

'I think we're going to walk. Or maybe there's a bus.' They stare along the deserted road, the houses flanking the green empty in the middle of a working day. 'Walking it is.'

'My house is a really long way from here.'

'Then we'd better get going.'

When Daniel takes her hand, obedient and uncomplaining, it hurts deep in her chest. She stops to pull him into a tight hug. 'You know who you remind me of?'

'Who?'

'Superman. Not because you tried to fly off the swings – I

279

think we'll leave the flying thing to him – but because you're strong and brave. That makes you a superhero.'

She kisses his cheek and takes his cold hand in hers again. They walk on.

'You'll need a superhero name, of course.'

'Super-Dan,' he says, his steps turning into hops.

'Sounds like Superman's little brother. Fantastic Mister Dan?'

He stops, holding up a finger as though testing the breeze. 'Dan-Fantastic.'

'Love it.'

'I can handle a poo-head like Lucas.'

'Of course you can, Dan-Fantastic.' She laughs, despite the ridge of unspilled tears in her throat. This is no time for weakness. 'The world is full of poo-heads. Sometimes even the people we love the most.'

'My mum can be a poo-head,' he says, testing out the idea, then adds hastily, 'But I still love her a lot.'

They've been walking for half an hour, the village and pavements left behind. The road is narrow, with blind bends that drivers take at hurtling speeds. Daniel keeps slipping, his flip-flops coated with mud. The roar of an approaching car makes Anna step off the road, pulling the little boy further back into the undergrowth. Her right foot is swallowed up, water circling her ankle. As the car slings round the corner, she turns her back to the road, bracing for the filthy spray off its wheels.

A few metres ahead, it grinds to a shuddering halt and she realises it's Gabriel's Defender. Getting out of the vehicle, he picks his son up in a fierce embrace.

'Were you looking for us, Daddy?'

Gabriel gives Anna's mud-soaked foot a quizzical grin, a fleeting moment of humour before the pall of midnight blue drops over him again. 'Yes.' But the word rises on an orange bubble.

Getting into the car, both she and Daniel notice Gabriel's rucksack on the back seat, the fastenings loosened to the maximum, straining to close.

She closes her eyes as the car bumps off the verge. 'Gabriel?'

He gives a distracted hum in response.

'How well do you know Billie?'

His colours withdraw, but not before a handful of ash blows across his crown. 'Not very well.'

She can't stare openly at him. He'll think she's looking behind his words because she doesn't believe him; one of the many reasons she never tells people about her synaesthesia. 'Did you and my sister ever...' She can't finish the sentence, the notion too outrageous. Gabriel takes his gaze off the road, catching the implication.

'God, no.' The smudge above his head, the appalled colour of barbecue sauce, confirms it. It hurts her, picturing Billie stabbing merciless fingers into her own belly and waist.

If there's a black store of hatred hidden in Billie, it's for herself, not Anna.

Billie doesn't hate her.

And yet for the first time in her life, her own colours disagree with her. There's a specific colour and shape for when a person is sick to their heart. Heartsick. A majestic, cavernous indigo that could swallow you whole.

Gabriel slows as they approach his house. A burgundy Jaguar is parked outside.

'Grandma and Grandpa are here.' Daniel opens his door, but his gaze returns to his father's rucksack. 'Are you going away again, Daddy?'

'Just for a day or two,' Gabriel says, and it is good that his son can't see the clementine circle rising away like a smoke ring.

'Surely you're needed at home?' Anna can't be under the same roof as Suzie without Gabriel there.

'Wait there a moment, Anna,' he says, getting out of the car to hug his son. He releases Daniel, then pulls him back into a second, desperate clutch until the boy starts to wriggle, giving his father a solicitous pat.

When he sits back in the driver's seat, dense, bloodied purples pack against his body like coffin silk. 'The trainers they found? I bought them for Lily. For her nineteenth birthday.'

She gives his hand a squeeze. There's no comfort in words. Her touch acts like a switch and he leans in with a swift motion that catches her by surprise, one hand behind her head, bringing her in to a hard, dry kiss. When he sits back, there's a discrepancy between the fervour of his kiss and his colours, the hot crimsons missing. Given the circumstances, it isn't surprising, but the kiss doesn't feel the same for her either, because everything is indigo. And Lauritz is back.

All those years, running into the arms of other men, never finding what she's looking for because it is always and only Lauritz. As she looks across at Gabriel, she still feels the same draw of attraction but through a screen, as if a paper partition has been placed between them, dimming the light. It ignites a small, panicked flame in her stomach. She has to hold on to Gabriel. He is real, whilst Lauritz is a dream of what might have happened in her best possible life.

'I can't be in that house with Suzie if you're not there,' she says.

He's staring into the rear-view mirror. She can't tell if he's watching the house or meeting his own eyes. 'Suzie has kicked me out. It's not because of what happened between you and me.

We're way past that. I need you to look after Daniel. Suzie's on the edge. It's only a matter of time before she lashes out at him.'

The thought opens a cold pit in Anna's stomach. She remembers the little boy sitting on her bed as she wrestled with her migraine, massaging a red mark on his arm like he could scrub it away.

Leaning his head back, Gabriel closes his eyes. 'Just a few days, until things settle, and then you can bring Dan to see me.'

He doesn't open his eyes as she gets out of the car. By the time she reaches the front door, he's gone.

A few days, for Daniel's sake, and for Gabe's.

Everything appears through a burnt-cinnamon lens as she walks into the hall, dreading the reception waiting for her. From the sitting room there's a murmur of voices like an untuned radio station. She takes a deep breath and enters the room.

Suzie is sitting on the edge of the sofa, her knees pressed together, a crushed tissue in her hand. Her parents flank her, the mother a bent stick of a woman, brittle and aggrieved, the father large and red-faced, his bald head gleaming in the light from the bay window. The room is overheated, a stew of sweat, clashing perfumes and recycled breath. Distress, dread, anger, all those seething, charcoal-edged colours reducing everyone to rubble. Daniel has wriggled himself between his grandfather and grandmother. He lifts his fingertips off his lap in a surreptitious wave.

Suzie greets her with a blank, flat look as though she is a stranger. 'You came back.'

Daniel climbs onto his grandfather's shoulders, tapping out a light pat-a-cake on his bald head, monkeying around to break up the room's atmosphere.

'Dan's fine here with us right now,' Suzie says, dismissing her.

Upstairs, the door to the box room is open, the bed stripped to its mattress, no sign of Ben's belongings; a single pinpoint of light in the dark.

She drops her bag on the floor in Lily's room. She has failed to escape.

Once the Jaguar has left and Daniel is sleeping, she ventures downstairs. The smell of fried food lingers, but the kitchen is empty, all evidence of dinner cleared away. There's an odd scraping noise coming from somewhere.

'Suzie?'

The noise stops, then resumes with increased tempo. She finds Suzie in the sitting room, kneeling on the hearth, her hands and face up close to the fireplace's wooden surround as though she is trying to peep through a hole. White scraps of paint like a fine scattering of snow lie on the hearth. A quick glance about the room, a sweep for clues, but there's nothing amiss or out of place: just a plate of plain crackers with a large dollop of butter on the coffee table.

'What are you doing?'

Suzie sits back on her heels, lowering her arms, a kitchen knife, blunt-tipped and glistening with melted butter, grasped in both hands. 'I always preferred the plain wood,' she says. 'Gabriel insisted on painting it with thick white paint. It suffocates the flowers.'

In the silence that follows, Anna prepares herself for the inevitable confrontation, but when Suzie glances over, the simmering red anger doesn't hurtle in her direction. Perhaps in the scale of things, a stray kiss is a pebble before a mountain.

Suzie gets up, choosing a random spot in the centre of the mantelpiece. Positioning the knife-tip, shoulders bunched, elbows splayed at an awkward angle, she scrapes away. A careless nudge to push aside the photo frames nearest her. One clatters to the floor, but the knife shaves on, gouging a little deeper, chipping off a large splinter. Her face and body are pinched with effort. The harder she grinds, the darker the red fanning out of her, like blood in water.

'Gabriel's gone. Off searching for Lily.' She abandons the central section and moves to the opposite side. 'All those trips away pretending he's looking for work when really he just can't accept she's gone. All lies.'

You're the liar, Anna thinks. *He's hiding the evidence of your violence. Protecting you, despite what you do to him.* Aloud she says, 'I think sandpaper would be a better idea.'

'Do you know what people say behind our backs, Anna? That he was fucking Lily and then killed her to shut her up.'

Suzie springs to her feet, her movements picking up speed, her lopsided ponytail shedding hair. With a sharp, martial swipe, she sends half the photographs flying, paying no attention as they hit the floor to the sound of splintering glass.

'And maybe he did. Maybe he fucked her and killed her.'

The reds have blackened, swarming around her. The knife slips and she flinches, clenching her left hand briefly, nothing more than a glance at the bloody-mouthed gash on the edge of her palm.

'Suzie, stop now. Let's do this properly, in the morning.'

'The last time I picked Dan up from school, I heard three bitches having a good old chinwag. *The girl was only fourteen when it started*, one of them said.'

'Gabriel's a good man,' Anna says, but her words are droplets of water against Suzie's storm-broken seas. 'Who cares what the bitches of this world think?'

Her sister being one of them. The thought chokes off her plea.

Back on her knees, Suzie is working the knife in tiny stabs

around the largest rose. With a quiet crack, it breaks away, hits the floor and rolls to a stop in the middle of the room.

'Ha.' She picks it up, bounces it in her bloody palm. 'A dirty snowball.' Then she lobs it with all her might through the open doorway. It cracks against the wall in the corridor with a noise like a pistol shot.

'OK, enough of—' Anna starts to say.

'I'm so done with my life.' Suzie bends over her knees, letting the knife clatter to the hearth. Catching her breath, rage spent. 'If only I could wake up as someone else.'

Anna leaves her there. The wooden rose has made a shallow dent in the plaster, a fretwork of fine cracks spreading out from it. It strikes her as odd that the noise hasn't brought Daniel downstairs. She runs up to his room and finds him awake in bed, driving an orange car along his arm.

'Can I sleep in your bed tonight?' he says in a matter-of-fact voice, travelling the toy car up to his shoulder.

45

Mud and blood resentment

Billie hates her. That's what Jonah implied. Even before she opens her eyes, the pain is there. She's waking to an injury. It doesn't make sense, but there's that circling bird-shadow, the truth waiting to land. Beside her, Daniel stirs and she becomes aware of how hot and uncomfortable she is. His hand is gripping the sleeve of her T-shirt, holding on even as he sleeps. She pushes his damp fringe back and then plants the lightest kiss on his forehead.

It wakes him and he opens his eyes, grinning around his thumb whilst scrubbing away her kiss with the back of his hand. 'Yuck.'

'What would you prefer?' she says. 'A manly shoulder bump?' She nudges his shoulder with hers and he jostles back, laughing. Daniel waking up safe and happy, something salvaged from the wreck of her life.

Suzie walks into the kitchen as Anna is giving Daniel beans on toast for his breakfast. Anna stiffens, preparing for an onslaught of gory reds, but only a faint play of colours rises from the other woman. Sitting down beside her son, she lays her head on her arm and tucks his hand under her chin, closing her eyes.

'Hi, Mummy.' With a frown of concentration he tries to cut

his toast one-handed, beans tipping off the plate with his fork's see-sawing effort.

The landline rings and Suzie lifts her head to send a silent plea in Anna's direction. It's Daniel's school wanting to know when he might be returning. She tries to hand over the receiver, but Suzie refuses it.

'Don't they listen to the local news?'

Returning to the call, Anna says, 'There's been a development... in Lily's case.' She stumbles through the sentence. She doesn't have the language for something like this but the mention of Lily's name is enough, Daniel's teacher in a sudden hurry to end the call.

'Dan-Dan, go and change out of that stuffy uniform,' Suzie says, straightening in her chair. 'Then you and me can have a fun day at home together.'

Daniel doesn't move, concentrating on spearing a single bean with his fork.

The doorbell rings as Anna is putting on her trainers to go to the supermarket. Jonah is at the door, a shiver of apologetic blues and purples rising from him.

'I'm sorry about how we left it,' he says.

Her fierce and sudden hug squeezes a startled laugh from him.

'I've known you for seventeen years and that makes you one of my oldest friends,' she says, ushering him inside. 'I don't know what's been happening between you and Billie, but it can't be good given how she's losing it.'

He blinks, scuffing his feet against the hallway floor. 'I'm not entirely to blame.'

'I know that.'

He's back in his shabby jeans and a blanched-pink T-shirt that hangs off him like flayed skin. Classic old Jonah attire, but it doesn't change the boastful definition of his arms or the fact of Lily's ring wedged under the passenger seat of his car. Something caused Billie to behave with a malice that isn't part of her make-up. Perhaps everyone harbours a dry store of hatred but it requires a sizeable spark to light it.

'I need to show you something,' she says.

'Your Danish friend came round yesterday, looking for you.' Jonah follows her up the stairs as if he's carrying a load of bricks on his back.

'His name is Lauritz.' They pass Daniel's room, where he and his mother are staring at the spread pieces of a jigsaw. Above Daniel's head is a rolling cloud of beige, but he pokes about, studying picture fragments, to please his mother. Suzie registers Jonah with a small flash of surprise, sending him a tired smile. He raises his hand, neither of them finding the energy for a proper greeting, though the current between them is a friendly carnation pink.

'This is Lily's old room.'

He stops on the threshold, reluctant to step inside.

'Have you been here before?' She ushers him onto the dressing table stool.

'Of course not.' His voice is quiet, petulant.

The photographs of Lily on the horse-head sofa are back in their original hiding place beneath the mattress. That had been Suzie's idea, having confiscated them from Daniel. *They belong in Lily's room*, she'd said, handing them over, keen to be rid of them. Crouching down, Anna feels about for the envelope. She lays the photographs on the bed, noting the first gentle breaker of orange as Jonah leans forward.

He gets to his feet, bending over the photographs. 'Whoa, Jesus.' Flinches back. 'Is that my sofa?'

'Looks like it, doesn't it?'

She watches the light-play above his head. 'Any idea who the photographer was?'

He sits down again, his eyes sliding back to the photographs. He doesn't want to look but he can't help himself.

'Jonah?'

'Sorry? No. No idea.' He massages his wrist, an old gesture. Hiding in the corner of parties, by the bar or the bowl of crisps, trying to look involved, rubbing his wrist. 'Do you think it's the same person who …' he waves a hand through the air, an inarticulate scroll of horror, 'killed her?'

It's the first time she's heard anyone say it. Speak the unspeakable. 'Maybe.'

'Has Billie seen these?'

'She tried to make light of it, for my sake.' She takes a breath, preparing herself. 'But do you know what I think, Jo? Billie suspects that you and Lily were involved.'

His shoulders hunch, his body concave as if he's been struck in the stomach. Breathing loudly through his nose, he reaches with a shaking hand to flip the photographs face-down. Through the fan of his murky greens and greys, there's a spark of red, like a little fish hiding in pondweed.

'Do you want to know why Billie hated that poor girl so much?' he says.

'Lauritz's wife turned up at your parents' house all those years ago.' He pauses, making sure she's taking this in.

'I didn't know that.'

A spatter of rain hits the window. She thinks how dark the room is. How grim and tired Jonah looks, a throbbing resentment above his head, a muddle of blood and mud.

'Billie was the only one at home. She was in the final year of her masters and uni hadn't started back yet. You were off at some festival with friends. Your parents were away too.'

290

She shuffles the photographs together. 'Billie never told me this.'

'Nope. Protecting you as always. She didn't tell your parents either. Being the grown-up for everyone.'

The thought that has been circling like a bird is within arm's reach. Billie said she and Lily were the same at nineteen. She hasn't said it outright but Anna hears now the implication that she and Lily had both been chasing something that wasn't theirs to take. She should have questioned why her big sister, a stickler for responsibility and accountability, had merely shrugged her shoulders over her affair with Lauritz. 'What happened?'

'The woman wouldn't leave. She raged at Billie for the best part of an hour. Saying nasty things about you, about your parents for turning a blind eye, and Billie just for being part of the family. Then she broke down and sobbed, which I think Billie found worse than the anger. You know how uncomfortable that would have made her.'

She closes her eyes. The picture is vivid in her head. She can see her sister sitting rigid, trying to soothe the woman with every clever thing she could think to say. It wouldn't have been enough. More than anything, her sister hates to feel helpless, out of her depth. 'Poor Bills.'

'Oh, it got worse. Before she left, she showed Billie scans of the unborn child she'd lost as a result of the stress caused by your affair with her husband.'

She swallows down on a rise of nausea. The child Lauritz and his wife had longed for. Her colours fly and jab at her like a lynch mob. 'Why didn't Billie tell me any of this?'

'You know why.' Jonah rests his elbows on his knees, head dropping forward with a sigh. 'Because you're her precious baby sister and it's her role to take care of you.' He looks up to meet her eye. 'When she looked at Lily, she saw you.'

The truth lands, digging in its talons. Jonah was right. Her sister hates her. There's no way Billie would have admitted to it – perhaps even to herself – and the rage needed to go somewhere so she had taken it out on Lily. It was Anna she was trying to hurt, not Lily.

'Billie's sick to death of being the only one who does the right thing. And I don't blame her.' Standing up, he points at the photographs she's holding like a hand of cards, a smear of barbecue sauce in the air above him. 'I did *not* take those pictures.'

'I know,' she says, but he's already left the room, his feet pounding down the stairs. She runs out into the corridor. 'Wait. Let me come with you. I need to see her.'

He stops at the bottom of the stairs. 'I don't know where Billie is.'

46

Maple syrup for guilty pleasures

Suzie agrees to Anna borrowing the car. She follows her to the door but goes no further, gazing at the sunlit garden, a primrose-yellow longing moving across the solid surface of her blues. The woman can't have forgiven her and yet the confrontation Anna is braced for never comes. Suzie watches her drive away.

The loneliest person in the world isn't Gabriel or herself. It's Suzie.

She winds the windows down, letting the air rush in. Speeds up, pressing hard on the accelerator, playing chicken with the bends.

This is what Billie does, Jonah said before he left. Takes off for a few days and won't say where she's been.

She turns on a whimsy, left one minute, right the next, wanting to get lost. After fifteen minutes she finds herself in a sunken thoroughfare with steep banks of ancient tree root, too narrow for oncoming cars to pass. Dares herself to go faster.

The pigeon tumbles out of the trees and there is nothing she can do. It explodes against the windscreen with a reverberating thwack, feathers bursting. The car swerves, the wheels catching and pinballing off the left-hand bank before she manages to bring the car to a halt. In the rear-view mirror the pigeon is a mound of gory feathers, the broken sail of a wing pointing straight up. Unclenching her fingers from the wheel, she wipes her palms on her thighs.

An oily imprint of the bird, remarkable in its detail, remains on the windscreen. Her hands are shaking as she takes a scrunched tissue from the glove compartment and gets out. Outside, all is still and quiet, as if she's locked in a bubble. She scrubs the imprint away, picking out feathers from the wipers. Back in the driver's seat, still shaky, she lays her forehead on the steering wheel, until she hears a car approaching and has no choice but to move on. She needs a black coffee to burn away her jitters.

There are places she could visit: a local RHS garden, any number of villages with cricket greens and curiosity shops, golfing hotels serving afternoon tea. But she chooses Kirkley, following her own ghost lights.

She parks by the playground, stopping first at the chemist on her way to the square. The shop floor is long and narrow as a tunnel, and dimly lit. She picks up both aspirin and paracetamol, a double whammy to keep the dull ache in her head under control. The woman behind the till gives her a friendly, open smile at odds with the aggressive red of her shift dress. A poster of Lily is taped to the counter. With a second glance, Anna realises it's one of hers.

'Where did you get the new poster from?'

'One of the poor girl's friends is bringing them round. Wasn't it awful about finding her shoes?'

Margaret, she thinks, and is disappointed to have missed her. 'Did you know Lily?'

'Not really. She came in here asking about a Saturday job once but she was too young, only fifteen.' The woman gives a shake of the head that is both amused and sorry. 'Little minx pinched a packet of condoms on her way out.'

Anna takes her change and leaves as the woman starts to wonder aloud whether she should have mentioned it to Lily's family back then, if it might have made a difference. Finding a small role for herself in the drama.

The Bandstand Café, with its prime view of the sinkhole, is packed. The outside tables have been removed, police tape halving the pavement and closing the road to motorists. Anna passes the old red phone box on her way, noticing a man shifting about inside, his back to the telephone. She tries not to take a second glance – she doesn't want to know what he's up to – but then she recognises Ben. He's taping the new poster of Lily onto the window. When she opens the door, he doesn't look surprised to see her, but then nothing seems to penetrate that bland, colourless exterior.

'Did Suzie ask you to do this?'

'No. I found them in the bin under the desk.' He bites off a piece of tape and fixes it in a crooked line to the top of the poster. 'They're better than the first poster. A bit more like the real Lily.'

'I never got the impression you actually liked her.'

'Probably more than she liked me.' With his thumbnail he scrapes at the creases in the tape.

She hasn't seen him since Lily's trainers were found, and something about him has changed. His self-satisfied drawl is missing, his body hanging slack off his shoulders. He barely glances in her direction.

'I didn't mean to walk into your room the other night,' he says, unpicking the edge of the poster. He smoothes it out, his thumb gliding over Lily's cheek, before reattaching the corner. Slate blue pulses around his head, a quiet play of colour, held close.

It hadn't been emotion Ben was lacking; it was interest. His attention towards her had been an act, a posture. He's no threat; just a young man searching for something to be part of, like everyone else. Like Anna herself.

She can't bear the thought of returning to the O'Keefes yet. She needs a friend, someone on her side.

Once she'd have called Billie.

The pain opens up her chest. She has never been so alone in her life.

She sends a text to Marni. *Hate the countryside.*

There's no answer when she calls Margaret, but she heads to East Mawsey all the same. She finds Margaret's name on the intercom in the narrow doorway beside the chip shop, and presses the buzzer. The shop's facade has a large cartoon trout with grinning teeth and a body painted the colour of revulsion, a glossy, distilled brown that sends a nauseous tumble through her stomach.

A faint tinnitus of music comes from the open window of Margaret's flat. She presses the intercom again, and when there's still no answer, she decides to take a walk; pick up some flowers or chocolates so she doesn't arrive unannounced and empty-handed.

Fifteen minutes later, returning with a bag of farm-shop fudge and Pink Lady apples, she spots the door opening. A man steps out onto the pavement, his build unmistakable, Margaret following in red fluffy socks. Her mouth is working, a beseeching tilt to her head like a baby bird asking for food. Gabriel looks down, saying nothing. As he walks away, Anna is torn between an urge to follow him and the knowledge that she'll learn much more from Margaret.

She stops the girl before she can shut the door.

'Anna, hi.' There's a high flush on Margaret's face. 'And it's

Greta, remember? I don't like Margaret. I'm not a thousand years old yet.'

'Is that Gabriel?' She points to his receding figure.

'Yes. He...' Margaret stops, bubbling away in a pumpkin soup of worry. 'Do you want to come in?'

The flat is minuscule: a single bedroom, a bathroom, and a living area with a kitchenette. Opposite a sofa, a flat-screen television is balanced on one of the two windowsills. Fried fat and the mustard tang of smoked fish pickles the air, seeping up through the floorboards. Anna catches herself running a hand over the sofa's seaweed-green material, rubbing her fingers together, checking for grease. Against the far wall is a small table, and on it a glass tumbler with a residue of maple-coloured liquid. That golden, syrupy tone, tarnished with a little brown, is for guilty pleasure. The colour inside her head when she thinks about Gabriel.

'I thought Gabriel had left the area?'

Margaret shakes her head, holding onto the electric kettle, which is rattling and bubbling as if preparing for lift-off. 'He's leaving now.'

She resists the urge to fire questions, letting Margaret speak in her own time. But as the silence stretches, she hastens things along, taking the glass to the sink and giving it a sniff. 'Strong medicine for this time of the day.'

'He's in a mess since they found Lily's shoes.' Margaret catches two tears on the back of her hand and slops boiled water into the mugs, one spilling over. She pinches the teabags out before the water's barely tinted.

'Well, he's lucky to have you as a friend.'

There's something in Margaret's posture that makes Anna wish she could see her face. This is what people do. They freeze, trying to shut down in moments of high tension, for fear their bodies will give them away.

'He asked me three times.' Margaret turns to face her. 'If Lily has been in contact. I kept having to say, *She's not coming back, Gabe. She's never coming back.* He couldn't care less how distressing that was for me.'

Anna rubs her shoulder, telling her to sit down, she'll finish making the tea. It doesn't make sense. Gabriel knows Lily isn't coming back. She'd seen it in his face, before he kissed her in the river.

But then she knows how it feels to wake up to a pain too large to fit inside your body. For months after Lauritz ended their relationship, she'd woken each morning to the vain hope that another letter might arrive, one to cancel out the first.

'He's in denial,' she says. 'The discovery of her trainers is killing any hope he had left.'

'Killing *everyone's* hope,' Margaret says.

There's a half-empty bottle of milk in the fridge. It gives off a faint sour smell, but Anna pours a dollop in each mug and hands the young woman hers. An angel doll is on the second windowsill, half hidden by the net curtain. A special angel wearing a tiny gold crown. Evangelista, Lily had called her.

'One of Lily's, isn't it?'

Margaret puts her tea on the floor and picks up the angel. The longing bowls out of her, a collapsing sandbank of crimson lust. 'This one was made specially for me.'

An odd thought hits her. 'Margaret, did you ever take pictures of Lily?'

The young woman presses her lips together, smoothing out Angel Evangelista's wings, refusing to reply, but Anna has her answer.

She lets the silence work on Margaret before she says, 'There's nothing to be ashamed of. You loved her.'

The girl tucks her feet up, curling into the arm of the sofa.

'The photos were her idea. She wanted to give them to Gabriel. That was back in the early days, when she still loved him.'

The idea horrifies Anna on Gabriel's behalf, imagining how he might have reacted on seeing those suggestive images of a girl he loved as a daughter. 'Lily stopped loving Gabriel?'

'Why not?' Margaret sucks in her cheeks, shrugs. 'She was just a kid, wasn't she?'

Anna can see her hesitation, the frantic scramble of green and dishonest orange as she tries not to give something away. 'You know more than you're letting on.'

Margaret picks at the glue holding the angel's crown in place. It breaks away and she slips the crown over her ring finger. 'We'd made a plan. Lily was going to run away that night. And I was going with her.'

She gets up, hesitates in the middle of the room, then opens the cupboard beneath the kitchen sink. Pushing aside a packet of toilet rolls, she takes out a rucksack with a pink camouflage pattern.

'She was supposed to come back and get her stuff after seeing Gabriel, but she never did.'

Anna stares at the bag in Margaret's hand. If only a person's possessions could be imbued with their feelings, a residue of emotion trapped inside the fibres for her to read. 'Why would Lily want to run away?'

'To start again. To not be that girl that everyone talked shit about.'

Anna turns away, facing the window. The need to start again, to move on and become someone new: that she understands. The high street is busy below Margaret's window. A boy on a bike, up on his pedals, threading through pedestrians, his eyes far ahead. A mum with a double buggy, toddler yelling, baby asleep, a chiding comment over her shoulder as the boy on the bicycle passes. Three teenage girls in school uniform, hair up, laughing too loudly, hungry for attention. It would be easy to put Lily amongst them. If she'd got away, she might at this moment have been walking down an identical high street far from here.

'What happened after Lily got her tattoo?'

When Anna turns back, Margaret is crying, soundlessly, wiping her face with the palms of her hands like a wretched child. 'She was going to go home, say her goodbyes. I wanted to come but she insisted on doing it alone. I waited with her at the taxi rank but there were no cabs. Of course.' The girl's words are hiccoughing out with her sobs, making it hard to follow.

Anna pours her a glass of water. 'It's OK, Greta. Slow down.'

Closing her eyes, Margaret breathes in through her nose, out through her mouth, both palms pressed to her chest, over Anahata, the unstruck heart, as Lily had called it. The gesture strikes Anna as showy, and she looks away to quell a rash of irritation, the colour of plastic cherries.

With a long, deep exhalation, Margaret continues. 'Someone Lily knew drove by and she waved him down. Got in the car with him. I never saw her again.'

'Who was it?' Anna's limbs ache with an electric rush of adrenalin. 'What kind of car?'

'Like I told the police, I don't know about cars.' Margaret gives a helpless shrug. 'It was small and grey, that's all I remember.'

Thanking the girl, Anna leaves the flat, forgetting her handbag until Margaret calls her back. All she can think of is Billie throwing the fish ring into the bushes.

✎ 47 ✎

Washed-out denim

It's one o'clock by the time she reaches April's. Her stomach is empty, a moment of light-headedness as she gets out of the car. She knocks on the kitchen door and is greeted by the smell of fried eggs, golden and crisp at the edges. It makes her queasy with hunger.

April ushers her in. 'Good timing, I was about to start on my coupons.' She points to a pile of cut-outs in a lidless biscuit tin, chuckling as she confesses that she's addicted to giveaways and prize draws. 'If you help me fill out my details, we'll split the winnings, ay?'

'Tempting, but I can't stay.'

April clears a stack of crinkle-edged newspapers from a nearby chair, but Anna doesn't sit down. A restlessness close to dread is rolling in her stomach. She read once that before a tidal wave hits, the sea is sucked far from the shore, receding to the horizon. That is the time to run.

'Do you know where Gabriel is?'

'Nope. Still haven't caught up with him.' A rare tremor works through April's emerald-green haze. She is worried about him.

Anna wonders if it would be rude to ask for a piece of toast to settle her stomach. 'Did you know that Margaret and Lily had planned to run away the night she disappeared?'

April shakes her head, listening intently. Something in her

expression suggests she's drawing her own conclusions, but thoughts don't have a telltale colour and she's keeping her emotions under strict guard.

'No comment?'

'No, my love. No comment.'

The blood drains from Anna's face as if her empty stomach has sucked it downwards, forcing her to take a seat after all. 'What was Lily like?'

'That girl had a golden energy. All the things she went through at such a young age, that could have crushed her or made her bitter. She was big enough in spirit to still be kind and compassionate. She used to do my coupons with me and we'd shoot the shit.'

April smiles, looking at Anna but seeing Lily; like a ghostly overprint.

'She had healing hands, that girl. Every one of those little angels blessed with her love and intention.'

Anna has never heard her speak so openly before without the self-conscious nettle of humour. 'I wish I could have met her.'

April positions her box of cuttings in front of her and puts on a pair of reading glasses. 'You want to help, Anna, and that's admirable. But the best thing you can do is go home and look after that little boy. And send a few loving thoughts to everyone involved.'

It's fine for April to sit on her high mountain and beam out loving thoughts, but Anna needs to find Gabriel. Heading back to the O'Keefes, she takes the lane that leads to the back of the paddock where Billie had picked her up a few days earlier. Here she can leave the car for a bit, knowing it won't be visible from the house. She walks into the woods, sucking a Polo mint from the base of her bag, a quick hit of sugar to keep her going.

The afternoon has turned humid and she is conscious of the damp patches beneath her armpits, staining the sky blue of her T-shirt a darker, unhappier tone.

The campsite is empty. The rain has washed away the fire pit, nothing but a scorched shadow remaining, their meeting in the woods already belonging to the past. Dizzy again, she squats down, head in hands. There's only one place left she can think of. After that, she'll have to face the dread in her chest that says she'll never see Gabriel again.

It doesn't take long to find the winding road to the coast. She drives too fast, steadies herself, reliving the crushing thump of the pigeon against the windscreen, then pushes forward once more.

She can't think about Lauritz, who will soon return to Denmark for good. She can't think about Billie, the person she thought she knew as well as herself, or Suzie's rage, or Daniel too afraid to sleep alone.

When she finds Gabriel, everything will be all right.

Cranley Marina is a different place in the daylight. People call to each other across their moored boats, drinking beer in the sun or hosing down their decks. A crane lowers a plump tub into the harbour. She knows before she reaches the clubhouse that Gabriel won't be here. As if he no longer belongs to places of sunlight and cheerful industry but has become a shadow, slipping away before she can reach him.

She checks the line of parked cars at the side of the marina, a plunge of disappointment in her stomach when his Defender isn't there. The clubhouse deck is busy, every table taken, the harbour breeze carrying the smell of roast potatoes and grilled fish. There's a metallic taste of hunger in her mouth as she heads inside. Just in case. Threading her way through the close-packed tables, with the heat of bodies and the smell of food, a claustrophobic spin descends. She bumps past two waiters placing drinks orders. Leaning against the high bar, she waits for the barman to acknowledge her.

Zdenko, as his name tag reads, greets each waiter's request with a smile, his movements quick and concise as a boxer's parry. Whilst he makes up two gin and tonics, she considers what to say, knowing she won't have his attention for long.

'I'm missing a husband,' she says when he asks what the young lady would like to drink.

'That is too bad.' He gives a diplomatic laugh. 'What does he look like? Maybe I have seen him.'

On her mobile, she still has the photograph of Gabriel holding Daniel above his head in his carnival strong man pose. She studies it through a soft glaze of antique rose. That happy evening seems long ago. Zdenko leans forward to look at the screen, eager to help.

'OK. Mr O'Keefe.'

Adrenalin surges from the pit of her stomach and down her legs. She shouldn't have referred to Gabriel as her husband. For all she knows, he and Suzie might be members of the club. To her relief, there is only chick yellow feathering out of Zdenko's crown, the name eliciting a good feeling but nothing more. Perhaps Gabriel takes the time to chat with the barman when he visits, or leaves decent tips.

'Your husband is a nice man. Can I make something to drink?'

She orders a gin and tonic, buying a little more time.

'I thought he said he'd booked lunch for us here.' Another mistake, minutes wasted as Zdenko checks through the bookings. There are no posters of Lily, she notices, and wonders why.

'Wait, one more picture. Maybe you've seen his niece?' Another gamble. 'She's joining us for lunch.' She finds the picture she'd taken of her new poster, drawing her thumbs apart so Lily's face fills the screen and the text is hidden.

'She is his niece?' Zdenko's tone is polite and neutral, but the play of colours above his head makes for interesting reading. From his hot pinks she knows he's recognised Lily, her beauty making her stand out. A splash of mild green curiosity and mustard amusement as he draws his own conclusions over her enquiry. But there's no darkness in his colours. He doesn't know she's missing. Forty minutes away and Lily's story is unknown. One of the thousands of nameless teenagers who go missing every year, according to her father. The thought hurts her. She understands then the reason for Gabriel sitting in his car, unable to go inside. He can't face the bullet of an innocent question.

'Actually, she's not his niece but the daughter of a family friend. My husband is teaching her to sail.'

'OK. Nice of him.' He gives another small laugh, shifting his weight, one of those people who can't stay still. He's also playing dumb, the mustard yellow taking over, enjoying himself immensely. Here is the wife, he is no doubt thinking, looking for the straying husband who has bagged himself a gorgeous young thing. If she hadn't been able to read him so well, she might have found herself warming to his cheerful, round face, thinking him kind and diplomatic when in reality he is canny and adept at concealing his thoughts.

These are the everyday moments that have kept her separate all her life. Whilst she can't imagine how flat and two-dimensional the world must appear to everyone else, she does envy the choice to take people at face value. To believe in an open smile, a flattering word, a protestation of love.

'So, have you seen them today?'

For one giddy moment as he scans the crowd, she thinks she

might follow his gaze and see them, Gabriel and Lily, together at a table.

'Not today, no.'

'But they come here together?'

There's a second's hesitation, no doubt considering how to answer. 'I see many people so it is difficult to remember. But I know Mr O'Keefe. He drinks vodka and tonic but no olives; he hate olives.'

He's chosen discretion. She has an urge to burst into tears, living up to her role as the desperate wife.

'I hope you find them for lunch.' His yellows have faded, a soft blue like overwashed denim in its place. He may have enjoyed the intrigue for a brief moment, but he's not malicious, any more than the people who gossip about Gabriel and Lily at the school gates. With the exception of her sister.

She takes a gulp of her drink, the liquid searing through her gullet, hitting her empty stomach like a bomb. The bar gives a sideways tilt.

'If you see Mr O'Keefe, can you tell him to call...' she pauses, 'home.'

Zdenko nods, looks away, then steps out from behind the bar. 'There are rooms upstairs,' he says, pointing to the ceiling. 'Do you want I check the bookings for them?'

'No. No, of course not.' His assumption horrifies her and she walks away, realising as she reaches the door that she has forgotten to pay for her drink. When she returns and asks for the bill, the barman gives a grave little shake of the head.

'It's on me.'

In the car, she takes a few deep breaths before switching on the engine, sick and light-headed. Hunger, the hit of gin, but most uncomfortable of all, the barman refusing to let her pay out of pity.

~ 48 ~

An orange spike of terror

On reaching the main road, the signal picks up on her mobile and it vibrates with incoming messages. From her mother and from Marni – *I warned you about the countryside, didn't I? Nothing but sheep and women in jodhpurs*. Nothing from Billie. She pulls over and sends her sister a text.

Call me. We both messed up. I still love you.

The house, as always, is rigid with silence. She finds Suzie sleeping on the sofa, hands tucked under her face like an angelic child. Closing the door to the sitting room, she listens for signs of Daniel.

'Dan? Calling Dan-Fantastic. Where are you?'

She runs upstairs, still calling his name, furious with herself for having stayed out so long. He is in his room, surrounded by drawings, which are spread around the floor like crazy paving. He tiptoes through the narrow paths between the pictures to reach her, then locks his hands around her waist, his head in her stomach.

'You were gone a really long time.'

'Have you had any lunch?'

He shakes his head. 'And no breakfast, but it's OK because I'm not really hungry.'

Normally she counts to five then disengages herself, as this seems an appropriate length of hug considering she isn't a blood relation, but today she needs comfort as much as he does. With a guilty pang she sees all those times she unknotted his little hands, stepping away, when he was probably feeling like she does now. She rubs his back.

'This is my picture collection. Want to see?'

'Absolutely yes.'

She smiles as he purses his mouth, giving serious consideration as to where to start. 'That one is my favourite.' He leans over and taps the corner of an A3 picture with an old-fashioned schooner bucking over a wild sea. The detail is astonishing, from the rigging to the grain of the wood and the scrolling mass of waves. Drawn with coloured pencils, but not in a child's hand.

'Who drew this?'

'Guess.' Trying to hide his delight, he points to the picture on his wall of the huge dragon curled around the tiny boy. 'Same person who did this.'

And then it hits her, making her sad all over again for the lost girl and the little boy left behind. 'Lily did these for you, didn't she?'

'Lily?' He laughs and scrambles on his hands and knees to retrieve a small lined piece of paper with two stick figures perched on a triangle of a mountain, a girl with blonde hair and brown eyes holding the hand of a little boy with dark spiky hair and black rabbit eyes. On the bottom of the page, in messy pen, someone has written, *Lily and Daniel go exploring.* 'This is Lily's. And those ones.' He points out more stick-figure drawings of Lily and Daniel.

She shakes her head. 'I give up. Who did those other ones?'

'Daddy, of course, silly Anna.'

'Silly billy yourself.' She lunges for him, tickling his ribs, making him shriek. 'I had no idea your daddy was so talented.'

*

Once they have tidied his pictures into a plastic art folder and played four rounds of Uno, they head downstairs. Telling Daniel to lay the table for dinner, she checks on Suzie, but the sitting room is empty, the dent of her body left in the sofa cushions. Through the window, she can still see the car, so Suzie hasn't gone out. Back upstairs, she finds the door to Gabriel and Suzie's room closed. Suzie must have crept upstairs while they were playing, shutting herself away as quietly as possible.

She hesitates outside the door, then knocks. 'Suzie? Would you like something to eat?'

When there's no answer, she tries again, a finger of anxiety drilling through her. She raps her knuckles against the door, the noise loud and obnoxious in the appalled hush of the house. Still no reply. She opens the door and looks in. Suzie is on her side, on top of the bedcovers, fully clothed, her eyes just visible between her eyelids, unblinking.

Anna takes a few panicked steps into the room. 'Suzie? Are you OK?'

Suzie rolls onto her back, a slow, involuntary motion, arms slack, going with it. Anna's stomach vaults at the sight. She rushes in, leaning over Suzie, her knee on the mattress.

'Can I just have some peace?' Suzie's lips barely move.

Anna turns away, her hand on her chest. The house is making her crazy.

Dinner is Marmite toast cut into silly shapes to amuse Daniel and conceal the fact of such a paltry offering. Neither of them eats much.

'I like you being here, Anna,' Daniel says. He takes a bite of toast and lets his hand fall back, coming to rest on her arm. She's noticed this, especially when he's near his dad: the unobtrusive contact of hand or knee or elbow, the small bridges he creates between himself and the people he loves.

'I like being here with you, Dan.'

'But I wish it was how it used to be. Like at Christmas when it was me and Lily and Mummy and Daddy. I got the best cracker present.'

She remembers last Christmas, her and Chris eating turkey crown with his parents in their undecorated flat – they regarded decorations for a single day as wasteful – wishing she was at Billie's. Christmas is a recent anchor in time. Lily hasn't been gone for long, and yet the aura around her memory is bleak and terminal.

How has everyone given up already?

After dinner, whilst Daniel watches television, she makes up his bed on the floor beside hers. Finding his teddies piled on his covers, he laughs and bats them around the room. He drags his mattress backwards until his pillow is inside the door frame.

'Now I'll wake up if you try to run off,' he says, a fat orange spike through his chick yellows.

'Why do you think I'm going to run away?'

'I don't.' He gathers up his scattered teddy bears, but she can't let the conversation drop, because his fear is real and growing deeper. She should have paid attention to it when he first started begging to sleep in her room.

'Are you scared in the house at night?'

'No.' His lie makes her own anxiety rush in. What has she been missing? He's getting busier and busier, arms full of teddies, laying them out in neat rows on his bed.

'You're frightened at night, aren't you? That's why your dad drew the dragon to watch over you.'

'I'm not scared. Only when I'm alone.' These words come out with a gush of ox-blood red. He glares at her, squeezing his lips together.

'But you're never alone, Dan-Dan.'

'I was one time.'

She sweeps him into a hug, lifting him onto her lap, making him safe inside the ring of her arms. 'When was that?'

'The night Lily went away. Everyone just disappeared.'

A cold rush across her skin. 'Daddy was out, wasn't he?'

Daniel nods, his chin buckling.

She takes a breath. 'And your mum?'

'Mummy was also gone.'

'Are you sure, Dan?' She rocks him as shivers travel through his thin frame.

'I ran all over the house in all the rooms and I shouted really loud, but she wasn't here.'

49

Aubergine bruises

She can't sleep, fizzing with feverish thoughts: Suzie giving her husband an alibi when her own whereabouts were unaccounted for, Billie currently God knows where; the angel-wing tattoo. Lily hadn't drawn it, Gabriel had. It shouldn't matter, she thinks, but she can't shake the feeling that it does. Something has started unravelling when she thinks about Gabriel, and it fills her with panic. All this time, he's been running through her like a clear, steady river, the sweetest tones of pink and violet. She can't bear for it to dry up.

If she could see him, everything might return to the way it was.

Daniel gets up just after six, wandering out with his thumb in his mouth, a teddy in the other hand. He comes back minutes later, a Fanta fizz above his sleep-mussed hair.

'Mummy says she's sick and can you look after me today?'

She hides her dismay. She has to find Gabriel. 'Well, sweetie. I think it's time you went back to school, before you forget how to count to ten.'

'But it's Saturday today.'

She leaves him to get dressed and heads to the sitting room, closing the door behind her. Gabriel hasn't been answering her calls or texts, but perhaps he'll pick up if she uses the landline.

When he answers, his voice feels nothing short of miraculous.

'Gabriel, thank God.'

'What's happened? Is Daniel OK?'

'He's fine. Suzie's fine.' A current of nerves runs through her empty stomach. She's not sure Suzie is fine at all.

'What is it then, Anna?'

It strikes her that his next question should have been about Lily and whether there'd been any new developments. But then his voice is so worn and weary, perhaps he can't bring himself to ask.

'I need to see you. Urgently. Daniel told me something about the night Lily went missing.'

In the pause, she hears the suck and crackle as he draws on a roll-up. 'How is my boy? I miss him.'

'Gabriel? Did you hear what I said? We need to talk about it face to face.'

Before the line cuts out, she hears the sound of distant bells, an irregular waterfall of chimes that seems familiar. It takes her a moment to place it.

'Daniel.' Her voice rings in the silent house. 'Are you ready? We need to go out now, this very minute.'

April is crossing her yard, pushing a wheelbarrow of grass cuttings. She squints against the rain that has started to fall, head to one side as she watches Anna approach, Daniel running to keep up, his fingers cold and clammy in her grip. She greets Daniel first, then looks at Anna. 'Someone's got to start taking care of this boy.'

Her stern tone and unsmiling face throw Anna. Bewildered, she looks down at Daniel and realises he's barefoot.

'We left in a rush, that's all.'

'That's the problem, isn't it? You're all so busy rushing

around, dragging this poor little fellow behind you. When did you last go to school, Daniel, my boy?'

Daniel shrugs. 'Yesterday. Or maybe two days ago.'

Anna hasn't got time for this. 'I need to speak to Gabriel, April. I know he's here.'

'Gabe's not here.' April's tone doesn't soften, but she's telling the truth. As if to taunt her, the wind chimes clatter and jingle.

'Daddy?' Daniel is twisting to look over his shoulder, his hand still caught in Anna's. Standing in the doorway of April's disused stables is Gabriel. Daniel breaks free and runs into his father's open arms.

'Well I never, crafty beggar.' April gives Gabriel a wry little wave of the hand, shaking her head. With a grunt of amusement, she turns away, taking up the handles of her wheelbarrow again.

'When you've said hello to your dad,' she calls to Daniel, 'help me collect the eggs and I'll make you my special scrambled eggs.'

She's not offering them a moment of privacy so much as reminding them to take better care of the boy. But then, despite her special gifts and insights, the woman has no idea what's been taking place behind the fortress walls of the O'Keefe family.

A green tarpaulin is laid across the stall's stone floor. It's filthy with fresh mud and old straw, a sleeping bag rolled out on top. Daniel sits between Gabriel's legs, threading his fingers in and out of his father's, holding on.

'Why didn't you tell me you were here, Gabe?'

He doesn't answer. Something feels different about him, but Anna isn't sure what. There's no space for her to sit down, so she crouches by Daniel, giving his leg a pat. 'Ready to collect some eggs?'

314

'Not yet,' Gabriel says. When he meets her eyes, she understands what has changed. Above his head, there is nothing at all as he looks at her.

'You're upset with me for coming here,' she says, though she knows that's not the case because there's no rash of irritation, only emptiness. The loss of his affection gives her a physical ache in her stomach. The rivers in her body are clogged with grit and stones and dead things.

'Not at all. You brought Dan.' He kisses the top of his son's head and love unfolds its wide fan above his head. Just not for her.

'I do have to talk to you, though, Gabe.'

He nods, but she has to wait while Daniel tells him about Suzie being in bed sick and how he might need to go back to school before he forgets to count to ten.

'Daniel showed me your drawings,' she says. 'I didn't realise you were such a talented artist.'

'A hobby, that's all.' He gives the boy another kiss and nudges him to his feet. 'Sneak me an egg, hey, sweetheart?'

Once his son has run off in search of the chicken coop, Gabriel pats the sleeping bag. Anna sits on the edge, hoping he might soften now that it's just the two of them. He doesn't speak, rubbing his knuckles where a shadow of aubergine bruising remains.

Aubergine is pretty much how she feels inside too.

'Does your hand hurt?'

'No more than usual. What's going on with Suzie?'

'She's falling to pieces. She's spent the last two days in bed.'

A disdainful puff of brown smoke lifts off his crown. Another change. She swallows. 'Why haven't you told anyone about her temper?'

His laugh is more weary than bitter. 'Who'd believe me? People only ever see my size.'

She remembers walking into the kitchen, knowing something had happened, something far worse than an exchange of angry words. Suzie collapsed in a weak huddle on the floor, abandoned to helpless weeping, while Gabriel nursed his sore knuckles at the far side of the room. Even she, the one person who sees who he really is, had experienced a moment of doubt.

'Most of the time I cover my head and wait for it to pass. I can't defend myself. One hard shove and she'd go flying.'

She takes his uninjured hand in hers and tries not to notice the indifferent weight of it, an inanimate object he's lending her for a moment. 'Tell me what I can do to help, Gabe. Anything.'

'What did you want to see me about, Anna?' His voice, whilst not unkind, suggests he doesn't believe that she or anyone else can help him.

'Suzie was out the night Lily disappeared.' Now she can look at him because the colours, or lack of them, no longer relate to herself. A faint clementine mist rises away, light and fleeting. Either he's not listening or he's failed to understand the implication.

'She gave you that alibi claiming you were home with her all night long, but the truth is, she wasn't in either.' She checks his colours, but they're sluggish and dim. 'Don't you understand what this means? Suzie was giving herself an alibi, not you.'

'I know.'

'What?' She gets to her feet, her own lemon shock clouding her view.

'Suzie was out with Lily the night she disappeared.'

She leans back against the stable wall, staring at him. 'But everyone thinks it was you. Why—'

'For Daniel's sake.'

She can't breathe. She turns away, unable to look at him as

316

she hurries outside. It all slots into place with a sickening kind of sense. How passive they had remained in their grief and anger. No radio appeal, no press conferences, no marching the streets searching for information, asking for help. Billie had seen it too, stepping in to help. And to assuage her guilt.

There's a light scuffle of footsteps, then his arms come around her and for a brief moment she surrenders to the warm cave of his embrace before stepping free of it. She needs to see clearly now, no longer blinded by her own wants and needs.

'You know what happened to Lily, don't you, Gabriel?'

There is no mystery. Not for the O'Keefes.

He puts his hands on her arms, their warmth seeping into her skin, a faint crimson around his crown.

'Yes. I know.'

~ 50 ~

Seething red

As she turns into the O'Keefes' lane, their roof comes into view and her heart jackhammers in her chest. She pulls over and tries to conquer the weakness of her body. One small task, that's all he has asked of her. She'll be in and out within three minutes. With any luck, Suzie will be in bed. She switches off the engine, covering the last metres on foot so the sound of the car doesn't alert her. Ochre wheels through her. She never wants to see that woman again. Closing her eyes, she allows herself a moment of stillness.

Gabriel had cupped her face, his forehead to hers. *If you're a good person, good things come into your life when you need them. You were sent to me, Anna.*

She opens her eyes. The rain is gone, the sun on her shoulders like supportive hands guiding her forward. Under a summer sky, the colour of innocence, there's nothing to be afraid of. The curtains of Suzie and Gabriel's room are still drawn. Her pace increases. At this rate she'll make it to the marina in time to join Daniel and Gabe for breakfast.

The one thing she isn't prepared for is Billie's car in the drive. Relief hits her first, then trepidation, olive green turning to rust. She retreats a few steps, but she's not going to be like everyone else and let Gabriel down.

She follows the towpath to the bridge, watching the window

of the empty kitchen, then breaks into a jog. The terracotta pot by the back door is filled with rainwater. It soaks all the way to her shoulder as she scrabbles for the key, a layer of ooze packing under her nails. The door opens with a loud, splintery crack and she hesitates, listening. For the first time, the silence is welcome.

Her pulse is an ocean in her ears as she moves towards the sitting room. The door is closed. Beyond it, the murmur of a single voice. Her sister's. No choice but to face both Suzie and Billie. Her throat dries, her nerves like a mouthful of sand. Picturing an umbrella above her in courageous gold, she opens the door.

The two women are on the sofa, facing away from each other. Suzie is a red candle of rage, straight-backed, fists clenched in her lap, right on the edge of the seat, spring-loaded. In contrast, Billie is slumped back, slack as a deboned fish, letting her colours have free play. Dirty snow shame, bitter blues.

For the first time in her life, Billie has had to admit to fucking up. Until now, Anna's particular area of expertise. A flag of olive-green relief from her sister as Billie sees her. From Suzie, the red flame reaches out to encompass her as well.

'The poison-bitch sisters reunited.' Suzie feeds her words through the grille of her clenched teeth.

'Are you OK, Bills?' Her sister's face is gaunt, her skin parched and pale as tissue paper, the lines around her mouth and beneath her eyes deeply engraved.

Billie nods without conviction, shifting her position so she is facing Suzie.

'I'm sorry from the bottom of my heart. I don't know what else to say.'

'That's not good enough,' Suzie says, her teeth still clamped. There's something comfortable about the way the woman wears

319

her fury, Anna thinks, and wonders how she never picked up on it before.

'All I can do is apologise.' There's a waver in her sister's voice. 'I don't know how to fix this.'

'Bills, stop. Don't apologise any more.' Anna points at Suzie. 'She's done far worse than either of us.'

Through the heart of Suzie's red flame, a spear of orange; fleeting, but she catches it. 'Suzie, do you want to tell my sister where you were the night Lily disappeared, or shall I?' She doesn't wait for the woman to respond, turning to face Billie. 'Suzie left Daniel alone at home, took Lily to the pavilion and got her good and drunk.'

'You know nothing.' Suzie gets to her feet and there's a dark magenta relish to her rage. It strikes Anna as a sorry thing, to have been angry for so long that it has become a perverse pleasure.

'You left her there, barely conscious, alone in the pavilion, and she never made it home. You punished her because she admitted how she felt about Gabriel.'

'How she felt? She was fucking him. Every moment my back was turned. Probably in my own bed.' Suzie isn't lying. No acidic tangerine halo hovers over her, because it's what she believes. There's no colour for being deluded.

'I knew it,' Billie says.

Anna shakes her head. 'It's not true, Bills. I asked Gabriel outright and I saw his colours. He's done nothing wrong.'

Heading over to the desk, she opens the sliding drawer of the filing cabinet. She mustn't get distracted. She leafs through the folders until she finds a slim leather case, the size of a laptop holder.

'What are you doing?' Suzie says.

'Taking this to Gabriel and Dan. He's asked for it and you can't—'

Swift as a diving bird, her long skirt rustling, Suzie crosses the room and grabs her wrist. 'You left Dan with him?'

With a sharp wrench, Anna frees herself, shaken by the slight woman's strength. 'With his *father*, yes.'

'Where are they? Give me the car keys.'

She hesitates, but she has no choice. The car belongs to Suzie. As do Gabriel and Daniel. 'Cranley Marina.'

Suzie takes the keys, snatching up her sandals from the hall floor and running out into the drive barefoot. She stops halfway along the path. Gives a little cough, patting her chest. Wipes her brow, shuffles another couple of steps forward, then drops her sandals. From the doorway, Anna can hear the air rasp out of her chest as she bends over her knees, staggering to keep her balance. It's Billie who goes to her aid, her rescue instinct clearly still intact, though she stops short of touching the woman.

'What's the matter, Suzie?'

'It's a panic attack,' Anna says as she slips the car keys from Suzie's shaking fingers. 'Get her to breathe in and out of a paper bag. They're under the sink. I'll bring Daniel home.'

Suzie straightens, her face ghastly white and shining with sweat, whilst fury blazes out of her undiminished. 'Pathetic,' she manages to say, her voice strangled and breathless. 'One kiss. All it took. Another of Gabe's little fools.'

51

Embarrassed coffee-brown speckles

She makes it to the marina by nine fifteen, having been gone less than an hour. Tucking the leather portfolio under her arm, she runs to the clubhouse. It doesn't matter what Suzie thinks. Gabriel had looked her in the eye that night in the forest and spoken the truth.

Her singular talent, to know when a person is lying or truthful.

The deck is empty despite the sun. Light glitters off the water, cutting silver streaks along the masts and turning portholes into golden discs. It sings inside her head, an electrical hum of brilliance. She almost misses the gentle shield of cloud. Inside the clubhouse, her eyes take a moment to adjust, blinking away dark shapes imposed on her retina by the scouring sunlight. Two tables are occupied, one by an elderly couple, the other by a single person hidden behind a broadsheet. The hands holding the newspaper are male, with manicured, feline nails. Not Gabriel's.

Her stomach lurches with relief as she spots a table in the far corner with the remains of breakfast: a bowl of soggy cornflakes and a half-eaten full English. Pushing the plates to one side, she sits down, the leather case positioned like a trophy amidst the mess. Gabriel will have taken Daniel to the gents.

'Good morning.' Zdenko gives her a broad smile of recognition. 'Come. I give you a clean table.'

'No, it's fine, I'm waiting for these two.' She indicates the place settings. 'Mr O'Keefe and his little boy?'

For some reason this elicits a rain of coffee-coloured beads, and she wonders what she has said to embarrass him. 'Is something wrong?'

'I haven't seen Mr O'Keefe.'

She shakes her head, her smile feeling odd and overstretched as she taps the table. 'His little boy is eight, dark hair.'

Pity, a cloying mauve, replaces the brown beads. His embarrassment had been on her behalf.

'Gabe *told* me to meet him here.' She picks up the portfolio. 'He asked me to bring this.'

Zdenko recovers his professional air. 'In that case I bring you a coffee or tea whilst you wait? This table was two ladies, the Pennyman sisters.'

She follows him to a clean table, glancing at the wall clock, its glass reflecting a crescent slice of light that cuts into her eyes. They're on their way. She's beaten them to it, having been far quicker than expected. Calm down and wait.

Fifteen minutes later, her mobile rings. She lurches for it, banging her knee on the underside of the table, shaken from a blank reverie of patience.

It isn't Gabriel, but Margaret.

'What do you want?' She has no time for the girl and her dramas right now.

'I just wanted to … Are you OK, Anna?'

'I'm quite busy, so shall we speak later?' Her thumb hovers over the call-end button. 'Unless there's something vital you need to share?'

'April and I are worried about you. We think you're getting kind of caught up with Gabriel.'

'Is that right?' She closes her eyes, reining in the temptation to fling the mobile across the room. 'Or is the problem that you're jealous of Gabriel, because Lily was so in love with him.'

There's a pause. 'I wouldn't say she was so in love with him, Anna.'

'No? She got his initial tattooed into her skin. Unless of course G is for Greta?'

The line goes dead. She ignores the brown scrap of guilt shivering in her sight. She'll apologise for her small unkindness next time she sees the girl.

Behind the bar, Zdenko is watching her, polishing glasses. Avoiding his gaze, she checks the wall clock. It's been almost forty minutes.

She gives them ten more minutes, then calls Gabriel's mobile. It rings unanswered and her brain offers up a series of morbid images: a wrecked car, bodies limp, suspended upside down by their seat belts. She puts the portfolio on her lap, fiddles with the zip. When she tries Gabriel's phone again, it goes straight to voicemail. She opens the case.

Inside it, there are bills – utility bills, phone bills, MOT bills. They date from a few years back, 2011 to 2014. She looks through them one at a time, slides her hand through the inside pocket and finds it empty. With care, her hand shaking, she zips the case shut.

A file of defunct papers. A decoy.

The sun shines, the water glitters, but the world is an ugly place, toad green and dirty purple.

52

Silver clarity

She stalls at the junction with the marina behind her as she waits to pull out onto the main road. There's no traffic. Through the confusion, a clarity is descending. It comes to her in a silvery light. She can't see the whole picture yet, but she understands two things. Firstly, that until this moment she has allowed herself to be a child, irresponsible, reckless and wanton, bold in the surety that her family will always pick her up and set her back on her feet.

The second, that with her help, Gabriel has run away with Daniel.

Suzie is sitting on the garden wall, hugging her arms, watching Anna pull in with a blank expression as though she hasn't recognised her own car. Gabriel's Defender isn't there, killing the last of her desperate hope. Her sister's car is gone. Just her and Suzie, then. She can't hesitate or her nerve will fail.

'I couldn't find them.' She comes to stand beside Suzie, a small voice in her head reminding her how volatile and aggressive the woman can be. But then she probably deserves a slap. 'Gabe told me to meet them at the marina, but they didn't turn up.'

Suzie nods, picking a piece of moss out of the stone, small as a pincushion, with tiny violet flowers on needle stalks. 'Do you know what I did before I left Lily in the pavilion?'

She waits for a response, making sure Anna is listening. Anna shakes her head.

'I gave her a pound coin. I told her to throw it in the well and make a wish. She could hardly stand.' Suzie digs a finger between the stones, gouging out the moss. 'I wonder why I did that. I think about it a lot. What do you think?'

'I don't know. But you need to get hold of Gabriel.'

Suzie studies her. Blank, almost colourless. 'He'd never take Daniel from me.'

A glitter of light catches Anna's attention. Sun on water. The canal has risen during the night's endless rainfall and flooded the side of the garden. It almost reaches the house, stopping the width of a child's foot away from the wall. She imagines it seeping underground, eating away at the foundations. Perhaps a sinkhole will open under the O'Keefes' house. 'I think it's time for me to leave.'

'Think you can just walk away?' Suzie says. 'You've played your part in all of this.'

A scratching noise makes them look towards the canal. With a stiff-bristled brush, Ben is trying to drive the water off the towpath and back into the canal, but his actions create a restless surge, helping the water reach the house.

Anna climbs onto the wall beside Suzie. Billie was right about the need for a reckoning. There's no walking away this time.

'No one knows what happened to Lily after you left, Suzie.'

'She tried to make a wish, of course.' A blue ribbon unspools above Suzie's head. 'My poor, poor girl.'

Anna says nothing, because it doesn't explain the tied shoelaces.

Each passing hour adds another layer of cement to her certainty that Gabriel isn't coming back. When she finally persuades Suzie to call his mobile, it goes straight to voicemail. Suzie doesn't bother to leave a message, and Anna fights an urge to grab the woman by the shoulders and shake the passivity out of her.

'He's punishing me, that's all.'

When the sun drops behind the trees, Anna makes pasta with garlic, onion and chilli. She can barely manage a mouthful, whilst Suzie methodically clears her plate, a void above her head. Once the dishes have been put away and the kitchen surfaces scrubbed clean, she faces Suzie across the empty table.

'It's time to call the police.'

'And say what? My son is with my husband?'

She follows Suzie upstairs, but the woman ignores her pleas as she climbs into her son's bed under the red eyes of the dragon.

53

Beetle-green determination

Someone is calling her name. She wakes fully clothed, crumpled on her side. She hadn't intended to go to sleep, but at some point she'd sat down on Lily's bed and her body had caved in.

'Anna?' Suzie's voice is pitched with alarm. 'There's a car outside.'

Not a police car, please not a police car. She rushes from the room, dizzy with fatigue. Suzie is at the top of the stairs, pinching the tips of her fingers like Daniel does when he's anxious. The doorbell rings and Suzie retreats to her bedroom, not quite closing the door so she can listen from behind it like the terrified child she's become.

The last person Anna expects is Lauritz.

'I am leaving in an hour for the airport,' he says. 'Can I speak with you first?'

He's wearing a white summer shirt with tiny birds on it, like distant seagulls in a winter sky. The daylight is powdery with early heat, a yellow haze of trapped pollen in the air following a night with no rain, no breeze. The sweet smell of pine resin enters the house along with Lauritz. In a different life, he might have been collecting her for a summer's outing.

She pretends not to notice Suzie watching them from the landing as she leads him to the kitchen and closes the door.

They sit opposite each other, and when he smiles at her, it sets off echoes of an old ache and she doesn't smile back.

'I am sorry for what I did,' he says, direct and to the point. 'I know it is a long time ago now, but it has been on my mind. I can't forgive myself.'

'What you did?'

'Me and you. It was unforgivable.'

She gets up and pours herself a glass of water, one for him as well. 'I knew you were married, Lauritz.'

'I'm not apologising for that. That is between me and Birgitte. But you were so young, Anna, and I was a much older man. I took advantage.'

With a sweep of her hand, she dismisses what he is saying. 'In my recollection, it was me who first knocked on your door. I knew what I was doing.'

'And I should have known better.'

He gulps down his water, pressing the back of his hand to his mouth afterwards. Always so neat and well presented, she thinks, with his crisp collar and clean hair. He looks like a man in control of his life. Even back then, whilst she lost her head, he reined himself in and nudged his life back on track.

'What I'm talking about is not so much your age in num-bers, but life experience. You were young, you were just opening your eyes to the world, and I was a grown man who had seen life and had many relationships. I had a responsibility to behave better than I did.'

She turns her glass between her fingertips, an eye on his colours. The conversation is making him uncomfortable, but overriding the orange wisps is a beetle-green wall, a vegetal, wholesome blend of sincerity, determination, bravery.

'Well. I hope that's made you feel better.'

'I don't feel better, Anna. But I can take responsibility for my mistakes.'

At which point she starts to cry.

'*Så så, lille Anna.*' He gets up, takes her hand and pulls her into a hug, soothing her in Danish. It is an embrace full of comfort and kindness, devoid of any reference to the way their bodies used to connect. She wants to say that she is sorry beyond words that his wife lost their baby but she is not as brave as him. When she draws back, she sees the crinkles around her eyes and smile lines bracketing his mouth.

'Why are you crying?' he says, gently teasing. 'There's nothing to cry about.'

'I'm crying because you're a good person and I'm not. I didn't care that you were married, Lauritz. All my life I've told myself I'm different, I don't belong, so the rules don't apply.'

'And Billie cleaned up after you.' His tone is kind, but it stings nonetheless. 'I saw it. You were like her little pet.'

'You always were so grown-up, Lauritz.' She sits back down and he perches on the table, a knowing smile on his face. She bites her lip to stop from crying again.

'You wouldn't believe how badly I've messed up.' She sweeps her hand around the room as if the evidence is there for him to see. 'Because of me, Daniel's father has managed to take him away. His mother refuses to call the police because ... well. She insists Gabriel will bring him home.'

Lauritz strokes the top of her head, once, then stands up, checking his watch. 'There's always a way to fix our mistakes.'

She gives a bitter laugh. 'How? Seriously, how?'

'For me, I go where it is uncomfortable to go. If there's something I don't want to do or I'm pretending it's not a problem, I make myself go there.'

She thinks about her sister, about Jonah, about Lucas bullying Daniel and how much she wanted to believe that Gabriel had felt something for her. 'Feels shit.'

'Then it's the right path.'

330

She laughs despite herself, and follows him to the door, where she kisses his cheek. 'How was I supposed to resist you? I didn't stand a chance.'

He smiles, drawing away. 'If I had waited until it was right and you were a proper adult and I was free, it might have worked out different.'

54

Rust and ochre

If it feels shit, you're on the right path, she tells herself. Back to Margaret's she goes. A fat droplet of rain hits her cheek as she waits by the door. The morning's heat has curdled and thickened into cloud the colour of ditchwater. Warm one minute, cold and miserable the next. The British weather and Suzie have much in common. She gives a sour grin, giddy with nerves.

Suzie had watched her leave from the shelter of the front door, seething and resentful.

'All this time, it was *me* who wanted to leave but Gabriel wouldn't hear of it. That fucking arsehole.' Her obscenities had added petrol, her entire body engulfed in a fireball of deep reds, the centre crusted black like dried blood. Anna could see its destructive hunger, the desire to inflict physical damage.

That Gabriel had stayed as long as he had was nothing short of saintly.

She rings the doorbell again. Both windows are closed, the curtains drawn. The rain comes and people hurry past, umbrellas bursting open. An abrupt movement in the flow of pedestrians catches her attention. Further along the high street, Margaret collides with a woman in her rush to get away.

She has to run to catch up, calling the girl's name. Margaret makes a sudden turn into a narrow alleyway between a butcher's and a furniture shop, stopping only when Anna is a few steps behind and she can no longer pretend she hasn't heard her name being called.

'Why are you avoiding me?'

'I wasn't. I was trying to get out of the rain.' A tiny orange halo above her crown as she holds out her hands, droplets breaking against her palms. They head for a low arch where the buildings connect above the alleyway. The floor is strewn with cigarette butts and pigeon feathers. Steps lead up from the arch to a car park on higher ground, and already a thin stream of filthy water is trickling down the stairs. Margaret looks as miserable as Anna feels.

'I have a gift, Margaret. I know when a person's lying.'

The younger woman puts one sandalled foot into the stream of water, letting it gush over her toes. Biting her lip as if to stop the words coming out.

'Do you know where Gabriel is?'

Margaret shakes her head. At this moment, telling the truth. 'I need to get home,' she says as a curtain of rain spills over the entrance of their grim little shelter.

'Tell me what you've been keeping secret.'

A man passes the entrance of the alley, staring at them from under his umbrella as if he senses something untoward taking place in the dark recess.

'If I do … you can't tell anyone.'

'It depends what you tell me. I don't know how bad it is.'

Rain blows against her face and bare calves, making her itch with moisture. She doesn't want to be here any more than Margaret does, but she can feel the girl wobbling on the edge of her resolve.

Margaret jabs the tip of her sandal into the stream again, and water splashes out over Anna's ankles. 'Lily lost her virginity to Gabriel when she was fifteen.'

The air leaves Anna's chest, making her breathless. 'I don't believe you.'

'Thought you could tell.' Margaret plays with the red stripe in her hair, fidgeting with discomfort. 'When someone's lying or telling the truth.'

'Say it again. About Lily and Gabriel.'

Margaret repeats herself. Not a trace of orange enters the cold, glacial lake above her head; the exact same colour as Gabriel's when he insisted he'd done nothing wrong.

Anna leans back against the damp brick wall.

Fifteen. At that age, she herself had kissed a few boys with the same experimental approach as trying a new and exotic foodstuff. She hadn't even graduated to tampons by then.

'It's not true.' She hears the raw plea in her voice. Margaret catches it too, a fine veil of mauve over her features.

Predators are a fact of existence, like rain and death. But not Gabriel.

'They were at it for years. I can't believe Suzie was so blind to it,' the young woman says. 'It was happening right in front of her.'

Anna sees again Gabriel's honest blue-green blaze in the torchlight. *I've done nothing wrong.* She'd believed him. Still believes him. But it doesn't stop the cinnamon twister massing in the pit of her stomach, threatening to rip everything to pieces.

What if she's been getting it wrong all these years?

'Who got Lily pregnant?' She already knows what Margaret will say.

'Gabriel's the only man Lily ever slept with. Ben was happy to let everyone think it was him at the time. He was also paid for it. Why do you think Gabriel employs the lazy little toerag?'

Fifteen years old. She feels sick, brushing the water from

her shins to avoid Margaret's pity. Running through it, a thin, cheese-yellow vein of enjoyment.

If she was wrong about Gabriel, she could be wrong about anything.

'Do you know why people thought Lily was a slut?' Margaret is saying, but Anna is struggling to concentrate over the clamour in her head. Pillarbox red flares above Margaret's head. It rises and dips because, unlike Suzie, the girl doesn't enjoy her anger. 'Your sister. Spreading rumours, telling lies to everyone she knows.'

'Oh God.' Anna closes her eyes. She'd pressed Margaret for answers, convinced the girl held the missing piece of information that would cut the link between this hideous mess and the people she loves – Billie, Gabriel, Jonah.

'Lily had been trying to end the affair for ages. Gabriel's too intense, too greedy. Forget making plans on a Thursday. On Thursdays she belonged to him.'

All she can do is shake her head.

'What was Lily supposed to do?' Margaret says. 'Stuck in his house, owing him everything. And she could hardly go to Suzie, could she?'

Anna straightens, trying to think clearly. 'But why get a tattoo with his initial?'

'His idea. His drawing. He wanted to put his stamp on her. It was Lily's idea for us to run away. She chose Valentine's Day, for the irony, and only had one angel wing done. Like a symbol, you know, to show him how he'd broken her and stopped her from flying.'

Anna's no longer certain she wants the truth. Too late now. 'What happened when you left Dragon's Ink?'

Margaret licks her lips, the smirk gone and in its place an ochre glow. 'Lily called Gabe and told him it was over. She was done with it. What's more, she was going to admit it to

335

Suzie because she felt so rubbish about it. She wanted to make it right. The last I saw of her, she was getting into a car, like I told you before.'

A small grey car. Maybe it was Jonah, maybe not.

'I didn't even get to say goodbye because Gabriel was calling and calling.'

'Did you tell the police...' Rust flakes off the air. She could choke on it. 'About Gabriel and Lily?'

'I had to, didn't I.' Margaret tugs her sleeve over her wrist, scowling. 'But there was no proof. Lily had been so careful to protect him. No diary, no texts, not a thing to link the two of them. Except that bloody tattoo.'

'And you told them Lily was heading home?'

Hunching her shoulders, the younger woman steps out into the rain. 'Yeah, but according to the O'Keefes she never made it back.'

It wouldn't ease the girl's pain to tell her what happened next. If she reveals Suzie's false alibi, Suzie will point at Billie – who had tormented Lily with anonymous threats and whose husband drives a small, grey car. The ground under their feet is made of lies. Sooner or later, it'll give way and a giant sinkhole will swallow them all up, including Anna herself.

55

Faded china blue

Anna takes her time driving home. Billie had repeatedly warned her what kind of man Gabriel was, but she'd ignored it, thinking it came from the same jealous place that made her sister point out the air bubble in her glass ballerina.

The thought of Gabriel's hands on that young girl is unbearable. And yet he'd radiated blue-green honesty as he insisted on his innocence. Distracted, she overshoots the turning to the O'Keefes' and has to make an arduous U-turn in the narrow lane.

When she pulls up outside the house, Suzie's face is at the bedroom window, watching for Gabriel's return. Anna parks, locks the car and is halfway along the drive when she has to stop walking. Bending forward, she retches over the grass, aware that Suzie is watching her. Nothing comes up, the thing making her sick refusing to dislodge. When she looks up, shaking and wiping sweat off her brow, Suzie is no longer at the window.

Having drunk a glass of water, she goes upstairs. Suzie looks as ill as Anna feels. The woman's hair is lank, eyes flat and lifeless as if they've been painted on, the skin of her cheeks papery. It reminds Anna of April's little speech about the body's rivers of energy. Suzie's rivers have dried out.

A glass lies in the puddle of its spilled water by Suzie's

337

bedside table. She's made no effort to pick it up. 'Are you hungry, Suzie?'

'Just thirsty.'

Anna avoids her own reflection as she fills the glass from the bathroom tap. Assumptions add their own colour filter. In the few hours she's been gone, her filter has changed. Suzie isn't a controlling, abusive monster; she's a woman broken by betrayal – real or otherwise – and the corrosive power of guilt. She wonders how often Suzie imagines Lily standing on the greasy iron rung to throw her coin into the flooding water and make her wish.

'Have you heard from them?'

Suzie shakes her head against the pillow, a strand of hair caught in her eyelashes. 'He's making me pay for all the misery I've brought him these last few months. Him and Daniel.'

'What about the misery he brought you?' As much as it hurts her, once the air bubble has been pointed out, it's impossible to feel the same again.

When the rain stops, she misses it. In its wake she can hear Suzie crying and her own footsteps in the empty rooms. Her armpits are damp, a pre-exam chill running through her body. When the post hits the mat, citrus birds startle across her sight.

As she sorts through the junk mail, a car pulls up outside. Calling to Suzie, she throws open the door to find Detective Adeyemi's blue Vauxhall parking in the drive. Her heart steps up a beat. Here, then, an opportunity.

Suzie rushes down the stairs, spots the car through the open doorway and ducks out of sight with a curse.

'Get rid of her,' she hisses from the staircase.

Anna watches the FLO take her bag off the passenger seat and tug the hem of her jacket. 'I can't send her away.'

'Tell her I'm sick with flu and I can't come down.' Suzie

peeks out, one bloodshot eye visible and an aura like broken, bloodied glass.

The FLO reaches the porch. Warm smile, shellfish-pink shirt, a sheen of gold across her eyelids, everything about Detective Adeyemi soft and mellow except the alert track of her gaze.

She points a thumb over her shoulder at the drive. 'No Gabriel today?'

'I don't know where he is. Or Daniel.' She has to be careful. Suzie is listening.

'But Suzie is home?'

'Yes.' Anna steps aside to let the detective in. *Look at my face, read me, even if you can't see my colours*, she begs silently. 'Suzie's here but I'm to tell you that she's unwell.'

'Ah.' Juliet makes a sympathetic noise and stops just inside the door.

'But she's upstairs.'

'I won't disturb her if she is under the weather,' Juliet says, taking her car keys from her bag. 'I'll come back at a more convenient time.'

Anna pictures Daniel the last time she'd seen him, racing off to help April collect eggs. Happy to have found his dad. But at some point, no matter what Gabriel says, he'll want to come home. She follows the detective out. 'I'm sorry you've had a wasted journey.'

'It's OK.' The woman gives an easy smile and heads to the car.

'Especially as you haven't been here for a while.'

The FLO stops, her lively bronze greens like flags in a breeze, paying attention. 'The O'Keefes feel they are coping admirably at the moment. They have expressed a need for privacy and family time.' She unlocks the driver's door. 'What would you say, Anna? Do you think they're coping?'

Above her, Suzie's window opens. She greets the detective, swaying and cadaverous with fatigue as she apologises for being too ill to come downstairs. Wishing her a quick recovery, Detective Adeyemi leaves. Suzie stares down at Anna for a long moment, but there's no aggressive burgundy or threatening red. There's no need. She and Suzie and Billie are bound together by their lies. Suzie lets her borrow the car again, her only question how long Anna intends to be gone.

When she pulls up outside Billie's house, she can't recall the journey, her thoughts caught in an anxious loop. She rings the doorbell, fighting an urge to run back to the car. It reminds her of bothering their neighbours when she was six and Billie ten, ringing doorbells and seeing how long they could hold their nerve.

Through the nearest window she can see the television on and a pair of men's feet on the coffee table amid newspapers and coffee cups. When she raps on the glass, the feet give a start, knocking a pile of papers off the table. Jonah isn't happy when he opens the door and sees her.

'Have you been fired?' she says.

Wearing shorts that might have fitted him when he was two sizes bigger and a crumpled T-shirt, he looks like he's just rolled out of bed. 'Working from home today.'

'And hard at it, from the looks of things.'

Still grave, he bobs his head, shying away from her attempts at light-hearted chatter. It gives her a pang of regret; she hopes their friendship will one day recover. This visit isn't going to help, she suspects. 'Is Bills in?'

'No. She's ... gone away again.'

She stares at him through a thin veil of disbelieving khaki green. 'Jo, what the hell is going on here?'

He stands back to let her in, not meeting her eye. His fussy little beard has grown out, eyes baggy with fatigue, returning to the old Jonah. 'Have you really not noticed how unwell your sister is?'

'I know she's been drinking a lot.' She meets his eyes, shamed.

He nods. 'We forget that Billie's a fallible human being like everyone else, not an indestructible robot with balls of steel.'

'Though she does actually have balls of steel.'

This time he smiles, and it releases a small knot in her chest. She follows him to the old part of the house, with its exposed beams and crooked, seasick timbers. The sitting room is snug but draughty, the whole thing tilting with age. Jonah slumps onto the sofa with an exhausted huff whilst Anna remains standing, gathering herself.

'Where is she, then?'

'Apparently she's been checking herself in at a spa.'

She gives a bark of disbelief. 'A spa? My sister?'

'More of a clinic. To help her relax, get some sleep. Deal with her drinking. They pretty much keep a room for her these days.'

Above him, rich purple shot through with orange, his concern rising and falling in a motion she associates with bewilderment. Then she looks away, remembering the contradiction of Margaret and Gabriel's icy blue-greens. They can't both be telling the truth.

'Can you give me a number for her?'

Jonah brings his thumb to his mouth, his teeth worrying at the skin beside the nail. She's not seen him do that in a while. Billie used to slap his hand away like he was a naughty five-year-old. 'She's not allowed outside contact. Their mobiles are taken off them. Immersive healing or something.' He lowers his hand, tucking his thumb inside his fingers. 'It's my fault. All of this.'

She holds herself very still. 'In what way?'

'Lily used to come to our house often. She was sweet, but damaged. She had a way about her with men. All men, not just me. She related to them in quite a sexual manner. A survival technique, I suspect, something she learned at a young age.'

Fifteen years old, Margaret had said, whilst Gabriel insisted on his innocence. Perhaps the person telling lies had been Lily, making up stories to impress her friend. 'Gabriel says she was a mini adult by the time she came to live with them.'

'I can see that.' Jonah nods, nibbling the edge of his thumb again. 'Billie simply couldn't understand why I was trying so hard to get fit. She decided it was because of Lily.'

'And was it?' Her voice is sharp and unkind, a red knife through his self-pity, a mournful blue like the faded pattern on a piece of china.

'Lily was little more than a child, for Christ's sake. Maybe I was flattered by her attention. I don't know.' He grinds his eyes with his thumbs. 'Billie's such a large presence. Sometimes there isn't space for anyone else. You must know what I mean?'

She presses her lips together, refusing to be disloyal by agreeing.

'I need to show you something.' He gets up, knocking the coffee table with his shin, sending another small landslide of newspapers onto the floor. 'I was searching for a receipt for a coat Billie bought for me because it was too big. I went through her desk, which is something I never do.'

She follows him to the study, where the blanket has been meticulously tucked back in place over the horse-head sofa, cushions resting over its arms so the pattern is all but concealed. She knows it was Margaret who took those photographs of Lily, but the sight of it still sends rust particles through the air. Jonah opens a drawer and takes out a handful of the new Missing posters, Ben's irregular pieces of tape still intact, the paper stippled with dried rain. On the topmost sheet, a handwritten message dissects Lily's face.

Ask Lily's rapist uncle where she is.

It makes no sense, the risk Billie is taking in persisting with her poison messages. 'Why is she still doing this?'

He sits on the sofa, the blanket untucking to reveal its tumbling horse's heads. 'To direct attention away from me.'

'Because you gave Lily a lift the night she disappeared.'

Under any other circumstances, the comic mask of shock on his face would have been amusing.

He'd picked up a Chinese takeaway on his way home, knowing he'd missed dinner. Passing Lily at the taxi rank, he'd been struck by how late it was for her to be out, but he only stopped because she ran into the road behind his car, flagging him down. He knew something was off from the moment she got in. He could smell alcohol on her. Her phone kept ringing and it was agitating her. She'd flung it into the footwell.

'And I thought, there's a phone-screen that'll need replacing.' Jonah nibbles at a hangnail on his thumb.

What happens, Anna wonders, when he finishes talking and she knows everything? What then?

'She put her hand on my thigh and started saying silly things about me being a handsome man, wanting to know if I ever played away. But she didn't mean any of it. She was trying not to cry.'

When he pauses to gnaw at his thumb again, head turned away, she wonders what he's seeing.

'Where did you take her?'

He hesitates. 'Home, of course.' But a tattered brown cloth like the sail of a ghost ship slowly materialises above his head.

'Jonah...?'

He closes his eyes. 'Actually, I dropped her at the end of the

343

lane. I didn't want them to see me – it was late, she was tipsy. It would have looked bad. I should have parked. I could have walked her pretty much to the front door and made sure she was OK.'

She allows him a moment to fold away his guilt. From the size of it, it's going to be with him for a while. 'I assume Billie had something to say on the matter?'

'I didn't tell her.' He rubs his face. 'Not even when Lily first went missing. I told myself it had nothing to do with me. It's only when I learnt the police were looking for the driver of a small grey car to help with their enquiries ...' He takes a ragged breath. She can see the rapid rise and fall of his chest. 'That I told Billie.'

'How did she take it?'

'OK-ish until I said I'd better contact the police and then she went mad, shouting and chucking stuff. Accused me of destroying the family, the children's lives, her life.'

'Very un-Billie-like.' Behind the theatrics, there would have been a cold logic. If Jonah became part of the investigation, Billie's own actions might be exposed.

'I still haven't told the police, Anna. You know what Billie's will is like. Made of the same stuff as her balls.' He gives a rueful smile that finds no colour counterpart above his head.

She can see her sister wrestling with the handle of the Golf's seat, slipping about in the mud, laughing like it was all a great game. Then finding the ring, her reaction to throw it as far from her as possible, in the hope that no one would ever find it.

'Did she believe you, Jonah? That all you did was give Lily a lift?'

'Yes, of course. How can you ask that?' But alongside the bruised purple hurt is a tiny flicker of orange doubt going on and off like a faulty bulb.

It still doesn't explain Lily's shoes in the water, their laces tied together, or April's conviction that someone hurt the girl at the Petrifying Well.

'Do you think they'll ever find her?' Jonah says.

Anna gets up to leave. 'No. Not anymore.'

56

Hope really is golden

The rain has stopped. Each day rises in glorious golds and loving pinks, mocking them. The sunnier the day, the darker, by contrast, it becomes inside the O'Keefes' house. Daniel and Gabriel have been gone for three days. Suzie's room is rank with unwashed skin and dirty hair. The woman barely speaks, never leaves her room. A colourless lump beneath the bedclothes.

'If we've still heard nothing by this evening, I'm going to the police,' Anna tells her, opening the bedroom window.

Suzie rolls away, pinching the covers over her shoulder. 'And I'll tell them about Billie.'

Anna glares at the huddled shape. 'What's your plan? As far as I can tell, it's lying there waiting to die.' She slams the door behind her, an impotent, pointless gesture. Heading to Daniel's room, she straightens his bedding, wishing she'd been more attentive, more affectionate. She should have thought more about him and less about Lily.

She should have given him her frog.

It's not too late. She'll put the frog on Daniel's pillow to wait for his return. Only she can't find it. It's not in her suitcase amongst her unpacked belongings, or in Daniel's hiding places. She thinks back to the day she heard April's wind chimes and realised where Gabriel was; Daniel trailing clementine sparks as she'd harried him to get ready and all but chased him out of the house. Instead of putting on his shoes, he must have squirrelled the frog away in his pocket, a talisman to keep him safe.

The sun is setting but the colours are lost behind the clouds. She puts on a pink jumper and her knitted yellow slippers – vastly reduced in last January's sale – in an effort to raise her mood. Her phone pings with a text from Marni.

Don't forget 16 October. Tequila and nachos at the Happy Piñata as per birthday tradition. My 33rd year of awesomeness. Love you. Even though you're a bit quiet and crap at the mo.

She pictures the Mexican restaurant with its mariachi-band trumpets and post-work crush, her friends jostling for cheese-laden nachos, flushed and happy. For one drowning moment she is certain it will never happen. She will never escape this house and find her way back to her old life.

If I miss it, it's because I'm dead, she replies. She's forgotten how to be funny.

Upstairs, a door opens, followed by a rapid thud of feet. The running stops.

'Anna?' There's a thin wire of panic in Suzie's voice.

'I'm downstairs.'

A moment of stillness in which Anna listens, her heart pounding, followed by a fresh stampede of footsteps. Suzie appears at the top of the stairs, her arm rigid, holding her mobile like it's a torch, the screen pointing away from her.

'It's a sick joke.' She skids and falters her way down the steps.

Anna's stomach vaults as Suzie pushes the mobile into her hand. She doesn't want to see what's on the screen.

'Read it. Read the name.'

There's a brief text from an unnamed mobile. *Dan and Gabe are at the Mill Tavern, off the A358, near Taunton, Somerset. Love*

Lily. A shock of blistering orange makes her blink and rub her eyes.

'Lily?'

Suzie sits on the bottom step, spine rigid, knees to her chest, her hands gripping her ankles. Holding herself together. 'Is it your sister?'

'No … no.' Misgiving opens a sinkhole beneath her until she remembers what Jonah had said about the clinic taking the clients' phones away. Nor was Billie given to hoaxes. At the core of even her most unhinged behaviour, there had been a hard logic. 'Of course not.'

'Then who is it?'

Their eyes meet, and in the silence, Suzie gives a vigorous shake of the head.

'Why isn't it possible?' Anna studies the space above Suzie's head, looking for that telltale brown cloth, the colour of guilt. But then even if it was there, she's no longer sure she can rely on what she sees.

'Lily would never have run off without letting me know she's OK. She would never, ever have done that to me.'

Anna takes Suzie's ballet pumps from the hallway and drops them by her feet. 'We've got no choice then.'

'Daniel had the biggest feet when he was born. This tiny little six-pounder, but his feet… Even the midwife was surprised. *This boy's got feet for going places*, she said.'

Suzie can't stop talking, released from the suspended half-life of the last three days. 'Dan's going to surprise everyone and grow as big as his dad.'

Worse than her manic energy is the glow of hope, a golden halo around her head. Checking the map on her mobile, Anna tries not to think about what they might – or might not – find at the end of their three-hour journey. It'll be late by the time they arrive. With every passing mile, her uncertainty grows. Why would someone send a text pretending to be Lily? Suzie's initial reaction might be correct. This may be a sick hoax.

'Is it possible the text came from Ben?'

Suzie dismisses this suggestion with a curt shake of the head, her nose wrinkling with distaste. 'You know what I think of him, but Lily's trainers being found down that hole shocked him. It's like the reality of it finally hit him. He actually asked if there was something he could do to help.'

The strident red of Suzie's jumper and the black of her trousers bothers the corner of Anna's eye. If she felt less anxious, she would cope better with such aggressive tones.

'Try the number again,' she says. Suzie has sent two texts and tried calling several times. It rings but no one answers.

'We'll be there soon enough.'

'And you don't recognise the number?' She pauses, unwilling to burst the fragile bubble of Suzie's mood. 'It's definitely not Lily's old mobile?'

A brief shake of the head and then Suzie returns to reminiscing about Daniel's baby days. When she moves on to Gabriel, Anna grows quiet as Suzie confesses to her parents' initial coolness – they were hoping for an office professional, not a bloke who messed about with a chainsaw for a living – and how she and Gabriel couldn't keep their hands off each other.

In the silence that follows, Anna swallows on a dry throat. 'I've been meaning to say sorry.'

Suzie holds up a hand, cutting her off. 'In the grand scheme of things, a kiss is pretty paltry. Obviously a bit of me still hates you for it.' She sends Anna an odd twist of a smile. 'But I can see how it happened. You've been kind to him when not many other people have. Not even me. He says he lost his head for a moment.'

349

Anna wonders if Lauritz had told his wife the same thing.

They drive on in silence. The countryside has changed, the forest replaced by acres of farmed pasture and bald hills, a grey dusk sitting over it.

'I haven't been easy to live with,' Suzie says after a while. 'I can't forgive myself for that night with Lily. My anger spills over and everyone gets hurt.'

Anna pictures Daniel rubbing his arm, and as if seeing the same image, Suzie adds, 'Except Daniel. I'd never, ever hurt my son. But once I threw his school shoe and it hit him by mistake.' She draws in a shuddering breath. 'All of that's going to change now. I needed a wake-up call. I was holding on too tightly, making the three of us miserable. But no more.'

Anna nods but doesn't trust herself to speak. She keeps thinking about all the times Daniel asked for her frog. Why couldn't she have said yes?

'Lily was in a crazy little mood,' Suzie says, addressing her words to the passenger window. 'I was pretty unimpressed when she admitted to this obsession for Gabe all these years. He was like a dad to her, so ...' The memory still sets off bitter bloody fireworks. 'I wasn't impressed,' she says again.

'And did Gabriel feel the same about Lily?' Anna's vision is ochre-stained, but she has to know who's telling the truth, Margaret or Gabriel. When she thinks about him, there's still a tiny spot of golden hope, like a firefly, telling her he might be innocent. After all, everyone except Billie thought Anna a thief.

'Oh.' Suzie waves a dismissive hand through the air as though swatting away a lazy fly. 'Lily was all upset and defensive. You know what teenagers are like. Can't ever be in the wrong. So she started suggesting Gabe *had* felt the same. That they'd actually had some sort of ... thing. But that's ridiculous.'

Anna's neck and shoulders are beginning to ache, her fingers gripping the wheel too hard. The sun has disappeared and there are no street lights. She can't risk taking her eyes off the unfamiliar road with its unexpected twists. At least not long enough to catch some subtle play of colour. 'You seemed to believe it the other day.'

A quick glance across to find Suzie staring at her, her colour smeary avocado-green disapproval. 'I see where you're going with this. If Gabe's that kind of man, it lets you off the hook for kissing him.'

It's time to give up. One day perhaps she'll read about it in the papers: the truth of what happened to a young girl who vanished one night without a trace.

57

Black swarm

The Mill Tavern is a sprawling building set at the inter-
section of two busy roads; a 1920s monstrosity with faux
wattle-and-daub walls and prison floodlights. Everything about
it makes her depressed: the cell-like windows of its guest rooms,
the playground with chipped fibreglass elephants for children
to clamber on, the empty beer garden facing the traffic lights.

Neither of them makes a move to get out of the car.

'They're not here, are they?' Suzie says.

Gabriel's Defender isn't among the cars parked outside. A
sign points to the side of the building, where the river runs,
offering extra parking for guests only.

'I'll take a look round the back,' Anna says, and is pleased
with how calm she sounds. Of course they're not here. It's a
malicious joke, or worse.

The river reaches high up on the bank, but it is sluggish,
barely moving. There are no birds, no brush of air through the
branches, only the drone of traffic on the other side of the trees.
Rounding the corner, she finds a small car park by the kitchen
bins and a single car. Gabriel's Defender. She runs back and
knocks on the passenger window, beckoning Suzie out.

'What?' the woman mouths, shrinking into her seat like a
terrified child. She opens the door an inch to hear what Anna
is saying.

'Gabe's car is at the back.'

'Thank God, oh thank God.' In her sudden rush, Suzie leaves her door open and Anna has to close it before following her to the pub entrance.

'Wait, Suzie, please.' It doesn't feel right. They still don't know who has led them here, and why.

'I have to find Dan.'

Anna isn't sure she can face Gabriel. And if, against all possibility, Lily is here, what then? 'Are you sure you want me to come in?'

'Well...' Suzie hesitates.

She isn't wanted here. She never was.

The hectic yellows issuing out of Suzie darken to burnt sienna. She too is afraid of what she'll find. 'You can mind Daniel whilst Gabe and I talk things over.'

At the bar, Anna has to shout to make herself heard over the football match on the screen above the fireplace. The barman winces in his effort to hear what she's saying, a pumpkin splash of irritability above his crown. Suzie scans the tables but Anna already knows Gabriel and Daniel aren't in the bar. She's always been able to pick a familiar face from a crowd with ease, as if knowing a person's colours helps her home in on them. The barman disappears through a door behind the bar, returning with a black leather book. 'What was the name again?'

'O'Keefe.'

He follows his finger down the page, already shaking his head.

'Where's Daniel? I need to see my son,' Suzie says, pushing in, being no help whatsoever.

'Their car is at the back. A black Defender,' Anna says. 'The man's big, tall, and he has his eight-year-old son with him.'

She sees the man recognise the description. He holds up a finger. 'Wait a minute.'

Suzie glares at Anna, her colours a finger-poke of blame, as the barman disappears into the back office again. He returns with a loose collection of papers and a pink smile of admiration.

'The little lad wanted us to print his pics for him. A whizz-kid millionaire in the making, that one. He showed me all about AirDrop. Admittedly it took me a while to figure out how to get the photos from my phone to the printer.'

Suzie doesn't give the papers a second glance, seething in her burnt orange dust devil as she demands the room number. Anna takes them, flicking through grainy print-outs of photographs similar to the ones in Daniel's secret scrapbook; Mum, Dad and Daniel.

Relief breaks over her. Daniel is here.

Suzie runs ahead. The corridor is narrow and windowless, the red carpet runner the precise tone of violent lust, a blend of anger and sex, the walls a shade lighter. It makes Anna claustrophobic. Suzie stops outside number 22 with a backwards glance, still afraid to do it alone.

With a single knock, the door opens wide, making her drop back in surprise. Gabriel is in the doorway and Anna catches the gold starburst above his head. The sight of the two of them snuffs it out. He's waiting for someone else.

'What are you doing here?' Even if Suzie can't see the full extent of his disappointment as Anna can, his tone is heavy with it. He puts an arm across the doorway, barring entry. A brief hesitation before Suzie ducks beneath it. Gabriel sends another glance along the corridor, his look passing straight through Anna as if she no longer exists. His hair is wet and he's wearing a shirt with burgundy stripes, still holding its crisp shop folds, straight out of the packaging. She's never seen him in a shirt before. She waits to see if he'll acknowledge her, but he disappears back into the room.

'Where's Daniel?' she hears Suzie say, the panic in her voice sending knife-edge slices through Anna's vision. She stands in the doorway. Gabriel is sitting on the bed, head in his hands. Suzie is opposite him, her back pressed to the wall, disbelief shivering out of her as she scans the room. 'He's not here. Where is he?'

'He's fine. Calm down.' Gabriel hunches over his knees, picking at a livid mark on the tender inside of his wrist. At first Anna mistakes it for a fresh injury, but then she sees it's a tattoo, raw and raised against his skin. A rose, the word *Lily* bedded inside its petals.

The tiny golden firefly is snuffed out.

Margaret, then. Margaret was the one telling the truth. The blood drains from her head. She grips the door frame, blinking away dizzy spots of light.

Lily and Gabriel.

She can't bear to look at him. A screen of tears fills her eyes and she glances down to hide them. Not that anyone is paying attention to her. She pretends to study the photographs, blinking until her eyes clear. The top photo is of Daniel with an uncharacteristic grin, eyes squeezed shut with joy as he hugs his mother. She blinks again, clearing her sight. Not Suzie, but Lily.

'Gone? What do you mean gone?' The tone of Suzie's voice makes her look up. The woman's colours have changed, reds bleeding into the air, forming a slow, darkening swarm like a cluster of flies above her head.

'He's been taken home,' he says.

The black swarm thickens, spinning harder. 'What? He's not at home. What are you trying to do to me?'

'Go home and you'll find him.' Above Gabriel's head, nothing but a vast flat sea. The Lily Blues.

She looks away. She can't bear to see it, Gabriel's love and loss for a girl who was pretty much his daughter. She focuses on the photograph instead and notices how, in contrast to Daniel's jubilation, Lily is not even smiling. She hugs the little boy, but meets the camera's eye with a wary, unhappy glance.

Without warning, Suzie launches herself at Gabriel, her fist raised in the air. He drops his head against her blows but makes no effort to shield himself, grinding his thumb back and forth across the tattoo. Droplets of blood pop under the track of his nail.

'What have you done with him?' she shrieks, over and over, locked in her violence, deaf and blind to everything but the jarring contact of her fists against his body. She wouldn't hear him even if he answered.

Anna leaves the room. Kneels in the corridor with the pictures beside her, fingers shaking as she scrolls through her contacts looking for Detective Adeyemi's number. Trying to keep her colours clear so she can think over Suzie's hysteria and the flat, meaty slap of her hands.

Something green appears in the picture beside her knee. Her mobile drops to the carpet. Leaning over the photograph, she studies Daniel's right hand, the one resting against Lily's shoulder as he hugs her.

Inside his clenched fist is her frog.

'Suzie? *Suzie!*' She runs out of breath, dizzy with shock. There's too much colour in the room, hers and Suzie's and Gabriel's, darting and swooping like bats, making her sick and dizzy. She can barely see straight. Suzie has stopped throwing punches but she's got hold of Gabriel's collar, tugging and wrenching at it as she sobs incoherent words.

'Stop now, Suzie.' No one hears her voice.

By the bedside there's an open bottle of beer. She tosses the contents at the woman, catching her by surprise. Suzie steps back, her clenched fists drifting slowly to her sides. Gabriel turns his head to stare out of the window. Past caring.

'Look.' Anna holds the picture up but Suzie bats it away. She tries again. 'Would you just bloody look. It's my frog. Daniel's holding my frog.'

Suzie's not listening, shivering in the fever of her rage as she tugs beads of brown ale from her hair, her shaky breath filling the room.

'Lily's alive.' Anna turns the picture towards Gabriel, who drops back against the bed, slow as a felled tree.

'You chased Lily away, Suzie,' he says. 'You took her from me.'

Suzie has grown very still, her eyes glazed with confusion but present again.

Anna shows her the photograph, points it out one more time – Lily and Daniel and her frog. Comprehension rises like the sun over Suzie.

'She's alive?' It comes out as a cracked whisper.

Gabriel looks at Anna. One eye the colour of leaves in sunlight, the colour of kindness; the other the colour of coffee grounds, for guilt, regret, self-loathing. The feelings that leave a stain. 'Clever, clever Anna.'

It frightens her when a person's colour sucks inwards, hiding their intent. She swallows, reaches for Suzie's hand and encourages her towards the door.

Gabriel points a finger at his wife. 'You hit Lily, slapped her across the face as though that girl, that angel, was something you'd scraped off your shoe.' His voice is tight, an artery visible above his temple like a worm cast under the sand. Straining to keep control. 'You shamed her. She wouldn't even look at me when I got to the pavilion.' He pushes his hands into his hair. 'As if *I* was the monster.'

357

This is how Margaret and Gabriel were both telling the truth. From the core of his being, Gabriel believes he has done nothing wrong.

She tugs Suzie's hand, inching towards the doorway.

'You *are* the monster, Gabriel,' she says, but he doesn't hear her because she is irrelevant and always was. Billie had been right about him. He'd been aware of her infatuation and worked it like reins in his hands.

'Lily was fifteen when it started. That's not love, that's abuse.' She tries to meet Suzie's eye and snap the woman out of her daze.

Gabriel makes a disdainful noise. 'I saved her. I gave her the love that had been missing her entire life.' And there it is, the blue blaze of his conviction.

'It's not true,' Suzie says. Anna's exact words to Margaret. How Gabriel had blinded them all. 'You're saying this to hurt me.'

Anna gives Suzie's hand another surreptitious tug. 'What about her trainers, Gabriel?'

'Still snooping, Detective Anna?' He gives a bitter laugh. 'Lily called me from the pavilion. She wanted her favourite boots. She could barely string a sentence together she was so wasted. And so angry. She tied her trainers together and tried to loop them onto a nail so they could be turned to stone. She thought that was funny.'

'All this time?' Rage bursts into the air above Suzie's head, a disturbed hive, seething and black. 'You've known she's alive all this time?'

He doesn't speak, his sightless eyes boring through the ceiling. 'I meant to punish you. Just for a day or two. Let you suffer for what you had done. But then off you ran to the police, telling your lies.'

Suzie is shivering in convulsive bursts. 'Why would Lily want to hurt me like that? No word, nothing.'

'I was supposed to tell you she was leaving. Lily's not vengeful like you.' Gabriel's drowning colours make a protective spike. 'But you didn't deserve it.'

'You let me think I killed her.' The words shake out of her.

'You may as well have.' Gabriel rolls away from them. 'Because she's never coming home.'

Anna is driving too fast. Blinking and rubbing her eyes, a futile reflex that won't clear the cement dust and drowning blues from her sight.

'Do you think she'll be there? At home?' Suzie says, as if Anna has the answers. Suzie is past tears, her body upright and rigid, the seat belt straining and catching as the car careers through dips and bends.

'I hope so.'

They hadn't got much sense from Gabriel after a while. All that ash raining down on him. Lily had contacted him, he said, out of the blue, suggesting they meet, but it was a trick. She just wanted to bring Daniel home, trying to fix the wrongs she'd committed against Suzie. How Lily knew that Gabriel and Daniel had gone away together, he had no idea.

Anna imagines how it will be. The ghost she has lived with, coming to life. She mustn't hug Lily or behave as if she knows her. She must remember they are strangers.

The blare of a horn travels past them as she struggles to keep control of the car. Her eyes keep returning to the rear-view mirror, but Gabriel won't be following them. They'd left him on the bed looking as though he might never move again. All she can think of is Daniel. In her haste, she'd reversed into the wooden fence surrounding the beer garden, the jolt and crack of the impact making them both gasp, but she'd kept going.

'What if they aren't there?' Suzie says, voicing Anna's fears.

'Call the house.'

Suzie does as she's told, but there's no answer. She replaces the mobile in her bag and stares at the road ahead.

Lily is alive.

Before they left the hotel room, Anna had taken one last hard look at Gabriel. Flat on his back, those powerful hands lying useless on the bed, like leaves curling in on themselves. The vein in his forehead pulsed, his face red, straining against slow, agonised tears. He seemed smaller, and ordinary. Now that the lens was smeared, she could no longer recall how he used to look.

Suzie opens the passenger door before the car has come to a halt. The front door is closed; the trembling in Suzie's hands prevents her from getting the key into the lock. Anna takes the keys from her damp grasp and realises the door isn't locked. A dragonfly flutter of gold lifts in the air.

The hall light is on.

'Dan?' They call his name at the same time. A yawn of silence and then, like a vision, Daniel appears in the hallway and his mother is sobbing and pulling him into her arms. Anna drops to her knees beside them, taking his hand in hers and kissing his small fist. Clasped in his fingers, keeping him safe, is her ceramic frog.

'Lily? Is Lily here?' Suzie says, looking past him towards the kitchen. Anna follows her gaze, her heart working its way up her throat.

'No,' says Daniel, and a toad-green curtain falls back in place.

58

Old anger is the colour of healed wounds

It's late October. Summer is long gone, a distant place where the O'Keefes still live. It couldn't feel further away as Anna faces Lauritz's house with the winter sea behind her. She's standing in the exact spot she stood thirteen years earlier, when she was just nineteen. Lily's age. It looks the same. She can't shake the notion that if she waits long enough, Lauritz will step out onto his porch and his wife will join him a moment later, and she'll have to witness all over again the brief exchange of intimacy, the pennies of a long, solid relationship. She's ready to lose her nerve again, as she did all those years ago.

If it feels shit, you're on the right path.

Scrappy flakes of snow have started to fall, brushing about in the air. It wasn't snowing last time. The looped moment passes. She crosses the road, unlatches the gate and walks to the front door, her legs feeble as though pushing through deep water. Woven paper hearts in white and red hang in the downstairs windows, but up on the first floor is a haphazard arrangement of gel stickers – Christmas trees, presents and cartoon reindeer. A child's decorations.

Lauritz's wife, Birgitte, opens the door. She blinks, pushing her hair behind her ear. The recognition is instant, the battle of colour above her head confirming what Anna already knows. This is going to be a difficult encounter.

'My name's—'

'I know what your name is.'

The woman is not going to invite her in, so she will have to make her apology on the doorstep in the falling snow.

'I'm not here to see Lauritz.'

'Good. He isn't here.' Her accent is harsher than Lauritz's. It makes her sound angry, and whilst anger *is* present – a scab-coloured red, slowly unfolding – there is also green curiosity. The door isn't about to be slammed in her face just yet.

A television is on in the background. The smell of roasting meat and aromatic herbs reaches her. A pair of shoes, pink with leather flowers, sits beside the doormat. They're smaller than Daniel's shoes and the sight of them sends an irrational poke of pain through her. Their child can be no more than four years old. The memory of Lauritz is going to be a boulder around which the rest of her life will have to flow.

She gathers herself. 'I wanted to apologise for all those years ago. I'm truly sorry. I was young, selfish, and I didn't think about anyone else.'

Birgitte gives little away, her colours settling. Crossing her arms, head to one side, she considers Anna. 'You have a lot to apologise for. You did a lot of damage.'

Anna nods, holding the woman's gaze. She can't imagine how Birgitte must have felt, showing Billie the pictures of her unborn child, the baby she never got to hold because of her. She can't imagine how her sister felt, the shield that took the blows.

'You lost your baby. I can never make it up to you and I'm not here for your forgiveness, just to let you know it is something I'll always carry with me.'

'Mor?' A little girl runs through the hall. Catching sight of Anna, she wraps her arms around her mother's leg, regarding the stranger for a second before losing interest. She has dark curls and brown eyes, unlike her parents' fair colouring. She tugs at the hem of her mother's jumper and Anna can't help but smile, understanding the little girl's demanding tone if not her language.

Birgitte swings the little girl up onto her hip. 'This is Mette.'

Anna smiles, touched by the introduction, knowing it is time to leave. She thanks the woman for listening.

'The picture of the baby,' Birgitte says as Anna turns away. 'It was old. From some years before you and Lauritz.'

'Was it really?'

The woman gives a curt nod. As she steps back to close the door, she hesitates. 'This house belong to me. Lauritz hasn't lived here for ten years.'

59

Salad-leaf contentment

She and Billie arrange to meet at the farmers' market close to Anna's cottage, choosing as always an activity and a setting with noise and people to fill the pockets of silence where they keep all the unsaid things. It's easier to walk side by side rather than face each other across a table. They never meet in Kirkley. Nor has Anna been to her sister's house since last summer. Billie's therapist is helping her work on boundaries.

'It's been nine months since you left the O'Keefes, and still no rescue call. It's a record.' Billie sends her an arch sideways glance. She's cut her hair, the sharp edge chipping at her jaw-line, and whilst she's wearing no make-up, she looks well.

'I rescue myself these days. Isn't that what us grown-ups do?' Anna smiles to hide an old ache. Those days of tight, inter-woven dependency are gone, their conversations pond-skating the surface of their lives, and for the moment that has to be enough.

It is the first time Billie has mentioned the O'Keefes. Anna resists the urge to ask questions. They pause at a cheese stall. A plate of blue cheese crumbs is on offer and Billie takes one, the smell turning Anna's stomach. The old Billie would have bombarded the cheesemonger with questions, taking it all in, an expert within minutes. As she takes a second piece, chewing slowly, savouring the taste, a thin, crenulated green, like salad leaves, opens above her head. Contentment looks like it would tear easily, but it's a good colour, one Anna is noticing more often from her sister. She gives Billie's hand a squeeze.

'Come on, Bills. I'm struggling with the smell.'

Her sister nods, snapping back into herself. 'So. What have you been up to?'

Her palm goes to her stomach, though there's nothing to feel as yet. 'Mostly eating tomatoes and being sick. And then eating more tomatoes.'

Billie's eyes grow watery. She is close to tears often these days, their mum says, but so far the bottles of wine have not returned to the fridge. 'Well at least I can help there.'

'Heat soup, fold socks, play Uno. How hard can it be?'

They share a quiet smile. 'Thought of any names yet, or is it too early?'

'Carsten if it's a boy, Liselotte if it's a girl.'

Billie nods. 'All things Scandinavian. How on trend.'

They fill the gaps in conversation with updates on Lucas's footballing triumphs and Maisie's gymnastics. Anna wants to ask if Billie ever sees Suzie, but she can't tell how her sister will react. Suzie had replied to a couple of Anna's emails. Brief lines about Daniel and nothing else. Once in a while Anna puts the name O'Keefe into the search engine, but the articles that come up are old, celebrating the unexpected return of a girl who'd been missing for five months. Gabriel's name never appears.

They buy scalding herbal tea from a refreshment van, watching the Saturday crowd push past. Billie nicks pieces of polystyrene from the cup's rim with her fingernails. 'Looking back, it's like I lost my mind.'

Anna puts her tea on the shelf, feeling the grit of spilt sugar beneath it. 'I think we all did.'

Her sister shakes her head. 'I didn't realise how angry and resentful I was.'

'Still hate me?' This at least they can joke about, because the roles have switched and now Anna is the one taking care of her big sister. A brief call every few days to check that Billie's taking her antidepressants, to ask if she's tried the new recipe she sent, to tell her she loves her.

Her sister gives a derisive laugh and a shake of the head, a brief flash of the old Billie. 'My expensive therapist says not.'

Anna picks up her tea again, hiding behind it. 'Shall we head home?'

'You know, I used to get tanked up when Jonah was working late,' Billie says, addressing her words over Anna's shoulder. 'Then I'd get restless and go online and shop about. Inevitably I'd take a little look at Lily's page. I had this insane dread that she'd boast about shagging my husband.'

'Jonah would never—'

Her sister holds up a hand. 'Like I said, I lost my mind.'

'Did ... did the police ever speak to you about those messages.'

'They never traced me.' Billie chews her lip, an uncharacteristic sweep of anxiety showing itself. 'I used a site called Ten-Minute Messages. It lets you send an anonymous message and then deletes all reference. See what an awful, sneaky bitch I am?' Her laugh releases a bitter aubergine tinge, her expression growing hard.

Here it comes, thinks Anna.

'I had to sit there whilst Lauritz's wife sobbed, cursing you, cursing Mum and Dad. I was there alone and I never told any of you.'

'I know, Bills.' She accepts they have to walk this ground until they've seen and discarded each sharp pebble, every snaking vine.

'That was my job, wasn't it? To shelter you so you could run

366

around without a care in the world. I told myself that made me happy, but actually it was eating me up inside.'

Billie opens out her palms as if to show she has nothing more to hide or to offer.

'We both played our roles, didn't we?' Anna catches herself watching a young mum with a buggy navigating the aisles between the browsing clusters. Feeling guilty, she looks away, in case the happiness inside becomes too visible and hurts Billie by contrast. 'I told Mum and Dad about my colours the other day. We should have told them a lifetime ago.'

'That's good.' Billie throws the remains of her tea in the bin, getting ready to leave. 'There's no hate left in me, Anna. You know that, don't you? I've set you free, little sister.'

Anna gives her hair a playful tug. 'Silly Billie.'

~ 60 ~

Happy candy stripes

The signpost for Beding is peeling, the white paint curling away under the hot sun. She turns into the lane. It couldn't look more different to a year ago. The spring has been dry and the shallow ditch alongside the road is full of last winter's brittle leaves.

She pulls over as the top floor of the house comes into view above the trees, spreading her hands across the small mound of belly, afraid her rapid heartbeat will alarm the baby. Every time she thinks of that tiny life safe inside her body, her head fills with candy-stripe pinks and yellows.

There are new curtains in the window of what was once Suzie and Gabriel's bedroom. Salad-leaf green. A good colour choice.

Gabriel never returned home. She knows this from speaking to April, just the once, some months ago. It was April who helped bring Lily back. The girl had called the older woman, wanting to know how Suzie and Daniel were doing and if they'd forgiven her for running away. April had persuaded her to make contact with Gabriel. To ask him where he and his son were.

She closes her eyes. Gabriel, waiting for Lily in that bleak pub room, hoping she'd changed her mind and was returning to him. Despite everything he'd done, she can't stop the anguish of pity, imagining the moment when he lost hope.

Unclicking her seat belt, she blows away the maudlin purple, pushing it out of her lungs like the last ever drag of a cigarette. On the passenger seat is a present wrapped in joyous yellow-and-green-striped paper.

To the one and only Dan-Fantastic, the gift tag reads. She hopes Daniel still loves frogs, because inside is a whole family of ceramic figures, in all shapes and sizes. She has imagined this visit countless times, an empty ache in her arms as she pictures herself giving Daniel the biggest hug. She wonders how he'll react when she tells him that autumn will bring her a baby and that she'll visit him before Christmas so the two of them can meet, her big boy and her tiny one.

She gets out with the present, and tulips for Suzie in sweet coral, wanting to approach the house on foot, taking her time. Bunting is strung around the front lawn and in the centre is a small gazebo with balloons and a birthday spread. Sandwiches in precise triangles, home-made fairy cakes with silver hundreds and thousands, bowls of cherries and watermelon slices. In the middle is the birthday cake, a chocolate-coated battleground with a Superman logo and a dozen little plastic superheroes.

A chorus of children's voices comes from the back garden. Apart from the new curtains in Suzie's room, the house is unchanged, but somehow it looks like a different place. A house full of life. A couple of boys stumble into view, chasing each other with water balloons. A third joins the chase, catching them both with a giant arc of water from his gun. It takes her a moment to recognise Daniel. He's taller, of course, and Suzie may be right about him reaching his father's height one day. His hair is tufty on top, with shorter sides. She'll tease him about how handsome he looks, ask him if nine years old isn't a little young to try and impress the ladies. She waits for him to notice her, but he's thrown aside his water pistol and is grabbing a handful of balloons from a tub whilst his friends scatter looking for cover. He bolts after them and is gone again.

She hesitates by the edge of the house. When he next appears, he's no longer the pursuer but the pursued. A woman runs after him, her long white-blonde hair flying, laughing as she grabs him around the waist, swinging him in a full circle before putting him down with a casual kiss on his head. He makes a show of wiping it away in front of his friends.

Anna raises her arm to catch Suzie's attention, but then realises the woman is younger than Suzie, her hair longer, face fuller.

Lily.

Her first thought is how ordinary she looks, the wild girl who had existed in her head, sabotaging her thoughts during the day, her dreams at night.

Lily takes Daniel's hand, and the two of them disappear behind the house once more. Anna puts his present on the garden wall, the tulips on top, and sends a kiss into the air for Daniel, for Suzie. And for Lily, who will hear her name from time to time, as Anna once heard stories about Lily. Returning to the car, the air is full of yellows and pinks and a touch of blue nostalgia for the eight-year-old who used to climb into her bed at night.

She turns the car in the narrow lane and pauses to look back at the house, hoping to catch sight of Daniel one last time. Something white and irregular that doesn't belong to the trees or the bushes catches her eye. She studies it, waiting for it to take shape and make sense. An amber glint of hair appears as a shaft of sunlight falls through the trees, picking out the crown of a man's head and his shoulder in a white T-shirt. Despite the distance, and the trees partly obscuring him, she recognises Gabriel.

Watching the birthday party from afar, trying to catch a glimpse of his son.

Or perhaps it is Lily, still drawing him back.

Anna drives away, stopping only when the house and the forest closing in around it have disappeared. Taking out her mobile, she sends a quick text.

Home in an hour, my love. In need of a Viking hug.

Author's Note

Synesthesia is a neurological condition in which a thing can be experienced through a combination of senses. A synesthete might taste sounds, see scents or smell colours. How it manifests is personal to each individual though sometimes similarities occur, for example, many synesthetes associate particular colours with letters of the alphabet. During my research I came across an online forum of people who associated particular colours and textures with their own emotions. It seemed plausible that someone might experience other people's emotions in the same way and so Anna was born. There's no magic to Anna's skills. She is just particularly adept at reading people – facial expressions, body language, tone - and her synesthesia adds colour and texture to the information she gleans.

Acknowledgements

This book came out of nowhere as I wrestled with an entirely different novel (which I loved but did not love me back and which has now been set free so that it may see the error of its ways and come groveling back). A huge thank you to my agent Rowan Lawton for her unerring support and belief as I parked that troublesome book and embarked on *The Colour of Lies*. An equally enormous mountain of gratitude to the lovely folk at Orion for their continued support and especially to my editor Laura Gerrard whose enthusiasm kept my own spark alive.

For offering a personal insight into synesthesia, much gratitude to Laurie Hill who experiences it as a gift, which I think is wonderful. Thank you for your candid and detailed responses to my many questions and for sharing your beautiful canvasses – a gorgeous visual source of inspiration!

A big thank you to Fiona Martin at Mother Shipton's Cave in Knaresborough for your help and for very kindly opening the Park out of season so I could visit the Petrifying Well – a source of water with such high mineral content that it coats objects in a 'stone' casing. A magical, mysterious place.

To Kit de Waal with much love for all the hours spent dissecting the big stuff and the minutiae.

To Sal Worringham, for your wisdom, inspiration and above all your friendship.

My gratitude to all the big-hearted warrior goddesses I am lucky enough to call my friends. For your time, company and wicked humour. You've steered me over the bumps and around the potholes and you have my love. You know who you are.

And to my family, always.

About the Author

Lezanne Clannachan was born in Denmark before moving to England when she was fourteen. After university, she lived in Singapore for several years before moving to London to work in marketing and event management. Lezanne has three children and lives in West Sussex.